CONJOINED

K.T. GEORGE

CONJOINED

© 2024, K.T. George

Dedicated to those who suffer
from some form of mental illness or
have struggled in the past,
I see you. You are enough.

1

WONDERLAND

{ANDREA}

An aging fluorescent bulb buzzed, and an incessant plip-plop noise stirred Andrea awake. She kept her eyes shut as she stirred and yawned. The musty scent of mildew made her lungs sting. When she attempted to stretch, white-hot pain shot through her shoulder joints. Her eyes grew wide, and she cried out, "Oww!"

She twisted and shifted to alleviate the pressure. Hardened mascara flaked off and crumbled into her eyes as her false lashes peeled away from each other. Blinking several times, she looked around. "Where the fuck am I?"

A ghoulish chartreuse-tinted light glinted off mint-green tile walls. "Jesus, did I time-travel back to the 1970s? If I didn't feel like puking before, I do now."

Andrea often woke in a stupor with little to no memory of how she got there. Her favorite form of self-care was oblivion through debauchery. "Argh," she groaned. "I'm getting too old for this shit."

Her head hammered as if a metronome had taken up residence inside it, and when she swallowed, her throat burned like a metal playground slide in the noonday sun. Her mouth was so dry, her tongue felt chapped, and her entire body ached. Shrugging internally, she accepted her fate and moved to rub the sleep from her eyes.

"What the hell?" she croaked. She couldn't move her arms! Her wrists were bound behind her back. Startled, she checked her feet. Her ankles were stuck together with . . . "Duct tape?" she whispered.

Squirming to free herself from her bonds, her skin touched cool, hard steel. She shuddered. Andrea lay on a table similar to the kind found in a morgue.

Panicked, she bent her knees and kicked out, trying to right herself and figure out where the hell she was. Instead, she lost her balance, free-falling before hitting the concrete floor with a hard thud.

"Oomph," the air whooshed from her on impact. The room spun as she landed on her back. She shut her eyes and sipped quick gulps of air through her gritted teeth until the pain subsided.

Rolling to her left side, she reopened her eyes. "Shit! Fuck!" She was face to face with a body, pale and lifeless and missing an eyeball.

As she scrambled to escape, she bumped against another body. She had fallen into the center of at least a dozen corpses thrown in haphazard piles. Sucking her lips into her mouth, she stifled a scream and scanned the room. She'd woken in some rank places over the years after a particularly fun bender. However, this place won all the terrible first-place prizes.

She was in a windowless storage closet, no larger than a bedroom. Two mobile metal carts containing various medical supplies lined one wall, while the opposite had a door with a narrow, frosted window above its handle. It promised a way out. To her left sat a stainless-steel utility sink she recognized from her forensic sketch artist days and the source of the plip-pop noise. A rusted rack occupied the remaining wall space. Its wire shelves were stacked with unmarked boxes, linens, and jars containing cloudy liquid. Her mind wanted to conjure all the disturbing things they held. She wouldn't allow it, and she shook her head, turning her focus on the door instead.

Dragging herself over the bodies, she wormed her way forward. Her stomach churned, and acid crawled up her throat as she considered they were once human beings. Then, her arm brushed against one. Its texture was rubbery, and its face held a queer, nonhuman expression. She examined another nearby. They were not corpses, but macabre, life-like dummies. Some were nude, while others wore hospital gowns. Glancing at her own body, Andrea gulped, and a cool sweat broke out on her forehead. She was dressed in the same threadbare smock. She'd bet her freedom this was no hospital, and if anyone had peeked into the room while she was unconscious, they would've spotted no difference between her and the other bodies.

Her teeth chattered, and her limbs quivered as she imagined what would happen next. Determined to fight the fear building inside her, she concentrated on baby steps, even though she wanted to curl into a ball and sob. "Free yourself first, then escape." Surveying the room, goals in mind, she flipped on her back to maneuver her body better.

"OUCH!" she shouted and sat upright at once to soothe a sharp, burning pain in her left big toe. She'd sliced it open on the wheel edge of one of the rolling carts. In her quick motion, she banged her head on its leg, and the full weight of the heavy cart crashed on her, dumping its contents onto the floor.

"Jesus. Could you be more clumsy and noisy?" She snapped at herself. With her arms behind her, hands at the small of her back, and the cart's extra weight, Andrea's shoulders shook from the strain. Struggling for relief, she writhed until she found a new position. There, she glimpsed a scalpel an arm's reach away. Wrestling for mobility, her long brown hair tangled in a dark, oozing liquid leaking from a small plastic bottle. The more she moved, the more ensnared her locks became. Yet she was determined to get her hands on the scalpel. Pulling her legs up as close to her chest as she could, she kicked out, raising the cart enough for her to roll out from under it. Shimmying once more across the floor, she made headway towards her goal.

"Son of a bitch!" The scalpel was a fake, made from the same material as the dummies.

Casting it aside, she focused on the door. Grunting and groaning, she struggled forward, moving her body like a human-sized earthworm. After a few attempts, she managed to pull herself to a standing position, the door supporting her back. Aligning her hands with the knob, they slipped off each time she attempted to grasp it. Whatever ooze her hair absorbed before was dripping down her arms, coating her hands. Even if they were dry, the bindings on her wrists were so taut she couldn't make the turning motion to move the handle.

"Free yourself, then escape," she chanted, closing her eyes to refocus on finding a solution.

If the same materials were used on her wrists as her ankles, pressure might stretch the tape enough for her to slide her hands out. Squatting, she used her body weight as leverage and tried slipping the door handle between her skin and the bindings. With help from the slippery goo, she eventually succeeded in liberating one hand, then the other.

Freed from their unnatural position, her arms trembled while her hands tingled from the surge of blood returning to them. Sliding to the floor, she hung her head and took a moment to rest before picking away at the tape around her ankles. "Fucking fingernails! Why haven't I stopped biting them," she cursed. Between her short nails and quivering arms, she couldn't make headway on her remaining bonds. As blood dripped from her cut toe, it occurred to her that if the wheel edge was sharp enough to slice skin, it should slice the tape too!

With her bindings gone, she turned toward the sink in the corner, tempted to wash the goop from her body. Her twin sister, Allyson, would be using it as a bathtub if she were in this situation. She liked things clean and structured. Everything had its place. Andrea preferred messy and unorganized.

Squaring her shoulders, she plastered a coy smile on her face. "Why change now?" Then she yanked open the door and staggered into the adjoining space. Her legs wobbled as she inspected the area. If she could find a phone or computer, she could get in touch with the outside world and call for help.

From the storage closet, she entered an operating room with a table, more instruments, and bloody gauze. Yet to her right was a spacious interior made to resemble a bus or airport terminal. Straight ahead was a short hallway with exposed wood framing supporting a semi-finished office. False windowpanes covered a painted sprawling city scene that reminded her of Atlanta, where she'd lived briefly after college. Spotting a laptop on the desk, she stumbled forward.

She stabbed at the power button, but it didn't budge. The buttons were fake. Every item she touched on the desk was a replica of the real thing! The phone, books, stapler, even the paper clips! Picking up the laptop prop, she threw it across the room, screaming in frustration. Terror seized her as it skittered across the floor. Whoever bound her and left her in that room might be watching and waiting. She must be smarter. *Quieter.*

Taking a deep breath to settle her nerves and racing heart, she tiptoed towards the next area. Soft music played overhead as she entered a mock hotel room. A table for two, dressed for dinner, sat against a floral-papered wall. Another false window showcased the same city skyline from a different perspective. "Definitely Atlanta," Andrea murmured. A bouquet of ruby-red roses rested in the table's middle as the proud centerpiece and a silver floor-length ice bucket stood beside it, holding a bottle of champagne. Four covered dishes rested on a room service cart, the aroma of real food filling her nostrils. Her stomach growled.

Intuition told her to exercise caution, yet her watering mouth and gurgling stomach argued it was worth the disappointment if the dishes were empty. Yet there was another reason for her hesitation. The whole scene tugged at a lost memory. It was familiar in the way a forgotten fashion trend returns and reminds you how much you hated that period in your life.

"Fuck it," she spat, stepping forward and lifting one of the lids. A loud bell broke the silence like a sensor alarm on a hot ticket item at the clothing store. She jumped, dropping it. The clang of metal crashing into metal reverberated. The echo hit her in the chest as she swung around to face the way she'd entered. A crawling sensation trickled up her spine. *Was someone behind her watching?* She half expected a cameraperson and a cinematographer to be standing there when she turned.

"Hello?"

When she spoke, the ringing stopped, only to be replaced by the sound of creaking floorboards. "What the?" she bit back as she looked at the floor and her bare feet, her toes automatically curling into the soft shag carpet.

She whipped her head back up to locate the source of the noise. As she did, a sharp pain above her right eye took her by surprise.

"Ugh! What is happening?" she whispered, gripping her forehead in her hands.

A buzzing sound began in her ears, low at first but increasing in intensity until it forced her to lay on the floor. Curled in the fetal position, her head still in her hands, a moan escaped her lips before she could gain any control over her roiling emotions.

Anger replaced pain, and fear replaced anger. Was someone playing a deadly game with her? As she drifted into unconsciousness, a hand smoothed the bangs from her forehead.

"Shhh. It's okay, Dre. Relax."

"Lyssy?" Andrea whispered, confused.

"I've got you. But it's time."

"Time? For what? I don't understand." Andrea slurred, which further baffled her. Why couldn't she speak properly?

"It's time to make things right."

2

A NEW PLACE

{ALLYSON}

Allyson was overjoyed with her little one-bedroom unit in a building filled with people at different re-entry phases in their lives. Each floor had an average of three apartments. On her floor, the neighbor across the hall was a recovering addict, and at the end lived a woman who suffered a mental breakdown during menopause, leaving her divorced and penniless. The other floors were comprised of assorted mental and emotional illness subcategories.

Moving here was the next step in their collective journey to healing. Being relegated to the dilapidated section of town was either a punishment or a reward for graduating from the program. The perspective varied based on how much Kool-Aid one drank while in treatment.

"The area has an authenticity lacking in the more gentrified neighborhoods," Allyson's transition coach commented when he showed her the space. She struggled to check an eyeroll. In his world, placing the mentally ill in the same community as criminals and others operating on society's fringe was reasonable.

Later, she wandered a few blocks and witnessed a beatdown, a few drug deals, and sex workers busy making a living in a nearby park. The remainder of the neighborhood included low-income families trying their best to make ends meet. No home remodeling shows would be coming this way to help refurbish the place any time soon. People didn't want *"disturbed individuals"* hovering around their innocent children or walking by their BMWs.

Allyson didn't care about those people. Her family were those people. Look where it got her. She would play the rehabilitation game and ignore the judgmental sneers. She was excited to live on her own again, where she could decorate her place as she wished. Make it feel inviting. Safe. No more concrete walls. No more soft edges or plastic. The rules were strict at the psych hospital where she'd spent the last six months. Here, she had control.

Allyson filled her kitchen with real silverware, ceramic plates, and sharp knives. She couldn't wait to have a steak. Six months was too long to live on mushy foods and pre-cut bite-sized nuggets. In the bathroom, she was giddy over a genuine glass mirror hung over the porcelain pedestal sink. And metal fixtures to hold her towels and toiletries. She longed for a glass shower door, yet a shower curtain in the pattern and color she chose made it feel less institutional. The best thing about having her own space again, though, was the privacy. Gone were the days of nurses and orderlies indiscriminately entering her room, dispensing pills without consent, and enforcing a routine based on someone else's schedule.

Allyson jumped at Jon Bon Jovi's voice, crooning about "Bad Medicine." It was her alarm—time for her meds.

"Are they really what I need?" she questioned the words to the song and tapped snooze. She needed a minute to decide which liquid was best to help choke down her concoction of antidepressants, mood stabilizers, neuroleptics, and antipsychotics—another freedom she needed to relearn.

Walking to the fridge, she asked her voice-controlled smart speaker to update her on the latest news. She needed a distraction from the task at hand, and hearing how people had it worse usually did the trick.

Popping open a can of mango-flavored sparkling water, she half-listened to the female computerized voice run through the news highlights. As she took a deep gulp, an unexpected mood swing took hold, not from the sad stories and disturbing trends the news pedaled, but from memories triggered by the *pshh* sound the can made upon opening.

"Please don't make me do this, Ma! Pa! Pleeaassee. I'll be good. I promise I won't hurt myself anymore," she appealed, sobbing to her parents. She was twelve years old.

Anselmo and Patricia Marta stood there as the zombies Allyson would eventually become under the influence of her first medicinal cocktail. They nodded, emotionless, as the administrator spoke in a hushed yet authoritative voice. Andrea hung back to the side with a slight, satisfied smirk and a soda can in her hand. Anyone else would think it was passivity or even shock, but being her twin, Allyson knew how Andrea felt. *Smug.* Andrea was pleased another scheme had worked in her favor and thrilled Allyson would be out of the picture, even if it were only temporary.

Allyson was disgusted with Andrea as she popped open her drink. The *pshh* sound as air escaped the can and her sister's loud, accompanying slurp had Allyson balling her fists tight while her arms hung by her side. What she wouldn't give to punch her twin in her conceited little mouth. It was Andrea who had driven Allyson to self-harm. And it was Andrea who went to their mother with false concern over the cut marks on Allyson's abdomen. Naturally, she left out the part where she was the one who made the first mark . . . the one who gave Allyson the idea self-harm equaled self-regulation, a way to even out her anxiety and fear. Once their mother surveyed the damage, no explanation or defense would satisfy her. No promise or begging stopped Patricia Marta from employing the best physicians and psychiatrists money could buy to fix her daughter. The ones who could work the fastest and keep it secret won her business because the only thing worse than having an unwell child was everyone in their social circle finding out about it. They'd become pariahs. And Patricia hadn't made herself into something from nothing to lose it all over *mental illness*.

Allyson tried to be the model patient and played the game, hoping it would get her dismissed early on good behavior like a goddamn felon. The medical staff all saw through her efforts, though, and punished her. For six months, she was allowed no visitors and no contact with anyone from her old life. Those were the people who got her into trouble, in theory. They weren't wrong—the powers that be making those decisions— but hell, if she wasn't lonely. At twelve years old, lacking contact with anyone other than medical professionals and other mentally unstable patients made it easy to slide down the rabbit hole into insanity. Thank God for art therapy.

An instructor came twice a week and taught Allyson how to relinquish her rigidity and get her hands dirty. Before, bright colors hurt her eyes, and she had an aversion to things overlapping or touching when they shouldn't. Making anything other than food with your hands was an aberration. Even Ma disapproved.

"Only poor people work with their hands and get grease under their fingernails, dirt in their cuticles," she'd said.

Ma wasn't around to encourage her to keep things clean and simple, though, which freed Allyson to let go and explore. Connecting with different textures of raw materials and feeling the density or even aliveness of an object evoked an unexpected passion in her. Despite having to experience all the horrible events before this discovery, it birthed her talent as a mixed-media artist—a gift all her own.

The voice crooned from her phone again. With her eight minutes of reverie over, she lined up her pills and swallowed them one by one, catching herself from wanting to lift her tongue and open wide for inspection. While she performed this new ritual, the smart speaker rambled on:

> *"In entertainment news, streaming service giant HORR Studios has announced a billion-dollar deal with Iceland to move its operations to the island nation by year's end. Iceland has been an increasingly popular location for big and small-budget films, with its diverse landscape and open access to all the country offers. A 25% return on investment doesn't hurt either, thanks to the country's job creation stimulus. This announcement follows on the heels of H0rr Studios' wildly successful video game launched this past Christmas, based on its franchise hit The Caretaker. What will the streaming giant think of next? Try a theme park based on cult classics, popular horror shows, and movies."*

Allyson swallowed hard. *The Caretaker* series was Andrea's project. Andrea hadn't mentioned a move to Iceland the last time they spoke. What did that mean for its employees? Were they expected to move with the company? She grabbed her phone, tempted to call her sister and find out the details. However, Andrea wouldn't answer, and even if she did, she'd lie and say she had no idea what Allyson was talking about; ask her if she'd taken her meds today. Andrea would brag about some famous person she partied with, then pretend to be interested in what Allyson was doing while simultaneously demeaning it.

"Aren't you supposed to be working on an art installation, Lyssy?" Andrea would quip with condescension.

"Fuck!" Allyson shouted, startling herself. "My project! And now I'm talking to myself in Andrea's voice. Just fantastic. Add that to my growing list of symptoms! Maybe it will buy me six months more in treatment. Or another pill! Christ, I'm a mess."

"Only a work in progress, Dawling," Grace drawled as they walked through the door and plopped on the couch.

"Ha! Come on in! Can I get you something, Your Highness?" Allyson laughed when greeting her neighbor from across the hall.

Grace was a six-foot-two, non-binary, recovering prescription pain med addict with a penchant for feather boas. They met at the hospital and were fortunate enough to have been assigned to the same floor in the out-patient residence. They had become close friends.

"What is this about an art exhibit?" Grace asked.

"I signed a contract over a year ago with Holger Beitin to create an art piece for an installation by the Space Needle. It is part of a larger exhibit with multiple artists contributing. My agent, Vince, was able to buy me some time while I was in treatment, but they'll be banging on my door soon if I don't at least show them a sketch!"

"Oooh. Holger Beitin! I'm impressed." Grace clapped.

"Do you know him?"

"No, honey. However, his name sounds like someone who would be an art curator. Now, come sit," Grace directed, patting the velvet cushion next to them. "I brought you inspiration!" they sang while holding a tightly rolled joint in one hand and a lighter in the other.

Younger Allyson would've gagged and declined to share anything you had to put in your mouth. Then she discovered kissing and other things you could also do with your mouth, and sharing a joint seemed relatively clean.

Relaxing into their chemical enlightenment, a soft *tap tap* sounded from the exterior wall that shared the hallway. "Psst. Hermana," someone whispered through her hollow-core door. "A suit headed to your suite." It was the middle-aged woman from down the hall. "Put your shit away and look alive!" she called louder before her light footsteps retreated.

Panicked, Grace and Allyson hid the evidence of their self-medication. Marijuana wasn't illegal in Washington State, yet getting caught using it would be more than frowned upon by their treatment supervisor.

Allyson's heart raced. "Why would anyone be coming to my apartment?"

"Shh. Relax, sweetie. Follow my lead. We haven't done anything wrong. At least, nothing I'm aware of," they arched an eyebrow. "Let's see what they want."

Bang. Bang. Bang. The door rattled like a 7.0 earthquake.

"Allyson Marta?"

"Yes?" she croaked, placing her hand on the doorknob.

"I'm Detective Davidson. I need to ask you a few questions. May I come in?"

Allyson's neck and shoulders visibility tightened as if she could magically shrink herself into a tiny ball.

Grace went over and placed a hand on her back. "Just breathe."

"I'm too stoned for this," she whispered.

"Ms. Marta?"

"Yeah, yeah. Give me a second." Allyson paused, her hand on the knob, before yanking the door open to an average-height, middle-aged man dressed in the typical off-the-rack suit he probably bought at some big box retailer on sale. She leaned against the door jamb, blocking his entry.

"ID, please." She trusted no one and always assumed the worst in people. Once he proffered his credentials and she gave them a casual glance, she allowed him to enter. Even though he was average on the outside, his presence filled the room. She and Grace observed him scanning her shelves neatly lined with knickknacks and failed art projects as if he were Hercule Poirot.

"How can I help, Detective?" she asked, scratching a nonexistent itch on her arm.

Davidson walked toward a console table with pictures arranged by size and age. Picking up a 4x6 gilded frame, he turned and held it out. "Is this you?"

"Who does it look like?" Grace hissed.

"I'm sorry. You are?" Davidson asked.

Ignoring his question, Grace cautioned, "Listen, Detective, unless you have a warrant, state your business, and go. We are a protected class. Hispanic and emotionally *challenged*. Harassment is frowned upon by our treatment teams."

Glowering, he turned to Allyson. "Is this your sister, Andrea Marta?"

"Yeah. That's her and me at my last exhibit. She loves the camera." Allyson played with an errant string on her shirt hem, noting to clip it later. Biting her lip, she lowered her head where her eyes caught the misaligned seam of her left sock. Suddenly, everything seemed malapropos.

"It's hard to believe we are identical twins when you look at that picture. It was like five years ago, and I've been going through a rough patch," she admitted, rubbing her hand along the top of her head.

Allyson had gained thirty pounds from the drug cocktail she'd been prescribed and chopped her long tresses, leaving only an inch or so in place. Most days, it stuck out in random spikes. To add dimension and fun, she'd dyed it her favorite color, a soft lavender. She had also plucked her eyebrows and eyelashes out one by one as a non-scarring form of self-harm six months prior. They had yet to grow back. Slow hair growth was a surprise, unadvertised side-effect of her meds.

"What's this about anyway? Is she in trouble?" she edged, chewing at a cuticle on her right hand.

"Your sister's employer, H0rr Studios, has reported her missing. Have you heard from her or seen her recently?"

"I moved in six days ago. Before that, I was in treatment for six months, nine if you count the ninety-day hold at County."

"Do you have any idea where she might go? Anyone she would stay with, off the grid, say?"

An icy chill hugged her shoulders despite being seventy-five degrees inside her apartment, and she narrowed her gaze at Mr. Average. His questions didn't feel right to her. "Let me check my wonder twin powers and see," she scowled and pretended to check her smartwatch.

"I told you my life was rather tragic this last year. Did I mention her visiting? Just because we share the same DNA does not give me insight into her life. If her employer reported her missing, they have more information on the ins and outs of it than I do. However, leave your card, and if something comes up, I'll call," she offered dismissively.

Grace regarded Allyson and grinned, appreciating her out-of-character assertiveness.

Detective Davidson handed the picture frame to Grace before giving Allyson his business card. "My cell is on the back. If anything comes to mind, no matter how small, text me along with her case reference number."

"Sure," she answered in an "I'll get right on that" tone. Then she opened the door to encourage Davidson's exit.

Before stepping across the threshold, the detective stopped and turned to face the two occupants, "Oh! I almost forgot. Do you know Roger Wotke?"

"*The Caretaker* guy?" she asked, curling her lip and wrinkling her nose. "Yeah."

Allyson shrugged. "He works with Andrea. Oh, and I think he's in town. Comic Con's this weekend."

"Yeah, he is. That freak of hotness," Grace added dreamily. "Got me tickets for a meet and greet!"

"What does he have to do with my sister missing?" Roger and Andrea had a relationship but kept it casual and confidential. As much as she hated Andrea, she wasn't about to give out anything that wasn't anyone's business but their own.

"It's hard to say. Yet a guy who has played a psychopath for over ten years and wears his costume in public to hide his real identity is someone worth looking into, I'd say."

Grace laughed. "Don't kid yourself, Detective. We all wear costumes to hide our true nature. Even you." Then they shut the door in his face.

3

THE ALBATROSS

{ROGER}

"**M**ay I have your attention, please: Federal Aviation Administration guidelines . . ." blah, blah, blah.

Roger hated that female public service announcer's voice. It sounded like his ex. Everything about the airport held a connection to *her*, from the frazzled and rushed travelers to the scent of body odor mixed with fast food and alcohol. Then there were the large, over-the-top art installations. They all defined pieces of her personality—a woman he planned on forgetting for good. As soon as he was on the plane to Uzbekistan, Roger would erase her and this wretched place from his memory by exchanging them with only dreams of the future.

"Why Uzbekistan?" his valet asked as they drove to the main airport from the offsite check-in facility reserved for the rich and famous.

He wanted to say, "Uzbekistan is one of two double landlocked countries in the world, which meant no easy access to the high seas, and handshakes were only acceptable between two men." Women's hands made Roger's skin crawl with their long, painted fingernails and soft texture. Hands were for work. They should be rough and calloused, not decorated with precious metals and gemstones. That's one thing he *did* admire about his ex. Her hands were perfect in that regard because she was an artist.

What he answered was, "Work." It conveyed the right amount of finality. Just because they were in a car together didn't mean Roger welcomed conversation. His abruptness was highly effective, for the man said nothing afterward. Not even a customary, "Have a safe flight."

"Oh, Mr. Wotke! I didn't recognize you," the airline attendant exclaimed as she verified his information while boarding the plane.

"I shaved," he quipped, rolling his eyes. Everyone knew Roger Wotke as *The Caretaker*, but few knew his true visage outside his on-screen persona. *Caretaker* fans were an extreme bunch, and he liked it that way, except in his day-to-day life. It took work and diligence to have two personalities. The reward was he could move about the world as any other nameless shmuck. It also made transportation easier on his wallet. Even though he'd made millions, he was thrifty and selective with his purchases.

"Once you arrive in Dubai, an airline representative will escort you to your connection to Uzbekistan."

He inclined his head and took his seat in first class on the double-decker Airbus. As he fidgeted with his belongings, the individual TV screen in his pod came to life. Ignoring the usual talk about Emirate's accommodations, destinations, and services provided, he closed his eyes and smiled. "Home free," he muttered and heaved a sigh.

Then his eyes snapped open. To enjoy the journey in a fully relaxed state, he needed his pills. He rifled through his designer leather carryall to find the correct bottle and selected mineral water from his exclusive wet bar. Flying had come a long way from when he took his first plane ride thirty years ago, and Emirates knew how to spoil the wealthy.

"Excuse me, sir," a twangy voice interrupted his brief reverie.

He couldn't help regurgitating a little at the manicured hand resting at the entrance to his private cubicle. Long fingernails filed in the day's fashion, painted in a gaudy, stereotypical red, and accented with tiny crystals.

"I think this is my seat. 10B?"

Sliding his sunglasses down the bridge of his nose enough to make eye contact, he scrutinized her appearance before baring his teeth in a sadistic smile. The woman squirmed, squinting at the crinkled paper ticket in her trembling hand. Her mouth opened and closed, reminding him of the sea bass he'd ordered for dinner the night before—overpriced and overdone.

"Ummm . . ." she stuttered, peering back at him through eyelashes better served as a feather duster.

"No," he barked.

Her shoulders jumped to her ears, and she fumbled with a giant handbag draped over her free arm. She sucked in her bottom lip, nibbling at a loose sliver of flesh before looking for help. Flicking his gaze across the aisle, he held back a laugh as realization hit her. Following his stare, she glimpsed the seat across from where she stood.

"That's right, deary. That one is 10B."

He waved his hand in dismissal, then slid his dark-tinted shades back up his nose with his middle finger. He closed his eyes again, sinking into his seat. The woman had no clue how fortunate she was that his meds were already performing their magic. He barely held back his disgust and irritation. He bought the best seat they offered on this flight for a reason, and it wasn't to be bothered by dim-witted passengers.

"Breaking News: A pair of men's sized 12 athletic shoes containing feet washed ashore near Pier 86 and Centennial Park. The gruesome discovery shocked a local jogger who thought his dog had found simple debris until he saw what was inside. More now from our TV-12 Investigative Journalist, Ram Helm."

Roger's eyes flicked open a second time. The noise blaring from the TV was coming from 10B. But the clamor didn't grab his attention as much as what was said.

"Could you turn that down? For Chrissake, there's a reason we have individual pods!" Roger snapped.

"I'm trying. I can't seem to find the thingy that controls the volume!" The woman cried.

"Thank you, Tricia. Since 2007, over twenty extremities, mostly feet ensconced in athletic shoes, have been discovered along the Salish Sea shoreline. In the past, scientists and health officials explained how a specific phenomenon is at play. However, this scene is slightly different."

Flaring his nostrils and gritting his teeth, Roger pointed to the iPhone-looking device stored to his left.

"It's on the opposite side as mine. This," he picked up the device and waved it at her, "is your '*thangy.*' Now fix it."

"Usually, Salish Sea Feet, as they've been nicknamed, appear as a singular shoe. With these turning up as a pair, investigators are processing the scene as a crime, along with forensic divers and other authorities. They want to ensure all remains have been recovered and any evidence that could explain their appearance has been collected. The public should be assured there is currently no threat to their safety. The authorities are simply following protocol. In the meantime, what we do know is that the feet came with a clue pointing to the identity of the person last wearing them. We'll update you as this story continues to unfold. For now, I'm Ram Helm for TV-12."

The woman's face turned a deep red as she bungled the remote control.

Roger pretended to ignore the noise and the report. However, the discovery was unnerving. Cramming his noise-canceling headphones in his ears, he programmed his viewing screen to play soothing jazz music, then he leaned his head back and tried to relax as the remaining passengers found their seats.

Even with the headphones on and music playing softly, he could make out the overhead bins closing as travelers wrangled their oversized carry-ons into the small compartments. Their shrill chatter drowned out the rumble of businessmen's voices finalizing deals before taking off on the long journey. He did some deep diaphragmatic breathing and chanted his personal positive affirmation: "*I am at ease with my life and am safe where I am.*" Except he wasn't fooling anyone, especially himself. His stomach was in knots.

Should he try calling *her* one last time? Maybe a message through that app she insisted they use. It was less personal, and its contents less traceable.

After a brief internal debate on what to say, he typed: "An Albatross is found at sea. Love from your former devotee."

4

WONDERLAND CONTINUED

{ANDREA}

Footsteps woke Andrea from her stupor. They were accompanied by a dragging noise as if something heavy was being pulled across a concrete floor. Her muddled brain tried to recall where she was again. At least this time, she wasn't bound up and left for dead.

Ah, yes. The fake hotel room. And her twin sister. Was she here?

"Allyson?" she called out softly.

The noises ceased. Andrea stood, her balance still a bit wobbly. She strained her ears to pick up on any other sounds. However, aside from the few emergency lights illuminating the walkway, there was only silence.

Did she imagine Allyson here? And what about the threat? That's how she perceived Allyson's statement about making things right. Despite the tenderness in her actions, the ultimatum was menacing. It made sense. The girls never loved one another. They were not typical identical twins, no matter how many matching outfits they wore or how much time they spent together. Admittedly, Andrea did drive Allyson nearly mad. Without her actions, her twin may be a married mother of two, with the white picket fence and golden retriever in the yard. Instead, she was a headcase, spending large swaths of time in and out of facilities that would never fix her. However, if anyone asked her what happened to Allyson, even St. Peter himself, she'd have a *very* different version of events.

The pain in her head pinged again, and her attention became unfocused. She was in a car, driving through a narrow two-lane highway with freshly fallen snow stacked on either side. The world seemed bright, yet the sky was a dismal gray. She commented on the contrast, or it could've been something she thought. The car was silent. Where was she headed, and with whom? Was she alone, or was Allyson or someone else with her? Did she hit her head in an accident? Nothing made sense!

"UGH!" she growled, shaking herself as if the action would clear cobwebs away like in cartoons.

With her pain threshold peaking, it was hard to focus. However, her instincts urged her back to the present moment and to figure out how to escape the current predicament. Was this a revenge scheme Allyson dreamed up? If so, she was in for a rude awakening when Andrea emerged, ready to face off.

She left the hotel room set, forgetting about her hunger, and stumbled into the next area. It was a small park scene with a bench, fake grass, trees, and a lake in the background. It was similar to a place she used to frequent when she lived in Georgia as a forensic artist. Then it all clicked. The storage closet was like the morgue she frequented for her job. The office might have belonged to her old boss. The terminal could have been the Atlanta airport. And the hotel room. Was it like the one she stayed in before she found an apartment? "I'm trapped in a fucking film studio," she snapped.

Why would anyone build sets based on her life? Allyson was a successful artist, yet going to such expense to exact retribution? That didn't sit right with her. She knew little of Andrea's life in Georgia, and these places held no significant meaning to her. What would be the point?

Furthermore, equipment such as cameras, boom mikes, and additional lighting was absent. If this were a nefarious plot against her, why an abandoned film studio?

Dread weighed on her as she treaded warily through set after set, hallways, and construction areas. A sound stage was built to control noise. Sound, or the lack thereof, was of utmost importance while filming in a closed location. The odds of anyone hearing a cry for help from the outside were nil, and obtaining an active Internet signal through the soundproofed walls was improbable. She might get lucky finding an old landline phone still activated as an accounting oversight. Otherwise, access to help would have to come from finding her way out.

While trying to keep her footfalls light, she tiptoed towards an apartment setting. It must have been for a male character, with its décor in cool neutral browns, deep reds, and taupe. A gourmet kitchen with stainless steel appliances, granite countertops, and all the gadgets you'd use to cook a meal flowed into a family room. She smoothed her fingers over the lush leather furniture as she walked by, trying to gather as much intel regarding her surroundings as possible. Whoever owned this studio was successful, allotting its art department with a large budget. If this were the set she'd woken up in, she would've believed she was at a lover's house. Designers spared no expense on staging, and the thoughtful detail in everything, from the trinkets to the book titles on an entertainment center shelf, conveyed a personality. Time was money, especially in the entertainment world. This set was for a big-budget film or a popular TV series. If she could place the stage or the work, she might be able to figure out exactly where she was and plan an escape.

Continuing her perusal, she spotted a bedroom off the living room. The same colors and materials adorned the space. In the center was an unmade bed and a pillow with an indentation. Moving closer, she patted the sheets and found they were still warm. She gasped, pulling her hand away as if burned, and glanced around the room.

"Hello?" she called, instantly cursing herself. Shouting was the last thing she should do, considering she was basically a captive and possibly left for dead.

She considered grabbing the comforter and bolting but noted a door ajar along the opposite wall. She bet it was a closet. Since the designers were so detailed about the other props, perhaps clothes hung inside, and she could change. Before she could put her hand on the handle, an unexpected voice had her staggering backward. She lost her balance and landed ass-first on the floor.

"Who's there? What do you want?" she croaked.

Lifting back to her feet, she spun around, searching for the source. A large screen television in the living room flashed with light. She inched her way back there, cautious and hyperaware of any movement other than her own. A poor-quality video played on the screen. It was a press conference from at least a decade ago, she guessed, based on how the people were dressed. A sheriff stood at a podium, answering questions from unseen interviewers and witnesses. Flanked by people in various uniforms and credentials around their necks, one person stood out: a figure dressed in all black with their back to the camera. They were staging something along a lakefront, like the set she passed earlier from Georgia.

"What are you doing?" she asked the screen, speaking directly to the dark figure.

Ignorant of the scene behind them, the shadow focused on their work. The way they moved about was like a mysterious, sinister dance. Andrea was drawn to them and ignored the ones talking. It was as though this person was a stagehand, setting the scene for the next act while the performers distracted the crowd with their current segment. Yet to her, they were the main act. With equal parts fascination and dread, she sat on the couch's edge, unable to look away from what was unfolding before her. As they stepped off screen, the camera panned toward the now vacant spot.

Rows upon rows of shoes in various sizes and styles lined the shoreline. The camera panned closer and zoomed in on a particular athletic shoe. A small, white, laminated card placed under the heel read "John Doe, Lake Lanier, right foot, August 2007, US 12."

The sheriff's voice disrupted her trance of gruesome fascination. "Experts have tried to allay our fears that body parts washing up on various shorelines across the country over the last fifteen years are a unique phenomenon. Everything from jet streams and suicidal tendencies, to the materials shoes are made with these days. All these make body parts easier to float. The 'scientific' findings have been interesting. Too much time and money has been wasted to debunk what we, as investigators on the front line, feel intuitively. Based on the consistency of the findings in this area alone: Men's size 12, right feet only . . . Folks, we have concluded we are indeed dealing with a serial killer."

Without warning, the TV blinked black, and the lighting in the room dimmed before growing bright twice in quick succession as if the building had experienced a power surge. Following the strange light display, a mechanical hum sounded from the bedroom. She jumped up and skipped towards it, both inexplicably frightened and exhilarated. When she arrived at the doorway, she found a man standing there, although he was more like an image from an old movie projector. Wavy lines made him appear like one of those balloon people flapping in the breeze.

It wasn't this appearance that terrified Andrea. Nor was it how one side of his head was sunk in as if he'd been battered with a wrecking ball. Not even his shiny eye sockets that glittered like glossy, deep, miniature black holes bothered her. It was his voice.

"Hola, querida." The man smiled broadly, exposing blackened nubs where teeth once were. "You've seen better days too." He waggled a bony finger at her head.

The *plip-pop* of water dripping from his clothes onto the hardwood floor caused her to break eye contact. A puddle formed where his feet should've been. Instead, his damp pant legs brushed the surface. Andrea's hand shook as she reached up to pat the side of her head, where he indicated. She cried out when her fingers dipped inward where her skull should have been smooth. Hers was a mirror image of his. Without hesitation, she pulled it away, holding back a scream when her hand came away sticky and wet. Counting to four to steady her nerves, she found her fingers covered in a dark ooze. She tried to reason it was from the bottle that spilled on her back in the storage closet. Bringing her fingers to her nose, she gave them a quick sniff before flicking her tongue out for a taste. It was blood. Andrea's insides flipped as she turned to flee.

"Run, little rabbit," the man's baritone voice bellowed with a distinct Spanish accent. "You know . . ."

"How I love the chase!" she finished, surprised at her outburst. At this revelation, the lights flickered one more time before she was immersed in complete darkness with a ghost from her past.

5

THE DECISION

{ALLYSON}

The waiting room at the Solomon Center, where Allyson met with her psychiatrist, Dr. Dean Santoli, once a week, gave her the creeps. The walls and flooring were the bright, bold colors of a pediatrician's office, complete with a fish tank and a TV that only played rom-coms and corny Christmas movies.

She was thankful it wasn't fairytale princesses or superheroes. There was nothing happy about stories involving deceased mothers abandoning their female offspring to a horrid fate. She could testify to that!

Disgusted with the furniture choice, she plopped in a lime-green beanbag chair with a huff and crossed her hands over her body. She was preparing herself for an onslaught of cheesy romance when the local news reporter caught her eye. He was tall and slender. Probably a runner. His thick, wavy blond hair was slicked back in a rockabilly style, and his eyes were as black as hers. Although he was handsome in the classical sense, with a Roman nose and high cheekbones, it wasn't his looks that grabbed her attention but what he was reporting.

"The feet washed up along a downtown shoreline earlier this week have been identified as the remains of Billy Walls, a Nisqually Indian Nation member, reported missing five years ago. According to his family, he vanished without a trace. Struggling with substance abuse and depression throughout his life, authorities believed he succumbed to one or both illnesses and closed his case after a brief search. The roughly 600-person First Nation tribe is mourning the loss collectively and questions whether more could have been done to locate him and the many other minorities like him that go missing every day in the United States."

Allyson found irony in sitting in her therapist's office waiting to discuss her mental illness while witnessing her fate if she, too, succumbed to it someday. The report didn't go into detail on how he did it. However, considering his feet were along the shoreline, he no doubt chose one of the high bridges dotting the coast. She would choose the Fremont Bridge herself. If being an identical twin wasn't cliché enough, jumping from the famous bridge would be. Authorities attempted to secure its sides over the years, but it was doable if you were determined.

"Allyson?" Dr. Dean's voice called from a bright orange door.

Startled from her musings, she half-rolled and half-fell out of the beanbag. Embarrassed, she avoided eye contact with her doctor as she made her way inside.

His office was more subdued in décor than the waiting room. Allyson guessed he loathed it as much as she did, based on the cool color palette and the lack of children's furniture.

"Now that you are in the outpatient residence, it's important you focus on maintaining your mental health, Allyson. You are what I call a 'repeat offender.' You've spent your life in and out of programs. It's time to break this cycle, and I'm here to help you get there."

"Excuse me, Dr. Dean. How is the failure of mental health professionals my fault? I come to you for help, paying a goddamn fortune, only to come back in a few years with the same issues. If you are offering a cure, and the cure doesn't stick, I should get a refund. Your ROI is horrendous, and if you were any other business, you would be unemployed!"

"Don't you want to enjoy your life? Being heavily medicated and confined in isolation is no way to live. Not to mention the stigma and shame you must face. You are a talented artist and an attractive woman. Haven't you considered a life where you get married and have children?"

"The medication, isolation, and humiliation? Those are a product of your profession's treatment methodologies. I don't want them, yet what are my choices? Besides, perhaps I enjoy being depressed and cutting myself. It's an art form. I'm Lauren Collin. Her medium is watercolor paper; mine is skin. I am a living canvas."

"Allyson . . ." sighed Dr. Dean.

"Regarding marriage and children, your ideologies are sexist and outdated. Just because I'm a woman doesn't mean I want kids or need to find a husband. I can't keep a fake plant alive or manage my relationship with my twin sister. You know, the kind that is pretty much automatic? I enjoy torturing myself. I wouldn't wish me on anyone."

"Ah. Your sister. You always manage to sneak her into the conversation. Let's talk more about her."

"What's to say? She's the reason I'm so fucked up. She's one-half the freakshow that makes up the Marta twins!"

"Excellent start," he replied, scribbling something on his notepad.

"It's the beginning, middle, and end. Andrea made me and everyone around her crazy. We all got help. The End."

"It's not, really, though, is it? You are still 'getting help,' as you put it. What about her? Has she sought help?"

Allyson barked out a laugh. "Andrea seeks attention any way she can get it. If someone offered her therapy, she'd play along until it no longer fulfilled her histrionic needs."

"Interesting. Let's stick to you. You call yourselves a freak show. What makes you use that specific term?"

The doctor ran his long, delicate fingers through his muddy-brown hair. It was his tell when he found something she said interesting. Was it Andrea or her? Either way, she loved watching his mind work. They shared an intimacy more profound than a sexual relationship. He saw her through a shallow point in her life. Rather than looking away, he held her gaze. She was someone who mattered.

"Allyson. I asked you a question."

"Sorry. I was trying to devise an astute answer," she lied. More like fantasizing about how he was in bed. "Why did I use the term freak show? By definition, it means a grotesque display to entertain the ignorant. It's exactly how I see identical twins—how all people see us. We're half of a whole or, at best, our mirror image. Clones. The same person in stereo. As far back as I can remember, we were on display—a pretty little carnival sideshow. 'See how cute the twins are in their matching outfits?' or 'Have you ever switched identities? Go to each other's classes, kiss each other's boyfriends'? No one sees us as individuals. Not even ourselves."

"You don't see yourself as an individual?" Dr. Dean uncrossed and recrossed his legs before scribbling more notes.

Allyson caught a peek at his socks. He always wore colorful ones with amusing sayings. Maybe the waiting room *was* his idea. "How can I possibly see myself as an individual when no one else does? When I look in the mirror, the person staring back is someone I hate! And I don't mean self-loathing. I mean my sister."

"And this is why you cut."

"And it's therapy like yours that drives me to drink or worse. Jesus. I can't believe this shit." Allyson crossed her arms over her chest, struggling against the urge to leave. Or cut. Her skin crawled for a bite of something sharp.

"I'm sorry. However, it's important you understand these connections. Self-acceptance goes a long way in recovery. You won't ever see yourself as an individual without accepting every part, including your twindom. Let's try a few self-compassion exercises. It's called Dialectical Behavior Therapy, or DBT. With practice, you will see how your perceived flaws and qualities are what make you different from anyone else, including your sister. It can help with your self-harm tendencies and other disorders too."

Allyson groaned and tipped her head back to look at the ceiling. "I'm counting to ten before I leave. Your recommendation is pointless. As long as Andrea exists, the world will see us as freaks. No special therapy will change society's reaction toward us."

"You're telling me you don't believe I can help you—that no one can. What do you believe in? If there was one thing in your life you could flip a switch and change, what would it be?"

"I'm sensing some frustration, Doc."

"How perceptive," he snapped. "We've been together a year, plus or minus a few sessions. I've guided you through terrible lows as well as successes. If I haven't proven my abilities to you by now, I'm unsure what will. And, if I don't have the answers, you must. Tell me, Allyson, what will it take for you to accept your life's circumstances and move beyond all your psychoses?"

Allyson didn't even hesitate. "Andrea. Gone."

"Gone as in dead?" Dr. Dean leaned forward, elbows on knees.

This question made her hesitate. Did she honestly want her sister dead? Sometimes she did. However, if a magic switch did exist, could Allyson flip it with a clear conscience?

"No. Like tucked away in a hidey-hole. Somewhere safe where she could no longer hurt anyone but still live out her life. Similar to purgatory without the dying bit. A place where she relived the hell she'd wrought on this world through her victims' perspective. Then, I could become someone worthwhile. I'd still feel her in my bones, yet she would no longer hurt anyone, and I would be free."

Allyson met Dr. Dean's stare. It was as if their souls were communing and their heartbeats synching.

"What if that happened?" he asked.

Allyson's breath caught in her throat. "What do you mean?" She didn't recognize her voice. It sounded forced.

"What if Andrea disappeared?" Dr. Dean edged.

Allyson remained silent.

"I've been waiting for you to mention she's missing."

"How do you find out?"

"A Detective Davidson contacted me."

Allyson's face contorted with red-hot anger. "He has no right to talk to you!"

"Why not? It's his job to investigate any leads involving his caseload."

Allyson stood and paced around the room.

"What did you tell him? What did you say? What did *he* say?"

"Allyson," Dr. Dean commanded. "Sit down!"

Surprised, she immediately complied. Dr. Dean never raised his voice. It was as if she was in her father's company instead of her therapist's. It unnerved her. Stuffing her hands between her legs and squeezing them together, she stared at the floor as if it were covered in diamonds.

"You're spinning. Let's recenter before I tell you everything, including my plan to help you. Then you can decide if you want it or not."

Walking her through meridian tapping exercises, Dr. Dean was able to assist Allyson in regulating her emotions.

"Excellent, Allyson. Now, let me answer your questions. Detective Davidson contacted me and asked if it was safe to question you about Andrea. He explained she'd been reported missing by her employer, and her immediate family was difficult to locate. He called me after his visit and told me you were uncooperative yet not hostile, unlike Grace, who won zero points with him. I'm pleased Grace was there when he came by," he smiled in a warm way that crinkled the corners of his eyes. "And I'm proud of you for omitting the full rundown of your sister's wrongdoings."

"It's none of his business," she interjected.

"Precisely. What we talk about here is to help you become the best version of yourself without judgment or getting anyone into trouble. Our conversations are protected, as you are aware. Therefore, I provided the detective with no further information. I also asked him to give me a heads-up on any future contact since this period in your therapy is especially tenuous. That way, we are both prepared. I'm sorry I didn't do that before. Selfishly, I wanted to see how you'd react to the news."

"She's gone incommunicado before. She does it for attention. Or boredom. Or even for fun. Although, she hasn't done it in a while. Probably not since she's been working on *Caretaker*."

"What I find interesting is why you didn't take the opportunity to tell the detective everything about your sister."

Allyson shrugged and remained silent but released her arms from their leg prison and fidgeted. "What she did . . . what she continues to do . . . she's sick. However, I'm skeptical that punishment is the answer. She needs someone like you to help her. She deserves a chance to be fixed . . . if it's possible."

"How empathetic, Allyson, considering all you've shared," Dr. Dean encouraged. "Do you have any idea where she is?"

"No! I don't, and I don't care. It's possible she found that hidey-hole or someone put her there already."

"Are you truly indifferent to what happens to her? Didn't you just say you didn't want anything bad to happen to her?" Dr. Dean asked.

"Stop putting words in my mouth. I said Andrea needs help. Or left in purgatory."

"And what will happen to *you* if she's there? Can you move on and become Allyson Marta, the award-winning artist without the added label of identical twin?"

"Possibly. I've never allowed myself to imagine life without her, even after everything. It's always me wanting to fade away. If it weren't for her, I wouldn't even be alive. Is it fair that I thrive if she can't?"

"What do you mean, 'you wouldn't be alive'?" Dr. Dean asked.

"I've never told you our birth story?"

"No. It's not in my notes, anyway." Dr. Dean glanced at a thick file on his desk but didn't move to open it. "Tell me."

"It's nothing," Allyson held her hands out, palms up. "We were born prematurely. Andrea was first, of course, by eight minutes. She was perfect in every way. When I came, I was weak and in distress. The story goes that I was whisked away to the NICU, where they attached me to machines, wires, and tubes. I was in rough shape. A neonatal doc suggested they put Andrea in the incubator thingy beside me. Since we were in the womb together for thirty-two weeks, I might do better with her there. Sure enough, I started to perk up. However, Andrea declined. They couldn't figure out why. It was as if I was sucking the life force from her to survive. Obviously, it all worked out. Yet, I always wondered if it were true . . . did I take a piece of Andrea? Would she be different, better, without me? Don't I owe it to her to help her *survive*? Don't I owe her everything?"

"This is huge, Allyson. What a breakthrough!" Dr. Dean cheered.

"In what way?"

"You've identified your core misbelief. The false ideology that has been driving your life decisions. In essence, you suffer from survivor's guilt.

You've tolerated your sister's bad behavior because you felt you owed her your life. And it is simply untrue!"

"How can you say that? I could've died."

"Or you would've lived anyway. The point is, no one can prove it was Andrea's presence or a medical protocol that saved your life, which is why it is a false belief. With your newfound knowledge, you have a big decision."

"Which is?" Allyson asked, confused.

"Do you want to live a life without Andrea or not?"

6

A DELAYED FLIGHT

{ROGER}

E ven after popping a pill to make him relaxed and sleepy, Roger was keyed up. He couldn't control his racing mind between the woman across the aisle from him and the news report. Rubbing the back of his neck and bouncing his foot, he counted the minutes until the announcement for pushback came.

"Ladies and Gentlemen, this is Captain Ellen Montoya. The control tower has signaled that a delay at our destination airport, Dubai International, will keep us grounded for a few minutes. Please bear with us while we confirm our scheduled arrival time."

"A woman pilot?" he muttered. "Could this flight be more of a disaster?!"

Contemplating an exit strategy, he peeked out the plane's window. Workers in bright green safety vests milled about. There were more than the usual amount dotting the international gate. However, the Airbus A380 was the largest commercial plane and could accommodate more than 800 people. A huge staff was required to load everything and everyone according to schedule.

What he needed to do was take another pill. Usually, he would stick to one, yet to avoid an all-out panic attack, desperate times called for more self-medication. Grabbing his carry-on bag, he headed to the small bar area close to his seat. Mercifully, an attendant was there, as well as one other passenger.

"Wodka," Roger barked, avoiding eye contact with either person.

Emirates' flight crew members were known for their poise. It was the nature of the air travel business to come across people in varying degrees of emotional distress, so his abrupt nature didn't create a reaction from the bartender. Instead, he slid two fingers of vodka—no ice, in a cut crystal glass toward Roger, who almost cracked a smile at the man's anticipation.

His hand shook as he lifted the glass to his mouth, the pill already melting to a bitter taste under his tongue. Setting the glass back on the rounded counter, he locked eyes with the stranger standing to his left. It was an accident on his part. He'd left his sunglasses at his seat and happened to look just as the fellow passenger mirrored his movements.

Those eyes. He gazed into similar eyes before. Shiny obsidian. Dark, mysterious, and the capacity to frighten while simultaneously showing great compassion. The man was dressed in the traditional Emirati kandura. Roger couldn't help but smirk.

"You caught me, Sir. Yet, we can keep this our little secret, yes?" the man winked and put a jeweled finger to his lips.

He was Muslim, and consuming alcohol was against their beliefs. However, he wasn't the first faithful follower Roger witnessed skirting the limits of proscribed holy texts. His mouth twitched, reversing its attempt at a smile to one of disdain. It wasn't because he was offended by someone weak in their faith. It was the fact that the foreigner felt entitled to exact silence over his personal choice. Roger was burnt-out on making promises to dark-eyed devils.

He turned and bolted back to his seat, fumbling with his safety belt and the air vent. The enormous aircraft's walls seemed closer. The space was cramped, and the air was stifling. Popping in his earbuds and sliding his darkened aviators back in place, he settled into his personal nook, awaiting the barbiturates and alcohol's magic pull.

"Sir? Sir!"

Roger's shoulder shook. He brushed it off as turbulence.

"Excuse me, Sir? You must vacate the plane immediately."

As he swam toward blurry consciousness, Roger became aware of someone shaking him.

"Mr. Wotke? You need to exit the plane at once. Leave your belongings and follow me, please."

"What?" he groaned, struggling to open his eyes. He squinted, trying to focus on the person standing above him.

"Sir, you need to exit the plane now. There's been an emergency."

The voice sounded like nails on a chalkboard—a sickly-sweet pitch feathered with a Middle Eastern accent.

"Are we there already?" he croaked, beginning to stir.

"No, Sir. We haven't left the ground. There's been an emergency, and everyone must deplane at once."

He glanced to his right. The red-headed shrew from earlier was stuffing her belongings into her pockets. "It's her fault, isn't it? You won't ruin my plans, you wench!"

"Sir, please," the flight attendant reprimanded.

"Please, what? I need to get to Uzbekistan, and I need to get there now! She won't ruin my plans again! I promise you!"

"Once we deplane, you can talk to a ticketing agent about rebooking travel. However, I'm afraid you will miss your connection to Uzbekistan. Now, please, you must hurry. Leave your items, and let's go."

The woman moved to hook her arm under Roger's to assist him in standing, but he brushed aside her advance to avoid her touch, accidentally smacking her. She screamed, stepping back and cupping her hands to her face on instinct.

"What is happening here?" another female voice barked in a rougher accented English. "Oh my! Help! We need assistance here at once," she cried after seeing blood dripping from the flight attendant's nose.

In seconds, two male flight crew members rushed to the scene. Feeling threatened, Roger staggered to his feet, holding his carryall bag against his chest like a plate of armor.

"Sir, you will come with us now. Your bag stays on the seat," the crewman from the cocktail bar ordered.

"No. I need to get to Uzbekistan, and you people are ruining everything!" Roger yelled, spittle flying from his mouth.

"All luggage, including carry-ons, must be left for inspection."

"But . . . but," Roger stuttered, "It's mine!"

"Sir. Hand over the bag," the second male crew member commanded. As he grabbed for it, a short tug-of-war ended when Roger punched him.

Across the aisle, the red-nailed woman was using her phone to video the altercation. He launched at her before being tackled from behind and thrown to the plane's floor. With his arms forced behind his back, a crew member duct-taped his wrists together. Not only was his freedom at stake, but his life too. Kicking his feet out, he attempted to squirm away, only to be caught by the foot. A short wrestling match earned him bindings at the ankles as well.

In a bit straight out of a celebrity gossip show, Roger was carried off the plane by the two men, his first-class passenger mate filming the entire time. It wouldn't be long before his real identity was revealed and his face splashed all over social media and news outlets.

The airport was in chaos. Several hundred disgruntled and scared passengers were forced to deplane at once. Yet when Roger was spotted being hauled off like a six-foot-four potato sack, the terminal went silent.

"Help me! I'm being abducted! I'm being denied my basic human rights! Do you know who I am, for Chrissake? Call my attorney! Call the Studio. Vanessa Rapaporte. I'm the goddamn *Caretaker*. You can't do this!"

Roger's shouting and vitriol continued until he was delivered to a closet-sized windowless room in the airport terminal's back halls. These rooms were reserved for TSA and FBI interviews of travelers suspected of everything from shoplifting to terrorism.

Despite all the drama, once left alone, he laid his face on the cool metal table and fell asleep.

It was night along the Vancouver harbor banks. Roger was sipping his third pint of draft beer at a nearby watering hole, Remorse & Co. The crowd thinned as the nearby Waterfront Train Station sounds ramped up. A few yards down the block was a shipping container terminal. It too was busy loading and unloading cargo ships filled with consumer goods bound for destinations all over Canada. The air was heavy and humid, which made Roger all the more dejected about the trajectory of his existence. He received word earlier in the day that the part he auditioned for was awarded to another lowlife with similar acting origins. This project was supposed to resuscitate life back into his controversial and faded career.

He threw two bills on the table, stood up, and swilled the last dregs of his drink. Swiping the back of his hand over a horrible mat of coarse facial hair, he belched and staggered into the courtyard cul-de-sac outside. Three months, he'd been growing the disgusting beard in preparation for the role. Its only saving grace was that he was unrecognizable as the guy who used to be famous.

Unsure where he was headed, he wandered out onto Water St, the main attraction in the Gastown neighborhood. A cruise ship departed from the Canada Place terminal a few hours before, taking with it the regular touristy traffic littering the area. In fact, the street seemed eerily empty.

Ahead of him was the silhouette of two people, clearly a man and a woman. He could hear their raised voices bouncing off the building facades and he slowed his pace to eavesdrop. Knowing women the way he did, Roger assumed she'd probably wronged the poor guy somehow. Flirted with another man at the bar or spent too much money shopping. Or maybe she hoarded all their money like that old woman in *Crime and Punishment*, and he was sick of her selfishness.

Slipping his hand into his front pocket, he pulled out a pack of cigarettes. It should've been his last. He swore to himself if he got the part, he'd quit. At least, there was one good thing about being denied this opportunity. Sliding one out, he rolled it between his fingers, examining it as if it held all the answers to his future, before flipping it into his mouth and lighting it. He lingered, feigning interest in something in the shop window facing him before proceeding forward on his route as the couple moved on. When they turned onto a side street, he followed at a decent pace to avoid arousing suspicion. They turned again and stood in the shadows, their shouting increasing in volume and intensity. Roger debated whether he should intervene. When he caught their arms flailing and the echo of skin hitting skin reverberating in the darkness, he lurched forward. He'd witnessed enough. However, he skidded to a complete stop when the man dropped to his knees under the spotlight of a lamppost. Something glinted in the woman's hand. Roger sucked in air through his teeth. He had just witnessed a stabbing and possible murder.

He was close enough to the scene that his reaction carried. The woman turned to hurry off down another alleyway when Roger ran after her. Glancing at the street sign as he passed over the body and under the light, he barked a laugh. *Blood Street.* "How synchronistic," he muttered, quirking his lips into a wry smile.

He seized the woman by the arm, and she swung out wildly, ready to take his life too, if she must.

"Hey! Hey. It's okay. I only wanted to make sure you were all right. I heard you guys arguing. It sounded like someone got hit."

Her eyes twinkled in the reflection of the streetlight. They were shiny obsidian, black as night, and full of dark mysteries and terrifying tales.

"It'll be our little secret, yeah?" she asked, with no regret in her tone. Then she stepped forward, dropping her knife arm to her side. She grabbed the back of Roger's neck, yanked him to her, and kissed him hard—with tongue. He had never been more stunned or more turned on in his life.

"Wakey-wakey, Mr. Wotke," a female voice singsonged.

Roger scanned the room, disoriented from sleep and the memory haunting him for the last ten years.

"I brought you a coffee. Black. You look like you could use it." A petite Asian woman in a black pantsuit pointed at a Styrofoam cup on the table.

Roger narrowed his gaze at the woman. "She thinks she can spoil my plans, but I won't let her," he mumbled, lips moving imperceptibly.

"I beg your pardon? Is there something bothering you, Mr. Wotke?"

"You might say," he began. "You obviously know my name. So quit this shit and cut me loose. Then you can get your boss in here to apologize before getting me on another flight to Uzbekistan. NOW!"

"I'm afraid . . ."

Roger interrupted her. "I also need my bag returned to me at once."

"All bags need to be inspected due to the nature of the threat. It's for everyone's safety."

"What threat?" he growled. "The only threat I see is your agency's blatant abuse of power and overreach. At a bare minimum, I want my lawyer here."

"We need to ask you a few questions. Your cooperation is appreciated. However, as a Homeland Security agent, I have the authority to hold you without counsel," she stated, looking him square in the eye. The woman explained her position as she stood there, hands clasped behind her back. It forced her to stand straighter, like a soldier at ease.

"I will ask you again because you seem to avoid my questions, yet expect me to answer yours. What. Threat?!" he demanded through gritted teeth.

"Your flight was canceled due to a credible security threat."

"And you think I'm involved?" Roger asked.

"You *did* punch two flight crew members on an international flight. The FBI has been notified. You are already in serious trouble. You could help yourself by explaining to me why you were with this man," she slid a picture from a folder and placed it on the table, "during the boarding process."

Roger studied it. It was the Emirati from the airplane bar, and he explained as much to his inquisitor. "It's not a crime to get a drink on an eighteen-hour flight!"

She put the photo back in the folder. Her hands were bony yet smooth, the nails well-manicured and short. The veins protruded slightly, and Roger could perceive her pulse through her translucent skin. The sight made him gag.

"No, it's perfectly legal to get a drink," the agent replied, quirking her head in a way a scientist might observe a test subject. "However, possessing illegal or controlled substances without a proper prescription is a different matter."

Roger narrowed his eyes. "Who has the credible threat now? By the way, I'm losing blood flow to my hands, and an old rotator cuff problem could get aggravated if you don't get this tape off me soon. I'm smelling a lawsuit."

"What is your relationship with the Emirati?" she asked.

"Relationship? Like we were fucking or something?" Roger grinned.

The woman groaned. "Look. I don't give a flying fuck who you are. The airport is in lockdown, and thousands of scared and angry passengers are out there wondering how they will make it to their destinations. If you answer the questions honestly, things will go much smoother."

Roger teetered to his feet, trying to regain his balance thanks to the duct tape. "Well, you *should* give a flying fuck because I'm the one who is going to end your career if you don't cut me free right now. I'm *The Caretaker*. I'm on every fucking billboard, bus, and park bench in this god-forsaken city. I just came from headlining the largest comic book and pop culture convention in the Pacific Northwest. I'm not a terrorist or any other label you want to assign me. What I am is a very pissed-off famous person who should be treated with some goddamn respect!" His chest heaved as he tried to catch his breath.

The door opened in a silent *whoosh* behind him. The only indication another person entered the room was a man clearing his voice.

"Mr. Wotke, *Caretaker*, whichever you prefer, please sit. Your face is purple. We wouldn't want you to fall ill. Quite the opposite, in fact. And to prove it, I'm going to free your legs first. Then, your arms. However, you must agree to restraints . . ."

Roger protested.

"Please, let me finish," the man asked in a soft, grandfatherly voice, waiting until Roger complied. "Good. Agent Wu will handcuff you in the front to relieve the pressure from your shoulders. However, we reserve the right to return to the standard fashion of behind your back if you act out aggressively. Do we have an agreement?"

Roger inclined his head.

The man produced a pocketknife. "If you would be so kind as to sit." He turned the chair in a position allowing easy access to Roger's legs.

Defeated, Roger dropped into the chair with a thud.

"I am Dr. Signori, and I work alongside Agent Wu in Homeland Security. My job is to assess detainees. I consider myself a human lie detector. I can also spot personality disorders and other psychological disturbances."

Agent Wu handcuffed Roger as the doctor promised before relinquishing her role as the interrogator, leaving the two alone.

"*Finally!*" Roger whispered as the woman retreated.

"I've been asked to talk to you due to the medications found in your carry-on. Is this okay?"

Roger made a loud gasping sound and nodded once in affirmation.

"Do you mind me asking how long ago you were diagnosed with your condition?"

Roger had no condition. He struggled with staying asleep and went through bouts of anxiety and depression. Still, nothing was labeled on his medical record as a condition.

"Mr. Wotke? I asked you a question. How long have you had your particular disorder?"

Roger eyed the man. He didn't have the countenance of a doctor. "That bitch agent called you in because I refused to talk to her, didn't she?!" His mind was roiling. He wouldn't play their game of good Doc, bad cop. He knew his rights. HE KNEW HIS RIGHTS, goddammit! "This is preposterous! Lawyer. Now."

"Agent Wu already spoke to you about our authority to question you without legal representation."

"Then I'm exercising my right to refuse to answer. This is nonsense. I have done nothing wrong! And now you've all ruined my plans. You've ruined everything!" Roger screamed again.

The doctor lowered his chin to his chest and blew out a long, low sigh. He assessed Roger one last time before straightening his tie and shuffling out the door as wordlessly as he had entered.

Alone in the windowless room, Roger paced around the 6x9 space. It wasn't a large area, especially for a six-foot-four, two-hundred-pound man. But his mind was restless, which made his body tense. He occupied himself with scenarios and countermoves he could use to escape before another visitor entered the room.

This man was dressed in a dark blue uniform with the TSA logo on the sleeve. He held Roger's carry-on and set it on the table. Pulling out a small, ornately carved wooden box, like something you might find in East Asia, he placed it next to the bag. An awkward silence ensued until the man finally spoke. "Due to the nature of the security violation, TSA is authorized to take extra precautions with any containers. The normal X-ray scanner saw nothing but a blank space inside this box, which was odd. Why would someone place an empty box inside their carry-on? The carry-on he didn't want to surrender when ordered to by airport personnel. Imagine our surprise when we opened it and discovered the liner was made in a special material impeding the X-ray machine."

Roger examined the box, keeping his expression neutral while fighting the urge to grab and hold it close. His memory forced him to recall her face, and he closed his eyes to resist the visage of an angel, the work of the devil. "The box is filled with mementos. Invaluable only to me."

He pictured the gold locket, its long, thin chain seemingly too delicate to hold the weight of the sizable charm. Inside, a woman's photo and an engraved message read, "Two coins with the same side."

"Roger Adolphus Wotke, a.k.a. *The Caretaker*, you are being charged with three counts of felony battery and six counts of felony assault. The FBI will take you into custody shortly. Do you have anything further to add?"

"L. A. W. Y. E. R."

The man moved to place the box back into the bag. Roger tensed, anticipating the agent's next move.

"Leave my stuff," he ordered. He was used to having things done his way.

"I'm afraid that can't happen."

"You've already inspected everything. Did you find your credible security breach inside?"

The agent narrowed his eyes at Roger and quirked his mouth into a menacing grin. "We found some interesting stuff. I'm sure your fans would love a little glimpse inside their demented anti-hero's world."

Jumping from his seat, Roger charged forward, baring his teeth. Before the startled agent could move, he was thrown against the wall. Roger's shoulder planted firm into the man's chest, a move learned from years of being a lineman during rugby matches as a youth in Argentina.

"Help! Help me!" the agent cried.

Several men dressed in black suits rushed the room. The last thing Roger heard as an electrical charge surged through his body was his *Caretaker* catchphrase, "You're out of time, shit-bird."

7

DANGERS SEE
AND UNSEEN

{ANDREA}

Andrea moved through the dark labyrinth of the film studio's obstacles and pitfalls as if she were the studio's designer rather than the rat trapped within its maze. Her temporary blindness wasn't a hindrance. Instead, it pushed her other senses to come alive. She never stepped inside a film studio before and only speculated on her location because of all the props and various soundstages.

Soon, she was overcome by a noxious odor. It was like a swamp of a thousand rotting rodent carcasses mixed with the sweet smell of cheap perfume. The aroma grabbed her by the throat and burned her nostrils, triggering her gag reflex. Her whole body tensed and jerked as she lost the contents of her stomach.

With her hands on her knees, she took a moment to recover. A buzzing noise started behind her and grew so loud it overwhelmed her ears and made her whole body tense. She shuffled forward, her direction uncertain, while her skin tingled in warning. All she could imagine was a swarm of flies gathering around her to feast on whatever dead things lay about. She'd seen and smelled some rancid settings in her role as a crime scene sketch artist, and this refreshed those memories.

A rustling nearby urged her to move faster. Increasing her speed as much as she dared, she flailed her arms out to ensure she didn't run into anything. Or *anyone*. Gooseflesh popped up all over her body as she entered an area where the air temperature went from cool and dry to warm and sticky. At first, she considered it a physiological reaction to the vomiting and overall anxiety of the situation. Yet as she continued to move, the change was more definitive. The terrible odor increased tenfold. More nausea brought her to her knees as she retched and gagged. Her response surprised her. She'd always had a strong stomach. It was a joke among her colleagues, teasing her about her lack of emotion in their challenging work.

"Check out Andrea's face. What do the profilers call it? Flat affect? Do you feel no empathy, Andrea? Or is your olfactory broken?" A coworker jeered.

"Maybe she's just a psychopath," said another.

Those words replayed in her mind as if they happened yesterday. Yet she couldn't figure out how and why she was stuck in a movie studio. She clenched her jaw and ran her fingers through her hair.

Another whoosh close by caused her muscles to tighten while her hands turned clammy. Was she being watched? Or was something standing directly behind her? Bending low, she used her fingers to search for a crevice or anything to crawl into and reconnect with her sanity. She needed to hide. As she scooted forward, she touched a moist, grainy substance, like wet dirt. Taking a fistful, she raised her hand to her nose and inhaled deeply.

"Yes, I can smell, you jackasses," she mumbled, referring to her earlier memory. Relief swept over her as the earthy aroma replaced whatever rot still clung in the air and to her nose hairs.

Standing on shaky limbs, she resumed her steady slog, only to trip over a tree root a few feet later, which sent her sprawling back to the ground. Her hands and knees splashed into a viscous-like puddle.

"For fuck's sake! What's next?!" she cried, slamming her fists in the slushy mess. "Would some light be too much to ask?"

It was stupid to shout, even to speak aloud. But she was tired, hungry, and sore. Not to mention scared shitless. The fear was the least of her worries, though. She could handle fear.

"Stuff it in a box and throw away the key," her mother always said. "Fear is a useless emotion leftover from cavemen days. It only serves to hold you back."

"For all Patricia Marta's faults, she was spot on there," Andrea muttered before rising again.

This time, as she continued forward, she shuffled her feet closer together to protect her from any further accidents. As if someone heard her demands, low lights clicked on as she passed by. Perhaps they were motion-sensor safety lights. They gave off a bluish, smoky glow, similar to twilight in the hills. As her eyes adjusted, her surroundings became more apparent, and another memory stirred.

An island oasis nestled deep in the woods north of Vancouver. Her island. A place all her own within a small forest of ancient evergreens, where she could step away from all the demands of modern living and just be. She half expected to see her house off to the right. Her she-shed would skirt the edge of the tree line, with her chopping block outside its entrance and her various canoes mounted along its side. Her eyes watered in a momentary sweep of emotion and vulnerability. Stopping to lean against a fake tree, she tugged her hospital gown's collar to wipe away the involuntary moisture while also clearing her thoughts and vision. With renewed purpose, she assessed the surroundings to carve out a new path with a possible exit.

Something in the dim distance caught her attention, and a warm adrenaline rush surged through her limbs.

"Is that a building? How can this be? Everything I think about suddenly exists! Why can't I imagine an exit sign?" she berated herself.

Andrea smacked her palm against her temple to clear her mind, causing pain to shoot through her eye. "Oiy, my head!" she gasped, recalling the dent. Cautiously, she poked and prodded the area, soft and gentle at first. Then, with more clinical determination. Everything felt normal, and her hand came away clean—no blood.

"What the actual fuck?!" Andrea cried out as her heart jumped in her chest, its beats booming loudly in her ears. Her legs wobbled as her imagination churned wild theories and worst-case scenarios. She wanted to lie down, to give herself a moment before she hyperventilated. Yet she felt too vulnerable and exposed. She could turn around and head back to the apartment setting, where she could sleep in an actual bed. Only, other things she didn't want to revisit lurked there too. Her intuition pushed her to keep moving forward. Perhaps the building ahead would allow her to rest safely. This *was* just a soundstage. She had no real elemental exposure risk, and it might make a good hiding spot.

Arriving at the small building, its outside appeared identical to her shed, right down to the complicated lock. Entry was reserved for her alone.

"How? How is someone doing this? Recreating events from my life?"

Tentatively, she unlatched the door and stepped inside, filled with expectation and anticipation.

Even with little lighting, Andrea could tell it was different. Relief mixed with disappointment as she stepped in, leaving the creaking door open a sliver to allow ambient light to shine in. Something tickled the crown of her head, and she swatted at it on instinct, imagining cobwebs and orb spiders getting tangled in her hair. It was a string attached to a single bare bulb hanging from the ceiling. Pulling it, she was half surprised when it illuminated the cramped space.

She stood in the center, taking inventory. Rusted lawn equipment dangled from rotting nails protruding from the wall. Shelves filled with dusty, empty beer cans and motor oil lined another wall, while the third held pinup girl posters from various eras. This wasn't her shed at all, but a regular caretaker's shed—something found on the edge of a property where the man of the house might go to tinker. It even had a built-in workbench, which jutted out about a foot from under the shelves, its top littered with sharpening tools, a wrench set, and an opened tool chest. Underneath it, wool blankets were piled, as well as more jugs filled with cloudy liquid.

The back of her neck pricked as she thought back to the supply room. Bending to inspect its contents, a gap in the floorboards caught her eye. A polished stainless steel recessed pull handle, hidden in plain sight, glinted in the overhead light. Unable to resist the urge, she tugged it. The protesting hinges of the secret door screeched, piercing her eardrums as she lifted it slowly to reveal a staircase leading into a dark abyss. She feared the noise was loud enough that its reverberation could be heard miles away. She didn't dare move, waiting for a reaction from anyone lurking nearby. When nothing happened, she continued to investigate. Looking around at the items again, she spotted what she'd hoped to find: an old-fashioned lantern. Except this was a movie studio, so naturally, it wasn't just a lantern but a battery-operated one made to mimic something from the 1950s. With a bit of luck on her side, it flicked on the first try.

She laughed at the absurdity of wanting to continue exploring. However, she lacked few options other than to continue through her personalized hellscape. She was bound to find an exit sooner or later. Despite behaving like the dimwitted girl in a typical horror movie, Andrea lifted the lantern over her head and descended the cold metal steps toward inevitable danger.

Half expecting to hear chainsaws and people being tortured, she shivered at the drastic drop in temperature as she stepped on the dark tunnel's damp floor. The light from the lantern only extended a few feet before her, but it was enough to give her a quick layout.

The right side of the tunnel was smooth concrete in varying shades of gray. White and dark imperfect circles painted the walls in natural moisture petroglyphs. The left side was fortified with irregularly shaped stones of various sizes. The floor was solid and gritty, like hard-packed earth. Above her ran several types of piping attached to the arched ceiling. As she walked forward, spray-painted markings, including arrows and numbers, appeared on the concrete side. Yet it was unclear what they were trying to convey. Next was an abandoned folding ladder laying on its side against the wall and six five-gallon buckets filled with hammers, crowbars, and other tools. Rounding a corner, she came to a decision point. To her left was another opening she assumed led to a different arm of the tunnel. Straight ahead, she spotted a stack of two-by-fours and a wheelbarrow. Shining her light to the left, she stepped in a few feet and came across vertical steel bars blocking forward progress. It was like a hollowed-out cave, deep enough; she couldn't make out its dimensions. Something shiny glinted in a far corner, and as she fiddled with trying to shine the light through the bars, she froze. It was a hospital gurney.

Her shoulders tensed as her grip tightened on the lantern handle. Turning back the way she came, she continued past the building materials and an alcove filled with spare pipes, a spool of electrical wire, and various construction supplies. Further still, a metal railing about a foot wide appeared on the wall to her left. Spray cans, hand tools, empty water bottles, and other trash led the way forward like a trail of litter instead of breadcrumbs. Another alcove opened to the left and housed the same medical supply carts from the storage closet stacked on top of each other. She wet her dry lips and shrugged off ideas about why those carts were in the tunnel.

Another alcove a few feet further led to a steel door with hinges mounted on the outside and a wheeled handle similar to those on a submarine ship. Her lantern's light reflected off a small circular glass window towards the door's top center. A cold shiver crawled down her spine while her arm and leg hairs stood at attention. She would pass on the temptation to look inside, her mind already spinning with terrifying scenarios. Turning on her heels, she hurried back to the main walkway.

The further she shuffled along the corridor, the more evidence of human activity was revealed, raising her hopes of a nearby exit. As she continued, she passed two more alcoves with identical doors and a third with vertical bars. She didn't dare explore any inlets.

When she was about to abandon her search and return to the shed, her light shone on another set of steel stairs. Taking them two at a time, she was immediately disappointed when she hit a dead end. Weak and shivering with a chill in her bones, Andrea sat on the top step with a thud. Setting the lantern beside her, she placed her head in her hands, trying hard to remain calm. She was tough. However, exhaustion and disappointment were winning over her need to escape.

"Who would build stairs to nowhere?" she murmured into her hands. "It's like I'm stuck in the fucking Winchester Mystery House in San Jose!"

Her left shoulder ached, and her back was sore. To soothe the built-up tension from this whole experience, she massaged it vigorously and groaned. "Think, Andrea. Where would the exit door be if this movie complex was built around your life?"

With a rush of inspiration, she grabbed her lantern and ran back down the stairs. Energized, she shone her light on the surrounding walls, looking for clues.

"This is a tunnel. A tunnel is underground. Its purpose is to allow travel between locations that might otherwise be blocked or made difficult based on terrain and weather. Or it's a secret passageway to move about an area undetected. Where things are kept concealed except to those in the know." She recalled the first cove with the gurney inside and shuddered. "I've got plenty of secrets that need to remain hidden and ghosts that will haunt me forever, as evidenced by what I saw earlier in the apartment set. Still, this can't be from my life."

The voice in her head mocked her. Swatting her doubt away with a physical wave of her lantern hand, something caught her attention on the stone wall to her left. It was a deep crack in the mortar, obscured without direct light. Setting the lamp on the ground to face the spot, she pressed and pushed around the area, hoping a secret opening would emerge. When her frantic search didn't reveal anything, she pounded her fists into the wall before sliding to the ground with a defeated thump.

"Fuck," she hissed, pinching the bridge of her nose and closing her eyes. Her big toe throbbed from the cut earlier, and her fingers ached from the cold.

Scanning the area one final time and finding no exit strategy, she stood to head back the way she came. She could always warm up in the stinking swamp and crash in the shed with the moth-eaten blankets. Rolling her head around to relieve a crick in her neck, something in the ceiling caught her eye. Lifting her lantern, a metal grate was revealed.

"Ventilation," she considered. "If airshafts exist, they eventually lead to somewhere outside. Only, how do I get up there?"

Running through her options, she considered the numerous five-gallon buckets she'd come across and the metal carts.

"Can I stack them high enough to reach the opening?"

Retracing the way she came, she paid closer attention to what was left behind. Emptying a bucket, she filled it with items she might find useful. A screwdriver, a crowbar, a hacksaw, and an unopened water bottle all went in the bucket.

"The ladder!" she yelled, remembering it from when she first entered the tunnel.

The whole way back, she debated whether she was foolish for wanting to explore the vent shafts versus returning to the shed's safety. Once she got there, running through the details and physical effort it would take to search them seemed too daunting. Setting her bucket on the ground, she climbed the stairs from which she descended.

"What the?"

The hatch from the shed was closed. Pushing on it tentatively at first, then more forcefully, she determined it was locked.

"Who the fuck is messing with me?" Her anger swelled. She wanted to scream and demand whomever it was to show themselves, but self-preservation won out, and her earlier mantra rang in her ears. "Free yourself. Then escape. I guess my decision is made. The ladder and vents it is."

The first vent she encountered was right near the room with the iron bars. Her body ached with effort as she set the ladder, climbed with her bucket of supplies, and surveyed the opening. She removed the cover using her screwdriver and peered inside the shaft. Cold air rushed from the galvanized ductwork.

"Nothing," she grumbled.

Next was the vent across from the first submarine door. As she set the ladder, Andrea studied the mysterious portal. Walking over to the door, she tried turning the wheeled handle. It wouldn't budge. On further inspection, its edges were welded shut. Pressing her ear to the door, she held her breath to focus on any sound coming from the other side. Andrea held out as long as she could, praying inwardly she wouldn't hear anything. When no sound returned, she moved onto the vent.

Exhausted and disappointed, she checked two more vents before returning to the tunnel's other end. Climbing the ladder with her bucket, she stopped to break open the water bottle. As she tilted her head back to drink, the final cover caught her eye. Clips and a hidden lever secured this one.

"It was right here all along," she shook her head before working the mechanisms to reveal an opening to a room above. "I'm a fucking idiot."

Hoisting herself into the room, she leaned back down to grab her lantern and supplies in case she might need them. The bucket handle caught the cracked top cap of the ladder, spilling the contents onto the tunnel floor and knocking the ladder over.

"Shhhiiittttt!" she yelled, grappling for purchase around the opening. The last thing she needed was to fall back through along with the items.

Scooting away from the cavity, she rolled onto her back, haggard by her near miss. Again, she waited and listened to see if the racket raised any new dangers or her unknown assailant. When no one came, she sat up and took in her new surroundings.

She was in a workshop with large windows installed just below the ceiling, similar to a warehouse or factory space. Two long wooden tables filled the center of the room. Small, funky lamps made from spare copper pipe fittings sat on each end, lighting the room in an amber glow. Drawings, random papers, and lumps of clay were strewn over the tabletops. She walked over and gasped as she traced the lines of a sketch. They were from the beginning of her career . . . crimes and bodies she was hired to detail for investigations, drawings from her imagination and dreams, and a half-carved hunk of clay shaped into a human face—a face with a dented skull.

"Fuck!" she hissed, jumping away from the sculpture as if it was electrified. It was the ghostly image that chased her from the apartment set earlier. He must have been a hallucination! He was dead—dead, disposed of, and fish food.

Memories stirred inside her and cramped her stomach. Looking past the tables, a leather couch was shoved against a corner wall. A colorful knitted afghan was thrown over its rounded arm. Perpendicular to the sofa was a door left cracked open. More soft light leaked out onto the wide planked wood floors.

Tiptoeing towards it, she was relieved to discover it was a full bathroom with a shower and towels. Unable to resist, Andrea took full advantage of its facilities, taking the time to wash and assess her physical state. She might be the corrupt one of the Marta twins, but she wasn't uncivilized. Her body needed a thorough cleanse.

The water was warm and comforting, like a hug from a lover reunited after a long separation. Or the kind a mother might give a child after they'd been hurt. Although, in Andrea's case, it was more often a nanny or the housekeeper. She washed away the aches, pains, and dirt from her various excursions. The experience provided ablution, making it almost religious—a symbolic baptism.

Wiping steam from the mirror above the sink after her shower, Andrea was startled by her reflection. Her face was swollen on the right side, and a hematoma sat above her eye. What makeup remained made her resemble Alice Cooper, and a reddish rash ran from her cheekbone into her hairline. If she'd been in an accident, she was the passenger, considering only her right side was affected.

"Is that why I can't remember how I got here?" she asked her reflection.

With no answers forthcoming, she took the towel from her body, wrapped her wet hair, and padded naked to the couch, snuggling into the warm blanket. Curling into herself, she settled into the soft leather, staring ahead at the tables. Her eyes landed on the lamps and their vintage Edison bulbs. "Steampunk" was the word that came to mind, and then her sister Allyson. The buzzing in her ears from earlier started again as the room spun.

"Why does this keep happening?" Andrea whispered as she disconnected from reality.

"You came! I didn't think you would," Allyson rejoiced.

"Don't read into it," Andrea replied. "I was in Seattle anyway. Besides, whenever we are in proximity to one another, my insides itch until I see you. It's maddening. You're an invisible layer of skin weighing heavily upon my shoulders. No matter what I do, the weight doesn't let up until I see you."

"Awww. I love you too, sissy," Allyson mocked. "You're always so dark and brooding. I thought I was the shadow. Is that why you always seek the limelight?"

"I don't go looking for it; attention just comes to me naturally. Besides, you don't do too bad yourself with these large art installations and exhibits. Everyone in the Art World knows Allyson Marta. When I started on *The Caretaker*, someone actually asked if I was you."

"How horrible. What did you do?" Allyson laughed.

"I fired them."

"Good call," Allyson grinned. "So anyway, I asked you here for a favor."

"I figured as much. How much do you need this time?"

"Oh, it's not money. I want to show you something and see what you think. Come with me," Allyson waved her hand as she turned her back to Andrea and walked down a hall.

Andrea followed. Her footsteps were heavy and slow as if she were wearing cement shoes, which made it hard to keep pace with her sister. The air shifted into a dream-like haze, and Allyson became a fuzzy blur as she skipped happily along. Andrea blinked in rapid succession to clear her vision and focus on the way forward but wound up tripping over her feet. Fortunately, she caught herself on a handrail.

"Be careful, silly! Just down these steps," Allyson called in an echo, sounding far away.

"Wait!" Andrea tried yelling, but her voice didn't seem to work.

"C'mon, Dre! Hurry!" Allyson urged.

"I can't . . ." Andrea gasped and fell face-first onto a hard, scratchy surface.

Rolling onto her back, she groaned and swiped away debris from her face. Was that gravel and dirt? When she opened her eyes, she was startled to discover she was encircled by teenagers who looked vaguely familiar.

"What have you done, Andrea? What have you done?! You always ruin everything!" Allyson sobbed. "Look at what you've done! You have to make this right. You have to fix this!"

It was twelve-year-old Allyson. How did Andrea move from her adult sister to her childhood one? Did she time travel? Or was this another hallucination?

Trying to place the exact moment in time she was currently revisiting, the memory punched her hard in the solar plexus. It was the summer before middle school and the night of her first murder.

8

A TENTATIVE TRANSFORMATION

{ALLYSON}

Allyson bounded from her therapist's office with an unusual smile on her face and a lightness unfamiliar to her. She refused to entertain life without Andrea before today. She considered freedom from her twin to be like erasing her reflection. She didn't dare to dream about having her own identity. It goes without saying that she did fantasize about Andrea's untimely demise from time to time. Those were silly fantasies, though. She didn't mean anything by them. She hadn't been strong enough until recently to consider independence, and the idea excited her.

A cold, brisk wind blew in her face, sending a chill through her clothes. Stuffing her hands in her wool coat pockets, she hunched her shoulders and hurried towards the light-rail stop that would deliver her back home. As she arrived at the entrance to the building, her phone vibrated. Pulling it from her coat pocket, she hesitated before looking at the caller ID.

"Aww, shit!" she moaned, placing it to her ear. "Hey, Vince. I was just thinking about you."

"Bullshit. Unless you were looking at your empty bank account and wondering where all your money went. Where are you right now?"

"Leaving downtown and heading back to my hovel. Why?"

"You know why. I need sketches, Allyson. And I need them five months ago."

"I sent you sketches five months ago."

"Yeah, and they were unusable! Millions will see this installation. '*A Day in the Psych Ward*' doesn't speak to a broader audience."

"Well, it should, Vince. That's what's wrong with this fucking world. No one wants to see or talk about the real shit. The ugly shit. Mental illness is rampant, and all people want to prattle about is what handbag is hot this season or which celebrity housewife got into a drunken fistfight this week."

"I agree. However, unless you want to return your sizeable retainer fee, you must stick with the elements detailed in the prospectus. Please reassure me you've got this. I don't want to sell all my belongings and leave the country in embarrassment!"

"They won't make me give back the retainer, Vince. Beitin came to me, remember? He couldn't stop talking about the SeaTac installation and how it spoke to him. More people travel through the airport daily than wandering around the Space Needle."

"Your art was different then. You need to find your muse again."

"I am sought after for my mixed media methods, not because I'm a Starbucks. Each piece is unique to a time in my life and where my imagination takes me. It would be boring to continue doing what I've already done."

"I get it, honey. I do," Vince grumbled. "Would you look at the prospectus again and see if you can get me an idea or two in the next few days, huh?"

"Yeah, sure. I'll whip it right up. First, though, my chariot has arrived."

"You're taking mass transit?"

Allyson could hear the disgust in Vince's voice. "Yes. It's all part of my creative process. Now, let me absorb the inspiration."

"More like perspiration. Ugh. Goodbye."

A double-beep and Vince was gone.

"Shit," Allyson murmured as she stepped into the train car. She popped in her earbuds and selected a playlist to help ease her anxiety while opening her mind to the creative muse.

Dozing off, she dreamed of contorted faces and bright flashing lights. Fortunately, two arguing aunties who sat across from her woke her with their racket in time to hop off before the train moved on. As she approached her building, she spotted two unmarked white vans, often used by electricians, construction workers, and serial killers across the US and Canada. They were parked haphazardly along the sidewalk, which put her on edge. Was there an emergency? She didn't need any more drama.

Two residents she recognized from another floor whispered inside the entrance as she passed to the elevators. This behavior wasn't unusual, considering the building's clientele, but something about their posture turned her mouth dry, and her heart fluttered faster. Hitting the call button, the digital display showed it was coming from her floor. A noise came from behind her. Turning, Nina, the woman who lived down the hall, was standing in the small alcove by the mailboxes. She was the resident busybody.

"They say they are pest control . . . ," Nina murmured.

"What?" Allyson asked, unsure what the woman said.

"The men in white. They were in your apartment. Grace was hollering at them to get out, but they weren't cooperating. You might want to get scarce while you can."

Allyson chose the opposite and took the stairs, two at a time, arriving on the third floor wheezing and huffing. The neighbor followed much slower to see Allyson and Grace enter her opened front door.

"What's going on? Why are you people in my place? Who let you in?"

"They let themselves in," Grace pouted.

"The Supe let us in," replied a tall man in white coveralls.

"Why?" Grace demanded.

"Pest control," said another, waving a wand in one hand while carrying a small opaque container with a hose attached in the other.

"This is a recovery house for patients suffering from various mental illnesses. You can't come in here, demanding entry to our private spaces. You risk upsetting the residents," Grace scolded.

"Actually, we can. Your manager requested our presence due to a reported roach outbreak. If we treat one apartment, we have to treat them all, or they just move on to the next place."

Dr. Dean stepped into Allyson's opened apartment door, with Nina hovering outside, her hands covering her mouth as if to silence a scream. He stomped towards the tall man who acted as the leader, their noses practically touching.

"You are full of shit. I own this residential building. It's a secure facility with protocols in place to prevent such things from happening. You need to leave before I call the cops, but first, I need your information, starting with who you say contacted you."

His voice was so low and menacing, both Allyson and Grace moved to hold hands in comforting solidarity.

"He's extremely hot right now," Grace stage whispered.

Allyson shivered. "Why would someone lie about being pest control?"

"To plant electronic bugs and spy on us, obviously," Grace winked.

Allyson suppressed a giggle. "The schizo's upstairs must be tripping out. I'm thinking you need to move there too!" she teased, elbowing Grace in the ribs.

They stood by as a silent standoff occurred between their therapist and the workers. It was as if it were the Rose Ceremony from *The Bachelor* TV show.

"Fine. Dan? You got the work order on you?" Tall Man asked, keeping his eyes locked on Dr. Dean.

"I left it with the Supe."

"Well, I guess we need to go speak with Marv. You first, gentlemen," Dr. Dean directed, waving his hand towards the door.

Nina slipped away as everyone's attention turned towards the vacating men. Dr. Dean put his hands in his pockets and tipped his head towards his shiny black leather loafers, blowing out a long stream of air through his pursed lips. Then he whipped his head up and met Allyson and Grace's gaze.

"I'm sorry this happened. I promise I'll find answers and call a group meeting in the basement as soon as I get a handle on what is happening here." He touched Allyson's exposed arm. "Are you okay? You look shaken."

"I've got her, Dr. Dean. You go whoop some ass," Grace encouraged.

Dr. Dean headed toward the door, pausing to look back at his patients. He frowned and turned, quietly closing it on his way out.

"Everyone back to your rooms until further notice!" he commanded. "I'll text out meeting details once I have some answers."

"Apparently, we had an audience," Grace smirked as they made their way to Allyson's sofa. "How about pizza?"

"What do you think those guys were really doing?" Allyson questioned, rubbing her hands up and down her arms. She was chilled to the bone despite having her coat on. "And how did Dr. Dean get here so fast? I was with him at his office only an hour ago. Isn't Link faster than the Interstate?"

"Good question, sugar. It's possible Marv called him when the guys arrived, and he high-tailed it here right after you left. However, I don't think those guys were legit. Bug spray has a distinct odor, and I smell nothing in my apartment."

"So, they went in yours too?" Allyson asked.

"Yeah. Mine and Nina's. Not sure about any others. I'm assuming they went floor by floor, top to bottom."

"What time did they come?"

"They were at my place about forty-five minutes ago. I was taking my evening meds when I got a knock through the wall from Nina. The stranger-danger code," Grace explained while fiddling with their phone, presumably to order their dinner.

"What's the stranger-danger code? And why don't I know these things?"

"Because you refuse to make nice with your neighbors. Nina has her finger on the pulse of this place. She's got your back if you let her. By the way, do you want Jersey-style or Detroit-style pizza?" Grace asked.

"I've already explained to you how I feel about making friends with other crazy people," Allyson joked, walking to the fridge. She needed her favorite flavored water to choke down another round of medication. "Also, Jersey and Detroit are both square, so you pick. However, vodka sauce and garlic knots are a must. Wait! Who the fuck delivers around here?"

"Door Dash. They drop it outside the entrance and dash before their car gets stolen," Grace laughed. "Also, we don't call crazy people crazy anymore, Dear One. We are all afflicted with mental illness."

Allyson laughed about the Door Dash comment as she plopped on the couch beside Grace and grabbed the TV remote. "You're right about being more sensitive to the words we use. I always see myself in those terms, and if I can refer to myself that way, it's natural to call others similar to me that too."

"We are all learning to be better at addressing each other in more respectful ways. It should start with how we address ourselves," Grace patted Allyson on the thigh. "You are a beautiful, damaged soul, just like the rest of us."

Allyson scowled and grabbed her sketch pad and charcoal pencils from the coffee table.

"News?"

"Nothing else on at this hour unless you want to binge something."

"What I need to do is find inspiration. Vince called on my way home. He tried to emotionally blackmail me into getting him something turned into Holger Beitin in the next twenty-four hours. The news guarantees something terrifying to trigger my inspiration."

"Oh, Holger. He has the best name. I want to meet him. What intrigues me more, though, is how can you find inspiration in the world's ugliness?"

"Honestly, I don't understand how any of it works—my creative process. Ideas literally appear in my mind's eye, and I go with it." Allyson forced a smile. "It's weird and magical. Andrea is inspired by her time as a crime scene sketch artist too. Those experiences are what allowed her to do the lauded work on H0rr Studios projects. I guess it's one more thing that makes us freaks."

"Again, with the language!" Grace admonished.

"Sorry, Mapa," Allyson said, peering through her lashes.

"Mapa?"

"Yeah. In our culture, our traditional parental names are Ma and Pa. Since you are neither, you can be both!"

"I love it," Grace smiled.

Allyson leaned her head on Grace's shoulder and clicked on the evening news.

"Breaking news from the entertainment industry tonight: actor Roger Wotke, known worldwide as The Caretaker, has been arrested at SeaTac airport. Ram Helm has more details. Ram . . .

Thank you, Tricia. An FBI spokesperson has confirmed that The Caretaker star has been taken into custody and is facing charges of interference with a flight crew and three counts of assault related to an incident last evening on a flight bound for Dubai. His arraignment in US District Court is scheduled for tomorrow morning. Other charges may be added pending the results of an investigation into the unspecified security breach that canceled his Emirates Airlines flight. Footage of Wotke's removal from the plane and unruly behavior has gone viral on several social media sites. Along with his antics, his true face was unmasked after hiding behind his nearly decade-old persona."

"Holy shit!" Grace shouted. "I saw him last Saturday at Comic-Con. He was a complete asshole and did the bare minimum at the roundtable discussions. Everyone expected it, though, and loved him all the more. And man, I thought he was a smoke show in his crazy costume, but he's drop-dead gorgeous in real life. Why would someone with those looks want to parade around as a fiend?"

"I guess he takes his method acting too seriously. I wonder if he's a murderer in real life too?" Allyson commented before gasping.

"Oh. My. God!" Her hand flew to her mouth. "What if he killed my sister and was running off to Dubai to get away with it?"

"You haven't heard anything since the detective came by? It's been what, ten days at least since she was reported missing?"

"Yeah, and I've heard nothing. I've avoided thinking about it until Dr. Dean and I discussed it today in therapy. I felt good about life without Andrea. Yet I told him I didn't want anything bad to happen to her. What if something bad *did* happen? What if Roger killed her in a crazed psychotic episode?! And I've been sitting here rejoicing, dreaming about Allyson Marta, beloved artist and individual, not the twin of a murder victim!"

"Oh, love. Don't put those thoughts out there. Wouldn't you have, I don't know, felt it?"

"Due to our wonder-twin powers? Ugh! Not you too, Grace!" Allyson jumped up and stormed across the room.

"I'm sorry, Allyson. Come. Sit. We can figure this out. Hey, wait! I'm friends with Ram Helm. We can contact him and see if he can help you somehow. He can report on Andrea's disappearance and do his investigative journalism thing. What do you think?"

Allyson chewed at a fingernail as she tried to rein in her spinning thoughts. "Detective Davidson asked us about Roger. Do you think they suspect he's involved? Why wouldn't they have questioned him before now? I should take action. Davidson is getting nowhere and probably doing the bare minimum. Get in touch with Ram. Let's see what he has to say about everything. He could probe his connections with higher-ups in the police department. Or even the FBI, if he has any!"

"Texting him as we speak," Grace replied.

Ping!

"Wow! He's responsive. What kind of friends are you two?" Allyson teased, remembering him from earlier when she was in the waiting room at Dr. Dean's. "He's hot!"

Grace arched an eyebrow. "It's the doc. He wants us all to meet in the basement in ten minutes."

Ping!

Ping!

"Jesus. Why is your phone blowing up?"

"It's not mine. It's yours. Here," Grace handed Allyson her phone. "It fell from your pocket. I have to pop over to my place for a few. Meet you in the basement?"

"Yeah, sure," Allyson replied, distracted by the messages on her screen.

Detective Davidson: *Allyson. Have you seen the news? Roger Wotke has been arrested. Trying to get time with him to discuss Andrea. Will update you soon.*

Dr. Dean: *This Pest Management business isn't adding up. Let's talk after the meeting.*

Grabbing her sketchbook and water, Allyson made her way to the basement, again choosing to use the stairs to avoid being trapped in a confined space and at the mercy of mechanics.

The basement was more for storage than group meetings based on the boxes, crates, and construction supplies scattered around. Yet it managed to hold the thirty-plus people gathered there comfortably.

"Thank you for coming. Let me start by apologizing to you all for the intrusion today. Honestly, I'm still trying to figure it all out. However, from what I've gathered in the last few minutes, two trucks arrived at our building around 3 p.m. today, each carrying three men claiming to be Burns Pest Control employees. They entered the building by some means, which I'll review in a second, and immediately went to the top floor. There, they treated two of the three apartments before heading back to the third floor, which didn't make sense based on their reasoning presented in Allyson's apartment. Apparently, a crew member was in training and misunderstood the assignment. I've unsuccessfully attempted to contact Burns' owner to gather more information. In the meantime, I want to remind you this is a secure facility, which means no one enters this building without their passkey. If you've forgotten yours, you call Marv to buzz you in. You don't ask another resident or wait for someone to leave and sneak in. And you must never, ever let someone in, no matter how official they look. Am I clear? Today's mishap could have been avoided if those simple rules were followed. Are there any questions?"

While Dr. Dean continued his speech and answered questions, Allyson stood in the corner, sketching away an idea that occurred to her as she descended the concrete steps to the basement. Before she was aware, the room was empty, aside from Grace and Dr. Dean.

"Ale . . . le . . . son," Grace sang.

"Hmmm?" she answered dazedly.

"Grace. Do you mind giving me a few minutes alone with Allyson?" Dr. Dean asked.

"Sure. Sure. I'll grab our food from the front. See you upstairs, girl?" Grace asked, attempting to gain Allyson's attention again.

"Yep," Allyson replied.

"Whatcha drawing there?" Dr. Dean questioned, slowly approaching Allyson.

"An idea for my Holger Beitin project by the Space Needle."

"Can you stop for a sec?"

Allyson's hand moved furiously across the page. "Need a minute," she muttered, obviously in the creative zone.

"It's about those men. They might be tied to your sister's disappearance."

Allyson stopped and lifted her eyes to meet Dr. Dean's. "How?"

"One man was visibly upset about being questioned as to why they were there. I overheard him speaking with another who was trying hard to silence him. He said something about being an actor and staying out of trouble."

"How strange. Why would someone hire actors to enter a building filled with craz . . . residents struggling with mental illness? Did they want us to lose our minds?"

"They were looking for something, or someone, in a creative way to avoid any attention."

"How does this relate to Andrea?"

"Well, she worked for H0rr Studios, right?" Dr. Dean confirmed.

"Yeah."

"And they are the ones who reported her missing. Could they be conducting a search and investigation, using their access to actors as a way to keep it confidential?" Dr. Dean questioned.

"Why?"

"Well, you've told me about Andrea and her past actions. The studio execs might have insight into that too, and they are trying to cover their ass. What do you think?"

Allyson returned to sketching before announcing, "I'm going to talk to a news reporter. The one who is covering Roger Wotke and the Salish Sea feet. He might help me find her and clear this all up."

"How is *The Caretaker* guy connected?"

"Oh, haven't you heard? He was arrested—freaked out on a flight destined for Dubai. There was an incident, and the flight never left the ground. He and Andrea worked together, but there is more. They were on-and-off lovers. Anyway, the detective, Davidson, texted and said he would try to talk to Roger while in custody and see if he could shed some light on Andrea's whereabouts. Perhaps Ram Helm can help pull it all together. He *is* the star investigative journalist, after all," Allyson smirked, then bit her bottom lip and resumed drawing.

"So, your sister goes missing, Roger gets arrested, and someone uses a fake excuse to enter your building. You don't see a connection or think it's all a little coincidental?"

"Oh. I don't believe in coincidence," Allyson replied, keeping her head bent and her hand moving.

"Yeah, neither do I. Can I see your drawing?"

"Yes. It's a work in progress, but it's a good start."

"Wow. Allyson! You drew this from your imagination in the space of a few minutes?"

"Yep."

"What is it? A maze?"

"A labyrinth. There are no dead ends or wrong choices, only a center. It begins where it ends and ends where it begins."

"What inspired this? It's fantastic. Your agent will be thrilled."

"Thanks. I'm unsure. It just came to me in flashes as I took the stairs. Something about being underground, I guess. I think labyrinths are great fun. It's all about the journey and what you discover in its center."

"Labyrinths are often used in therapy. They are metaphors for our life's winding path. Many patients find they can confront their traumas and achieve mental clarity. Or face their demons," Dr. Dean commented.

"I think I have heard that before," Allyson replied with a wide smile.

9

NOT GUILTY

{ROGER}

"How does the defendant plead?"

"*Not. Guilty*," Roger's voice boomed, bouncing off the walls within the US District Courtroom. He channeled his best Jack Nicholson impression because a man had nothing without his honor, as the character he portrayed in *A Few Good Men* believed.

After the usual pomp and circumstance, he was released into his legal team's custody.

"They had to give me the female judge, didn't they," he sneered at his attorney once they settled in a conference room. "They always have something to prove. How dare she speak to me as if I were a child?!"

"Roger. Show some respect. It's her job. Although, between you, me, and the walls, she is a particularly nasty sort. I don't know who you pissed off to get her assigned to you. This one will keep the billables up," his attorney chuckled.

"Thankfully, I'm not the one paying! I should send a thank you note to Vanessa," Roger smiled, slapping the attorney on the back.

"Highly recommended. Oh! And as the CEO, she wanted me to mention your NDA. If you wind up doing jail time, which is unlikely, your agreement stands, with an addendum, naturally."

"Yes. Yes. Keep the old trap shut. Fulfill my contracts and commitments for *The Caretaker* spinoffs, then fuck off into the sunset. I understand it, and it's exactly what I was trying to do before this fuckery happened. Did they ever tell you what the flight's security breach was about?"

"The rumor is TSA was profiling an Emirati—one of the six ruling family members. I highly doubt it. Those oil-rich bastards wouldn't fly commercial! I wouldn't be surprised if *they* were behind the cancelation, though. A simple anonymous phone call to the proper authorities would stop any plane from getting off the ground. If they want something to happen, it happens. Including preventing a flight from landing in their country," the attorney explained.

"Oh, I almost forgot. Aside from the flight crew filing suits against you, another woman in first class, one Abigail Williams, filed as well. She's seeking damages due to your verbal assault before the flight was canceled and when you lunged at her during the altercation with the crew. She'll require therapy."

"That twat needed therapy way before she met me. For Chrissake, she was filming them carrying me off the plane! You should subpoena her! That footage proves their brutality," Roger exclaimed.

"Absolutely. Great idea," the attorney replied, fidgeting with a fountain pen before coughing delicately into his elbow. Pulling out a piece of paper, he continued. "You'll need to surrender your passport and sign this affidavit. I've assured the judge you will remain in the studio security team's custody while we prep for the preliminary hearing. We aim to either get the charges completely dismissed or at least devise a plea bargain to satisfy the prosecution's office."

"My passport and other belongings are with TSA. It was tucked into my carry-on bag. I only have the clothes I'm wearing," Roger stated, standing to stretch. "I need to use the facilities. Can you see I get a change of clothes and something to eat? I'm starving."

"Anything you need. The bathroom is down the hall on the left. A security guard will escort you."

"Like hell! I can't take a shit with some asshole staring at me!"

"He won't be staring at you, Roger, simply standing outside in the hall-way to ensure your safety and that you don't accidentally get lost. This mess is costing the studio a fortune, and they want to keep their investment safe."

"I've made them billions! They wouldn't exist without *The Caretaker*! They owe me this and more," Roger spewed as he yanked open the confer-ence room door, nearly plowing into the waiting guard. "Get the fuck out of my way!"

"Roger, wait," the attorney placed a hand on the door. "There is one more matter we need to discuss before you go."

"I'm just going to have a think. I'll be right back. Can't this wait?"

"It's about Ms. Marta."

Roger stepped away from the door and walked over to the window where the Space Needle and Elliot Bay were visible. Stuffing his hands in his pockets, he rolled on the balls of his feet and swiveled his neck side to side as if to crack it. Blowing out a loud puff of air, he whispered, "Okay."

The conference room door snicked shut. "I'm guessing you are aware Andrea is missing. We've filed a report with the local police both here and in Vancouver. Do you know where she is?"

Roger folded his arms across his chest. "We haven't talked since the internal Iceland announcement and the *expansion* of *Caretaker*."

"I want to believe you, Roger. However, your intake sheet with the Feds says you had scratches and bruising consistent with a struggle on your torso and arms. Don't forget, attorney-client privilege stands if you want to tell me anything."

"Yeah? I want to tell you to fuck off! I don't know where the hell she is. It wasn't quite the fairytale ending the last we spoke. Turns out she was still employed while I was getting shipped off to fucking no-man's-land. Nasty cunt, she can be. I have neither seen nor heard from her since. As for this stuff," Roger waved his hands at his body, "I'll tell you what I told the Feds. It's none of your goddamn business!"

"Roger. Roger! Wait!" the attorney shouted after Roger's retreating figure. It was too late. He was out the door, slamming it hard enough to make the interior walls rattle.

As he stormed down the hall, someone cleared their throat. "Sir? Sir. Mr. Wotke! The restroom is this way," the guard directed.

"Fuck!" Roger shouted before turning around and stomping back in the opposite direction. His heart was racing, and perspiration from the last twenty-four hours clung to him in an invisible stench.

"Oh, my God! Caretaker! It's really you. Can I get your picture?" a young woman called from his right. She stood outside another courtroom door with files and a briefcase stacked in her arms.

"Sorry, ma'am. No photos," the security guard replied, waving off the fan.

Roger's skin crawled at her appearance. It reminded him how vulnerable he was now that his true visage was out in the world. He'd never feel safe again from people like her. For the last ten years, he cultivated the *Caretaker* persona in a symbiotic co-existence. When he wanted to be seen, he went out as his character. When he didn't, he assumed his real-life image. It's how he could fly commercial without being bombarded with crazed fans. It's how he moved around in daily life without interruption.

"Mr. Wotke. Care to make a statement about your case?" a young man with journalist credentials strung around his neck asked. He held a cellphone, most likely already filming the interaction.

Darting his gaze around the hallway and back at his security detail, Roger pulled at his collar and swallowed a hard lump in his throat. Vanessa's voice buzzed in his head, directing him on how he might help with this situation. He was a goddamn award-winning actor, after all.

"Yes. I'll make a statement. I do not take these serious allegations lightly and look forward to proving my innocence in court and to the *Caretaker* family." Locating the door to the washroom, he ducked inside, thankful the security guard he previously begrudged was there.

With the door closing swiftly behind him, he was temporarily plunged into darkness. Disoriented, he waved his hands around wildly. A cool sweat beaded on his forehead and trickled down his face as his muscles tensed for a fight.

Click.

"For fuck's sake!" Roger shouted. Black spots flashed before his eyes as the automatic lights came to life like a blinding camera flash.

"Everything okay in there, sir?" his guard called from the hallway.

"Fine. Fine. Fucking peachy," Roger replied, rubbing his eyes as he stumbled towards the sinks. "Fan-fucking-tastic," he muttered to his mirrored reflection. "You look like fucking hell, old sport. You need to pull yourself together and figure a way out of this shit show. Christ, you've really done it this time."

He stuck his hands under the faucet to trigger the water to turn on, yet nothing happened. Moving to the next sink, he tried again without any luck. Then he tried a third and finally the last. None worked. "You have got to be fucking kidding me!" Pulling at his hair, he backed against the wall and slid to the floor, placing his head between his knees. "Get it together, Roger. This is not the time to lose your shit. What would the Caretaker do?"

Swoosh.

A toilet flushing made him jump to his feet, fists raised in a boxer's pose. "Hello? Is someone there?" he asked, looking under the stall doors for feet or any other telltale sign someone was in the room with him. "This is nonsense," he hissed to himself, pushing open each door to confirm he was alone before turning towards the sinks to attempt another go-around with the auto-sensors.

Whoosh.

"Finally," he sneered as cold water rushed out. Splashing his face, throat, and neck, he took time to enjoy the soothing balm on his overheated skin. "Ahh. Much better." Inspecting his reflection once more, he caught movement coming towards him from his left.

Several things happened all at once. The lights cut out, a cloth was thrown over his head, and a striking pain pulsed at the base of his skull before Roger's knees buckled. A loud sizzle rang in his ears as his body involuntarily relaxed. "Christ, did I just piss myself?" he slurred before he blanked out. For the second time in twenty-four hours, Roger had been tased.

Sometime later, he awoke with a start, bewildered by his last conscious memory. "Where the fuck am I?" He was lying on a fully made, unfamiliar bed, and his clothes were new. As he sat up and swung his legs over the side of the mattress, the room spun.

"Whoa," he exclaimed, gripping the covers. When he regained his equilibrium, he attempted to stand. His body weaved and swayed. He took a few tentative steps toward a circular wall mirror with a built-in light that illuminated the room in an eerie pale-blue glow. Deciding to brighten the mood by avoiding his reflection, he moved to a wall of heavily draped curtains. A space between them revealed floor-to-ceiling windows and a dark-blue sky. Pulling them back further, he recognized Seattle's sparkling skyline. "At least I'm still in town," he said to himself as he staggered towards an open door.

Orienting himself, Roger registered the generic space as a hotel suite, with a neutral plush couch in one corner and a wall-mounted TV in another. Continuing his exploration, another opened door revealed a small bathroom appointed with basic amenities. A sign on the sink told him they valued the environment and some other millennial bullshit when the name caught his eye. Hôtel Ändrean.

"And someone has a sense of humor, I see. Fucking Vanessa," he bit out, turning on the shower. "At least it's not sensor-based," he barked, recalling his difficulties in the courthouse bathroom.

As he undressed, his smartwatch flashed the date and weather conditions. Two days had passed since his court appearance. How could he lose two whole days of his life? Was the studio really behind his kidnapping? Before he could answer those questions, he needed a thorough wash.

Taking his time, Roger appreciated the quality of the shampoo and skin conditioners the hotel provided. Even though the facility was far from the Four Seasons, where he stayed during Comic Con, he was oddly grateful to whoever chose this place as his hideout. It was inconspicuous, with agreeable amenities. He could make it work while he awaited his fate with the judicial system.

In a more humble, subdued mood, Roger finished his shower. Wrapping his lower body in a plush white towel, he reconsidered his reliance on five-star hotels. This place wasn't so bad. As he stepped out onto the cool tile, his mistake registered a moment too late. The shower mat was missing.

"Son of a bitch!" he cried out as his wet foot slipped on the tile, sending him sprawling across the floor, his head making a loud thwack as it slammed into the unforgiving surface.

"Ow," Roger groaned, rolling over on his side and attempting to sit up. His vision was blurred, and he was nauseous. "Ugh. I'm such a fucking idiot," he moaned, holding his head. There was a huge lump where he'd hit the floor. Considering he could be concussed, he gave up on standing. He crawled towards the bedroom, hoping to get to the phone he spotted earlier, placed conveniently on the nightstand. He only made it halfway between the bathroom and the common area when he threw up. His entire body tensed and convulsed in pain.

"Help!" he cried out, but in his weakened state, it was more a gasp than a shout. "Someone, please . . ." he raised his arm as if stretching towards an invisible figure. "I can't be the shitbird."

10

MOST IMPORTANT WORK

{ANDREA}

Andrea was startled out of the past by laughter. Her laughter. It echoed in the room's high ceilings. She was prone on the floor instead of the couch, where she fell into her crazy dream/memory.

"What the fuck is happening to me?" she moaned and rubbed her eyes. "I'm losing my ever-loving mind!"

Sitting up, she stretched and took inventory of her aches and pains. As she stood and grabbed the afghan by her feet, she wrapped it around herself again. Searching the room, Andrea went to the worktables where a sketchbook lay open. A lake surrounded by tall fir trees, an ambulance, a sheriff's car, and dark figures hidden in the background were all depicted in the detailed drawing.

"There's one every year or so, it seems," the paunchy bald sheriff remarked as if he were standing beside her. He and the emergency medical team, who arrived moments before, were convinced the girl named Calliope accidentally drowned. She was discovered a little after midnight under the light of a full moon. Reaching out to the image on the paper, Andrea closed her eyes, embracing the full memory replaying in her mind.

She stood in the tree line near her cabin, the shadows hiding her well. The sheriff shook his head and frowned while scribbling in his notepad before struggling back into his late-model trooper sedan. She braced herself, concerned a fellow camper might point a finger at her. She had a plan if caught, but the idea excited rather than worried her. She wanted them to know how dangerous she was.

The EMTs zipped up the small black body bag, placed it on a stretcher, and slid it into the ambulance, setting off for the morgue or funeral home or wherever they take little preteen girls who died too young. The vehicle's lights stayed off as they pulled away. There was no longer an emergency. The camp's adults gathered, comforting one another as the brake lights from the retreating vehicles reflected a sinister red glow on their clothing.

A subtle movement to Andrea's right startled her. As she glanced over, the little hairs on the back of her neck stood, the intensity painful. Across the parking lot, along another thicket, stood Allyson, her hands crossed over her budding chest, face contorted with betrayal and sadness. She was staring straight at Andrea. For an instant, it appeared Allyson would run toward the adults and confess everything she knew. They would lock her away somewhere for what she'd done, and Allyson would rejoice in the freedom. However, she wouldn't snitch. She feared Andrea more than the devil himself. Humming a little tune, Andrea snuck back into her cabin as if she'd been there all night.

Andrea was overcome as she returned to the present moment. Everything was crystal clear. She had seen herself as a victim, trapped in a horrible game, until that memory, filled with such intensity and unspoken truths, emerged. Now, she was the hero of her own story.

Picking up the sketchbook, she flipped through its pages, stopping occasionally to appraise something that caught her eye. Each drawing represented a pivotal moment in her life. It captivated her. She'd locked away much of herself, and it all flooded back in a torrent. As she considered everything, she continued turning the pages until she stopped on one that hit her like a gut punch. A man she knew inside and out. No one affected her as he did.

"Roger," she whispered, wincing as her heart twisted when she spoke his name.

Roger Wotke was a narcissistic psychopath who struggled to attain his one true desire: superstardom.

"I have an idea," Andrea recalled saying to Roger as they snuggled in bed the night after meeting under a streetlamp in Vancouver.

"I bet you have a thousand ideas bouncing around in that brilliant brain of yours."

"I've been working for this new streaming service, H0rr Studios. It will fold soon if we don't develop some original content that resonates with our viewers. I've been in pre-production on this script. It has enormous potential, but it's missing something. You. If you help me, it will benefit us both. Though, you'd have to trust me implicitly and do what I say without question. It would be our dirty little secret."

"Similar to the secret we already share?" Roger crooned, licking and kissing the indent at her throat. "Can't get much bigger than being your alibi in a murder."

Andrea laughed, enjoying the affection Roger showed her. She related intimacy to a cat's purr when contented. She wished she could purr in moments like these. "Maybe a smidge," she smiled, showing how much with the space between her thumb and forefinger.

Roger pulled her tighter to his hard, naked body. "You set my soul alive. I'd do anything for you."

"I hoped you would say that," she nipped at his bottom lip before pressing her open mouth to his.

Present moment, Andrea swept her fingers across the cheekbones of the drawing, trying to hang onto the memory. She'd never believed in love, especially love at first sight. Roger showed her things she didn't think existed, feelings she regarded as not meant for her. Andrea did the same for him too. They were so similar in all the best ways. There were occasions when he felt more like her twin than Allyson. At times, they acted as one, bound to each other as if conjoined.

"This is Roger Wotke. Roger, this is Vanessa Rapaporte, CEO of H0rr Studios," Andrea said, making introductions. "Roger is the secret sauce we've been looking for. He is the perfect Caretaker."

"As nice as it is to meet you, Roger, I'm afraid I need to remind Andrea we've already cast the role. It was awarded to Lonny Black," Vanessa replied coldly.

Andrea's countenance remained ambivalent to Vanessa's deliberate move to embarrass and degrade her. "Haven't you heard? Lonny met with an unfortunate accident."

"No! My god. What happened?" Vanessa gasped.

Her reaction sent a secret pleasure through Andrea as she delivered the news. "Stabbed. An apparent mugging gone bad. He's alive, but the last I heard, he wasn't expected to survive. He lay on the street for some time before he was discovered. Blood loss and infection will presumably get him in the end," she explained clinically.

Vanessa's lips thinned into a straight line, yet she never broke eye contact with Andrea as she spoke. "I forget you were in forensics before you came to us as creative director," she said, turning her back away from the twosome to look out the window. "It's no secret losing him could benefit the company. He was demanding much more in salary and services than what we can afford with our current performance numbers. Still, the reward would have been an instant hit."

"Let Roger test with the team and see how he does. He has name recognition and demands less than Lonny. Plus, he dated that hotel heiress for a moment a decade ago."

"Oh, I know who Roger is. How could we all forget you masturbating off your hotel balcony? The video circulated for years," Vanessa said, turning back to glare at Roger. "Or the domestic abuse allegations. As a matter of fact, you already tested with the team, and they gave a hard no. What are you doing, Andrea?"

"I'm saving this goddamn company, Vanessa. We both know if this project fails, which it will without Roger as the Caretaker, we are all out of a job. I'm sure I will bounce back because I'm just the creative director. What about you? CEO of a failed streaming service and a woman? Where would you land? And will it come with a parachute? Also, raising Roger's painful past is a bitch move. Yet one that proves my point. The Caretaker character is the basest of men. He's a murdering fiend who enjoys what he does. Who better to embrace that essence than someone who has been there? Not that you are a murdering fiend, Roger. Not yet, anyway," Andrea winked at him while flipping her hair over her shoulder.

"All right, you win. He can test. If the team says no, I expect you to move on and stay in your lane."

"Absolutely." Andrea's eyes flashed with victory as she turned towards the door.

"Thank you, Vanessa, for the opportunity to prove Andrea right and to help save this company," Roger added as he followed Andrea out the door.

"That went well, especially your little ass-kissing moment in the end," Andrea smirked as Roger caught up with her. They brushed hands for an instant before flinching away from one another. She grinned wider, appreciating how in sync they were with the littlest things. She had found her equal—a true twin flame.

"Let me show you my studio and what I've created for the series so far. It may help you get into the mindset of the Caretaker. Then I'll make some calls and get you into casting for a table read."

Present day, Andrea opened her eyes and really took in the room. Her room. This was her workshop. The one she brought Roger to. The one where she did her most important work. This was H0rr Studios' movie lot.

"The place where I unleashed Roger's hidden talents and put the Caretaker on the map of Pop Culture."

11

MISSING PERSONS

{ALLYSON}

Seattle Center is a large campus of buildings and attractions, including the Space Needle, family friend exhibits, and a museum. The city has produced some of the world's most recognizable creatives and has a thriving art scene. That inventive climate drew Allyson to the area from Southern California upon completion of her Associate's degree in Art. She eventually earned a Master's degree, and several well-known pieces are on display worldwide.

"This is the spot." Allyson's agent, Vince Sasso, stuck his arms out and spun like he was in *The Sound of Music*.

"It's smaller than I envisioned." Allyson placed a finger on her lip and squinted her eyes. "I can't visualize the labyrinth here. Especially with all the other individual contributors."

"Holger thought so too, after seeing your labyrinth concept. He's devised a workaround and is negotiating with the other artists to place their creations *inside* your design. A truly mixed media art display," Vince clapped his hands.

"Second puberty, Vince? Your voice actually cracked there," Allyson teased.

"I'm overcome with emotion to think your piece in this installation is the focus while all the others are mere additions. I mean, Allyson! This is huge!"

"Do I get paid more?"

Vince winced. "We'll see. You did cause a significant delay to the project. Many of the artists are nearly complete with their pieces. Asking them to pivot and incorporate their creations into yours may have significant financial ramifications."

"But if I carry the whole design, I should benefit more, financially. Let's look at the original agreement and see where we can renegotiate. If I make more, you do too, Vince. Remember that."

"I could never forget, dear. Say, who's the Luke Perry circa 1990 fella standing over there? He's been watching us the whole time. He with you?"

"I never understand your '90s references. I'm a millennial! But I came alone. Wait a minute! That's Ram Helm from the news. Grace said they could introduce me, but I didn't expect him to be the stalker type. I wonder how he found me?"

"Uh, duh. He is doing his job and chasing the story. My inquiring mind wants to know about that gorgeous hair and body, though."

"Down, boy," Allyson laughed. "Are we done here? I should go introduce myself and chat him up."

"And I should come with you," Vince replied. "For your safety, obviously," he added, quirking his lips.

"I'm a big girl. In more ways than one these days." She ran her hands over her curves. "I can handle myself with a news reporter."

"Can you, Allyson? Are you really okay? A lot is going on with your sister missing and this project. You're still in recovery from your last hospital stay."

"Oddly, I'm in a good place. I can't point to any one thing. Maybe it's the new medicinal cocktail I'm taking. Maybe Dr. Dean is a sorcerer. Maybe it's all of the above and more. Whatever it is, I feel . . . optimistic. I hope I didn't just jinx myself."

"No. No. No jinxing. I see it too. You look . . . tethered. Not your flighty self, yet not completely grounded. It suits you."

"Tethered," Allyson laughed, picturing herself bouncing around in the wind with a ball and chain tied to her ankle.

"That's the perfect description. I have just enough space to feel free." Kissing Vince on each cheek in a goodbye, she turned to go, her steps a hop as if springs were attached to her shoes. "Oh, Vince! Tell your sister hello from me, would you?"

"Ugh. I will absolutely not, you heartbreaker! Go! And call me later with *allll* the details," Vince waved.

"Hey, Ram, right? I'm Allyson. Fancy meeting you here."

"Grace gave me a lead," he answered in his familiar authoritative broadcaster voice and quirked a lopsided grin.

"Right. Well, do you want to grab a coffee? There's a popular shop nearby. It has a radio station that broadcasts from inside!"

"I'm familiar. I actually got my start in radio," Ram offered.

"I bet you did. You have the voice for it."

They silently walked past a few buildings before Ram began, "Grace said you are headlining an important art installation."

"Yes. Holger Beitin commissioned a few local artists for a new project on that green space where my agent and I were walking. I've designed a labyrinth. We're thinking waist-high, low-maintenance shrubbery. Holger is getting buy-in from the other artists to include their pieces within the labyrinth's path to contribute to the design's meditative appeal. It's a nod to my public struggle with mental illness. I mean, seasonal affective disorder and suicides are the poster children for the Pacific Northwest, next to Starbucks and Microsoft."

"Don't forget Pearl Jam!" Ram interjected.

"Oh, never. Eddie Vedder's voice is a balm on my soul," Allyson hummed.

"Your idea is incredible, and you are brave for bringing awareness to such an important cause."

"Thanks, Ram. I appreciate it. I'm unsure how much Grace has told you, but I'm currently in a treatment program; thus, having this project to concentrate on is helpful."

"They did, and they mentioned your missing sister. She is your identical twin? That's gotta be rough."

After entering the coffee shop, they placed their order and found seats by a gazebo-styled nook with a huge vinyl record collection.

"Yes, Andrea's my identical twin. However, you might have to squint to see that these days." Allyson cringed, pointing at her short lavender hair.

"Your hair is fantastic. It fits the artist's persona. I bet it saves you time getting ready too! Unlike mine," Ram chuckled, running a hand through his thick, wavy hair.

"And money on expensive products," Allyson grinned. "I was never one to spend inordinate amounts of time primping. It drove Andrea crazy growing up. As much as I prefer things in a specific order, I don't care about physical perfection. She was all about looking flawless, and because I represented her . . . ergo, I needed to, as well. I think flaws make the character. Imperfections are art."

"Agreed. Sounds like she has a histrionic streak. Does she also struggle with her mental health? I know little about twins and identicals specifically, but I do know it can be hereditary."

"She's never been officially diagnosed. The focus was always on me. My first stint in therapy happened around puberty, right after my twelfth birthday." Allyson pulled her sleeve to her elbow to expose raised lines along her arm. Some were only an inch long, others longer, or in shapes and words.

"What does 'sin' symbolize?" Ram asked, catching the word carved on the inside of her left wrist.

Allyson pulled her sleeve back down and tucked her hands in her lap. "None of us are without it. Although it has other, deeper meanings too."

Ram flexed his right hand and acknowledged her sensitivity to the subject. Allyson recognized the faint white lines of scars across his knuckles and along the delicate bones of his hand. She traced them delicately with her forefinger.

Without pulling his hand away or waiting for the question everyone always asked, Ram explained, "In a fit of grief, I punched the tiles covering my bathroom wall. It felt so good, I kept doing it until I broke nearly every bone in my hand. I tried to continue, but the noise brought my brother, who was strong enough to grab me in a bear hug and drag me from the room. Took a few surgeries, yet the doctors were able to fix it. Unfortunately, I can't say the same about my memory and the grief. It pains me when it's damp. Which is nearly every day here." The corners of his mouth turned down.

"Pain is a self-regulator. You can control it when you can't control anything else, like loss. It's what attracted me to self-harm. It redirects the spiraling emotions dominating my thoughts. Seeing the blood reminds me I'm alive," Allyson whispered.

"Did you lose someone before you started cutting? Is grief what triggered it?"

"Yes and no. I'm reluctant to talk about it. I'd rather discuss my missing sister, and that's saying something."

"I'm sorry. I get it. I'm a stranger to you. However, if it helps you to trust me more, Grace and I have known each other since childhood. We identified as cousins because our moms were best friends. More like sisters. We've stayed in proximity to each other all these years, even with career changes, life changes, and identity changes!" Ram laughed. "I look up to Grace—their courage to walk through life as their authentic self is admirable. Many don't. You want to feel alive? Hang with Grace. They'll make you feel things you haven't felt in a while, if ever."

Allyson laughed, her eyes crinkling at the corners. "Don't I know it! I love Grace and am incredibly grateful they latched onto me in treatment. I needed unconditional love and support. Our friendship has forever changed me. I owe them for this introduction too. It speaks to the depth of your friendship that you took time from your busy schedule to chat with me. I'm hesitant about what I want from this meeting, other than it felt right to talk to someone with a pulse on the public. Andrea has been missing for over ten days. I learned from Google the first forty-eight hours are critical, and seventy-two hours is the crucial decision-making deadline. I've missed both because I felt, and still feel, she is being her ridiculous self. I imagine her on an island somewhere partying her ass off or holed up with a sadistic sex group. You laugh; however, I'm dead serious. The girl is not just the life of the party. She is Bacchus incarnate. Yet, I question my assumptions. The what-ifs start floating through my head. I've seen your Salish Sea feet coverage, and I half expect hers to come washing ashore any day now."

"If it helps alleviate your fears, the feet are typically men's, size 12." Ram glanced under the table. "Looking at your Dr. Marten's, I'd say, with confidence, neither of you fit the profile. Love the whole lavender theme, by the way. You don't see pastel-colored Docs every day. I'm assuming the artwork is yours?"

"Purple is my current passion, as you can tell." She rubbed her hair again. "Anyway, thinking about Andrea's disappearance, two things bug me: One is her employer, H0rr Studios, reported her missing, and two is Roger Wotke was arrested attempting to leave the country. He would've been in the wind if his flight wasn't canceled. My trust meter is flashing in the red."

"H0rr Studios *has* been in the news a lot lately," Ram admitted. "I didn't realize she worked there. What is her role?"

"Creative director. Her big claim to fame is *The Caretaker* series."

"Wow. I had no idea. They've certainly got their hands full between their move, expansion into gaming and merchandise, and Roger's fiasco. However, an employer reporting one of their own missing is common. With our hustle culture, work people know us better than our family and friends. They are typically the first to see us in the morning and the last to see us at night."

"Sounds like you speak from experience," Allyson smirked. "Here's what's bothersome . . . Roger and Andrea have a thing. Were a thing. An on-and-off thing. I honestly never understood it, but they have a powerful connection. She brought him on *Caretaker*, saving his career and, ultimately, the Studio's existence. It's no secret both were sinking fast until *Caretaker* took off in the ratings. That was all Andrea's work behind the scenes. I never learned their origin story. However, I always felt like they were magnets, meant to find each other. They are bound together somehow. He gets drunk on her creativity, and she feeds on his ability to carry out her vision. They fuel each other physically and emotionally. I dare say I'm a tad jealous of their connection. Still, if anyone asks me, I'll deny it, so don't publish that anywhere," Allyson threatened. "It's like he's her twin sometimes. Oddly, they keep their *relationship* . . . for lack of a better term . . . under wraps, and they're not exclusive. What are the odds he did something to my sister and was fleeing the country to avoid being caught?"

"Well, then, he isn't the criminal mastermind his character portrays him, is he? He didn't make it far and is facing serious charges."

Allyson scoffed. "Do you think he'll face any real jail time? It's almost as if the Studio choreographed it. The only part that truly bugs me is the revelation of his true face. He hid behind his Caretaker persona for so long, no one recognized the real Roger. Can't say that anymore. What I do know about him is how much he values his privacy."

"Why hurt her if they are so close?" Ram asked.

"He has a wicked temper, which the world saw a few days ago. Andrea probably pissed him off. She is working on the *Caretaker* spinoff, and word is, he is being put out to pasture. He is aging and not well. And even though the fandom adores him, the studio execs despise him."

"I've heard the same rumor. Anything is possible. Probably wouldn't take much to make him snap. There's a fine line between insanity and reality when you are a method actor like him. How can I help?"

"You're an investigative reporter. You know the entertainment industry. And you've covered missing persons before. What should I do that the police aren't? I get the feeling little is being done unless they can pinpoint an obvious criminal aspect to her disappearance. If Andrea were a white suburban housewife, instead of a Hispanic woman with a certain reputation, a nationwide search would already be underway. Instead, the authorities seem to be waiting for the case to solve itself. Detective Davidson did the minimum by tracking me down and asking questions. He can move on to his next donut break."

"Ouch. That's harsh. I admit the sense of urgency in cases involving marginalized individuals isn't there. However, Andrea's case is a bit more complex. She is a US citizen living in Canada on an extended work visa. Two international agencies have to coordinate, and that alone can take time. I'm sure everyone is doing their best."

"Except me. I'm sitting here, wringing my hands. Should we run a story on her? Get media attention with Roger in the news. What about creating flyers, a website, or posts on social media? It's all overwhelming." Allyson rubbed the side of her face. "Plus, I'm in self-preservation mode. I don't want to do anything to upset my equilibrium. Selfishly, I'm in a good headspace, and a lot of good is coming my way. Dealing with Andrea's antics is a low-priority item. Needless to say, I'm not a sociopath. I do have empathy. What if she's in danger and needs my help?"

Ping. Ping.

Both Allyson and Ram grabbed their phones.

"Must be yours," Allyson observed.

"Yes. And you won't believe what it says." Ram's eyes met Allyson's, his eyebrows raised.

Allyson coughed, attempting to swallow a lump in her throat. "What is it?"

"An FBI source says Roger has vanished, and the authorities suspect foul play. I need to go and see what I can uncover."

"Foul play, as in something happened to him?"

"Yes. The authorities are processing Roger's hotel room as a crime scene now. If I don't get there first, someone else will get the jump on the story. I promise I'll get back to you when I can."

"Wait! Can I come with you?"

"Why would you want to?" Ram asked, shrugging on his wool overcoat.

"Morbid curiosity? Maybe I can help. I'd bet I know Roger on a personal level better than the rest of you."

"Okay, then. Let's go!"

12

SOMETHING FISHY

{ALLYSON}

"You mentioned Andrea was behind *The Caretaker*'s success. How exactly?" Ram asked Allyson as he drove them to Roger's hotel.

"The traffic is terrible. We could walk faster!" Allyson answered like a seasoned politician.

"Nice try, Allyson."

"I forget you are a prized investigative journalist." Allyson nibbled her lip while studying the passing storefronts and building facades. Rubbing her palms on her pant legs, she started, "Andrea worked closely with the scriptwriters and production team to get the gore just right."

"Whoa. How did she get into that kind of work?"

Allyson picked at a piece of nonexistent lint before forming an answer. "She worked in crime and forensics before turning to the big screen. She drew from those real-world experiences. Conjoined with her perfectionist tendencies, the result lured the freaks who like watching people being tortured and slain in sickening ways. I always wondered how they could tell which scenes held more authenticity."

"Because it isn't just everyday people watching. The horror genre grabs the interest of every profession, including the people she used to work with. You can easily recognize what is fake when you watch how things are portrayed in a show or movie. Take *Grey's Anatomy*. Ask a medical professional their opinion about the creative license taken with its portrayal of medicine and surgeries, and you'll get an earful *Caretaker's* accuracy is commendable. Kudos to your sister."

"Yay, Andrea," Allyson fake cheered. "Way to make people fall in love with a murderous fiend."

"Hey, it's escapism. We all need that from time to time."

"We should be more evolved from our ancestors and the Coliseum days of watching people getting ripped apart by wild beasts," Allyson offered.

"We have! It's now a huge money-making industry employing millions worldwide."

"Is that evolution or opportunism? Regardless, it's still a distraction sanctioned by the powers-that-be to keep us lowly peasants entertained and focused on something other than revolution."

"Wow. You have unexpected depths, Allyson. I'd hate to cut this conversation short; however, we are here," Ram announced, pulling into an open spot along the curb opposite the hotel entrance.

"Who are all those people? Fans?"

"Shit. That's a bad sign. Word has gotten out," Ram scowled.

"I doubt it. If it had, we'd be looking at a siege that hasn't happened since the Capitol Hill riot of 2021."

"Remind me to talk to you about *The Caretaker* fandom. For now, you are my producer in training. Don't say anything. Just observe. My contact is at the door."

"If those fans catch you talking to someone official-looking, they are going to realize something is up, and social media will have the jump on you before you can whip out your pad and paper."

"I use my phone's voice recording feature, but I get your point. Shit. Perhaps we should go around the back."

"No, follow my lead. Open my car door. We'll walk hand-in-hand to the entrance as if we are any couple popping into the hotel for a late lunch or an afternoon delight. Best case scenario, they'll assume we are having an affair, not reporting on a crime involving their favorite antihero."

"Is it 'bring your girlfriend to work' day, Laramie?" Federal Agent Irving Kingsley teased as Ram and Allyson approached hand-in-hand.

"It's for the fans," Ram laughed.

"Yours?" the agent teased, pointing to the small gathering.

"Mine aren't quite as rabid."

"Ha! He obviously hasn't seen the looks every middle-aged mom, and even some dads give him when he walks by them on the street. I'm Allyson, Ram's new production assistant," Allyson waved at the FBI agent, avoiding the customary handshake when he offered it encased in a rubber glove. "Perhaps we should step inside to prevent any unwanted attention."

"Nice to meet you, Allyson. Interesting hair."

"Thanks," Allyson beamed, rubbing her palm over it. "It's like Buddha's belly."

The agent scratched his chin and shared a lop-sided grin with Ram.

"It's a joke, Irv. You rub it for good luck. Never heard that one? Right, anyway, what's going on?" Ram asked as they stepped into the well-lit lobby.

"Over here, behind this pillar," Irv directed.

Allyson teased, "Laramie? Is that your real name?"

"Yeah. An early mentor thought Ram sounded better," he grinned. "Irv and I go back longer than that."

The three huddled behind a large white column, blocking the view from the street.

"We were called in about an hour ago by the studio attorney. The nighttime security guard went to wake Mr. Wotke thirty minutes before the seven o'clock shift change. He was startled when he found the room empty and blood on the floor. The guard immediately called his employer, who followed their chain of command. We were asked to be discreet with our arrival due to the fans."

"How did those people even find out Roger was here?" Allyson asked.

"Usually, there's a leak on the team—someone in charge of PR. No publicity is bad. Especially with a guy like Roger," Ram answered.

"Why hire security and hide him if you're going to leak it anyway?"

"It gives them control over the situation," Ram answered. "Irv, can we see the room?"

"My team is still processing the scene, but I managed to snap these." Irv handed his phone to Ram. Together, he and Allyson flipped through the pictures.

"It's like he never slept in his bed, although the comforter looks disheveled," Ram assessed, zooming in and out of each frame. "That's the suspected blood? It's outside the bathroom entrance. It's possible he had an accident."

"Then where did he go? Was the guard there the entire night?" Allyson asked.

"He isn't talking. We're holding him and the attorney in the hotel's conference room with instructions to stay until we can get a statement. It's a favorite tactic of law enforcement. Waiting makes people anxious. Anxiety makes people act unexpectedly, like talk themselves into a corner or reveal an accidental truth."

Ram and Allyson agreed, but for different reasons. "I'm glad I've never been in that kind of situation," Allyson remarked.

"I'm waiting on access to the hallway security footage. It should give us an idea of what went on from the doorway to the exits," Irv said.

"Excuse me, sir? The footage is ready." A woman with a power bob hairstyle and legs for miles appeared from a side door off the lobby desk area. She waved the trio towards her in welcome.

"Thank you, Alma. You are welcome to join me," Irv offered to Ram and Allyson. "However, I must warn you both, if we discover anything pointing to a crime, you need to give us time to work the case before you report specific details. Deal?"

They assented in unison as they followed the FBI agent to the small room behind the check-in counter.

A man with little black eyes and a bulbous nose turned from his chair facing a bank of monitors and greeted them professionally. Allyson couldn't look away from the angry red boils dotting his face. She rolled her shoulders and shuttered in discomfort.

"I've cued the footage from Mr. Wotke's floor. It begins from his arrival until agents came about an hour ago."

"Did you find anything?" Irv asked.

"See for yourself. I programmed the system to play the specific segments. Watch here on this screen," the tech replied, pointing with a crooked finger resembling an overcooked sausage.

Once he clicked play, the first segment showed several men getting off the elevator, one in the center with a hoodie pulled over his head to hide his face. That was presumably Roger. His back remained towards the camera view throughout the few seconds it took his team to process the door and enter. After their initial arrival, there was nothing other than the guard fidgeting outside the door until around 3 a.m., when commotion around the elevator briefly drew him away from his post. He was confronting three women clutching papers in their hands.

"Fans," Irv guessed. "I thought the elevators were secured for hotel guests only?" he asked Alma, who stood behind the group.

"Correct. You need a room key to make the elevator move from the lobby. Perhaps these women are guests. If we can identify them, I can confirm whether they were here for legitimate reasons. If they weren't, we will press charges for trespassing. We value our guests' privacy and safety first and foremost," Alma responded in a curt, clipped tone.

After the women were sent on their way, nothing appeared on the footage until the guard entered Roger's room at 6:30 a.m. Ten minutes later, he rushed out, taking the staircase door. Without coverage of the stairwell, they could only assume he was headed toward the lobby.

"Can we view clips of the various building entrances during this same period?" Irv asked the man at the controls.

"Certainly," the tech replied, flipping through screens, clicking, and typing at a practiced speed.

Each frame showed no evidence Roger left the building through any covered exit between when he arrived and when the security guard discovered he was no longer in his room.

"A man doesn't just vanish into thin air!" Allyson cried.

"There are no adjoining rooms to his, correct?" Irv asked.

"Correct. Mr. Wotke was assigned the Presidential Monarch Suite. It's fifteen hundred square feet with no entrances other than what is here on the footage."

"Wait. We are processing a regular room!" Irv exclaimed.

"What do you mean? That is the only room we would have given him, considering his status and requirements for privacy," Alma insisted.

"What room is this?" Irv asked the technician, pointing to the screen.

"The Presidential Suite," he confirmed.

"The security guard led us to the eighth floor, room 810."

"Impossible. The Presidential Suite is on the top floor." Alma paled.

"Go check your system. I need a card to that suite now!" Irv barked.

"You two stay here. Bob will show you footage from the eighth floor during the same time frame. Stephen!" he shouted into his phone, "Get your ass to the conference room and make sure the attorney and security guard don't move a muscle until I get there!"

Irv left the small security room with Alma, while Ram and Allyson stayed with the computer tech.

"You heard the man. Show us the eighth-floor view from the same time frame," Ram commanded.

"What do you think is going on?" Allyson whispered to Ram.

"It's possible the studio booked two rooms to avoid crazy fans trying to catch a glimpse of Roger." Ram scratched his head, considering all the possibilities and angles.

"And *they* didn't release his whereabouts. Someone else did," Allyson jerked her thumb at the man in the chair.

Ram inclined his head yet kept his eyes on the security system programmer. "Roger has fans all over the world. Literally, anyone between the courthouse and the hotel could have spotted him and blasted out a location to the fandom. That's the thing about *The Caretaker*. People are so obsessed, they follow its stars like it's a full-time job."

"What do they expect to gain from it all?" Allyson asked.

"A minute to interact, mostly. An autograph, a photo, maybe give them something to show their devotion. I've heard of several gruesome interactions with Roger. *Givers*, the more devout ones, call themselves. They've offered him jars packed with animal parts and lockets filled with their blood! There's a whole social page dedicated to tattoos, scarification, and other body art. One guy was arrested last year for giving him a finger in a Ziplock baggie. Roger told him he hated hands, and the guy went ballistic. It turns out it wasn't even his finger but something he got from a buddy who worked in the morgue."

"Jesus. That's wild. I can't grasp why people idolize celebrities to the point of obsession. Yet, the body art thing, I get. I guess I should be thankful I never fell victim to hero worship." Allyson shivered.

"Did Andrea mention interacting with the fandom or the Givers?" Ram asked.

"Not to me. I suppose it's probable, considering their obsession. Why?"

"Let's talk about it later," Ram answered, tilting his head toward the computer guy. "Hey. What's that?" he asked, pointing to a screen.

"Delivery truck for the Italian restaurant," the man answered, zooming in on the logo. It advertised fresh fish delivered daily.

"What about it?" Allyson asked.

"I'm unsure. Something about it caught my eye. What's the timestamp on that?"

"That's the live feed from the service entrance. You want to look at this screen here for the recording you wanted," the man directed.

"How often does the hotel get deliveries back there?"

"Every day. Sometimes a couple a day for linens and other supplies."

"So, this specific truck and company is a routine delivery?"

"No," stated the technician.

Moving forward with the footage, they found it was identical to the one from the suite view. The only difference was the décor and number of doors along the hallway.

"Were there other guests in those rooms?"

"I'd venture they were empty since there is no other activity on video. If the studio booked decoy rooms, they probably booked the whole floor for privacy's sake. Alma can confirm that."

"Everything appears to be staged," Allyson whispered, watching the guard run from the room like the other guard did. "I wonder if they are even real guards or actors? Because this weird thing happened at my building the other night—"

"Thank you for your time and expertise," Ram interrupted, grabbing Allyson by the elbow and leading her out. "Sorry, but there is something fishy going on here, no pun intended. We should discuss this away from Bob."

Heading back out into the lobby, more FBI agents were visible.

"What's going on?" Ram asked a passerby.

"Sir, you both need to have a seat over by the fireplace. At the moment, the building is going into lockdown."

"What the fuck?" Allyson whispered, closing the gap between her and Ram, who still had his hand on her arm.

Doing what they were told, they huddled together on a couch.

"Here's what we've learned," Ram began. "Roger, who may or may not have even stepped foot in this hotel, has been reported missing by the studio or its representatives. The evidence points to nothing other than a coordinated stunt."

"Oh my god!" Allyson blurted out before covering her mouth.

"What?"

"The fish truck. You pointed it out, and I should've immediately seen the similarities!" she said, slapping her forehead.

"What are you talking about?" Ram shifted to give her his full attention.

"I started to tell you in the room this weird incident happened a few nights ago at my building. These men, posing as pest control, were caught searching our apartments. They claimed someone contacted them about roaches, yet Dr. Dean couldn't corroborate their story. Weirder still, they only 'treated' select apartments, including mine. And they drove vans nearly identical to the fish truck. I mean, it's generic enough that every laborer has one. However, the name. Wasn't it Burns something?"

"Yeah! Burns Fishery or Hatchery." Ram's eyes went wide.

"It was Burns Pest Company at my place too! This *was* planned."

"In all fairness, Burns is a pretty common name. Could you positively ID them if they were stupid enough to use the same guys from your place?"

"I think so. Let's go find out!"

"Where are you two running off to?" an agent shouted at them.

"Restroom?" Ram suggested.

"Laramie!" It was Irv. "It's okay, Bryan, they are with me," Irv waived off the agent, attempting to stop Ram and Allyson.

"What's the latest?" Ram asked.

"Both rooms were empty and staged in the same manner. The attorney and the security guard are in the wind."

"That matches what we saw too. However, while we were reviewing the footage, we caught something else. A delivery truck at the service entrance. It looked suspicious, so we're headed there now." Ram shot a look at Allyson to keep her from explaining further.

"I'll join you. Let's go."

"There was no fish delivery today, sir," a man dressed in kitchen staff garb replied. "We are closed tonight for a private party. Vegans. Can we hold the event?"

"Fuck!" Irv shouted. "Sorry. Yes, we should finish our investigation before dinner. Someone will inform you when it's completed." Turning to Ram and Allyson, he said, "Let's get back to the technician's office and ask if he can pull what the camera caught from the delivery. I have a hunch they were doing a pickup instead."

"I can't explain why it didn't record," the technician stated. "Other than it must be a glitch."

"So, you're telling me, Bob, there is nothing from that location? For how long?" Irv asked.

"Let me see. Hmmm. Only the last hour. Notice the timestamp?" Bob pointed with his sausage finger. "Then it jumps to the next hour, to the second."

"Is it possible someone erased it?" Irv asked, moving to place his hand near his handcuffs.

Bob raised his hands in defense. "I can't control what gets recorded. I can only log into the cloud and retrieve read-only data."

"Who has the administrative rights to delete stuff, then?" Ram demanded.

"My boss? The head of IT? Or Alma? She's the manager."

"Alma was with me the entire time. Where is your boss, this IT guy?"

"At corporate. I'm just an on-site tech, called in for things like this and simple troubleshooting stuff, like when a TV doesn't work, or the main computers freeze, I swear! Don't arrest me."

"You are not under arrest . . . yet . . . But we will hold you for questioning until we confirm everything with your employer." Irv turned to Ram and Allyson.

"This has turned into a regular shitshow. What I thought was a simple dip-and-slip from an overprivileged actor has turned into a major clusterfuck of a crime scene. I'll ask you to hold off on any reporting until we have a complete picture of what's happened here. In the meantime, Bryan will walk you guys out so you can get on with your day."

"Call or text me when you have an update," Ram slapped his pal on the shoulder. "Nothing is ever cut and dry. You know that!"

"All too well, buddy. Nice to meet you, Allyson."

"Likewise," Allyson smiled and gave a mock salute before heading out the door towards the lobby.

The crowd outside grew as they sat in Ram's car, taking in the day's events. A few carried signs with Roger's pictures as the Caretaker, while others held their phones out as if recording something.

"Probably vlogging their experience," Ram commented.

"I still don't get how they knew he was there when it appears the hotel staff had no fucking clue a celebrity shell game was being played right under their noses." Suddenly, she hopped from the car and ran across the street towards them.

"Allyson! What are you doing?" Ram called after her.

"Did any of you notice a delivery truck come or go from here about an hour ago?"

"What's going on inside? Is Caretaker okay?" a fan asked, fear evident in their voice.

"Caretaker? Is that why you are here? Who told you Roger was staying here?" Ram asked.

"It was on the 'Givers' app," another fan showed them.

"There's an app for that, really? Anyway, do you have any video of the vehicles coming and going from this direction?" Allyson asked, pointing to the place where deliveries would enter and exit.

"Only a few unmarked cars," a third piped in, flipping through their phone's camera pictures.

"Wait, go back. There. Can I see that?" Allyson asked.

Using her fingers, she zoomed into the picture. It was an unmarked white van leaving the area. The driver was clearly visible. "Ram, I'm 99 percent certain this is the same guy from my building." Allyson showed him the screen.

"Can you read the license plate?"

"No front plate, and the sign is gone. It was probably magnetic."

"What's going on? Who are you people? Wait! I know you! You're Ram Helm. What's a reporter doing here? Has something happened to Caretaker?"

Swiftly sending the video to his phone via Bluetooth before anyone noticed, he flipped it back to its owner. "I'm usually the one hearing this, but . . . no comment. Come on, Allyson, let's go." Ram grabbed her hand and turned towards the car.

As they sped away, Ram said, "There's definitely a link between your sister and Roger's disappearances. My investigator instincts say there are too many coincidences. The question is, how do you play into this, Allyson?"

13

SCARED LITTLE GIRL

{ALLYSON}

C losing her eyes tight, Allyson began practicing the calming techniques Dr. Dean taught her to use in moments of high stress. "I don't believe in chance. Andrea and Roger worked on the same production, and they were linked romantically. The fact they've both gone missing is no accident. How I fit into everything confounds me." She scratched at her arms before rubbing her hands on her thighs. "God, I need something sharp," she murmured before turning her attention out the passenger window.

She pressed her forefinger to the glass, tracing a singular raindrop as it trickled in a zigzag pattern down the window. Ram was driving her back to her apartment. The splashes fell far apart at first as if the sky were crying. By the time they entered the highway, a steady stream splattered all the windows.

"Hey," she turned to Ram. "Can you bring me to Dr. Dean's office instead? You can get off at the next exit. He's near 5th and Union."

"Yeah, sure. You okay?"

"I don't think so. My thoughts are spinning, my skin is itching, and my chest feels tight as if I'm having an asthma attack. Yet I'm not asthmatic."

"Should we go to the hospital instead?"

"No. No. It's a panic attack. I'll text Dr. Dean. He'll fit me in. I think everything is just hitting me. I'm feeling really vulnerable and probably shouldn't be alone."

Ram hit the accelerator and navigated expertly off the highway and back into downtown, not far from the hotel. Allyson gave him directions and thanked him as he pulled in front of the building's entrance.

"Umm. I'm sorry if I said or did something to upset you." Ram leaned across the passenger seat to talk to Allyson as she stood holding the door edge. "Will you call me later and let me know you are okay? I've got to get back to the station and prep for the evening segments. While I'm doing that, I'll also look into any other ties between Roger and Andrea."

"Sure," she smiled, yet it didn't reach her eyes. Her face was flushed, and her chin quivered. "Today was strange, disturbing, and somehow wonderful in the most unusual ways. Thank you." Then, she slammed the door and bolted between raindrops into the building.

"Welcome to Hollywood Tonight. I'm Gail Beekers, and that's Courtney Shaw. Here are today's headlines . . ."

The sound from the TV blared in the waiting room at Dr. Dean's office. Allyson appreciated the distraction since she had to wait while he finished with another patient. She loved watching *Hollywood Tonight*. It was real news to her. Nothing but fluff and stories to make you feel good about yourself because famous people were always doing dumb shit.

"Breaking news out of Seattle. Roger Wotke, star of The Caretaker *series, is missing. If you recall, a few days ago, the FBI arrested the embattled actor for allegedly assaulting Emirates crewmembers on*

board an aircraft destined for Dubai. Sources say he was staying at an undisclosed hotel under tight security awaiting legal proceedings when a member of his team found his room empty. No further details are available at this time."

"How the hell did they find out already?! Ram will be pissed!" Grabbing her phone, she fired off a hasty text while continuing to listen to the report.

"That man is a menace to society, Gail. Why they didn't leave him in jail to await his day in court is beyond me."

"You're right, Courtney. About twenty years ago, when he first tasted fame, he escaped serious jail time after he was accused of striking his girlfriend repeatedly, then peeing in her Birkin Bag during a drunken tirade."

"Mmm. Hmm. I remember, Gail. He basically victim-blamed the poor girl, saying something along the lines that his relationships were always conducted with open communication and a dedication to mutual agreement and satisfaction. Anyone who suggested otherwise did so out of misplaced shame. He doubled down on his ostentatiousness when fans reacted, claiming they were jealous it wasn't them on the receiving end."

"History shows people love a bad boy. He has made it work in his favor. What I resent, Courtney, is if we acted like that, we'd be labeled and canceled!"

"Girl, hello, Scarlet Letter! It's hard to believe he wasn't caught up in the Me Too movement."

"By then, his popularity as the Caretaker was soaring."

"That kind of behavior is probably what landed him the job. Who else could pull off such a nasty character with such precision and gusto? And it's been proven time and again how much power and pull these big entertainment conglomerates have. I bet they paid a pretty penny to silence anyone who could put a wrench in their successful franchise."

"Allyson? Earth to Allyson!"

She was so absorbed in the broadcast, Dr. Dean's voice was more like background noise. She didn't even acknowledge his presence until he tapped her shoulder. "Sorry! Coming," she replied, gathering the coat and handbag she had flung to the floor when she first arrived. "I appreciate you seeing me on such short notice," she added as she stepped into his office.

"I am here any time you need me. Sit. Make yourself comfortable. What's going on?"

"Did you see that?"

"No, but I saw how absorbed you were. Honestly, I think I should pull that thing out or leave it on a blank screen with white noise. It has caused more arguments and anxiety than it's worth! What's happened?"

"Roger is missing."

"Roger? As in the Caretaker?"

"Yep."

"Wow. I can't say I'm terribly shocked. Is that what brought you here?"

"No. I was with Ram Helm, the investigative reporter, earlier. We met to discuss how I could get more involved with Andrea's case when he got a call from an FBI friend. They were alerted this morning that Roger was missing from his guarded hotel room." Allyson continued explaining the situation to her doctor, including the complex emotions she was struggling with.

"Honestly, I'm scared. Ram asked how I'm connected to all of this, and it got me thinking. What if I'm next?"

"It's natural to feel anxious with all this uncertainty in your life at the moment. Realistically, though, Roger probably slipped away to avoid facing prosecution versus falling victim to a kidnapper. "

"After the group meeting in the basement the other day, you asked if I saw Andrea's disappearance and Roger's arrest as a coincidence. Now that he has vanished too, I'm spinning out! Yet, you make a great point about Roger. I could see him squirming his way out of his legal mess by choosing to run away. It's probably what he was doing when he got arrested. The two incidents could be completely unrelated, and I am making this all about me."

"Why don't you share some of your worries?"

Allyson rubbed her face with shaky hands. "The fake exterminators may have helped Roger get away from the hotel today. We saw a similar white van, and the driver could've been the tall man you confronted in my apartment. As Ram drove me back, I thought, what if they weren't helping Roger escape, and instead, his lifeless body was rolling around in the back? Then I thought how that could've been me if Grace and you weren't there to scare them away."

"Why would someone want to hurt any of you?"

"I'm unsure! They worked on *Caretaker* together, and I'm the identical twin. Maybe they want to make sure they grabbed the right Marta girl? Or perhaps they are targeting people from Argentina. Then there's the revenge angle. I've told you about Andrea's propensity to violence. Could someone be retaliating against her and Roger? Or even trying to hush them up? But why come after me?"

"Who said they are?"

"Someone snuck into my apartment building and entered my place under false pretenses!" Allyson shrieked.

"Is it possible they were only checking to see if you were hiding Andrea in plain sight? Or truly a misunderstanding?"

"It could've been a warning. 'We can get to you, if we need to.'" Allyson fidgeted more by running her fingers over the word 'sin' on her wrist. "Honestly, I want to cut right now," she whined, balling her hands into fists before slamming them on her legs. "I want to scream, to jump out of this twelfth-story window and end all this nonsense. I wish I'd done it the minute I discovered my dead friend at summer camp when we were twelve. I've hidden Andrea's secrets for eighteen years at great expense to my sanity. I should have had the courage to kill her, then myself back then. The world would have been a safer place."

"Whoa, Allyson. Hold on. You are speaking from your inner child. She is a scared little girl, and she needs you to comfort her—reassure her she is safe. Everything else is in the past. There's nothing to do but accept it happened and move on. You are an adult, and you can make different choices."

"I don't feel safe! Not until there's a sharp object in my hand and blood oozing from a wound."

"You cut because you need to regulate your thoughts. Your brain wants a break. Why don't you take one? With the information we have, I don't think you are in any immediate danger except from your thoughts. Let's shift our focus away from what you can't control and discuss the ones you can. Tell me about your labyrinth. Where are you in the process?"

"You . . . you're changing the subject? I tell you I want to die, to cut, and you want to talk about my labyrinth project?"

"Yes. Tell me everything about it and how you met Ram Helm. He's a fantastic journalist and my favorite on the evening news."

Allyson stood so abruptly she got light-headed and collapsed back in her seat. She wanted to leave and never come back. Sliding her hand into her pocket to call a ride share, her phone buzzed. "Normally, I would ignore this. However, since you've just ignored me and my needs, I'm going to answer," she hissed. "Hello?"

Allyson pulled the phone away from her ear as if she'd been scalded and stared at the screen before stabbing at the 'End' button.

"Are you okay? Who was that? Your face is white." Dr. Dean asked, grabbing her phone. "Unknown Caller. What did they say?"

Allyson fixated on the growing darkness outside the window. Her phone buzzed again—same caller ID.

"Hello?" Dr. Dean answered.

"Who's this?" questioned a preternatural voice.

"You first," Dr. Dean demanded. Their response was three beeps signaling the end of the call.

"They hung up. Did you recognize the voice? Did they threaten you?"

Allyson shook her head as she nibbled her bottom lip. The phone buzzed again. This time, it listed Ram Helm as the caller. Dr. Dean handed back the phone.

"Hello?" Allyson answered.

"Hey. How are you doing?"

"I'm still with the doctor. We're . . . taking a little break." Allyson scrunched her nose and narrowed her eyes at Dr. Dean before turning her back to him.

"Breaks are good, I'm guessing?"

"Sure."

"Anyway, I got approval to head to Vancouver to survey the sound-stage H0rr Studios rented. I was wondering if you wanted to tag along. Your sister owns a place there, right?"

"Yes. She keeps an apartment in the city. Both she and Roger do. They are in the same building. Different floors. Do you think we can get in?"

"You'll probably hate this idea, but . . ."

"Let me guess. You want me to pose as my sister? Have you seen me? We don't exactly resemble each other anymore."

"Only in *your* eyes. I think you could pull it off with the right wig and a little makeup."

"Don't you think the police searched both places already?"

"Certainly hers. Yet the police lack perspective. They look for signs something criminal happened . . . blood, a suicide note, and clues along those lines. As for the movie lot, they would need a search warrant. A missing employee wouldn't qualify, especially since the studio execs are the ones who reported it. They'd need evidence pointing at the studio."

"What makes you sure I can help? Besides, I'm unstable at the moment."

"Ram, this is Dr. Dean." Allyson took the phone from her ear and placed it on his desk, hitting the speaker button.

"You're on speaker." She scowled at Dr. Dean and crossed her arms over her chest.

"I apologize if I've crossed a boundary. However, I'm close enough to overhear your conversation, and I wanted to add my professional opinion. I think it might benefit Allyson to immerse herself in her sister's world. It might dissolve the antipathy she holds toward Andrea."

Allyson muttered something unintelligible while shaking her head. "I don't see what I can do to help. Besides, if I resurface as Andrea, don't you think someone will report me? Or put us in danger?"

"We'll slip in under the radar. Based on your characterization, Andrea might vanish for a few days, then reappear, pretending it was no big deal. A concierge or a security guard would expect that. If they balk, a little cash, and they'll keep quiet," Ram suggested.

"Seems as though you've done this before," Allyson replied, distaste in her voice.

"Look, Allyson. You asked me to help. This is how. If you'd rather I file a report tonight about Andrea missing, say the word. Then, you can go about making posters and websites with telephone tip lines and rewards. I happen to think investigating on our own will get us further along. If we don't find anything in a day or two, we can go the traditional route with publicity."

"*Hollywood Tonight* is already reporting on Roger. Did you see my text?"

"I did. Did you hear the Studio's rebuttal statement?"

"What? No! What did it say?" Allyson's mouth slackened, and Dr. Dean raised an eyebrow.

"I'll read it to you. 'A false story is circulating about the whereabouts of our beloved actor Roger Wotke. Due to the nature of his crimes, the conditions the court has set forth, and the privacy required while the legal process runs its course, Mr. Wotke will remain out of the public eye. H0rr Studios guarantees there is no validity to the rumor at this time.'"

"At this time? Seriously? What does your friend at the FBI, Agent Kingsley, say about this?"

"Funny you should ask. I called Irv the minute I heard their spiel. He says the FBI is still working the case. They are scouring CCTV footage for the white van you caught leaving the place and following what few leads they have. He thinks issuing a denial was simply to keep the Givers from going berserk. After all, it was H0rr Studios or their representative who called in the FBI in the first place. Listen. I've got to run. What do you think? Should I mention Andrea, or will you come with me on a little field trip first?"

Allyson hesitated, locking eyes with Dr. Dean. He winked and flashed a hundred-watt smile to seal the deal.

"Okay," she blurted. "When do you plan on leaving?"

"Tonight, after my shift here. I figured I would drive. It's two hours and change, depending on the border crossing. At that hour, I wouldn't expect any delays. I can pick you up at your place. Pack a weekender. We may only stay a night. We may stay two. Depends on what we find out and how successful we are at our little subterfuge."

"All right, see you soon." Allyson turned to Dr. Dean. "What have you gotten me into? What if I lose my shit there?"

Dr. Dean placed a hand on her shoulder. "You've got this. I'll explain which meds you can take if you feel unstable. And I'm always a phone call away. Besides, Vancouver has a fantastic healthcare system. If you need anything at all, I have several colleagues there. I think you'll find it fun embodying your sister. Didn't you guys ever swap places when you were kids? If I had an identical twin, we would've done so all the time!"

"All you singletons are the same," she snorted.

14

EXIT STRATEGY

{ANDREA}

Roger, Andrea, Craig the cinematographer, and the girl—victim *numero uno* were the only ones on set. They were on location a few miles from the studio on a rural road to film an outdoor scene. The remaining film crew was on dinner break while Andrea led a walkthrough of her vision with the threesome. The director radioed ahead, saying he was running late and to move forward without him.

The scene involved a young, beautiful woman whose car broke down on a desolate road. She would set out on foot toward the next town to seek help, leaving her headlights on to light her way through the cold, moonless night. She was underdressed in a tank top, jeans, and flip-flops. The Caretaker's rickety old pickup would round the corner and hit her. To cover his misdeed, he would wrap her body in a tarp and throw her in the truckbed, then bring her back to the house he cared for, owned by a billionaire entrepreneur. Once she was hidden away, he would head back to dispose of the car. Another marginalized individual in society vanished into thin air. No one would care. No one would search. It was the perfect crime.

Andrea ran them through the scene half a dozen times while Craig played with lighting, filters, and angles. Roger practiced driving erratically in the pickup. The victim, a stuntwoman new to the film world, stood by, absorbing what she could from Andrea, Craig, and especially Roger. Even with his questionable past, he was someone to admire and learn from. Only the movie's casting agent was aware Andrea sourced the woman specifically to fill the role, promising her a career on the big screen. However, nobody imagined what she planned. Something so big, its consequences would reverberate for decades.

"Let's run through one last time with the cameras live," Craig ordered.

"Sure, Craig," Andrea assented. "Roger. Let me ride with you back to the set point," she suggested, hopping in the truck.

"Listen," she began as Roger drove them about a mile to his mark. "Remember when I told you to trust me regardless of what I might ask you to do regarding our work?" she asked.

"Yes," Roger grimaced, gripping his hands tighter on the steering wheel. "And I can guess what you are going to say. I can't do it."

"You will do it—without any debate. She is my gift to you, and I made sure only you, Craig, and myself would be involved."

"You recruited Craig too?!"

"Once you play your part, I trust him to fall in line. He needs this job with three kids heading to college and ten years of future alimony payments to cover. Not to mention that pesky gambling habit he's developed. Now, I'm going to hop out as you set yourself. Am I clear?"

Roger locked eyes with her, repulsion coloring his face before it turned to indifference, followed by self-loathing. He said nothing as she got out. "Welcome to your new life," she said, and a wicked smile spread across the Caretaker's face. In that instant, he had transformed into his character, and she was as proud as a doting mother. Double-tapping the side door when

Craig sent the signal that the cameras were live and ready, Roger peeled out and sped away. And the rest, as they say, was history.

Andrea ran her fingers over the open sketchbook page again like a long-lost lover before placing it back on the table. She'd been in another time while holding it, each page a personal time machine. People often discussed the chance to revisit their past and what they would do differently. She wouldn't change a damn thing.

"You're a killer! For the sake of killing," Roger screamed at Andrea after the deed was done.

"Oh please, don't get all sanctimonious. You knew that already. It's how we met!" Andrea countered. "Besides, now you are too," she quipped. Smoothing the back of her hand over his cheek, she stared at him lovingly. "It's the ultimate creation, to make someone in your image. Godlike. It's a heady feeling. Almost better than taking a life. You feel it too. Don't you?"

"I could go to jail!" he cried.

"It was an accident," Andrea countered, rolling her eyes. "You lost control of the truck. She was a stuntwoman who should've been faster on her feet. These action sequences are always risky. It's why we run through them a million times and still get waivers signed. This will make *The Caretaker*. Future ones like this will guarantee its success and, therefore, ours."

"This was no accident. You told me to do it!" Roger countered.

"Prove it, you entitled shitbird! I'm trying to save your career and this company, and you want to blame me? Was I behind the wheel? The one who was so preoccupied they confused the gas for the brake?"

He swung out, striking her in the mouth with his open hand. She was surprised and lost her balance, stumbling into an armchair. She tasted blood in her mouth as it oozed from the left corner. Righting herself, she stood before him, her shoulders squared, revealing her amusement at his violence with a wide smile. He examined his hand as if it were someone else's before turning his focus back to her. Her expression sickened him, driving him to scurry from the room.

Shaking her head, Andrea snapped herself back to the present one final time. The memory was so solid and realistic, she raised her hand to her mouth, half expecting to find it swollen and bleeding. "Why have I forgotten so much of myself?" She scratched her head and immediately regretted it. She'd hit the bump she discovered earlier in the mirror's reflection. Feathering her fingers around the area, she winced at the dual pains in her shoulder and head.

"Fuck," she groaned, "I should rest." She looked longingly at the couch. This space was her creative sanctuary, after all. She'd be safe.

Suddenly, keys rattled outside her office door, jolting her as if she'd touched a live wire. Her body tensed, and she froze in place while her mind hunted for a way to make herself small, invisible. In a split-second decision, she grabbed a chair from the worktable to wedge it under the knob as it turned and twisted. Slipping into the bathroom, she closed and locked its door.

Someone was whistling a melody she recognized as *The Caretaker* theme song while they continued to rattle their keys. Pressing her back against the door, her eyes scanned the bathroom. She needed a weapon or a way out to appear magically. At a minimum, she needed to trade the afghan for the hospital gown, which she had rinsed out in the shower. It was still damp yet gave her more mobility and protection. Then she waited, chewing a fingernail and cocking her head to the side to listen.

The chair scraped across the floor, breaking the silence. Immediately, the whistling stopped, its sounds replaced by heavy footsteps.

"Hmm. What do we have here?" an accented baritone voice questioned.

Andrea unlocked her door, quietly cracking it open to see if she recognized the person speaking.

"An artist's den. Interesting," the voice continued.

Andrea spied from her hiding spot as the nondescript man, dressed in medical scrubs, walked around the room, inspecting items as he went. He kept his back to her as if he were aware he was under surveillance. When he lifted the sketchbook, something in her snapped. Channeling her inner animal, she growled and leapt from her spot, barreling toward him like a linebacker rushing the quarterback on any given Sunday.

Stunned, the man turned, yet too slow. Her momentum crashed into his chest, sending him reeling back into the gaping hole in the floor leading to the tunnels below. His surprised yelp turned into a scream as a sickening thud and crack echoed below the minute his body hit the hard ground. Crouching over the opening, Andrea squinted to see if he was moving.

"You little bitch!" he cried out.

Andrea stumbled backward at his vitriol as if he'd struck her with his fist. She couldn't make out his face, yet his voice suggested they were acquainted. Scrabbling away from the opening, she rose and raced toward the exit.

Her office opened to an expansive warehouse filled with building supplies, tools, and half-made film sets. Paint cans and lumber were stacked in one area, while fabric rolls and home furnishings littered another. Closing her eyes briefly, she envisioned teams of people happily chatting with each other as they worked on various projects under her and the set designer's direction. She kept her back to the wall and sidestepped along its edge, stopping periodically to discern any sounds from the man in the tunnel or any accomplice with him. She was having trouble staying grounded in the present moment as her mind continued to flash back to a time when her surroundings meant something different.

"Is it because of the head injury?" she whispered, closing her eyes tight and opening them several times to force herself to focus and remain in the present.

Metal clanged as something dropped to the concrete floor. She gasped and pressed her body tighter against the wall to minimize the visibility of her vulnerable position. Across the room, she spotted a door similar to her office. It might provide cover and safety—if it was unlocked.

Breaking into a run, she slammed into it, shoulder first, fumbling with its handle before it gave way, allowing her inside. Securing it behind her, she took in the space. It was the set decorator's office, no bigger than a large bedroom. Two lit floor lamps provided enough illumination to reveal its contents. Scaled floorplans of the various *Caretaker* sets plastered the walls, while easels crowded the floor, holding storyboards filled with sample colors and fabric swatches. Rummaging through desk drawers, she hunted for a potential weapon to fend off another threat. "Who the fuck is this guy, and what in the hell does he want with me?" she whispered as she found all the drawers empty.

She searched a credenza and checked a coat closet; they both turned up the same . . . nothing. The high windows, like the ones in her office, revealed no light, and there was neither a calendar nor a clock anywhere. She was left to assume it was either nighttime or early morning before sunrise.

"Naturally, we all wore watches or carried phones on us at all times," she grunted. "Okay, this trip down memory lane has been fun. Not. However, I need to refocus on the goal. Escape. I can't stay here forever. How do I get the fuck out of here? What's my plan?"

A chill ran through her body from the damp hospital gown and her bare feet on the concrete floor. Then, her stomach growled. No, not her stomach, but a tool or motor firing up.

"Shit! I've trapped myself again. And this time, there's no hole in the ground to stuff a body. Think, Andrea! Think."

"Little rabbit . . ." a man called. It was the same accented baritone as before.

"How? He was in the tunnel!" she said, astonished. "Wait. It . . . it's the same voice from the set earlier too. But, but," she stuttered, pinching the bridge of her nose and shaking her head. "That was a ghost. A hallucination. From my head wound. He's dead. Dead and gone."

Bang. Bang. Bang.

Cracking lumber echoed in the open space as collapsing structures rattled to the ground. Concerned the office door was the next target, she shoved the credenza across the floor to block it. The makeshift barrier wouldn't hold a maniac bent on coming in. However, it would buy her time until she could figure something else out.

Slipping inside the coat closet as an additional layer of defense, it hit her. It was an interior room. Its walls were drywall screwed into two-by-fours. If she could break through it the way he was destroying the half-made sets, she could escape before he discovered her. Surveying the room with new eyes, she cast about for anything she could use to punch a hole through the backside of the closet. She'd use her fists if she weren't exhausted and weak from all she'd been through thus far. However, she wanted to conserve her strength as much as possible. Moving around the room, she assessed each object, weighing its ability to create a large hole. Her hands grew clammy, and her legs shook the longer it took her to find something. In the meantime, the man's voice grew louder and closer. Then, her attention fell on the floor lamps. With their heavy base, they would do the trick.

She made a small runway to charge forward with the lamp's base out in front as if it were a spear or lance, hoping the momentum would make a hole. Timing her movements, she waited until more destruction sounded from outside before slamming her makeshift tool into the drywall. It made a big enough hole that she used her hands to pull away the debris. From there, she used the lamp again. This time, to break through to the other side just as the office door rattled.

Andrea emerged into another storage room—this one full of furniture. Thinking to cover her tracks, she slipped back into the closet to shut the door before sliding a large armoire over the hole she'd made.

"That should at least stall him," she panted in a whisper. "But where do I go from here?"

Finally, an answer to her prayers. A door with a glowing red 'Exit' sign shone like a beacon from across the room.

"Little rabbit! I'm coming for you!" the voice boomed as the wood from the credenza splintered.

Hurdling over couches and side-stepping tables and bedroom sets, Andrea pressed the bar to the exit door just as her pursuer broke through her last blockade. Turning to flip him the bird, it wasn't a *him* at all, but a woman—a doppelganger.

"Oh, you know how I love the chase!" it said with a sinister laugh.

15

GETTING TO KNOW YOU

{ALLYSON}

A llyson was waiting in her building's lobby later that evening when Ram pulled up to the entrance.

"Here, I'll pop your bag in the trunk," he replied, seeing Allyson's hands were full.

"Thanks. Grace made me bring this casserole. Supposedly, it's your favorite. They said you probably hadn't eaten all day, and that's how you stay so 'Goddamn thin.' Then they said to tell you they love you and keep me safer than their dark secrets, whatever that means."

"I will text them a thank you. However, how am I supposed to eat it while I'm driving?"

"They sent plasticware and napkins. I guess I can feed it to you?" Allyson smirked as they both got inside. "By the way, tonight's report on H0rr Studios was fascinating. I didn't realize conspiracy theories were actual news, though."

"Ouch. Everyone's a critic. I'm assuming you mean my reference to the rumor they murdered people for their productions? I thought it was worth mentioning in connection to Roger's latest legal challenges."

"Do you find it odd that nobody ever looked into those claims?" Allyson asked as she fiddled with the casserole dish.

"I mean, the idea is ludicrous. Why would anyone waste their time? Didn't Andrea ever discuss it with you?"

Allyson tugged her left earlobe. "She talked about her 'very important work' and her obsession with authenticity. That's if we talked at all. As artists, we discussed our creative processes more than anything, even though our mediums are different. If we were face-to-face, we either sat in uncomfortable silence or bickered."

"I'm fascinated by your relationship with Andrea. You always seem rather negative."

"Andrea is pretty disturbing!" Allyson moistened her lips. "If I told you even half the shit she's done, it would open a Pandora's box I'm not sure I'm willing to open. Not with you. I am her twin. Her sister. That makes me the keeper of her secrets."

"Naturally. We all want to protect our families, even if we don't particularly love them. I'm only asking for insight into how you are together."

Allyson inhaled and blew out slowly through pursed lips. "Well, we *are* on a mission to find her or find out what happened, so I guess it makes sense to fill you in. Where to start . . ." She tapped a finger to her lips.

"What's she like? Are you guys identical in every way?"

Allyson flashed a smile. "Why does that sound pervy? Do you have some twin fantasy you hope to play out here, Ram?"

"Absolutely not!" he chuckled. "I'm simply twin-curious. I know practically nothing about you or them."

"*Right.* Well, physically, we are identical, except for fingerprints. We do luck out there. It's true everyone really does have unique prints, including identicals! Which blows my mind, considering the planet is home to over eight billion humans!" She flipped her palms up and stared at her fingers for a minute. "However, our similarities end with our looks. My mom used to say we fought in the womb. We were that contentious. Andrea is older by a few minutes; thus, inherently, she is the boss, a natural-born leader. I like the shadows. Although, I'm getting better about embracing the spotlight as my success grows. I wouldn't call it shyness, per se, only an extreme dislike of being scrutinized. People always stare at us when we are together like we are a museum piece. Or perhaps a zoo animal is more precise. Or both," Allyson snorted. "Andrea is the Statue of David, and I'm an Aardvark."

Ram grinned. "Why an Aardvark?"

"I did a book report on them once. They are considered one of the shyest animals in the world due to their nocturnal nature. They have large, sensitive ears, making them hyperaware of noises, which helps them stay alert against predators like big cats and humans. They are my spirit animal."

"You don't have large ears," Ram teased, taking a hand off the wheel to caress the object in question. Allyson shivered, then swatted his hand away.

"Hey! Keep those eyes on the road, mister."

"And my hands on the wheel?" Ram's face lit up as he tapped out the beat of a song. "I love that one. Okay. Back to seriousness and the topic at hand. You and Andrea have this Dom/Sub dynamic. Can you elaborate?"

"Again, with the innuendo, Ram. Did you pack the whips and paddles?"

A flush crept across his cheeks. "Sorry. I didn't mean to make you uncomfortable."

Allyson's body shook from amusement. "I'm just messing with you. Thank you for being considerate, though. Anyway, yeah, like I said, she's the leader, and I'm forced to follow. It's caused a lot of problems for me. I blame her for my mental health issues and almost every bad thing that's ever happened to me. She is a sociopath with no remorse for anything she's ever done and always gets away with everything!"

"Like what?"

Allyson hesitated. "Stuff." Sucking in a sharp breath, she continued. "She has to be the center of attention and the first at everything. You wouldn't believe how pissed she got when I discovered art while in therapy as a teen. She didn't find her talent until she saw my work and wanted to prove she could do it better. Our mediums wound up being different, but she wouldn't have picked up a charcoal pencil if it wasn't for her need to be the best at everything."

"She's a bit histrionic, huh?"

"Uh, yeah. Like the gold standard. I could fill ten car rides with stories about her quest for being recognized as the best, like how she tried to drown me once in the ocean because I found more seashells than her. Or the time she stole my mom's credit card and charged up five grand in one day, then blamed it on me. Pa took me shopping after I was released from treatment. I needed new clothes due to a growth spurt, and Patricia was too busy to take me. It was an amazing day until Andrea ruined it with her jealousy and determination to one-up me. It's not like I was trying to compete!"

"Patricia? That's your mother, right?"

"Yeah. Once she had me committed, I refused to call her Ma."

"Wow, I'm sorry. You don't think she got you treatment because you needed it?"

"Patricia was a lot like Andrea. She never did anything that didn't benefit her in some way. Even having us was for her benefit. She got pregnant while she and Pa were dating. Since he was raised in a strict Catholic household, he married her. I mean, she came from a good family and had the right pedigree, yet I always wondered if he would've married her if she hadn't gotten pregnant first."

"I never understood why women played that game. Speaking from the male perspective, if I'm not into her before kids, chances are I'm not going to be into her afterward. I appreciate how people can grow to love one another. Yet entrapment doesn't seem like a way to get there. As far as Andrea goes, other than the whole attempted murder bit, your relationship sounds like any typical sibling rivalry," Ram countered.

"Well, like I said, I could tell you *all kinds* of tales. But let's keep it light. Simply put, she is not a good person. We all make mistakes and wish we could do certain things differently. Not her. She's only ever desired more attention to feed her inner beast. She is literally the worst human ever."

"Ouch. No wonder you are conflicted about doing anything while she's missing."

"Also, I feel like if she were dead, I'd have felt it somehow. That sounds dumb because I'm the biggest naysayer regarding twin superpowers. However, there have been times when we connected on an unexplainable level."

"Do tell."

Allyson hung her head. "Okay. Don't laugh, but like when she's near me, I can feel it. We both do. It's hard to describe. It's like a crawling sensation under my skin. Like all my nerve endings come to life."

"Like when your foot falls asleep?"

"Yeah, something like that. So, it seems like if Andrea were dead, I'd perceive it somehow. I don't feel anything either way. Not even a sense of urgency. I actually feel happier than I have in a long time. Maybe in forever." Allyson pressed her lips together in a grimace before turning her attention out the window, trying to make out the passing landscape in the dark. Tapping her fingertips on the door's armrest, she tried picturing her life without Andrea. "I talked to Dr. Dean about self-acceptance and getting over my antipathy to being a twin in one of our last sessions. I felt incredibly light when we finished. I'd never considered a life without her in it. There's a piece of me who doesn't want to find her. It would make being an individual easier. That's why I'm at odds with her missing, to be quite honest."

"Do you think you will ever accept yourself, regardless of Andrea's outcome? Say you're right about your hunch, and Andrea is not dead, but out there, somewhere," Ram said, waving a hand in the air. "Can you embrace your identical twin-ness as something that makes you as unique as your artwork? Because you're not like everyone else. Everyone else is boring. Trust me. I've met loads of people in my work. The majority have one or two exciting events worth celebrating in their life, and that's it. We are all too busy trying to be 'normal.' You were born with two extraordinary gifts. Twindom and talent."

Allyson didn't answer right away. Instead, she shifted her gaze from the passenger window to the road ahead. "I'm not sure. I guess only discovering what happened to Andrea will fully answer that for me."

"I think you already know the answer."

"Shut up and drive, you quack." Allyson gave Ram a playful shove before turning on the radio for a much-needed distraction.

"Hey, how about some casserole?"

"Oh, yeah. Sorry. It smells amazing," she raved, opening the container and scooping some out to feed him. After tasting some herself, she continued, "Our housekeeper, Maria, would make something similar from time to time while we were growing up. However, Pa was big on integrating American culture into our lives as much as possible and didn't allow too much Hispanic and Latino influence. It just made it that much more special when we did have something from home."

"You guys are from Argentina, right?"

"Yeah. We came right after Andrea and I turned six. The Great Depression hit, and Pa thought it best to leave with his riches before the corruption could get him. My grandparents and uncles weren't as lucky."

"Your father is in mining?"

"Mmm. Hmm. How did you . . . Oh, yeah. Investigative reporter. Yes, Anselmo is a metallurgist by trade and has a knack for finding copper, which is important, especially in today's battery-centric, technology-dependent world. I hear life is good for him these days."

"So, you don't keep in touch?" Ram prodded.

"Only through messaging, mostly. We're all busy with our lives."

"I get it. I'm glad we are doing this, though. I'm hoping we get some answers for you. Dr. Dean seemed to think it was a good idea too. What you felt earlier tonight when you needed to see him—that's gone away?"

Allyson caught Ram's expression. He seemed to be assessing her face in a clinical way. "Yes, for now. Don't worry. I won't slit my wrists on your watch. You seem to have a calming effect on me. No pressure or anything, but you may be stuck with me the way we are with Grace!" Allyson chuckled. "Although, don't let that go to your head. Dr. Dean adjusted my meds, so the pharmaceuticals may be helping with the good vibes."

Ram cleared his throat and changed the subject. "So, I talked to Irv, my FBI contact, before I picked you up. He told me Chief Constable Jordie Sutter was the Vancouver detective overseeing Andrea's case. I'm hoping he will be a good contact once we do our own little investigation."

"I'm half afraid, half excited by us going undercover," Allyson replied, flipping the visor down and glancing at her reflection in the mirror.

"Undercover is a stretch. More like role-playing, similar to today at the hotel when you introduced yourself as my producer. I'd think you'd have more experience with this, though."

"Why? Seeing as I'm an identical twin? Seriously?!" she snapped. "By the way, was I supposed to get a wig and makeup for this farce? Because news flash. Ha! I didn't."

"Nope. I asked our makeup person to help me out with that. I have a little kit in the trunk they put together for us. Nice pun, by the way," Ram beamed. "Now, less talking, more feeding, woman. I'm starving."

16

ONE MISSED CALL

{ANDREA}

An arctic wind gust sucked the air from Andrea's lungs as she opened the heavy steel door leading outside. The startling blast had her questioning her hasty retreat. As she spun back around to face her pursuer, the door slammed shut in her face. She grabbed at the handle, only there wasn't one. She was locked out, dressed only in the shabby hospital gown and no shoes. Sharp, needling pain rocked the bottoms of her feet as she ventured onto the frozen concrete. The amount of snow and ice on the ground made it nearly impossible to know where to step, and the drifts stirring in the air filled in her footprints as soon as they were formed.

"It's a goddamn blizzard!" she exclaimed, rubbing her arms to ease the cold. The nighttime dimness and the lack of security lights added complexity to her situation. Someone was bent on tormenting her, it was dark and freezing cold, and she was utterly unprepared. Her next moves were crucial.

Andrea was between a group of large buildings that encompassed the film studio's campus. Dredging into knee-deep snow, she scrambled to different doors, trying each one. Her attempts were in vain, though. Most entrances required keycard access, while others needed a physical key or lacked an external lever at all, like the one she just exited. She kept moving to stay warm and away from her stalker while staying vigilant about any unexpected sounds. More importantly, though, she moved to maintain hope. She'd come this far since waking in the storage room all bound up, enduring all the strange obstacles and circumstances. It seemed silly to give up now. However, her optimism was fading as quickly as the feeling in her extremities.

"Who the fuck was chasing me? It wasn't Allyson. She didn't know my little . . . *catchphrase*. And honestly, she's too clumsy." She shook her head to clear the accumulating snow. "No, this person was not a mirror image, but a replica—like every other fucking thing in this place. Nothing here is real!" she shouted into the falling snow. Taking off in another direction, she continued to seek shelter.

Her body shivered violently. She would succumb to hypothermia if she didn't find help or safety soon. Andrea walked in wide circles, disoriented by the blowing snow and low visibility. She yanked at anything resembling a door and even retried ones she'd already visited. Disillusioned, she dropped into a snowbank, closed her eyes, and murmured a plea to any supernatural entity who might be listening. "Please send help. I'd promise to be good, but you know that'd be a lie. I don't want to die like this!"

Her respirations slowed, and her muscles relaxed. The unseasonably cold air combined with the heavy, wet snow was akin to a warm blanket rather than the stinging, prickling sensation she'd been trying to ignore since fleeing outside. Fragmented images flashed through her mind as if she was already dreaming. Their purpose was unclear as nameless faces and random scenery molded and dissolved like clouds in the sky. Then Roger appeared, larger than life. "*If you fall asleep, you'll die. Don't give up, you coward.*"

She peeled open her eyes. "I am not a coward," she spat and staggered to her feet.

Moving away from the buildings, she proceeded toward the main road. It was her only hope. The employee and delivery truck parking lot was on the opposite side from her current position. It led to a gated exit. Perhaps a security guard was on duty. If not, a few trucks were always parked nearby, available for various supply runs. She might get lucky and *borrow* one.

Her joints creaked, and her skin crackled like a rusted tinman as she shuffled her way through the snow again. Andrea tripped multiple times, falling once face-first into a drift. The cold, wet snow didn't even melt as she lay there wheezing. A sour taste developed in the back of her mouth, and as she tried to swallow it down, a painful lump in her throat blocked what little moisture she could muster.

Roger's taunt rang in her ears, pushing her to keep moving. As she trudged along, she caught the sky shifting to pale pink as the sun peeked over the horizon. The sight lifted her spirits, and shortly after, she arrived at the lot where one lone truck stood buried. Trying the handle, she found it locked.

"For fuck's sake!" she shouted.

Slipping and stomping to the passenger side, she found it locked too. Leaning against the truck, Andrea hung her head, shaking it in disbelief and holding back a sob. "Don't you dare cry!"

Rather than succumbing to despair, she sniffled and wiped frozen snot from under her nose, then scanned the area for anything she could use to bust the window open. Everything was blanketed in snow. In an endless field of white, the sole thing visible was security light poles installed every thirty feet. The only tool at her disposal? Herself. Mustering all her anger and desperation, she threw her elbow into the glass.

"Fuck!" The window didn't budge, and pain zipped up her arm. She bent over at the waist and held it against her until the throbbing subsided.

She tried again. "Owww! Motherfucker!" The window still didn't budge. Pain tore through her entire arm this time. It took several minutes before she could muster the courage and strength to try a third time.

"Ahhh! Yes!" The glass finally gave way. Her exhilaration was short-lived, though, when she realized there was a deep slice along her triceps. "Oh, shit. Like I need another complication!"

Stretching her arm inside, avoiding any further mishaps with the leftover shards, she hit the unlock button and ran to the driver's side to get in. Ignoring the ache from her slow, oozing wound, she bumbled inside the cab and snuggled into the cold vinyl seat as if it were a plush mattress. She took a moment and sat still, closing her eyes and releasing the frenzied emotions she used to get this far. Pine scent filled her senses. "Must be an air freshener," she grinned, relaxing into the moment and temporary safety. A slight breeze blew into the cab from the broken window, stirring the pine smell and tickling her nose while snowflakes landed softly on her face. The sensations triggered yet another memory.

Andrea stared at the black flip-phone in her hand as if she could make it ring by pure willpower. It was bound to, sooner or later. As a phone, its whole purpose was to ring! At least the kind one bought at the convenience store and loaded with minutes.

"The minutes!" she cried out. "Are there enough?" She flipped it open and scrolled through the options. "Yes. Yes. Plenty."

Next, she ensured the ringer's volume was audible, and she had service. It only displayed two bars. That was more than she could hope for in the rural area where she resided. Andrea snapped it shut and dropped it on the countertop, only to lift it immediately to ensure her carelessness didn't damage it. She was wound tighter than a guitar string.

"I need to relax. I gotta take something!" she said, patting her pockets. When she found them empty, she tried the drawers and cabinets. When those didn't deliver results, she ran to the bedroom and into the bathroom, rummaging through all the places she would stash her feel-good supplies.

"Fuck! Nothing," she groaned, pinching the bridge of her nose. Placing her other hand on her hip, she let out a long sigh and looked to the ceiling in a silent prayer. She promised herself self-medicating was no longer healthy. Drugs were crutches, masking her problems. And benders always ended in fuzzy memories, late appointments, and missed important phone calls.

Heading back to the main room, where the windows opened to a broad view of the property, Andrea stopped to appreciate the snowflakes floating lazily toward the ground. Only a few at first, then more and more. They were hypnotizing. Their gentle beauty brought back childhood memories. Innocence. Pure. Unique, unlike her and her sister, who were nature's clones of one another.

"No!" she snapped, turning away and gathering her sketchpad. She flipped through its pages, determined she could distract herself with work.

A loud gurgle sprang from her stomach, followed by an uncomfortable twisting feeling. The only thing she'd been consuming was wine and potato chips. Glancing around the kitchen, she counted the empty bottles, the stained stemware, and the crumpled bags lying around the trashcan, which was overflowing and stinking. Dried wine in a deep red color lined each dirty glass. It reminded her of blood, and she licked her lips. Another hungry growl snapped her away from those dangerous thoughts.

Rummaging through the fridge, Andrea discovered bacon, a fresh loaf of bread, and some vegetables free from rot and mold. "When did I last do a grocery run?" Scratching her head, she grabbed the contents and set them along the counter one at a time, then returned her gaze out the window. The yard was covered in at least a foot of snow, and there was no sign of footprints. When would she have been able to go anywhere?

"When did I get here, and how long have I been waiting for you to ring?" she asked the phone sitting nearby. She furrowed her brows and nibbled her bottom lip.

Selecting a serrated knife, she focused on slicing a tomato, pausing to study its red juice seeping onto the white marble counter. She appreciated the rivulets trickling along in a path of least resistance. The sharp knife's edge glinted in the light as she slid it through the thin tomato skin to observe the phenomenon again.

"Stop it!" She pressed her lips together in a slight frown and tried concentrating on assembling the meal. As a further distraction, she hummed a little tune, swaying her hips as she listened to the bacon sizzling in the pan. She grinned, imagining each sandwich component having its own particular melody. She didn't smile often, which had her bursting with a sudden giddiness.

"I'm ... happy?" She tilted her head and gave a short laugh. "Yes! I'm happpyyyyy!" she shouted as she pirouetted in her sock feet, then danced, plate in hand, to the small breakfast table overlooking the west side of the house. Tucking a leg under her, she sat and scooped up her sandwich.

Bang. Bang. Bang.

Her mouth hung open in mid-bite.

"What the hell was that?"

Holding still, she waited to hear it again. A peek outside showed the snow blowing wildly and the large evergreen limbs swaying. Attributing it to the wind, she resumed taking her first bite when it happened again.

Bang. Bang. Bang.

Groaning, she placed her sandwich back on the plate and shuffled to the window. She cataloged everything in the side yard. A freestanding lean-to sat perpendicular to the back edge of the house, where all her firewood was neatly stored. She admired the circular pile and recalled the lively debate with the delivery driver on the best way to pile it for seasoning. Further to the left was the caretaker's shed near the lakefront. From her vantage point, only two canoes were visible. They were stacked in a rack atop one another, leaning against its side and covered with a tarp. Its corner flapped in the breeze, yet it was too light to make a banging noise. Between the canoes and the wood pile stood a tree stump and an axe she used to split logs as needed. She reviewed each item on her mental list and recoiled in shock when the shed door flapped open with another wind gust. *Bang. Bang. Bang.*

"How the hell did that happen?" Clenching her teeth, she headed towards the front door. Wrenching it open, she stepped onto the snow-laden porch but recoiled from the cold and wet snow. Pulling on her boots and parka, she ran outside.

Slogging through the snow, Andrea approached the shed with caution. She halted, stiffening her stance in a defensive pose, when she spotted footprints leading to and from its entrance towards the lakefront. The best part of the property was the water surrounding the little island. It was deep enough that it rarely froze solid. It was a natural moat to keep trespassers at bay.

"Who the hell would come all the way out here in this weather?" she muttered, glancing from left to right. Her hands balled into fists, and her muscles tensed as she stared at the stump where her axe should be.

Bang. Bang. Bang. Smack. Smack. Smack.

The shed door rattled against the structure, reminding her why she was there. However, this second sound was new, and it came from the house.

Closing the remaining distance to the shed, she glanced inside. When all appeared in order, she grabbed the door and slammed it shut, setting the complicated locking mechanism back into its secured state.

"Did I come out here earlier and forget?" She rubbed her temple. Squatting to examine the footprints, she saw they matched her boots perfectly. Also, she was the only one who could open the lock. Standing, she placed her hand on the back of her neck and rotated in a circle, searching for anything askew. The sun was setting, and the increasing winds and blowing snow hampered her visibility. Sweeping her long hair from her face, she dismissed her possible forgetfulness, rechecked the shed door, and returned to the house.

"Ugh," she moaned, realizing she'd left the door open. The inside temperature was no different than the outside. "And now I have to restart the fire." She glared at the fireplace's dying embers. Cursing, she kicked off her boots and dropped her jacket by the drying mat. As she stepped further inside, her socks became soaked. "Fuck. Great!" she fumed. Snow had blown in and melted into cold puddles on the rare hardwood floors. "If I don't mop this wetness, it could warp the boards." Rushing towards the kitchen, she peeled off her socks on her way to grab tea towels to clean the mess.

"Hiya, Doll Face."

She gulped in shock and whirled around.

A man stood in the shadows by the table, her missing axe resting against one shoulder and her half-eaten sandwich inches from his mouth.

Andrea gaped in morbid curiosity as he chewed. His long black hair was covered in thick, coagulated blood and tangled as if he'd awakened from a restless night's sleep. He was graying at the temples, and hideous scars covered his face. He had high cheekbones, a squared chin, and distinct almond-shaped eyes with irises dark as midnight. As he stood across from her in a tank top and thin athletic pants, she considered how his clothes were out of season. His bare arms showcased tribal tattoos that ran from his neck to his wrists. Dark red splatter trailed from his matted hair to his running shoes, the same way the tomato juice did earlier.

"Who?" She didn't recognize her voice as she choked on the question.

"Does it matter? One in a long line, I assume. Thanks for the sandwich. I was famished." He grinned, revealing red swollen pits where his teeth should have been.

"You aren't real. You're my imagination," Andrea stammered.

The man leaned forward. "Could be. Or perhaps I'm your guilty conscience. Either way, you're about to find out," he teased, setting the sandwich down.

While he sucked his fingers, Andrea surveyed the area without moving her body. The cast-iron frying pan was cooling on the stove. She studied the man facing her. He was muscular for his average height, yet the pan would leave a mark if she could hit him where he was already wounded, and the heat would add a nice touch.

"I see your mind working out the probabilities with each escape route. I'm thrilled I have this effect on you with our roles reversed."

Andrea's stomach fluttered as he leered at her while making a suggestive motion with his hand. An open wound pulsated around his wrist like music at a discotheque. Her lip curled. "I watched you die."

"So now you remember me. You studied me as my very soul left my body. You wept. It hurt you to hurt me. Your pain touched me. You were probably the only one who shed a tear over my death. Even though you *were* the one responsible."

"It was . . ."

"Important work. I know. It was your mantra as you scribbled in your book every night."

"How is this possible?" Andrea questioned, running her fingers through her hair as if moving to put it in a high ponytail. "You're . . . you're," her mind struggled to find the right words. "Dead and gone!" She waved her fingers oddly as if suggesting he floated away somehow.

His features shifted from amusement to determined executioner as he positioned the axe, readying to strike. While he was distracted with his repositioning, she grabbed the panhandle from the stove. Swinging out wildly, she channeled all her fear and anger into one shot, mimicking a discus thrower or a major league batter.

A sickening thud rang out, and the man howled in pain. Following her arm's momentum, she charged towards the door, pausing long enough to kick him while he lay on his side. It wasn't as hard as she'd liked without her boots on, but hard enough to dislodge the axe from his hand. She grabbed it and sprinted out the door, across the bridge, and to the car.

It was locked! She bellowed in frustration because she lived in the middle of the goddamn woods, where getting her car jacked was improbable. "You're a fucking idiot," she growled. Looking back at the opened front door, a shiver ran down her spine. There were two choices: go back and finish what she started or run. Unsure if what she experienced was real or imagined, she rushed up the drive to the remote two-lane highway where the chances of a car passing were as good as the car being stolen or the shed being broken into.

She slipped and slid in her bare feet as they grew numb from the cold, wet snow. When she reached the road, she hesitated and looked behind her. The path to the house was clear and showed no evidence the man was in pursuit.

"Shit. Fuck!" Andrea yelled into the darkening evening sky as she stopped to rest. "The phone!"

Bending over, she took deep swallows of cold winter air and placed the axe across her thighs. Pine scent lingered in the wind. It invigorated her mind. She straightened and hefted the heavy handle, weighing and twisting it while calculating the options in her head if she were to return to the house. Adrenaline and sheer determination propelled Andrea forward as she squared her shoulders and tromped back to the house, hyper-aware of her surroundings and the slightest noises. As she crested the modest hilltop leading toward the footbridge, she was struck by her home's beauty. It was something out of a Thomas Kinkaid painting, including the requisite smoke billowing from the chimney.

"Wait. I never restarted the fire!"

Rushing back across the bridge, she headed toward the house, stopping to listen for any indication the man was nearby. Creeping onto the porch, she waivered at the door. Only the wind slipping through the trees responded to her silent inquiry. Skeptical of what she might find, she tiptoed inside. Her eyes landed on the fireplace first. A blaze of red warmth smiled at her. At the table, her sandwich sat untouched. The floor was covered in tea towels instead of a dead body, and the cast iron pan sat on the stove, bacon grease congealing in the bottom. Not a soul was in sight.

"What the?"

Tightening her grip on the axe handle, she gasped when her hands became fists. It was gone!

Rushing to the window, she peered out towards the back. There it sat, its head embedded in the stump, handle arched upwards, awaiting someone's firm grip. Andrea twirled, evaluating the room from every angle. Everything was in its place. No vile man threatening her, eating her meal. Rubbing her head, she whispered, "He was imaginary. It was a hallucination. You're losing your shit. Jesus! Get it together!" She padded towards the door and took one last look outside before closing and locking it despite the improbability of visitors.

Turning back to the large room, she gnawed her top lip. "What a fucking mess!" She threw her hands in the air and walked to the kitchen, where she spotted the cellphone on the counter. "Shit. Shit!" she ran to it, picked it up.

One missed call.

"Holy fucking shit!" Andrea gasped, waking from her dream-like memory. "I remember how I got here. Only here isn't really *here*. Help me!" she hollered. "Help! Make it stop! This isn't real! This is all a delusion!" As she screamed, something in her chest gave way. A heavy pressure, as if someone stood on her left breast, took her breath away. It quickly spread to her shoulder and into her left arm. She gasped and tried to move, but her body was paralyzed. Spots obscured her vision as she fought to remain conscious. "Help. Me!" she whispered. The words barely left her lips when everything faded to nothing.

17

FRESH PERSPECTIVE

{RAM}

Three hours after they set out on their journey, Allyson and Ram arrived in Vancouver. To play it safe, they parked their car outside Constable Sutter's precinct and proceeded to find a place where Allyson could transform into her sister. Instead of waiting until daylight, Allyson told Ram Andrea was more likely to show up at an ungodly hour and demand access to her place.

"For Chrissake, Mike, I lost my keys. Why is everything a fucking project with you?" she yelled at the doorman, who thankfully wore a name tag. The poor man shook as he retrieved the master key from its secure location. "Have you seen Roger?" she asked as they followed Mike to the elevators.

"No, ma'am. I don't believe he could get back into Canada considering all the trouble he's in."

"He's the Caretaker. He can go wherever the fuck he wants. Although, the border is no joke these days," Allyson quipped. Ram struggled to keep a straight face as they rode to the twelfth floor. Gone were the days of a simple border crossing between the two countries. It took them thirty minutes and a security sweep with German shepherds before they were allowed across.

Mike let them in without question yet remained outside as they walked in.

"Tip!" Allyson mouthed to Ram, who hurriedly slapped a fist full of bills in the man's out-turned hand.

When Ram returned, Allyson was standing in a long, dark hallway lined with shelves containing boxes, books, and jars of cloudy liquid. "Andrea's curiosities lean towards the morbid, thus her career choices," Allyson answered Ram's unspoken question. "I'm impressed with her newfound organizational skills. These boxes are actually labeled! I wonder if the contents actually match the description. Also, I wouldn't look too closely at those jars," she curled her lip.

"Thanks for the warning. Here," Ram handed Allyson a burner phone. "I popped over to the convenience store while you were morphing into your *evil twin*. I often leave my smartphone behind during an investigation where I don't know who or what I'm facing. Since we have little to go on with Andrea's disappearance, the safe thing to do is to avoid being traceable with all the apps on our normal phones. I programmed yours with my burner number too, so we can get in touch if we get separated."

"Thanks, Ram. I've been feeling quite vulnerable with everything going on. This eases my mind a bit," Allyson smiled warmly. "Now that you've endeared me even more to you, shall we see how my other half lives?" She waved her hand forward.

The hallway led into a small, open floor plan. The kitchen was on the left, and an entertainment wall was on the right, while straight in front was a wall of glass doors overlooking Vancouver Harbor. The narrow balcony was decorated in So-Cal style, with a rattan rocker and a fake potted palm tree adorned with twinkle lights. A small hallway, past the wall holding the flatscreen TV and accompanying equipment, led to two bedrooms split by a small guest bath. The interior bedroom was obviously Andrea's with its lack of windows, while the outer one was arranged as a home office. Two acacia wood tables nearly the room's length flanked its sides. They were the width of a standard dining table and left little walking space in between. Various art projects related to her job at H0rr Studios covered their tops.

"I'll go search her bedroom," Allyson said.

Ram nodded. "I'll look through things in here." A series of sketches halfway hidden by a large foam board of fabrics and paint swatches drew his attention. He waited until Allyson left the room before wrenching them free. The pages were on heavy cardstock, larger than legal-sized paper, and divided into quadrants. Each section felt zoomed-in, focusing on a piece of anatomy and its corresponding body art, as well as detailed diagrams of scars and injuries. To the untrained eye, the images were simply an artist's rendition of an autopsy of a male cadaver or a special effects artist's imagination. However, Ram recognized the tattoo immediately. It was Billy Walls's, the missing Nisqually tribe member whose feet were discovered recently. His foot was identified through a catalog of tattoos stored in a shared database created and maintained by hospitals and other agencies to help put a name to the unidentifiable.

Perspiration broke out along his forehead, and a pulse throbbed at his temples. Without his smartphone, he was unable to take pictures, and he didn't want to leave them behind. Thus before Allyson could reappear, he carefully rolled the pages and stuck them in the back waistband of his pants where his jacket would cover them. Then he continued rifling through the papers and drawings strewn across the table. His curiosity was piqued as to what else was hidden in plain sight.

"Anything good in here?" Allyson asked, popping her head around the corner.

"I don't know if I'd call it good. But I'm captivated by Andrea's dark imagination," Ram lied.

"Oh no. Are you a closet Giver?" she smirked. "Anyway, I found her keys, wallet, and phone. The phone was dead, but I plugged it in to charge. We could crash here for a few hours and save money on a hotel?"

"Sleep does sound fantastic, but my expenses are paid for. I could leave you here and grab a room nearby if you'd prefer.

"Nonsense. We should stick together."

"All right. By the way, I meant to congratulate you on channeling your sister. Is she really that crass?"

"You cannot imagine. So what do you think?"

Ram's eyes widened, and he rocked on his feet while taking in the room. "Andrea's talent is . . . compelling, but nothing pointing to her whereabouts."

"I meant about catching some Z's first."

"Oh! Yeah. Yeah. I'm good. I can take the couch if you want to take her room."

"Cool. I'm going to raid the kitchen to see if anything edible is left. All this covert stuff has made me hungry, and I need to take my meds with food."

Allyson turned, pulling her wig off as she padded towards the galley kitchen. He turned back to the tables, his investigator instincts pulling at him.

"Oh, gross!" Allyson groaned from the kitchen. Ram assumed she found some expired milk or moldy cheese and ignored her outburst.

Flipping through large sketch pads, he discovered more drawings similar to Billy Walls's, except they didn't contain tattoos. These were bodies in various states of trauma. A few were even decomposing. Ram's stomach twisted.

"Eggs don't go bad, right?" Allyson called.

"Crack them open. If you smell sulfur, they're bad," Ram answered absently.

He sorted all the drawings by theme and pattern, then tucked them inside a large artist's portfolio case he found leaning against the wall behind the table. He could alert Irv later if their investigation pointed to criminal activity. In the meantime, he'd hang onto the Billy Walls drawings. However, he needed to find a better hiding spot than his pants.

Hastily, he slipped off his jacket and stuffed the papers into a sleeve, then draped it over his arm. "Did you manage to scrounge enough to make us breakfast?" he asked as he returned to the great room. Ram carefully laid the coat across the sofa arm before joining Allyson in the kitchen.

"Mimosas and eggs with cream cheese over melba toast. It's about all I could rustle up. She has more alcohol than real food. A real bachelorette!" she forced a smile while tears welled in her eyes.

"What's wrong?" Ram asked, placing his hands on either of her arms.

"I got a twinge in my chest while scrambling the eggs, and I couldn't help thinking it was Andrea's pain I was feeling. I sound foolish when I say it aloud, especially after all the anti-twin talk I spew, yet what if it *is* Andrea, and something's wrong with her? What if she's in danger, and here I am playing house in her apartment?!"

"I thought you didn't believe in magical twin powers?"

"A couple of times in past treatments, I swore I had moments like . . . remote viewing. I was seeing and feeling things that were outside my current reality. My experiences were always written off as delusions or dissociative episodes. One time, I was found in the hospital basement and completely clueless about how I got there. The staff were just as confused, considering the security measures in place. My therapist dismissed everyone's version of events, outright accused me of lying, then changed my meds. I was always curious if they were Andrea's experiences I was somehow channeling, but as you said, I detest anything to do with supernatural twinning stuff. Thus I relied on the professionals' opinions. With Andrea missing, though, and being here, in proximity to her belongings, I can't help wondering."

"Should we get you checked out?"

"No, I feel fine. I can't accurately put it into words, yet I can confidently say the pain is not mine. It doesn't make sense, and you probably think I'm crazy."

"I don't. However, say something if it gets worse. There is literally a hospital right across the street."

"I saw that when we walked up. Has anyone bothered to verify whether Andrea is there?!"

Ram blanched a little. "Shit! Good question. Do you want me to run over there and pull my credentials? I might get lucky and charm a middle-aged, unhappily married nurse into looking into it! Use my fan club clout, like Roger. "

Allyson chuckled. "It works for him! Before you go, though, let's eat. You should investigate on a full stomach. I want to sink into her soft, cozy bed and take a long winter's nap with mine. Unless you need me to tag along."

"No. No. I do this kind of stuff for a living. You rest. If I find anything, I will come right back and wake you. By the way, I don't suppose you've found Andrea's keycard to get me back in the building? I'll go broke if I have to bribe the doorman again."

"Oh, yeah! It was with her other items in a basket on the end table. Let me get it."

"Do you mind if I check if her car is still in the parking garage while I'm out?"

"No. Help yourself. But promise me you'll sleep soon. I don't love to drive. It triggers my anxiety. I also don't love to ride with people who haven't slept in twenty-four hours."

"Promise." He made a cross sign over his heart and beamed at her.

While Allyson went to grab the keys and access card, Ram hurried to re-hide the drawings and replace his coat. He planned to conceal them in his car by the police station. If Allyson slept soundly, he would poke around more upon his return.

After stopping for some caffeine fuel, Ram went to his car and stored the drawings inside his overnight bag. He hesitated outside, where Constable Sutter was probably sitting at his desk, debating whether to pay him a visit. However, he was still piecing together a narrative about Andrea, Roger, and the rest. So he went to the hospital instead. Ram's curiosity made him anxious to return to the apartment and sift through more of Andrea's *treasures*. She was an enigma who challenged his investigator persona, while his empathetic human side was terrified at what he'd already uncovered. He needed to tread carefully before bringing his discoveries to the authorities.

The hospital was a dead end, as was the car, aside from a strong odor in the trunk. It was a sickly sweet aroma mixed with garlic and rotting soil seeping from a dark stain that didn't leave any residue by touch. He concluded Andrea, or someone hired by her, had previously attempted to clean it.

"Hopefully it's only a food spill," he muttered. "Note to self to add this to the potential evidence list should my hunch prove valid."

Back upstairs to the twelfth floor, he crept into the apartment as silently as possible and hung in the hallway to attack the boxes stacked there. Using a small penlight to aid his search, he sifted through the collection. If Andrea left drawings of Billy Walls in the open, what else was there to uncover?

"Any luck at the hospital?"

Ram jumped back a foot and dropped a box he'd just pulled from the shelf, spilling its contents onto the floor.

"Jesus!" he shouted.

"Sorry! I said hello when I walked up. I guess you were too deep in investigator mode to hear me."

"Yeah, sorry. I hope you don't mind." He groaned as he bent to put items back in the box. "I drank a shit ton of coffee and was too jittery to sleep. I figured I'd thumb through these boxes instead."

"It's okay. I asked you to help me find my sister. By all means, snoop away." Allyson scooped up an errant photo. "Oh my God. I forgot about this place!"

"It's a real place? It looks AI-generated."

"Oh, it's real alright. It's Andrea's little artist's escape hidden in the mountains northeast of here. The legendary cabin in the woods everyone wishes they had. It's where she goes to reconnect with her creative self."

"That billowing chimney smoke, tall evergreen trees, and rustic bridge . . . It's like something from a vacation rental site or an old-timey postcard."

"She took me there once. My first art exhibit with Vince was here in Vancouver. She surprised the hell out of me by showing up. Then practically kidnapped me and took me to this place. She was in such a mood that I was scared she would kill me and dump me in the lake. Yet it turned into a lovely day, and I found myself jealous of her little slice of heaven. Hey! We should go there!" Allyson's eyes widened, and her cheeks turned red. "What if she's hiding or needed a timeout from life? What if she's hurt and wasting away all alone, hoping someone might eventually find her? Maybe she's fallen, and she can't get up. It happens all the time!"

"With the elderly, yeah. Still, you're right. Accidents do occur, and this is a blind spot no one knows to investigate. Do you know how to get there?"

"No. She drove. I remember it's less than a two-hour drive northeast of the city limits, depending on the road conditions. It snows there due to the higher elevation, and you take this road through a narrow mountain pass, where sections are unpaved."

"You're not selling this, Allyson. My car isn't built for offroading."

"I'm making it sound worse than it is, I'm sure. The address might be in her car's GPS history. Maybe we can take hers instead."

"Umm. I don't think her car is much better. Which reminds me, if all of her essentials are here, how would she get there?"

Allyson tapped her chin. "Maybe she went with someone?"

"And she doesn't want to be found."

"Or they left her there! My gut says we have to go."

"Okay. Okay. But first, I need to freshen up. I've been wearing these clothes for close to twenty-four hours. " Ram sniffed his armpit and winced.

"Eww."

"That's what I'm saying!" he snickered.

Allyson gave him a playful shove, then looked at her smartwatch. "It's still early. Go shower, and let's crash in her room. I won't bite. Unless you want me to!"

18

THE MOUNTAINS ARE CALLING

{ALLYSON}

"**A**re you propositioning me?" Ram leered.

The room chilled with awkwardness. Allyson cringed inwardly and became fascinated with a stain on the white marble floor. She had just offered no-strings-attached sex, and Ram was visibly waffling. "Umm, yeah. Obviously. And somehow, I'm failing miserably." She could feel her ears burning red-hot as she crossed her arms over her chest in a self-hug. If only she still wore the wig, she could hide behind the curtain of long hair.

Ram grinned and placed his arms on her shoulders, pulling her into an embrace. He kissed her forehead, then tucked her head under his chin. "You aren't failing. We are too much alike, you and me. I completely understood why Grace was drawn to you the minute I spotted you across the green at the Needle the other day. You have this magnetism that pulls people towards you. However, you hit this barrier, like you're saying,

'Mmm. Just kidding.' I, too, attract only to repel. I know why I do it. Is your story similar?"

Allyson pushed away. "You've immersed yourself in my world over the last two days. You tell me."

Ram scratched his head. "'Immerse' is a strong word. I've gotten to *know* you through the parts you've wanted to share. And Grace gave me a Spark Notes version before we met. That's it. Being the kind of reporter I am, though, I *can* make assumptions based on what you've left unsaid. That's enough to understand we are kindred souls. Sleeping together will only complicate things."

"I just want to feel good, Ram. I'm not looking for a goddamn ring. Let's bond a little deeper, you know?" she teased. "I'm a straight shooter. I've hooked up with men, women, and all the ones in between. Feeling good keeps the demons in check. We're on this mission to figure out what happened to my sister, which makes me feel close to you. Sex is the next natural step. But I won't beg. If you don't want a piece of this," Allyson waved her hand over her curvy frame. "Your loss." She turned her back to him and straightened the boxes. Cleaning also kept the demons in check. *Everything in its place.*

"Listen. I'm a guy. Guys enjoy sex. Right now, though, I don't want my feelings to get in the way. I'll go and hit the shower. Afterward, I'm open to a nice cuddle while we catch a nap . . . And I sound like a cheeseball," he swiped his hand over his face, then turned on his heels toward the bedroom.

"I think a more appropriate word is 'pussy,' but cheeseball works too," Allyson called over her shoulder. She continued tidying up before crawling into bed and passing out. Ram joined her as she slid into dreamland. His strong arms wrapped around her and pulled her into the curve of his body. She slept for a sound four hours, the longest uninterrupted stretch she'd experienced in months.

"Holy shit, it's after one. We should get up," Allyson yawned, stretching away her sleepiness.

"You're right," Ram groaned groggily. "If we're headed into the mountains, we could run into interesting road conditions depending on where this place is."

"I'll look through her phone for an address while you get . . ." Allyson took in Ram's muscular physique as he stood and lost her words. He had a runner's lean frame and a bodybuilder's chest with pec muscles worth sinking back into. How did she *sleep* in those arms? He wasn't one of those guys who went crazy manscaping, either, with a nice hairy chest and a happy trail pointing to . . .

"Are you eye-fucking me? Allyson!" Ram scolded. The smile on his face told a different story. He made her laugh even harder when he tried to cover himself with his hands in fake modesty.

"I'm evaluating and appraising. That's all. But yes, finding directions needs to happen right now!" She grabbed Andrea's phone charging on the nightstand and unlocked it with Face ID. "I guess being identical does come in handy sometimes!"

She immediately found herself absorbed in the phone's photo library. Andrea was in various settings with different guys *and gals* in intimate poses but also snippets of her studio life and daily happenings. Yet nothing revealed a clue as to her whereabouts. Moving to her emails, Allyson grumbled, "She has thousands of unread messages. It will take forever to go through them all. Although, at a glance, they appear mostly business-related." The address book revealed nothing, either. "If I were my sister, how would I file away my hideout address in contacts?"

"You've searched all the obvious ones, I assume?"

"Yes, darling. I'm not a dingbat."

Ram tsskd. "How about a work address? Is the studio listed? She could've filed it in the notes section."

"Yep, looked there, too. Hey, should we stop by there first? I know you wanted to go there," Allyson pointed out.

"The urgency lies with her home away from home. The campus was relisted for rent by their landlord as soon as they announced their move to Iceland. It's probably empty and harder to get into without bending the law."

"I bet there's a keycard around here somewhere. Physical security is always last on the list," Allyson smirked. She jumped off the bed and snatched Andrea's handbag from a corner chair.

"Ah-hah! Bingo!" she waved a laminated photo badge in her hand. "I'll stick it in with my stuff so we can stop there on our way back from the cabin. Unless we hit paydirt first!"

"Great. Let's head out."

Allyson took the time to make Andrea's bed and wiped down the bathroom from their use before tucking the towels in a laundry basket. Glancing around the place, she sensed she'd return soon.

"Wow. What's that smell?" Allyson wrinkled her nose as the heater from Andrea's car blew in her face.

"I found an ominous stain in the trunk. I guess it's from that?"

"Why is it coming through the vents?" Allyson gagged and rolled down the passenger window as Ram maneuvered the car out of the parking garage. "It's been sitting inside a concrete tomb. The probability an animal crawled in somewhere under the hood and died is nil. Did you happen to check the gauges or the oil?"

"Why would I? It's an electric car! No moving parts."

"I'll never get used to that. Although I did expect flying cars by now. Thank you, Jetsons."

As they made their way out of the city, Allyson searched through the car's travel history. "Here we go. This looks right. It's on the water. Actually, her house sits on a small island with a footbridge attaching the property to the mainland."

"Sounds incredible. When were you there?"

"Hmm," Allyson tapped her chin. "Five years ago, during my exhibit, *Pretense*. Andrea, Roger, and Craig came on opening night, along with a few others from the studio staff. Two days later, she brought me to the cabin."

"Why?"

"She wanted some alone time with me, which was *very* out of character. She was hovering outside my hotel one afternoon. When my agent Vince and I left to grab lunch, she pounced on us. Vince, naturally, was enamored with her, having met her at the exhibit. Plus, seeing us together can be jarring. After a few minutes of chitchat, he went on his way. I remember Andrea shouting a promise to have me back in one piece. The way she said it gave me chills."

"And you presumed she wanted to kill you? You said that so casually earlier."

"I already told you about the near-drowning incident. There were others, too. I'm convinced I was born distressed because she tried to off me in the womb. Do you know there is actually a phenomenon called Vanishing Twin Syndrome? It's where one gets 'absorbed' into the other. It's a nice way of saying the surviving fetus is a cannibal and committed siblicide!"

"Disturbing. AND ironic now that she's the one who has vanished." Ram quipped. "I hope the cannibal piece isn't a part of her disappearance, though."

Allyson shivered. "You had to go there!"

"You brought it up!"

"Ugh. Anyway, she was in such a strange mood—quiet one minute, keyed up the next. I figured she was on something. It put me on edge. However, it was a great day, and she offered to let me use the place whenever I needed it. It was as if she was saying, 'When I die, this is yours.' I brushed it off, though, and forgot all about it. I've struggled since then emotionally, and I was preoccupied with my own shit."

"Do you think she was planning on dying soon? Was she ill, or would she—commit suicide?"

"Suicide? No way. She is too in love with herself. However, I could see her deciding Iceland was impractical. She made serious bank and could afford to disappear if she really wanted to. Hell, she could go back to Argentina and blend in with the locals. No one would ask any questions."

"Why would she leave without telling anyone, though?"

"That's what she does. It never occurs to her how anyone else would think or feel."

"Would she contact your father first?"

"I highly doubt it. They weren't close. I'm the favorite since I was the perfect child . . . neither seen nor heard." She circled her finger over her head to imply she wore a halo. "I earned his heart right from the start because I was the more fragile twin. He has almost lost me more than a few times."

"Must be nice," Ram chided.

"Uh-Oh. Did I hit a sore spot? Not the favorite child?"

"Nope."

"Nope, as in the sore spot or the favorite?"

"I'm the middle child. My brother is a war hero, and my sister was born with Down Syndrome. Then there's me."

"Lead Investigative Reporter, Ram Helm! That's something to be proud of!"

"Well, think about it in Andrea's terms. She's successful in her own right, yet your father still picks you."

"Yeah, I guess. However, there's history there. I don't want to justify his tendencies towards me. You'd have to know the whole story before passing judgment on him."

"So tell me. We've got nothing but time! What's the deal with your mother? She died when you guys were teenagers, right?"

"Nice work, detective," Allyson chuckled. "Yeah, she was unstable herself. Ironic since she made such a big deal about my mental health. The month before she died, she OD'd, then claimed it was an accident when they pumped her stomach at the ER. She supposedly confused her medications. Even if she did, you can't mix up knocking back a fist full of pills and chasing it with champagne. So when they found her car floating upside down in the ocean off Devil's Slide, in San Mateo County, Patricia still buckled in the driver's seat, they deemed it a suicide, end of story."

"Holy shit. That's unbelievable. She drove six hours to kill herself?"

"No, actually, my parents drove up the coast together. Pa had a meeting in San Francisco, and Patricia wanted to go to Wine Country. They could've flown, but Pa said they wanted uninterrupted time alone. While he was at his meeting, Patricia . . . did what she did. It didn't add up. That's why I don't have a high opinion of the police. They picked the easy answer. They didn't even do an autopsy. Open and shut. 'Rich housewife with history of mental illness offs herself in Thelma and Louise style off the coast of Highway 1,' was practically the headline."

"What was your father's reaction?"

"Obviously, Pa was devastated. He instantly became the sole parent to two teenage girls, who were always a handful. We had household help, of course, but you get my meaning. In all honesty? I think he was a bit relieved. Patricia wasn't easy. They were an unhappy couple. I never witnessed any affection between them. Then again, it could be cultural. It was evident he and Andrea were never the same. She said it should've been him, and he accused her of driving Patricia to such an act."

"Your father blamed Andrea for your mother's death?"

"Yeah."

"Why?"

"Long story. I shouldn't have brought it up. Listen, we all go through hardships, and they either kill us or make us stronger on the other end. What about you? What's your story?"

"Ahhh . . . Perhaps another time. I'm trying to stay focused on driving. The snow is starting to pick up."

"There's a turn ahead onto a road that, according to Google, doesn't exist."

"It's probably a logging truck road," Ram guessed.

"And there goes our cell service, just an FYI."

"It's okay. Everything is fine," Ram muttered as his knuckles turned white from gripping the steering wheel.

Thirty precarious minutes later, they turned into the sloped private drive of Andrea's picturesque cabin.

"Whose car is that?" Allyson asked rhetorically.

"Good question."

"Andrea implied nobody knew about this place. Perhaps it's a sign she's here!" Allyson shouted, jumping from the car before it came to a complete stop. She slid across the small footbridge connecting the island to the mainland and stumbled up the front porch.

"Andrea?" she called, knocking on the door. She attempted to peek into the blind-covered windows without success. "Hello? Anyone there?"

"Hey, Allyson. The car is unlocked, and there are groceries in the backseat. Ha! It's chips and wine! Good wine, too."

"Naturally!" She pounded on the door again, then tried the handle. The door was unlocked.

"Do you want me to grab this stuff?"

"No. Leave it," she instructed, stepping inside. Immediately, Allyson was struck by a crawling sensation up her spine, as if someone were lurking in the shadows. She turned abruptly, only to find Ram standing in the doorway.

"Is there electricity?"

"There must be. It's comfortable in here. There's a light switch on the wall beside you," Allyson pointed by the door.

Once the space was illuminated, she moved forward. "Hello?" she called, exploring the bedroom, bathroom, and even the walk-in closet. "No one's here," she held up her hands as she turned back to Ram.

"As you said, the house isn't terribly cold, which makes me think someone was here recently," Ram pointed out.

"Are the coals in the fireplace warm?" Allyson asked, walking back to the front room and tentatively touching the screen with the back of her hand. It was cold, and the ashes were gray. Taking a poker from a set of tools, she stirred the fragments around, confirming nothing was lit.

"Well, I found the heat source. Andrea has a dual gas and electric heating system. Probably to keep the pipes from freezing when she's not here. The thermostat is set to fifty-eight degrees." Ram called as he appraised the utility box mounted on the wall in the short hallway between the main living area and the bedroom.

"Hmmm. Okay." Confounded, Allyson eyed the great room she stood in. It contained a small dining table, the kitchen, and the living room, where she stood next to the fireplace. The ceilings were vaulted to about twenty feet, with no cobwebs or telltale signs the place had been uninhabited long term. "I'm going outside. She could've gone for a walk, and something happened."

Stepping back through the front door, Allyson was hit with a cold gust of blowing snow. It was coming down heavier, and the sun was dipping behind the mountain behind the house. To the right was the side yard, where the wood pile was stacked expertly, and a large tool shed sat off to the corner. Tromping into the snow, she was surprised when her legs were covered nearly to the knee. She saw no footprints around her, yet headed towards the shed anyway and fiddled with the complicated lock. She considered that if it was secured from the outside, theoretically, no one was on the inside. Still, she called her sister's name to be sure. Only her echo returned.

She continued to the property's edge and walked along the water until she reached the tree line. The wooded area was dark and dense. Perhaps they could spend the night and explore them more thoroughly in the morning. Circling back to the front, she spied the extra car again. Crossing back over the bridge, she inspected the water to ensure nothing obvious was missed earlier. When she got to the vehicle, she paused to consider the snow on and around it. "The sun probably melts the previous snowfall during the day," she muttered as she opened the door. When she sat inside, she realized this was the car her sister had driven years ago. Allyson paid no attention to the make and model or its exterior features at the time. However, she'd spent at least a few hours each way on the inside, allowing her time to observe and judge it. Allyson noted it was a late-model Crossover with a soft, velour interior and no bells and whistles, unlike Andrea's current vehicle, which could practically drive itself.

Allyson placed her hands on the steering wheel and closed her eyes. She would never admit it, but she was trying to tap into the Wonder-Twin power. Unsurprised, nothing extraordinary happened. However, the glove box did capture her attention when she reopened her eyes. Holding her breath, she pressed the panel's button. The dim lighting revealed the usual things . . . sunglasses, a car manual, and a Glock, fully loaded according to the indicator. "What the actual fuck, Andrea?" she whispered, as her shaking hand closed over the cold black metal. She stuffed the gun in her coat pocket and snapped the compartment shut. Then she continued her search by flipping each visor and opening the ashtray and the center console. A black flip phone similar to Allyson's burner and a key ring were hidden inside under a pack of tissues and a coin purse. She grabbed the phone and the keys, putting them in her other coat pocket.

As she got out, a cloud of steam left her mouth from the rapidly cooling air, yet perspiration formed under her armpits in anticipation of what she might find as she shuffled to the trunk. To her delight and relief, it was empty. Completing her outdoor investigation, she grabbed the grocery bag from the back seat and headed inside. She would discuss spending the night with Ram. They could open the wine her sister bought and make a plan for tomorrow.

"Staying is smart. I can't imagine navigating those roads in the dark. However, I don't see how to charge the electric car here, and with the temperatures dropping, we might have a dead battery on our hands. We should look for the keys to the other car. We may need to take that to the city tomorrow," Ram warned when he returned inside with an armful of split logs.

"I found the keys. They were in the car, believe it or not. That one is definitely hers, too. I came here in it. I didn't recognize it from the outside because I spent most of the time inside. What I can't figure out is how a car gets here without a driver. Or how does the driver get back to the city without a vehicle?" Allyson asked, her forehead puckered in concern.

"She wasn't alone? Or someone came to get her?"

"Possibly." Allyson considered different options as she chewed on her bottom lip. "The house is pretty tidy. Honestly, too tidy," she observed as she went into the kitchen and used her foot to open the trashcan. "For example, if Andrea were here over a long weekend, this would be overflowing." She whipped open the fridge door and gasped.

"What?" Ram straightened from his position by the fireplace.

"It's pristine. You can even smell a lingering bleach odor." Closing the door, she opened the upper freezer portion. It, too, was spotless and free from built-up ice or debris. "This doesn't feel right." From there, she went back to the bedroom and bathroom, inspecting the trashcans. Everything was empty and sparkling clean.

Ram followed her to the bedroom. "Is it possible she hired someone to come clean and winterize the place? I can't imagine she spent too much time here in the colder months. One could go stir crazy trapped inside with the unpredictable weather."

"I think that's what she loves most about this place. She can scream until she loses her voice, and no one can hear it." Allyson stepped from the bathroom into the walk-in closet. "Hey, look," she pointed. "Men's shoes."

Ram bent to examine them. "They are different sizes."

"What's the big deal? I sometimes go up and down in size depending on the style."

"By three sizes, though?"

"Her photo library did show her *entertaining* several different people. Maybe she brings a different boo with her every weekend she comes?" Allyson laughed, yet it died quickly as she spotted a strange garment falling off a hanger. "Whose is this?"

It was a tattered and stained overcoat. Ram straightened it and crinkled his nose. "Ugh. It smells like 'Eau de homeless guy.'"

Allyson chuckled. "Is that a new Tom Ford fragrance?"

"Why would your sister keep a stinky old jacket hanging in her closet yet have the rest of the place spotless?"

Allyson's body went cold as she considered the one option she didn't want to speak aloud. She simply shrugged and turned away. She pulled the nightstand drawers open and rummaged through various papers. She discovered a charging cable that most likely went to the phone from the car and stuck it in her coat pocket, too.

Smoke drew them back to the great room where the fireplace was left unattended. "Can we not burn the place down until we figure out what the hell is going on here?"

"Sorry. I wasn't thinking."

"No, I should apologize. I'm projecting my frustration onto you, and that's unfair. I was sure we'd find something pointing to Andrea's whereabouts," she groaned, pulling off her jacket and hanging it on the wall hook by the front door. Two other coats were already there. One was clearly her sister's, the other a man's jacket. Five pairs of boots lined a drying mat underneath the hanging area. Again, two pairs were women's boots and Andrea's type. The others were different styles and sizes.

Brrring. Brrrring.

The unfamiliar ringtone shook them both from their ruminations.

"It's mine," Ram announced. "Hey, Dan, what's up?" His face blanched as he held up a finger. "Wow. That's insane news. Yes, I will head that way as soon as I can tomorrow. Thank you for the update." Ram ended the call and stared at his phone.

"What? What is it?!"

"Another H0rr Studios person has been reported missing."

"Oh my god! Who?" Allyson cried, raising her hands in prayer over her lips.

"The cinematographer, Craig Guilford. Dan said he's been trying me for a couple of hours now. I get two bars if I stand over here," he held his phone toward the ceiling. "He's pissed I'm not there to break the news tonight. I'm sure you heard that I need to get back there tomorrow to file a special report. Rumor is the Givers are holding a vigil there."

"This is not a coincidence. Three core people involved in *The Caretaker* are missing! Has H0rr Studios made a statement?"

"Yeah. No. Comment."

19

CIRCLES OF HELL

{ANDREA}

Andrea's eyes fluttered open to an oppressive bright light.

"She's regaining consciousness, doctor," a honeyed voice called.

Beeping and whirring machines made Andrea's head throb to the beat of their mechanical rhythm.

"Welcome back, Andrea. We were worried," a guttural voice greeted. Andrea assumed it was the doctor the other person was talking to.

The lights made everything hurt, especially her brain. As she fought to keep her lids open, she caught a glimpse of the room. Mint-green tiled walls assaulted her memory, and her body tensed like a kick to the gut. She tried shifting her body, but it wouldn't respond. Licking her lips, she attempted to ask where she was, only to discover she had no control over her tongue. It flapped around in her mouth like a pet goldfish out of water.

"Her oxygen is good. However, she's still tachycardic. Her BP is 165 over 100," the sugary sweet voice announced.

"That's an improvement. Keep monitoring it, and alert me to any worsening change. I need to check on the others," grumbled the doctor.

A warm hand pressed against her chest, then slid to her arms and palpated her abdomen. "Relax," the sweet voice instructed.

There was something off about her new situation—the way the person spoke, coupled with the doctor's abruptness. Andrea flinched from the unwelcome touch as they continued to poke and prod her body without consent. Was her nightmare at the movie studio starting all over again? At least this time, she assumed, she was in an actual hospital with real medical professionals.

As if reading her mind, the medical professional reassured her, "For your safety, your wrists and ankles are tethered to the bed rails. We can't risk having you pull out your tubes. In the meantime, the doctor has ordered a sedative."

Andrea tried in vain to decline. An alarm rang in her mind while her scalp pricked with a warning. She didn't want to sleep. She wanted answers. The only response she received was a burning in her hand as though she'd been stung by a bee. Warmth quickly spread throughout her body, and everything went dark.

An eardrum-piercing beep brought her back to consciousness. She scrunched her nose, and her mouth twisted in discomfort. Unexpectedly, her body stiffened, her back arched off the bed, and a pins-and-needles pain swept through her. Then she dropped into a prone position, her muscles and bones as floppy as Jell-O.

"Sinus rhythm," someone announced. "That's the third time today. We may need to consider a pacemaker if her heart doesn't start cooperating soon."

Panic seized Andrea as the words infiltrated her muddled mind. Abruptly, the stinging in her hand returned, along with oblivion.

"She's doing much better after the last defibrillation overnight," the now familiar silky voice reported.

"That's good. She's stabilizing. Continue with sedation for another twenty-four hours. Page me if anything comes up. I'm headed to surgery with patient sixteen. It's time to remove his feet, a nice size twelve."

"Don't forget the tattoo this time. The authorities identified the last one too quickly!"

Andrea squirmed and tried again to protest, to ask for answers—instead, she found the void of unconsciousness.

"Right on schedule! Time for your meds, dear," her caretaker announced in a sing-song voice. Andrea was paralyzed in a fucked-up version of *Groundhog's Day* with no way out. She'd swim to the edge of reality, only to be forced into a blank numbness.

A whisper close to her ear called her name. A man's velvet voice and warm breath made Andrea's body tingle. She batted her eyelids open and tried to move. *How much time had passed since her last injection?*

"Lars? I've told you to stop messing around with her. I need you to help with patient sixteen. He's combative, and I've already given him the maximum dose."

"Maybe the doctor should've taken his arms too," a man's belly laugh trailed away.

Sweat broke out on Andrea's forehead. *What kind of hospital was this?*

"Oh, what do we have here? It appears someone is awake and has been stable for over twenty-four hours. Great job, Andrea. Now, the real work begins!" Warm hands lifted her eyelids and flashed a light that left black spots swimming across her field of vision.

"Pupils are reacting nicely. Can you try and speak?"

Andrea moistened her lips while attempting to keep her eyes open and focused. The mint-green wall was still there. In front of it stood a young, athletic-looking woman with short, spiky hair and a pug nose. Then Andrea's traitorous lids clamped shut. "Wha . . . Where?" was all she could manage.

"Here. Let's get you something to drink. We've sponged your mouth and lips while you were unconscious. However, those vocal cords are probably drier than beef jerky," the woman chuckled. "My name is Samantha. I have been your nurse over the last five days."

Something papery touched Andrea's lips.

"Take a small sip. Too much at once will make you gag," the nurse instructed.

Andrea forced her eyes open again. The woman was holding a cup with a lid and a paper straw to her mouth. As she sucked, cold, thick liquid hit the back of her throat with such force that she immediately fell into a coughing fit. The machines started beeping wildly.

"Oh, sweetheart. I told you to take a *small* sip. Exhale through your nose slowly and try again."

Andrea wriggled her wrists.

"I can take those off once it's clear you're coherent. You have an IV," the woman touched Andrea's hand. "A blood pressure cuff," and touched her arm. "EKG leads on your chest, sides, and legs," she tapped a spot near Andrea's left breast. "And a catheter for urine output. I don't think I need to show you where that is," she smirked.

Andrea blinked repeatedly to keep her vision clear as she focused on the nurse, who moved to a mobile work desk about four feet tall. It contained multiple drawers, and an open laptop sat on top. Samantha typed and clicked away as she hummed a strange tune. Her brow furrowed, and her eyes hardened. She snapped her attention back to Andrea.

Agitated by the sudden change in the nurse's demeanor, Andrea tried to speak. "Wwhaaat?" She wanted to please her. Ease her mood if she could. This woman was her lifeline.

Moving briskly about the room, the nurse slipped on blue latex gloves, then pulled a syringe and glass bottle from a pouch in her colorful scrubs. Andrea flinched as the nurse drew nearer, trying to shake her head no.

"It's a little pick-me-up to help wake you from all the sedatives in your system. You won't feel a thing other than an immediate heightened sense of well-being."

Andrea wriggled more in her bed. The machines responded to her movements.

"You need to remain calm, Andrea," Samantha scolded. She placed her hands on Andrea's arms. "If you can't calm down, you'll go back to sleep, which will make the doctor unhappy. You don't want that, do you?"

Andrea locked eyes with Samantha and relaxed. They were an unusual shade of gray, reminiscent of a stormy winter day. The more she stared, the more her ease turned to fear. She shivered at a memory itching to replay in her brain as Samantha plunged the syringe into Andrea's IV.

Her body came alive all at once, with each nerve ending blazing and prickling with blood flow. She writhed in response, twisting her body as much as possible with her wrists and ankles bound to the bed. A high-keening sound, similar to an animal suffering, filled the room. Her head pulsed with a tormenting pain as if her brain would burst from her skull. The physical onslaught besieged her while the nurse stood watching, her mouth set in a crooked grin.

"Oh, dear. Are you in pain?" Samantha asked. "Some patients describe a pulsating ache in their head with this injection. Don't worry. You'll be right as rain soon enough. Be a trooper and try to ride it out by taking deep breaths." The nurse mimicked her instructions. "That's it. We don't want your heart rate or blood pressure to get all crazy again. Otherwise, I'll send you right back to la-la-land. Keep it up. You're doing great. It'll end in five, four," she glanced at her wristwatch.

Andrea squeezed her eyes and fists as tight as she could while her lip quivered from the strain. Her jaw was clenched so taut her teeth ground together as if they would pulverize into dust. The high-pitched whine continued. Had she ever heard anything like that come from a human?

"Yes," she hissed aloud. Andrea *had*. Terror overtook her as she also remembered where she'd seen those eyes.

"You!" she rasped through gritted teeth.

"Three, two . . ."

As if a switch was flipped, Andrea's pain ceased once the nurse reached number one.

"You," Andrea panted. "Can't. Be. Here. Roger . . ." She shook her head and swallowed hard to push the memory away. "No," she huffed, glaring at the woman at her bedside. Andrea wanted to throttle her, to hide under her gurney, to rip out all the wires and tubes, and strangle Samantha with them. She wanted to run away—like a little rabbit.

"Oh, I'm here, all right. I wish Roger were, too. Alas, he found a different route to take. I'm sure you'll see each other soon though. Now, be a dove," Samantha leaned in as if she were about to kiss Andrea on the lips and purred, "and let me have some fun!" Next, she whipped a scalpel from her pants pocket, brandishing it in her captive's face. "Hmm. Where to start?!"

Andrea fought against her bindings. "Help!" she screamed. "Help me!"

Samantha ran her tongue over her bottom lip as she eyed Andrea. "Shall I start with your pretty face? Or should I go right for the heart, hmm? I am a little curious," she said, straightening her stance and tapping the scalpel to her chin, "How black is it?" Reapproaching her soon-to-be victim, she ripped open the paper-thin hospital gown, pulled off the EKG wires, and pressed the surgical knife against Andrea's breastbone. "This might hurt a little," she sang, baring her teeth as if she were a wild animal.

On instinct, Andrea fixed her focus on the blade as Samantha sliced into her skin. She expected immediate pain, yet she only saw blood and her flesh dividing. Samantha said the injection would make her feel euphoric, and she did feel a vague sense of pleasure at the sight of blood—until a bone saw materialized in Samantha's hands.

Andrea's eyes widened, and she writhed to get away. "You can't!"

"Why not? You did! For five days, you kept me in the crypt, filming Roger's very authentic torture, you sick bitch! All the while, I dreamed of revenge."

Andrea's back arched off the bed. She thrashed and twisted until everything started to fall away. First, the IV and catheter dissolved into nothing. Next were the machines, her bed, and the nurse. Even the room disappeared, until Andrea was floating in a lightless vacuum like the deep recesses of space. It was as if she were the Hubble telescope free-floating beyond the Milky Way. A singular sound, in a deep "OM" tone, reverberated through her body as she drifted, weightless, her limbs spread apart Vitruvian Man style.

"What's happening?" she whispered. Swiveling her head around, she saw nothing. It was disorienting, yet somehow peaceful.

After what seemed like an eternity, something shifted around her. A hazy outline of shapes and a distant pinpoint of light grew steadily brighter. She was moving toward them as if a tractor beam was sucking her in. The figures became more distinct. A strange slideshow of people's faces streaked past her. She only recognized one—the first victim she was tasked to sketch as a forensic artist. It was a partially decomposed body in the woods outside of Atlanta, Georgia. She had been fascinated by the long, bony hands and the caustic odor of rotting flesh. The case was unusual because the victim had been reported missing five years before, yet the state of decomposition suggested they'd only been dead a few months. The irregular shape of its many bones baffled investigators as well. The forensic pathologist theorized they were held captive and tortured before they were eventually discarded in the deep woods. Andrea couldn't imagine how someone could remain in such an abusive situation or begin to understand the thought process of the perpetrator. Yet the whole situation intrigued her. She became obsessed with the concept of the absolute power one gains by carrying out such a feat. Being the center of someone's world and holding complete authority over them was such a heady concept that the case became a precedent for her future *endeavors.*

"Andrea . . ." a disembodied female voice called. It was not Nurse Samantha. This voice was accented, and they pronounced her name the way her family used to say it. *On-drey-ah.* "Oh, Earth to Andrea. Time to rejoin the living."

"Oh, fuck," Andrea groaned. It was her mother! "Okay. Whoever is in charge of this sick game needs to stop."

Patricia Marta's mirth echoed in her ears. "Silly girl. Wasn't it you who was just fantasizing about your life's work? Aren't you the one who made captive torture the porn of the modern era? It's not as fun when you are on the receiving end, is it, *mija.*"

"What the fuck is going on?" Andrea snapped, attempting to wrestle her body back under her control. As she moved, her bleak surroundings took on form and substance. Again, the mint green tiles appeared along the walls of a windowless room. It was cold and damp, and she lay naked on a cot centered on stained concrete. A pool of stagnant water lay around a floor drain nearby.

Her mother materialized across from her, dressed in a flowing white gown. Her feet hovered off the ground, and she held her hands at her sides in a mudra foreign to Andrea. Patricia Marta smiled coyly as she tilted her head the way one would when speaking to a small child.

"Ahh, my little murderous *demonia.* Welcome to the inferno!"

20

BURDEN OF PROOF

{RAM}

The wind howled outside as Ram and Allyson stood frozen, staring at each other in disbelief.

"How can they simply say, 'No comment,' when three employees are missing?" Allyson gripped her head and shook it.

"The same way they claimed Roger was in safe hands and sequestered until his next court appearance. You, me, and the FBI know that's a lie. With Andrea's disappearance still private, it's clear there's a cover-up. Which is where my skills come in handy." The wind battled the home's exterior. "I only wish we stopped at the movie lot before heading here. There's no predicting the road conditions in the morning."

"Why? What do you expect to find? Besides, don't you think the police will push to investigate there with this latest development? Surely, Agent Kingsley has heard about Craig by now."

"Let's find out." Ram punched in his friend's number. Irv answered on the first ring. "Hey, Irv, it's Ram. I'm on a burner cell, in the mountains north of Vancouver, following a lead on a story. I got a call from my producer that another H0rr Studios employee is missing. You got anything?"

"Christ on a cracker, Laramie! I've been trying to reach you. I was getting ready to send a search party. Why are you calling from a burner?"

"I often do when I'm on assignment. I'm a little bit stuck at the moment and feel as if I'm missing out on something."

"Stuck, how?"

"Snowstorm. Unreliable vehicles. I'm hoping to get out by morning and head to the movie lot. Tell me a warrant has been issued to search the place."

"Chief Constable Sutter is coordinating with our FBI sub-office there, which has one agent and an assistant. With a small crew and H0rr Studios' deep pockets, it's imperative any evidence obtained is flawless. Otherwise, they'll block and deflect all day long. The government hates expensive, lengthy litigation. That's if Sutter can even find a judge to sign off on a warrant."

"That's bullshit. Didn't they rent the complex? How about going directly to the landlord?"

"It's a tricky situation, and our attorneys are heavily involved. All I can tell you is the wheels are turning in the right direction. As far as Craig Guilford is concerned—he was a no-show for a dinner date with his girl-friend two nights ago. She tried calling him, and when he didn't respond after repeated attempts, she contacted his eldest daughter through social media. No one had heard from him in over twenty-four hours. After con-sulting with the family attorney, they filed the report this morning with local LA authorities, where he's based. The FBI was brought in because the family raised concerns about his gambling addiction and lingering debts, along with his connection to Roger. Honestly, Laramie, this is a real shitshow we're dealing with. If word gets out that all three employees are missing, the fans will go berserk."

"I hear your frustration, but are you seriously asking me to hold off on reporting this? This is huge! The longer we withhold anything from the public, the more suspicious it looks. The optics wouldn't look great for you guys, either. The public has a right to know what's going on and could even provide valuable information to help resolve this."

"I get it, Laramie. We all have jobs to do. However, unless there is a genuine threat to the public at large, our obligation is to the victims and their families. If we fuck-up gathering evidence and intel, whoever is responsible for these disappearances could get away with it."

"Are there any leads at all?"

"No. Guilford's family was smart, mentioning the gambling debt. The local PD should get a warrant executed soon so they can search his electronic records. The big question is whether these three were in contact with one another before they went missing. Otherwise, they are simply adults who've decided to go ghost."

"Go ghost?"

"Yeah, willingly vanish—like a ghost. Get it?"

"Cute. Only days apart, though? That's a stretch. Roger slipping away while out on bail is criminal, right? Seems to me you could pull his electronic records to track his movements."

"It's all in the works. Everything is moving faster than we can process the paperwork."

"Well, shit. This sucks. Okay, I can leave out certain specifics in my next report. Which reminds me, I'm headed to the movie studio tomorrow, provided the roads are passable. The Givers are holding a vigil in the afternoon. They believe, and rightly so, that Roger is missing, and the execs are covering it up. If anything happens while I'm there, I'm going to report it. There's no professional courtesy if news happens live. Hopefully, Sutter's team can manage any chaos that erupts."

"Thanks for the fair warning. As for Sutter, I'm told he's stretched pretty thin. Why don't you contact him, if you haven't already, as a courtesy? He'll work with you. By the way, what story are you working on that would bring you to the BC mountains?"

"What's that, Irv? You're breaking up," Ram grinned at Allyson. "Hello?" he called, moving from the fireplace to the front door, where the signal wasn't as strong. "Irv? Are you there?" Snapping the phone shut, he shrugged. "Hmm. Call dropped."

Allyson nibbled at a cuticle. "Stop stalling. What did Irv say?"

"A whole lotta nothing."

"Three employees of the same company—on the same project—go missing, and they've got *nothing*?!"

Ram extended his arms to comfort her. Allyson slipped into the kitchen, where she rummaged through the grocery bag. "At least there's wine! I'm sure it will all work out tomorrow. The road coming wasn't terrible. It must get cleared after a big snowfall."

He returned to finish his job with the fire. It gave him a moment to consider the facts as he understood them. If only he weren't stuck overnight in a remote cabin on a useless wild goose chase. Time was being wasted. The perfect clue tying everything together was out there, waiting for him to uncover it. The wild wind outside forewarned blizzard-like conditions, and they were utterly unprepared. If he couldn't get to the movie lot by tomorrow afternoon, his job could be on the line.

"Earth to Ram!"

"Sorry. I'm spinning."

"It shows. I said, do you want the dark, dry red or the medium-bodied?"

"Dark and dry, like my sense of humor," he laughed. "Was there anything else besides chips to eat in that bag?"

"Yeah, M&Ms!" Allyson giggled, showing him the oversized bag.

"And they're peanut. Yuck. I hope you eat healthier than your sister. Who brings that kind of food to a cabin in the woods?!"

"Hey! Peanuts are protein, man! Besides, it's possible a mystery guest brought more nutritious items."

"Did you look through the cupboards? Ouch! Damn it, I've got a splinter!" Ram groaned, instinctively sticking his finger in his mouth.

"Don't do that! Do you know how many germs are in your mouth? Come and wash it out at the sink, and let me see."

As Ram's blood dripped down the drain, Allyson sniggered. "This is exactly what we needed to get a break in the case—a blood offering to the *Caretaker* gods."

"As long as I don't lose a body part, I'm good with that," Ram smiled.

"My first successful exhibit was based on body parts."

"What? Tell me more."

"I was committed to a treatment facility catering to those who self-mutilate two years prior to coming up with the idea. While there, I became obsessed with the 'how' and studied people in my therapy group. I sketched their scars, tattoos, and piercings—even twisted appendages. I met an individual who would break their bones and leave it to heal without medical intervention. Their hands and toes were all gnarled, and they walked with a cane due to knee injuries. I even met someone with brain damage from slamming their head into a wall to help self-regulate. When I got out, I turned those drawings into life-like people and parts."

Ram examined his scarred hand. He could relate. "It sounds fascinating. What was your medium?"

"Silicon and foam formed the skin, and then I added a little human hair. Viola! Perfect human replica."

"Whoa. Where in the world would you get hair?"

"Oh, that's easy. Hair salons! You wouldn't believe how much they trash in a day."

"Do you keep all your work the way Andrea does?"

"Yes. However, mine is organized. My shit isn't lying around in haphazard piles or in boxes in my hallway. I rent a special storage unit that is temperature controlled."

"How much does that cost? You must have a building all to yourself!"

"Oh, no! My sketchbooks, drawings, and a few small pieces are stored away. The rest are on display somewhere in the world." She waved her hand dismissively. "My agent, Vince, manages that stuff."

"I'd like to see your work sometime."

"Haven't you seen my website or social media? You did say you were an investigative reporter, right?! Tell me you've at least googled me?"

"Honestly, I've been a little busy," he shared a lop-sided grin. "Grace called and asked for my help. We've been on this whirlwind ride ever since. Are you offended?"

"God, no. I'm still unknown to most. The Space Needle installation might get me name recognition. I just don't want it connected to Andrea in any way. That would really piss me off. I'm always her fucking shadow. Can't have one without the other, and she's usually first. Ugh. You singletons don't know how good you have it!"

"Only you know you are a twin. Have you considered shifting your mindset about your identity?"

"Wow, Ram. I wish I'd met you when I was twelve. Would've saved my family thousands in therapy. I should call Dr. Dean and tell him you've cured me," Allyson snapped, stomping from the room.

"Shit!" Ram swore at the ceiling. He pinched the bridge of his nose and counted to three before heading after Allyson.

"Look. I'm sorry. I didn't mean to come off as a know-it-all," he called through the bathroom door. "My intention was pure. As an outsider, sometimes it helps to have another perspective. You fight so hard against something out of your control. Think of the Serenity Prayer. Accept what you cannot change. You can't change that you are an identical twin, but you can accept it."

"Not helping, Ram."

"Hey! You're not hurting yourself in there, are you?"

"Fuck you. Really not helping, Ram."

"I'm out of my depth here." He threw his hands in the air as if saying, 'I give up.'

"You should probably stop doling out advice, then. Go open the wine. I need a few minutes."

He hovered outside the door, listening for any sound that would suggest she was self-harming. Worry gnawed at him, and it made him uncomfortable. Why should he care this much about a woman he just met? Was it his obligation to Grace to babysit their friend? Or was there more that he refused to unpack?

When the toilet flushed, he wandered back to the kitchen to open the wine. A few minutes later, Allyson emerged, her long sleeves clenched into her fists. He searched her face and assessed her body language for evidence she'd hurt herself.

"I'm fine! You think I don't see you judging me? Stop it. I'm fragile like a bomb, not a butterfly's wing."

"Okay!" Ram raised his hands in defense. He turned to look for glasses in the cupboards. "I'm allowed to worry, though."

"Are you?"

Ram spun around to face Allyson. "Look," he pointed a finger at her. "I am here to help you. I've put my career on the line for this. You are dear to someone dear to me. Ergo, I need to ensure I'm keeping you out of harm's way, even if that means from yourself. If you don't like that, that's on you. Under my watch, nothing bad shall happen to you. Got it?"

Allyson closed the gap between them, placed her hands on his face, and kissed him hard.

Ram responded by wrapping his hands around her waist and pulling her tight against his body. Their kiss intensified while their hands roamed over each other as if mapping their contours by touch alone. He lifted Allyson and placed her on the counter by the open bottle. His lips moved to the sensitive spot between her neck and shoulder as he pulled her shirt collar away. A smile teased his lips as he explored her neckline's erogenous zone.

Allyson swept the bottle aside, moaning in appreciation. Wrapping her legs around his hips, she yanked at his sweater, urging it and his undershirt over his head. "God-like," she murmured as her shaking hands traced his torso's sleek lines.

Unexpectedly, Ram's stomach growled, bringing their play to an abrupt stop.

"You're hungry!"

"Not for M&Ms and chips," Ram hissed, burying his face back into her neck.

"We should move to the fireplace—have some wine and chocolate. Set the mood."

"I thought I was setting the mood. I'm losing my touch."

"Oh no. The eating is foreplay. And you should leave your shirt off. I need to see your muscles move with you."

Ram did as he was told, enjoying the calm and ease washing over him. Maybe he needed a good old-fashioned romp to reset his mood. His life was stagnant, aside from his journalism work. The Salish Sea Feet phenomenon and the H0rr Studios mysteries were exciting. Otherwise, he'd fallen into a dull attention-seeking and self-validation rhythm. He needed to feel worthy. A successful career helped, yet it wasn't enough. What if this time with Allyson was a chance at something more?

"See? A roaring fire, a blanket spread on the floor. This is romance novel shit," Allyson smirked. "Oh. Are you okay? You seem . . . distracted."

"Why would you think that?" he curled his lips in a seductive leer and arched an eyebrow.

Allyson handed him a glass. "Taste."

"This isn't a restaurant. I can't send it back if I don't like it," he smiled.

"Humor me."

He did as he was asked and smacked his lips in approval. "Mmm. Notes of black cherry and plum," he added dramatically.

"Very good," Allyson giggled and nodded in approval.

As she swirled the dark liquid in her glass and took her first sip, Ram admired her mouth and the way her throat moved as she swallowed. He couldn't help imagining what other things her mouth could do.

"Didn't you accuse *me* of eye-fucking you this morning?"

"Busted." He brushed the back of his hand across her cheek as another wind gust rattled something outside. "They say the weather has an energetic vibration we unconsciously tap into."

"Are you blaming your desire on the weather? And here I thought it was my natural seductive prowess."

"It's the perfect intoxicating mix."

Allyson moved to curl into his lap, feeding him chocolate, along with the chips. It was Ram's turn to moan in appreciation.

"Andrea knew what she was doing with this pairing. They are perfect together," she whispered against his mouth.

They nuzzled and explored each other through all their senses until the wine was finished and the food devoured.

"Let's have dessert in the bedroom," Allyson suggested, standing and offering her hand to Ram. He took it without apprehension, this time surrendering to the intimacy the atmosphere and the woman demanded.

They took their time getting to know each other's bodies. Ram was shocked at first when Allyson unveiled her body 'art' from years of self-harm. Soon, he discovered beauty in the heartbreak.

"It's okay to look. To touch. I actually find it soothing," she reassured him, taking his hand and guiding his fingers along the raised edges of her scars. Many hide their trauma and emotional baggage behind false smiles and external coping mechanisms. Allyson wore hers on her body, sharing her story with anyone interested in learning it.

Ram delighted in her involuntary shivers as he trailed his lips and tongue over the more prominent, intimate parts. They melted into each other, entwined in a lover's embrace, until they collapsed in exhaustion, side by side.

"I'm shattered," Allyson declared, trembling with the aftereffects.

Ram smiled, clasping her hand in his and bringing it to his lips. He couldn't speak. His mind swirled with various emotions he didn't want to label. Sex came easy with his looks and how he maintained his body. Appearing nightly on TV didn't hurt, either. However, true intimacy in the way he and Allyson connected scared him. It made him vulnerable and open to being hurt, which he avoided at all costs. Looking at the scars on his right hand again reminded him what grief and pain true intimacy could bring. As he drifted to sleep, he said a silent prayer to let this time be different.

A noise woke him hours later. His outstretched arm was cold and empty. Allyson was gone. He figured she'd left to use the bathroom, but when he rolled over towards the door, it was open and unoccupied. The noise came again—a banging from outside. Lurching to his feet, he stumbled around to find his pants. While stuffing a leg in, he leaned into the window, spreading the wooden blinds apart to check outside.

Through the blowing snow, he could make out the shed door flapping open. Rushing to the living room, he slid to a stop. Papers lay scattered across the kitchen table, and two burner cells sat charging side by side. A small travel suitcase sat open on the floor beside a dining chair left askew as if someone had pushed back abruptly. He edged forward to inspect the contents more closely when the creaking floorboards sent a warning shiver up his spine. He turned in time to discover Allyson standing in her snow-covered parka, the wood-chopping axe in her hand.

"Allyson! What the?!" Ram shouted as she raised her arm to strike him. He charged at her to stop her momentum when a shot rang out.

Ram bolted upright from the bed. It was only a dream! A nightmare. Except for the gunshot. That was real. He scanned the room. Allyson was gone! As if on repeat, he stumbled from bed, groping for his pants. He was wrestling with what was tangible and what was imagined when another shot rang out. Running towards the front door, it flapped in the wind as he slid to a stop, like in his dream, yet this time, there were no papers, cellphones, or an ominous suitcase.

Ram rushed out on the porch in his bare feet and without a shirt and found a silhouette standing in the steady snowfall by the bridge leading to the parking area. He assumed it was Allyson. Then a red flash flowed from the figure's outstretched hands, followed by a fourth gunshot. He traced the direction they were pointed and discovered the outline of another person running up the hill toward the road. He stood frozen while his brain tried to comprehend the scene.

An engine roared in the distance as headlights raced through the thicket of evergreens along the winding, rutted road back toward the main highway.

"Allyson?" Ram shouted.

The shape turned. "Oh, Ram!" she cried, tossing back her faux fur-trimmed parka hood. She ran across the bridge back to the house. "Thank God."

"What in the hell is going on?"

"Come on. Let's go inside." Her breath blew in clouds as she hooked her arm in his and pulled him toward the open door.

"Let me take that," Ram offered when they stepped inside.

Allyson gripped the gun tightly in her shaking hand. "I'm fine. I've obviously shot a gun before. I'm just c-cold."

"And in shock. What the fuck was that all about? *Who* was that?"

"No clue. A sharp cracking noise woke me. I tiptoed to the window and spotted a figure chopping at the shed's lock. Who fucking breaks into someone's shit in the middle of a snowstorm? Then, I recalled the gun I discovered in Andrea's glove compartment yesterday. It was in my coat pocket. So I slipped out the front with a plan to scare the intruder off when a man . . . I'm sure it was a man . . . large and burly . . . came running at me. I'm a better aim than I give myself credit because I'm sure I hit him. He turned abruptly, waded through the water, and ran toward the road."

Ram ran his fingers through his hair. "This is all kinds of fucked up."

"I know."

"What if you killed someone? We should call the police." Ram moved to get his phone.

Allyson snatched his arm. "Not so fast."

21

SHE SHED

{ALLYSON}

"Allyson! You could have just killed a man!" Ram shouted, his voice cracking in pitch.

"Who's going to know? They aren't here anymore, and they shouldn't have been in the first place. And let's not forget, we came in secret too. We don't know what's out there, and we have no idea the trouble Andrea may have gotten herself into. Let's think this through before we make any rash decisions."

Ram's jaw muscle ticked as he glanced about the room. "What's on the counter?"

"Oh. I found this in her car yesterday too, and it could be a major clue." Allyson grabbed Andrea's burner cell. "I plugged it in out here after you fell asleep and waited for it to have enough juice to check its logs. There was only one call in the 'recents' list from an unknown number, and this voicemail. Listen."

Allyson hit play, and a robotic voice spoke. "Hello, Andrea. It's time."

"Time for what?" Ram asked, his eyes wide.

Her face contorted into a frown, "I'm not sure. But that voice . . ."

"It's from *The Caretaker*," Ram finished.

"It's disturbing," Allyson shivered. "There's no caller ID. No way to trace it back to anyone. Only a time/date stamp. It was the day before she was a no-show for her meeting with Vanessa Rapaporte and the other execs. Who would have access to *The Caretaker* voice?" Allyson asked.

"Anyone. It's a function on their damn app!"

"Christ!" Allyson rubbed her eyes before scrubbing a hand over her face. "These fucking fans! They're nuts! Why would anyone need that capability?"

"Because people want to be like the Caretaker! Throughout the series, whenever Roger's character held a victim longer than a few hours, he would use this mechanical voice to speak to them. It was a device used to disorient and psychologically torture his subjects—foreplay before the physical abuse began. The sound was chilling to his on-screen victims and equally disturbing to the viewers."

"It makes no sense. Why would anyone want to sound like the person who scares them?"

"Escapism! We've talked about this. It's fun dressing up in costume and playing the psychopath sometimes."

"No thanks. Not me. There's nothing fun about terrifying people."

"You're a real bummer on Halloween, aren't you?" Ram laughed.

Allyson flipped him the bird. "I like any holiday that involves free candy, but you don't have to be a cold-blooded killer to participate."

"Agree to disagree. Back to the voicemail . . . On the positive side, this *is* a clue. I mean, it could be anyone who left it. But to me, it means there's a *Caretaker* connection to your sister other than her being the creative director. Maybe our nighttime visitors are linked too somehow?"

"Only one way to find out. Give me the gun back." Allyson held out her hand and wriggled her fingers. "I'm gonna go search the shed."

"Umm. How about I get dressed properly, and we both go check it out," Ram suggested.

Brrriiinnnggg! Brrriiinnnggg!

"Saved by the ringing phone. Give me the gun. Meet me out there when you've finished. I'll give you a shout if I need you. You'll be able to hear me from the bedroom window."

"This is against my better judgment, but it's 2 a.m., and only three people have my burner's number, including you. It must be important. Please be careful!" He grasped her outstretched hand and pulled her into an embrace, planting a chaste kiss on her lips before handing off the gun and running towards the phone he had left on the bedroom nightstand.

Ram's retreating figure and subsequent "Hello" gave Allyson the cue she was listening for. Her intuition told her she needed to investigate this alone. As much as she resented Andrea, she was still her sister. An unexpected sense of loyalty and protectiveness held Allyson back from possibly revealing any secrets she might uncover in her search.

Once at the shed, it was evident the door had been broken with the axe Andrea had left out for chopping wood. "Didn't see that coming, did you, Dre?" she murmured, sliding the gun into her coat pocket to hoist the axe handle. She turned and scanned her surroundings before ducking inside.

Allyson gasped when she was abruptly immersed in disorienting darkness. "Gah!" she choked, "what's that god-awful smell?" She held her hand up to her nose and retreated outside for fresh air. Holding her face to the sky, she was grateful for the cold snowflakes alighting on her nose. "I'm going to need a flashlight!"

Darting back inside, Ram's excited voice, grousing in muffled tones, emanated from the bedroom, reassuring her there was still time to do a cursory inspection without interference.

She had found a spotlight-type light in the hallway closet earlier in the evening and grabbed it without interrupting Ram. Returning to the cold, snowy night, she lit the path back to the shed while also searching the nearby tree line to ensure she was alone. The sky always seemed brighter during a snowfall, but she couldn't help feeling uneasy. *Was someone watching them?*

She held the light above her head at the shed entrance to get a preview inside. Her mouth popped open as her wide eyes took in the scene. The inside wasn't a garden shed at all. More like a tiny house. *Or torture chamber.*

There were no windows or exits other than the busted door. A metal-framed twin bed covered with crumbled, soiled bedding sat in the left corner. An old fabric recliner on the right. Its seat and footrest were covered in dark splotches, and it appeared as if a wild animal's claws had attacked it, leaving threads and stuffing spilling out. Allyson's lips curled. The left wall, approximately twelve feet in length, featured typical shed tools such as shears, clippers, and handsaws hanging from pegs. The right wall was decorated with framed pictures of Allyson's artwork from her first major art exhibit—the one she had told Ram about earlier. "The fuck?"

Her hand moved to her throat, where her pulse hammered against her fingers. Stepping inside, she searched for the odor's source and discovered a bucket of human excrement tucked between the bed's footboard and the chair. She traced a rope dangling next to the makeshift toilet to the bed's corner leg. Lifting it carefully, she found a loop at its end, stained with a similar dark substance as the chair. The other corners had ropes too! Her hands shook from the ideas filling her head. She dared not touch anything else as she slowly backed away.

"Jesus. Were you hiding someone here, Andrea? Is that why those men were so interested in this place?" she whispered.

She shone the light on the hanging tools. They appeared rusted upon first inspection, but as she drew closer, it became more apparent the red residue was not rust but, more than likely, blood.

"What the actual fuck?!" she shouted in frustration and disgust. Then she clamped her hand over her mouth. Ram did not need a reason to come out here and see this. He would be on the phone with Agent Kingsley before she could utter a possible explanation. Yet she could use another's opinion without them having the context of her sister's dark past. Maybe Ram could devise an alternate explanation for what Allyson was filling in with her imagination.

Before she left the shed, she checked under the bed. What if there was a person still there, hiding, assuming she was Andrea bent on harming them? Allyson couldn't imagine anyone surviving in this gory "She-Shed" for long. Yet people defied terrible odds all the time, clinging to their survival instincts.

"Hello? Andrea?" *God, please don't be Andrea!*

As Allyson crouched and lifted the covers to get an unobstructed view, a loud bang sounded behind her. She screamed, dropped the flashlight, bolted upright, and turned towards the entrance. It was the door banging from the wind. "Holy Mary, mother of Christ!" she spat, returning to the bed.

"Hello? If someone's there, you're safe now. I can help." Although, in honesty, she didn't trust she could. To her relief, the spotlight only revealed a few empty toilet paper rolls, discarded chip bags, and a footlocker about two feet long by a foot wide.

"Allyson?" Ram called.

"Coming!" she replied, leaving the storage box where it was. Outside, she shut the door and wedged the axe handle under the locking mechanism busted by the intruder.

"Anything worth driving all the way out here to steal?" Ram asked.

"No," Allyson replied quickly. "Nope. Definitely not. But maybe we can secure this before we leave in the morning. It's late, and I'm exhausted." Not a lie. It had been an eventful twenty-four hours, between combing through her sister's belongings in Vancouver and coming to the cabin with

Ram. Not to mention the sex, the shooting, and this gruesome discovery. It was all a little too much for Allyson to process.

"Sure. Come on. Let's get back inside. I doubt those guys will be coming back tonight," he reassured her with an arm around her shoulders.

"I've still got nearly a full clip to greet them if they do," she smirked as they shuffled back inside. "What was your call about?" she asked, stripping off her cumbersome winter wear.

"You won't believe it! Another pair of feet was found along the shoreline. This time out on Jedediah Island."

"Is that near here?"

"No. It's way west. A tiny island between mainland Vancouver and Vancouver Island, near the Strait of Georgia."

"Okay. I have no context. Do you think it's connected to my sister or the studio?"

"It's hard to say. My producer wants me to check into it after the vigil tomorrow since I'm here anyway and have covered all the other occurrences in our area."

"This one is not in your area, though. Sounds pretty far away, actually."

"I've reported on over twenty instances. They are all along the Salish Sea. The professionals keep waving it off as a natural phenomenon. But what if it's not?"

Allyson groaned, kicking off her snow boots and walking towards the bedroom. "I don't even want to consider it right now! I'm on overload. Can you lock the front door before you come to bed? I'm keeping the gun on the nightstand. I hope you aren't offended, but I want to be prepared for any eventuality."

"Not at all, considering tonight's escapades. Hey, listen. If both cars run in the morning, we should head out separately. You can take your sister's car back to the apartment and hang out while I file my report. Dan arranged for me to work with a local crew, and they are meeting me in the studio's parking lot. I want to break the news about Andrea and Craig missing too, but Irv has warned me not to."

"It could get chaotic. I don't want any part of a surprise announcement."

"I get it. You don't mind, do you?"

"Nope. Happy to sit that shitshow out. I need to check in with my agent, Vince, anyway. Even though it's acting like the middle of winter here, it's spring in Seattle, and the hedges for my Space Needle art installation are scheduled for planting soon. I can't believe my life has other things to worry about besides missing people! It seems strange to think about 'normal' things."

"Normal is boring," Ram laughed, leaning in to kiss her forehead.

22

MEMORY LANE

{ANDREA}

Andrea stared at her mother's visage. "Inferno? As in Dante? What kind of bullshit is this?"

"How else did you plan on making things right? Issuing an apology? You've never held compassion or regret for anything in your life. You need to relive your sins through fresh eyes."

"Oohhh. I'm so scared! See me shake?" Andrea held out her steady hands.

"You can be as sarcastic and childish as you want, but you know what you've experienced thus far. How was it finding yourself bound and surrounded by mutilated corpses? Or traipsing through the movie set maze? Hell's tunnel? Seeing yourself as the pursuer? Facing death in the raging storm? Waking up here, in this 'hospital,' and seeing me again after all these years?"

"That's seven. I thought there were nine circles of hell?" Andrea flashed a cold smile.

Her mother inclined her head. "You always were brilliant. Too bad you didn't use your gift for more meaningful purposes. If you recall, the last two levels were where the real punishments were doled out. For the seven deadliest sins. I'll come to get you after you've had your walkthrough."

"I can't believe this fuckery. Why are you even here?" She shouted, spinning around in utter darkness as her mother disappeared. Her words echoed back at her as if she were in a closed chamber.

"This is *your* labyrinth. Take it up with your subconscious if you don't like it," her mother's disembodied voice laughed from afar.

Andrea flipped her middle fingers up, pumping her fists above her head like a concertgoer at a heavy metal show. Abruptly, a door opened, revealing a bright white light. It stung her eyes as if she had stared at the sun too long. Girls giggled and birds chirped from the other side while a wild burst of warm wind rushed through the opening. As the breeze hit her face, she detected hints of honeysuckle and pine. A second gust blew in wood smoke, sunscreen, cheap beer, and weed. Those clues told her where she was headed next. A knot twisted in her stomach as a force behind her pushed her through the opening. Before she could turn around, the entrance had disappeared. She was left standing on a gravel parking lot facing a clearing and a lake beyond.

"Come on, Allyson! You have to see this," a teenage blonde girl with a head crowned in tightly coiled curls, sun-reddened cheeks, and olive-green eyes called.

In answer, a perfect copy of Allyson at twelve years old ran right past her as if Andrea wasn't standing there.

"What is this? A goddamn rip-off of *A Christmas Carol*? Where's my ghost of Christmas Past?"

No ghosts appeared, but her body moved forward automatically, following the giggling girls towards the lake where two boys stood. One was holding a fishing line filled with his wriggling catch, a joint dangling from his mouth. Another was squeezing a giant frog between his hands.

"Don't kill it, Royce!" Allyson cried.

He lunged at her with the frog in his hands. She screamed and ran away. Everyone was laughing. Allyson acted so carefree and vibrant. Her whole reality had shifted the minute they arrived at summer camp. She was the popular one, the one holding everyone's attention—the one with friends. The strangest part was how they all seemed to like her for being her and not because she was a twin.

Andrea rolled her eyes, recalling the scene. She was about to turn away when she spotted the younger version of herself to her left. This Andrea stood in the tree's shadows, shifting uncomfortably, a scowl forming a deep crease between her eyes. Perhaps *adult* Andrea was the ghost in this flashback.

She wanted to call out to her former self, but what would she say? She wouldn't be able to provide any comfort. Andrea had always resented Allyson's existence, but her bitterness was strongest during summer camp. It vexed her then, and surprisingly, it still did in the present. Nothing she could offer would change those feelings.

Allyson tripped and let out a squeal. Royce caught her before she fell, dropping the frog in the process. He swung her into his arms, like in old movies, and held her against his bare chest. He leaned in and kissed her with familiarity. Young Andrea sucked in an audible breath and bared her teeth. This was a new development. *Allyson had a boyfriend.* The other children, Calliope and James, ooohed and ahhed and teased.

"Get a room, you two!" Callie cried, delight and warmth in her voice. The playful banter didn't bother either Allyson or Royce as she threw her arms around his neck and pulled him tighter.

"Hey, Allyson. Isn't that your sister lurking over there?" James called, pointing to a silhouette in the pine trees.

"Ugh. Probably. Don't ruin it for me. For once, she's in the shadows and not me!"

"I don't know how you guys are even twins. You're like night and day. And not just by the clothes you wear. I can tell you apart easily," Calliope sneered, folding her hands over her budding chest. She cocked her hip to the side and stuck her tongue out in the direction where they had spotted Andrea.

In turn, like mirror images, both Andreas balled their fists at their sides, embarrassed and angry for being caught. *Little cunt will pay for that.*

Suddenly, the scene changed. It was a few days later, and it was now nighttime. All the campers had been gathered around a huge bonfire. They were divided into several smaller groups while Allyson moved from pod to pod, handing out instructions for the murder mystery game she had invented with her new BFF. Calli and Ally. Everyone said they were more like sisters than Andrea and her. They finished each other's sentences, liked all the same things, and shared everything from the minute they met. If Andrea hadn't been stuck with the geeks, freaks, and losers, she would've been with Calli and not Allyson. She'd begged the counselors to keep them together, but they said it would be best to have them separated. "There's growth in being apart," they told her. They'd pay for their mistake. They all would.

Dressed in all black, including a balaclava she'd found in a counselor's closet one afternoon while skulking around the adult cabins, Andrea waited in the tree line until all the groups had dispersed. Not one person reported her absence or was even aware she wasn't there to participate—an oversight the camp's stakeholders would be fired for later on. She had set a trap with a clear fishing line and whatever else she could get her hands on. The plan was to lure Calliope into the woods, where they'd have a little chat about her relationship with Allyson and come to a reasonable understanding.

And it worked, to the point where Calliope threatened to scream and tell on Andrea. That couldn't happen. They'd send Andrea home and not Allyson. She was not going back with Ma and Pa all by herself.

She stuffed the balaclava into Calli's mouth and tied her hands with the fishing wire. Adult Andrea had forgotten all the details, the way a bride had trouble recalling her wedding day. There was too much excitement, too much she had done on pure instinct. She took pride in the patience young Andrea showed, torturing little Calliope while their peers laughed and carried on mere yards from them. She choked her until Calli passed out, broke her fingers one by one, kicked her, punched her, and held her face in the dirt. At one point, while Andrea paused to catch her breath, a small group passed within feet of them. It was dark, and they were so focused on sneaking away from the games that they didn't notice either girl. They giggled and splashed as they grabbed canoes and discussed plans for getting high out on the lake. What a great idea! She could cleanse herself and Calliope through a *Marta baptism*!

Andrea had tried to *baptize* Allyson in the ocean once when they first moved to Point Dume. She was convinced Allyson's birth was a sin, so Allyson must be cleansed. The belief that water magically removes immorality simply by holding someone under while besieging God's forgiveness bewitched Andrea. In Calliope's case, Andrea didn't need to beg anyone. She merely held the girl's head underwater until she stopped moving. Once Andrea was convinced Calli wouldn't call for help, she removed the fishing wire bondage and makeshift gag. Snagging a kayak off the beach, she paddled them out to the lake's middle, where she purposefully capsized the vessel, leaving Calli underneath. With her dastardly deed covered up, Andrea flipped on her back and floated leisurely toward shore, appreciating the three-quarter moon's light and the stars shining brightly above.

After Andrea got back to shore and changed her wet clothes, she joined her cabinmates, playing the role of angsty preteen. Everyone she came into contact with was like a judge or jury. Did they have any idea what she'd done? Did it show on her face or body language? She was jittery. Worry and fear about being caught threatened to expose her. Yet she was intoxicated by the power she held over her sister and anyone who stood in her way. If she were to get away with this, the sky would be the limit in removing obstacles.

Adult Andrea recalled feeling unstoppable for pulling off a caper that no one could pin on her. If only she could claim it—scream it from the rooftops: "I did it!" That's where *The Caretaker* came in. It was an artful ode to herself and her mastery over committing crimes without consequences—a flamboyant disregard for basic human decency.

"How is revisiting this point in time punishment?" she asked aloud. "These were my best years!" she laughed. "My first blooding."

"And you made me your unwilling acolyte." Young Allyson appeared next to her as Calliope's lifeless body was loaded into the ambulance.

"You can see me?" Andrea tilted her head.

"Sure, Dre. I'm your other half. I'm always with you. You've aged, by the way. Your face is worn. But not like a favorite pair of jeans or an old T-shirt—more like a footpath or a sidewalk. Do I look the same in the future?"

Andrea smirked and tucked an errant piece of hair behind Allyson's ear. "You're even worse. This loss was hardest for you. And keeping my secret. It drove you mad."

"Am I dead?"

"No. Why would you ask that?"

"Because I can't imagine living with this knowledge my whole life."

"Well, it's not for a lack of trying on your part. You've attempted to end it all a half-dozen times. But that just landed you in treatment centers for suicide, depression, anxiety, cutting, etc. . . . You name it, you've been treated for it."

"Because of you . . . and this?" Allyson pointed to the police car and the ambulance slowly rolling away from the campsite as the morning sun peaked through the trees. Camp counselors and administrators gathered on the gravel, consoling one another while clusters of campers looked on. Allyson's innocent accusations made Andrea's insides twist.

"Yeah, I think so. We could've worked out most of our shit in therapy or even forgotten as we grew. But losing your friend like this, having to go home and face Ma and Pa . . . having to face me? It was too much for you."

"How awful. How do I do it?"

"Do what, beautiful girl?" Andrea took in Allyson at such a younger, more vulnerable age. Something shifted inside her. What about her young twin cracked her impenetrable emotional shell?

"How do I live? How do I look in the mirror and see not only myself but you?"

Andrea grabbed for Allyson to shake her, to thrash her, to show her who was boss, but her hands slipped through the air. Allyson was gone. She was back in the dark void she'd been in before this trip down memory lane.

"Lyssy," she croaked, but her voice wasn't strong enough to make a noise.

The world tilted on its axis, and Andrea began to spin, like an amusement park ride where it turns so fast you stick to the walls when the bottom falls out.

"It's time to make things right, Andrea," Allyson's voice called from beyond.

"What is there to fix? I have all I ever wanted," Andrea answered the emptiness.

"Lucky girl." A man's voice came from Andrea's right side.

Shaking her head like an Etch A Sketch to clear her mind, Andrea found herself back in the mint-green tiled room, dressed in a threadbare gown, hooked to IVs and beeping machines. "Not again!" she groaned.

"Where you've been for the last ten days, silly. Right here with me. You don't recognize Lovely Lars? I'm hurt."

Andrea searched his face but found it unfamiliar. She guessed he was five foot nine and wore his brown hair in a sleek man-bun. He had wide, bright, brandy-colored eyes and a goatee. His medical scrubs stretched tight over his round beer belly, and his arms were covered in tattoos.

"I know you?"

"Yes, girl! I've been sneaking you extra chocolate pudding at lunch daily. I came to tell you old Lars has done you a solid, and your wish has been granted. The room by the water you wanted is yours. Instead, I find you talking to yourself and not remembering who your best friend is. I'm hurt."

"I've been here for ten days?"

"You sure have!" he frowned, turning her wrist to check her pulse rate.

"What about my heart? Did I have a pacemaker put in?"

"What are you talking about? You are in prime physical health. Besides, this is not that kind of facility. You came to escape the stress and mental strain you've been under recently. It's why everyone comes here."

"What is your accent?"

"Girl. You are really starting to worry me. Why don't we get you moving? A walk outside in the fresh air will do you good. It's a sunny, cloudless day. The mountains will be reflecting off the lake."

"Lake? My lake?"

"Oh, come on now, honey. Are you pulling my leg?" Lars laughed as he assisted Andrea to her feet. "Here. Let me get your sandals," he muttered as he prepared Andrea for her excursion.

She puzzled over what was happening and where she was. The room was much larger than she previously recalled. It was like an activities room. Men and women dressed in comfortable clothing lounged on couches or sat in reclining chairs. Why were they wearing regular clothes while she was in a hospital gown?

"Hola, Andrea," an older gentleman waved and smiled. He said her name like her mother did earlier.

She returned this gesture with a dark scowl. She wasn't the friendly sort to go waving at people, and anyone who knew her understood this. When the man caught her mood, he slowly lowered his head and returned to studying an elaborately carved chessboard. Two others made eye contact but slid their gaze away as she delivered the same expression she'd given Mr. Friendly.

With her shoes on, Lars hooked his arm under hers to steady her gait. "Let's go!"

"Wait. What about the wires and IV? And my clothes?"

Lars furrowed his brow. "Check your arms, honey. Nothing there. As for your clothes, you picked this outfit yourself this morning. Soft cashmere cami and pants. You said they were your favorite when I complimented you on the ensemble."

It was Andrea's turn to furrow her brow as her whole body seemed to morph before her eyes. Was Lars an illusionist?

Tugging at her arm, Lars encouraged her to take a few tentative steps. When they were both confident in her balance, they continued down a wide corridor and outside through a set of automatic sliding doors.

"You're going to love your new suite. The mountain views are exceptional. And it has access to the water, like you requested. It's our best guest quarters in the entire place. And if you want, I will continue as your concierge."

"My concierge?" Nothing made sense. Until the panorama her escort had touted came into view. Then, at least one question was answered. "This isn't Vancouver."

23

PUDDING

{ANDREA}

"I know this place!" Andrea gaped, and she placed her hand on her chest. "Palm Springs!"

"We have a winner, folks!" Lars laughed. "You've won a month-long stay at the exclusive retreat center for the incredibly rich and fucked up."

"I'm neither!"

"Oh, please. You are old money, honey. The kind earned from corrupt corporations who rape natural resources from the land, then deny global warming. Not to mention an oh-so-famous movie franchise attached to your name."

"You seem to know a lot about me."

"Well, you could say I'm your *Caretaker*," he laughed wildly. When she threw him a look like a cat about to strike, he stopped and stepped back from her while still holding her with a firm grip. "I told you before, I'm your concierge. It's my job to know everything about you. I become a subject expert on the guests I serve so that you feel safe and at home, away from home."

"There's no way I'd pay to come to such a hippy-dippy place."

"You wouldn't be here if you didn't. It's a healing center, not a psych hospital. Even though we offer similar services, like group therapy and medication management, we would never keep you against your will, and we don't take insurance. We have a two-year waiting list."

"I waited two years for this bullshit? I don't believe it for a second."

"Well—maybe *you* didn't wait, but most have to."

"Why wouldn't I have to wait?"

"If you know the right people, you can get anything on short notice. You must know *someone*."

"You mentioned medication management. Have I been prescribed meds while I've been here?"

"Sure. Everyone has. Nothing serious. Dr. Bouchard's treatment protocols include a microdose of psilocybin once a day to help modify the serotonin levels for all patients."

"Ha! Magic Mushrooms. I thought I'd never see the day they'd become legal, let alone used to treat illnesses."

"We're making strides with the fun stuff, aren't we?" Lars smiled.

Andrea sighed, taking in the breathtaking view. She'd been to Palm Springs several times before. She recalled the first time they visited as a family. Her father told them how the San Jacinto Mountain range was formed—a giant granite block in between two fault lines. "Intense pressure can build beautiful things, mijas," he'd said.

Why was that mundane memory indelible, yet she couldn't recall making plans to return on a retreat? "Why is my memory so fucked, Lars? It's disorienting."

"Let's ask the doctor," Lars turned his attention to someone over her shoulder.

"Hello, Andrea." A new voice greeted her from behind.

She swiveled to answer and found the most handsome man she'd ever seen. A jolt went through her as if she'd touched a live wire. As he walked forward to join her, his tall frame blocked the sun. He glowed like a full-body halo surrounded him.

"I've heard you are feeling a little agitated today. What seems to be the trouble?"

His guttural voice triggered an immediate reaction. Andrea's skin crawled, and the hair follicles on her scalp stood on end. She stepped back and crossed her arms over her chest.

"What is it?" he asked, moving forward and extending his hand.

"Don't touch me," she snapped.

"Andrea. It's me. Dr. Bouchard. We've been working together since your arrival. In fact, we've been meeting weekly over the phone for a month before you got here. Plus, we've known each other for years."

"I recognize your voice. You were the one who took the man's feet! And wanted to put a pacemaker in me!" She pointed her finger at him and shook it while backing away.

"What?" he smiled, revealing gleaming white teeth. "No, Andrea. I'm a doctor of psychology, not a medical doctor. All the time you've spent with me has been in talk therapy, either in a group or one-on-one. This is a safe space where no one is harmed."

"I don't believe you! I've seen people and had experiences . . . Look at the cut on my arm! You can't fake this!" she rotated her arm forward so they both could examine it. "What the?"

"See?"

"No, no, no!" She placed her head in her hands and shook it side to side.

"Think back. You arrived at the local airport via a private jet, where I personally picked you up. You underwent a thorough physical exam with my colleague, Dr. Wagner, the head medical doctor on staff, to ensure you had no underlying health issues before we even got started with your protocol. We talked about your mental health and a possible schizophrenia diagnosis based on a few troubling incidents you've experienced. You committed to doing the necessary work to return to a healthy, productive state."

"No. You're lying. This is all part of your schtick to keep me here."

"You are free to go whenever you like. However, in your current condition, I wouldn't recommend it. You could be a harm to yourself or others."

"Ha! Now I know you're full of shit! Even before I came here, I was a threat to others."

"Yes. I know. We discussed your . . . *predilections.*"

"*Rrright.* If we had, I'd be in jail, not living the life at a fancy resort!"

"Wellness center. And anything we discuss is confidential. It's part of our nondisclosure agreement. Our reputation is built on anonymity and discretion. Roger was here before. Remember?"

"No, he wasn't!"

"Yes. Right after *The Caretaker* was released, when the world became obsessed with his work, he was in crisis, struggling with his rediscovered infamy. You came with him. Dropped him off."

She spun around, taking in the grounds with fresh eyes. She *did* remember being here. She could picture herself walking with Roger, talking to him about getting his head on straight and how things would be different for both of them going forward.

"There's no putting the genie back in the bottle," she whispered.

"I'm sorry?" Dr. Bouchard asked.

"I told Roger there was no putting the genie back in the bottle, and he needed to get his shit together because his dreams were finally coming to fruition. He was losing it—threatening what we'd all worked for."

"That's right. It was a big deal. Vanessa Rapaporte came, too. The three of us counseled him on sticking with the program. Once he embraced it fully, he blossomed and stayed an additional month!"

Andrea stumbled backward and swayed as the memory resurfaced.

"Are you okay?" the doctor asked.

"Yes. I think so. I'm so . . . confused. Why am I having trouble with my memory? I have all these blank spots."

"We've been working through your trauma, big moments you felt shaped your life. It's intense work. We've also tried cognitive therapy to help with your other mental health issues."

"You said I have schizophrenia? For real?"

"It's a possibility. More tests need to be done, but it's not my area of expertise. I founded this Center to help those with a broad range of needs, such as stress, addiction, and weight issues. They can be dealt with in the short term. Schizophrenia is a lifelong illness. You can have good days— many good days, for years even. But there will come a time when an episode hits hard. That's when you need to seek treatment at a facility more adept at treating those symptoms. It is a complex mental illness requiring a support team familiar with all its unique characteristics and intricacies."

"Like where Allyson goes?"

"Yes, from what you've shared with me. You know, mental illness can be hereditary, so it doesn't surprise me, being identical twins, that you might present with similar issues."

"Issues? I'm not a fucking *Vogue* magazine! How am I supposed to believe anything you're telling me? I barely know my own name. How do I know you aren't a hallucination? I've heard stories of how people can hypnotize you and plant false memories."

"We could call your father. He knows you're here."

"My father? No. No. We don't need to bother him. He's a busy man."

"All right. We could go for a walk around the lake. You love the water. It soothes you."

"No. I'm not going anywhere with you."

"That's fine. Oh, I know. Maybe more chocolate pudding? I've heard it's your favorite."

"Fuck your pudding and your special treatment. I'm done here. Time to check out. Get my head screwed back on tight."

"This is the best place for you right now. You are safe here."

"Ha! I've used that line before. This is Gaslighting and Manipulation 101. 'Trust me. I know what's best for you.' Blah, blah, blah. Once I put my faith in you, I'm under your thrall. Then you're free to do what you want."

"This is your guilty conscience talking, Andrea. It may have worked for you in your day-to-day life, but it's not a successful business model. Think about Roger and how well he managed after his treatment. I've helped hundreds of people like him. He reached his full potential *after* spending time here. You can, too."

Another memory hit Andrea: Roger acting exuberant when he returned to the set. His rigidity gone. He was stolid and focused when it came to their important work. *The Caretaker* was truly born after he came back from treatment.

"It's time, Andrea." Dr. Bouchard said, holding out his hand.

"For what?"

"To make things right." A twinkle of light reflected in the doctor's eyes.

"What did you say?" She frowned and backed away further. "What did you just fucking say?" Her breath caught in her throat. Her eyes widened as she scanned the area for an escape. A walkie-talkie squelch sent a shiver through her.

"We have a possible situation on the veranda," a voice called behind her.

"Andrea!" Lars called. "Hey, look what I have?" He was juggling three small chocolate pudding cartons.

Like Pavlov's dogs, she salivated at the sight.

"Come on! Let's check out your new room. It has a TV with all the streaming channels. Including your favorite!"

Her feet moved automatically, following him in a stupor to a nicely appointed suite.

"Look. Your belongings have already been moved. Your clothes are in your closet here, your favorite soaps and conditioners in the bathroom, and I put your sketchpads and pencils on the side table for your convenience."

"I want to leave. Can you help me?" Andrea blurted out.

"I'm not sure you really want that right now. You're having a bad day, is all."

"I can give you money. Lots of money. But I need to go. Right now. If you know me like you say you do, you have to see that this place is not helping me. I'm losing my fucking mind, Lars."

"Shit. Okay," Lars rubbed his hand on his chin. "Look. Let me investigate what it would take. You can check out at any time, but it's a process requiring paperwork and sign-off from the doctors."

"But if I were to sneak out with, say, a staff member . . ."

"You'd forfeit any money you have already paid and trigger a review of our security measures. Not to mention the employee investigation. I love it here. The staff—we're like a big family. I don't want to be fired, and I definitely don't want to be charged with a crime."

"If you had enough money, you could find a new family, even move to a new city," Andrea reasoned.

"Look, if I were you, I'd stay in this secret little enclave and accept all the pampering and treatments we offer."

"Where do you go when your shift's over?"

"Umm, home. Why?"

"Where's home? You can't live in Palm Springs. It's incredibly expensive here."

"That's an unfair assumption. Do you think because I work here, I make minimum wage? I thought you said you weren't rich. Sure sounded like something a rich bitch would say to someone they perceive to be lower than them." Lars moved to go.

"Fuck. I'm sorry. Don't go. Listen to me. I need to escape."

"You've said. But the more you say it, the less convincing it is. You sound paranoid."

"You don't get it! The doctor . . . Borland. He's a monster. I heard him say horrible things."

"Dr. *Bouchard* is a miracle worker. Whatever you thought you overheard wasn't real."

"He wanted to put a pacemaker in me! He removed a man's feet!"

"That's ridiculous! He's not even a medical doctor. If anyone were worried about your heart, Dr. Wagner, our staff physician, would have been called in. But this place is not equipped to perform surgeries. There's no reason! Seriously, Andrea, the more you talk, the more unstable you sound. You are right where you need to be."

"How much is it worth to you to smuggle me out to a place I can rest—dry out from all the pharmaceutical bullshit they've been pumping into me? I only need a few days, then I'll disappear for good. No one ever has to hear from me again!"

"I don't know, Andrea. If you go missing from here, the first person they'll look to is me. I don't want any trouble. I'd be no good to anyone in prison other than as someone's sex slave. No one dreams of being a prison bitch."

"How much do you need in order not to work again? A million? Two?"

"I don't want your money. Besides, you told me you're not even rich!"

"And you reminded me how I come from old money. Don't forget all the coin *Caretaker* has brought me too. I've invested well. I could make you comfortable."

"Shit. I don't know. I need to think about it. And I have to go check on my other guests."

"You go. Have a think. I want an answer by dinnertime."

"Oo—Okay," Lars stammered. He placed the three chocolate pudding cups on the table beside her sketchpad and scurried out the door.

Andrea dropped back on the bed and stared at the ceiling fan until her eyes closed involuntarily.

"Psst. Andrea. Hey, Andrea. Wake up!"

Andrea awoke to a hand on her shoulder.

"Wh . . . What? What's happening?"

"It's me, Lars. You slept through dinner. Dr. Bouchard told me to let you sleep. I'm headed out for the night. Do you still want to go?"

Andrea rubbed her eyes, trying to get her brain working. "Yes! Absolutely. Are you willing to play, Lars?"

"Yes! But we need to go now. It's a shift change, so there's a gap in coverage. Here. Put these on. Quickly! Before I change my mind!"

Andrea jumped from the bed, snagged the clothes he had in his outstretched hand, and ran to the bathroom to change.

Scrubs. Compared to the cashmere she'd been wearing, they were *scrubbing* her skin raw. But she didn't care. She was getting out of crazy town!

"Okay. Ready. But what about my stuff?" Andrea waved her hand around the room.

"It stays here. Sorry."

She bit her lip. "Where are you taking me?"

"There's a motel about ten miles away. It's not fancy. But they won't expect you there. Come on!"

She paused, glancing at her closet full of clothes and creature comforts, then rushed after him.

"Slow down. You'll look suspicious if anyone sees you running," Lars whispered behind him.

"You're walking too fast!"

Lars guided her through a hallway and down a flight of stairs before exiting a side door. For a moment, she was back at the movie studio in the blizzard. She swayed on her feet, trying to keep her grasp on reality.

"Come on! Why are you staring at the door?"

Andrea shook herself and proceeded after Lars. Without any hiccups, they made it to his car, a luxury sedan, and drove towards the Center's gates.

"Get down. I'm going to put this coat over you. Cameras cover the exit, but they should only capture me when I swipe my card."

Andrea did as she was told. Within minutes, they were out on the main road, flying up Canyon Drive and away from Big Brother's surveillance.

"We'll be there in a little bit. Stay hidden. We don't need any CCTV cameras catching us."

"Okay," Andrea replied from under Lars's coat.

The car sped up and slowed down, taking several turns—a couple of lefts and a few rights, before it finally stopped.

"Okay. I'm parked at the fast food joint next door. Here's the key— room 213. I covered the expenses for two nights. Once you get inside, call whomever you have to for the payment arrangements. Two million, and freedom is yours. Here's the bank information," he said, handing her a bright blue sticky note. "Once I see the payment, I'll call your room, let it ring three times to confirm receipt, and you'll never hear from me again."

"Wait! How am I supposed to get away from here?"

"Not my problem. You wanted to escape the Center. I got you out. The rest is on you. Do we have a deal? Or do I need to bring you back and claim you were a stowaway without me seeing you?!"

"Shit. Fuck. No, we have a deal. But can you do me one more favor first?"

"What?" Lars snapped.

"Do you think you can score me some weed or coke or anything party-related?"

"You literally spent days being microdosed! Didn't you say you wanted to dry out?"

"I need to level up, is all. Clear the cobwebs."

"I think they had you in the wrong treatment program. You should have been in rehab, not stress management."

"Fuck off. Can you do it?"

"Yeah. Yeah. I'll have a buddy drop you some food with a little extra inside. But otherwise, I'm done!"

"Yes! Yes. Of course. Thank you, Lars. You are a saint. You may have saved my life."

"Sure. Sure. Get going before I change my mind."

Andrea threw off the coat and bounded out of the car, briefly disoriented until she spotted the motel sign ahead. She ran across an empty lot and up the external staircase, searching for room 213. Once she found it, she tapped the keycard against the reader and entered.

She'd been in worse places, but not by much. There were stains on the carpet, and the room smelled strongly of stale cigarettes and sweat. The bedspread was from the same era she was born, and the décor was from the 1970s. But she was free! Now she needed to figure out how to pay Lars his two million and arrange transportation out of this hole within forty-eight hours.

Walking over to the nightstand, she eyed the phone, which was at least from the current decade, before spotting the notepad beside it. She stared at its logo and contact information, committing it to memory. "What if I wire this asshat his money, and he hands me over to the police? Or worse, calls Vanessa? I have no idea who this man is or if he's reliable. But who else can I trust?"

She could call her father, but if he were footing the bill for the retreat, he'd be pissed to find out she'd fled. He might even send his goons to escort her back to Argentina. She trusted Anselmo Marta as much as she trusted Lars and Dr. Bouchard. But he *was* family.

Just as she grabbed the phone to make the call, a rapid tapping came from outside her door. With a huff, she replaced the receiver and walked toward it. The peephole revealed a man with his back to her.

"Who is it?"

"Delivery."

"I didn't order anything."

"Room 213, Lovely Lars?"

"Jesus," she huffed and opened the door.

The man turned and pushed his way into the room.

"What the fuck?"

"Shut up, bitch, and shut the door. I got the stuff you asked for, but I can't just hand it over to you."

"Why not? You said you were a delivery guy. It's not like everyone on this floor is waiting to witness a drug deal."

"No. But others might get pissed that I'm working in their territory. There are unspoken rules about this stuff."

"So if I don't like what you have, I can go bang on my neighbor's door and see what they've got?"

"Oh, you'll like what I have," the man said, licking his lips and touching his crotch.

"Ugh. Gross. Give me the shit and get out."

"Are you sure, baby? There's enough for us to party all night. It's no fun by yourself!"

"I'm pretty sure I can have way more fun alone. Now. Get. Out. Before I scream rape."

"Fucking slut." He threw a brown paper bag on the bed and walked to the door. With his hand on the knob, he gave her a withering, scrutinizing glance. "I can't believe Lars says you are Caretaker's friend."

"Fucker, without me, there would be no Caretaker. Now *take* yourself back to the cave you crawled from."

"Do you know where he is?"

"Who?"

"Caretaker. They say he's dead. That the studio killed him."

"Who is 'they'?"

"The Givers."

"They don't know shit. They're a bunch of whack jobs who live in this fantasy world where Roger is their best friend. Caretaker is not real. Not in the way you all believe he is."

The man waved his hand at her appearance. "Takes one to know one, I think."

Andrea scoffed. "Cute. Leave."

"Are you saying that shit he did was fake? It was all makeup, props, and CGI?"

"No. I'm saying the character isn't real. Roger is a scared little boy with a narcissistic complex. He needed his hand held through every take. Literally. Now, go!"

"Take that back!"

"No. What are you, five?"

"Roger is a hero!"

"Of what? Your fantasies? Get bent, loser, before I lose my shit. Where do you think all those twisted torture ideas came from? The writers' heads? No. They wrote, 'Gory scene goes here,' and left that shit to me. So if I were you, I'd turn around and walk out that door. Unless you want to experience what it's like to be a real Caretaker victim."

The look in Andrea's eyes transmitted the truth because the man scurried out the door, slamming it behind him. Through the curtained window beside the door, she laughed at his retreating figure running downstairs to an awaiting car. "Run, little rabbit, run. I like the chase," she whispered in a dark, gravelly voice.

Turning towards the bed, she snapped up the bag and dumped its contents. "Is this a fucking joke?"

Chocolate pudding cartons tumbled out onto the flowery polyester coverlet. One had a turquoise sticky note on it. In a loopy script, it said, "You didn't think it was the chocolate you craved, did you?"

"Naturally, they laced our food. How else would they be microdosing us?"

Collapsing on the bed, she used her finger to scoop out the rich, velvety substance into her mouth, savoring its flavor as she awaited the escape to oblivion.

"What do you think about Roger being dead?"

Andrea moved into an upright, crisscrossed leg position. "Hmm. That was quick."

A mirror image of herself sat across from her, mimicking each movement. "It's all we've been eating for the last three days."

"I can't help it. It's too good. Anyway, what do I care about Roger? He ran. Because he's a little rabbit, too."

"Then why do the Givers think he's dead?"

"He's in Uzbekistan. No extradition treaties with the US. Weird customs with women's hands. He's fine," Andrea lapped her finger.

"Is he?" her mirror image asked, smacking her lips.

"Do you know something I don't?"

"Maybe."

"Fuck. What if Lars was right and I was safer at the Center? Should I go back? I could say Lars tried to extort me for millions. Not far from the truth."

"Oh, don't worry, darling. Have another pudding." Her mirror image tilted her head, widened her eyes, and grinned a toothy smile while balancing another pudding cup on her palm.

As Andrea reached for the pudding, the scenery changed behind her reflection. A bright, white light glinted off the water as it peaked over the mountain range.

"Not Vancouver. Not a cheap motel. Where am I now?"

"Paradiso," her mother's voice whispered in her ear.

24

COVER UPS

{ALLYSON}

Allyson glared at her reflection in the mirror while gripping the counter. She took quiet, shallow breaths as Ram stormed around the bedroom, gathering his belongings. When the front door slammed and the snow crunched under the car's tires, her body went limp. She left the bathroom's safety, shuffled out to lock the front door, and slipped back into bed. Pulling the covers over her head, she squeezed her eyes shut, willing herself to go back to sleep. But her mind wouldn't stop spinning. Her intrusive thoughts were tormenting her and making her feel off balance. How could Ram be such an ass?

The morning got underway well enough with another quick round of satisfying sex and postcoital cuddling. They seemed to be an excellent fit and intuitively knew what the other liked. Then he had to spoil the whole thing by bringing up Roger! She didn't want to think about him or her sister while wrapped in her lover's arms. He and Andrea probably had been in the same position in the same bed! The imagery made her snap.

To make matters worse, he doubled down on his assessment and her "hang-up" on being an identical twin, reopening the wound from the previous night. It was too much.

"Who the fuck do you think you are?" she had snapped at him, throwing back the covers. "We fuck a couple of times, and now you're an expert on what makes me tick? Fuck you, Laramie Helm, and the white fucking horse you imagined you rode in on. I don't need your psychoanalysis. Get your shit and go! I don't care if there is a foot of snow. Figure it out and—Get. The. Fuck. Out!"

Her heart raced as the scene replayed in her head. Slipping from bed once more, she retrieved her handbag and the pill case containing all her prescriptions. Dumping out the morning's dosage, she studied each one, considering their purpose. There was one to calm her but not send her into a depression. Another to stimulate her but not cause anxiety. And two more that did God knows what. Which one would keep her from chasing people away from her who were only trying to help?

Tossing them back, she chased them with a palmful of water from the bathroom sink, then cleaned her mess. *Everything in its place.*

Back in the bedroom, she stared at the rumpled linens. Should she strip the bed? Maybe there was a spare set in the closet. It was the right thing to do if Andrea returned. "Or . . . I could let her sleep on sex sheets," she wrinkled her nose. The closet had those strange men's clothes hanging, and they reminded her of the shed.

"Goddamn it. Where the fuck are you, Andrea? I don't want to have to deal with your mess!"

Deciding to leave the sheets, Allyson made the bed, dressed, and headed outside. She was surprised by the sunshine reflecting off the snow. Whatever amount had fallen overnight had already melted, leaving behind a mushy Slurpee-like texture.

Pulling away the axe she had wedged under the lock, she inhaled deeply before opening the door. The odor hit her as it did last night, but this time, she was prepared. Even in the daylight, the place was disturbing, but she forced herself to examine each element thoroughly. Could it be this was a set design Andrea had recreated to help with her creative process? Allyson would believe it if it weren't for the toilet bucket, which was too real to be for inspiration. Or was it? Method actors did all kinds of crazy things to prepare for roles. Why couldn't horror show creatives do something similar?

She fished the footlocker out from under the bed and slid it towards the door to be closer to fresh air and daylight. Naturally, it had a complicated lock, like the one on the shed door. Following the example of their would-be thief, she whacked away at the thing with the axe until the lock busted open. Panting from her efforts, she stood leaning against the handle, staring at the box. She empathized with poor mythical Pandora. Her curiosity was nearly overwhelming, yet a part of her wanted to slide it back under the bed and leave. Once it was open, there was no going back, no matter what was inside.

Nibbling her lip, she closed her eyes and crossed her fingers before throwing open the lid. She turned her face to the sky in silent gratitude— no dead body or pieces of one inside. Instead, there were clothing items, a necklace in a velvet pouch, an inscribed lighter, a gold watch, and even a locket of hair. There were sketches of people and body parts, an area map, three hard drives, several flash drives in a baggie, and an old laptop.

At the bottom, a binder caught her attention. It was a script for the first *Caretaker* movie. Tabs marked specific pages, and highlighted sections had handwritten notes in the margins. The last page had Vanessa Rapaporte's signature and an official H0rr Studios approval stamp. Underneath the binder was a manilla envelope. It contained several official-looking documents, including NDAs for people Allyson didn't know, as well as pictures of Allyson's early work with her "human" series. Dread tickled her spine as she recalled talking to Andrea about the mediums Allyson used in her work.

Andrea was going on about making the perfect macabre, life-like dummies for their more explicit scenes and wanted to get it "right."

Allyson needed a moment to consider what she found, and there was nothing more grounding than walking in nature. The land surrounding the cabin was beautiful, with its evergreen, white spruce, and cedar trees. The parcel was shaped like an almond, with its pointy end connected to the mainland by a strip of earth no wider than a car, making it more of a peninsula than an actual island. It was surrounded on three sides by water, with the little moat-like brook separating the parking area from the house. The lake hugging the land was broad enough in certain places you couldn't see the other side. In other areas, it was narrow enough to easily wade across in the warmer months. Allyson imagined her sister canoeing or paddleboarding out on the smooth summer water and sunning herself as warm rays broke atop the tall trees at high noon. There would be birds singing and woodland critters chittering away. Unlike now, when the world seemed dead, and she, its sole survivor.

Shivering, Allyson headed back inside and planned her trip back to the city. She would make a point to stop by the police station and introduce herself to Constable Sutter and find out if he had any new information on Andrea's whereabouts. She also needed to retrieve her cellphone and other belongings from Ram's car. Talking to him would be tough after the way he left. However, things needed to be said, and going forward, firm boundaries needed to be set in place. If he were to continue investigating Andrea and the subsequent mysteries surrounding H0rr Studios, they would have to come to an understanding.

Patting her coat pocket, she verified the keys she'd found in the car were still there. She needed to find out if the vehicle would even start. She wouldn't be going anywhere if she didn't have transportation. At least not as soon as she'd like.

As she sunk into the driver's seat, her eyes were drawn back over the property. It really was an exceptional view. Except for the damned shed looming on its back edge. What was she going to do with the trunk and the broken door? Was it possible those items were simply mementos and trinkets from old lovers? If so, they might be better served to stay where Andrea had hidden them, especially if she were to turn up. However, the attempted break-in just hours before meant someone thought those contents had value. To whom remained open for debate.

How would she secure the broken door? There wasn't a utility closet around, and there were no building supplies, like nails and wood, inside the one place you'd expect to find such items.

Turning the key in the ignition, the car fired up right away, and the gas gauge reported three-quarters of a tank. Allyson let it run while she went back inside and tidied up. She gathered all their trash and put it in the trunk. With one final glance at the shed, she came to a decision.

Grabbing the coverlet from the bed, she set the footlocker on top of it, dragged it out to the car, and hefted it into the trunk. Not wanting to take the blanket with her, she tromped back to the shed one final time. As she fiddled with replacing the coverlet, she considered the framed pictures on the wall. It was odd for artwork to be hung in such a place. What was Andrea thinking?

"Nails!" she snapped her fingers. Removing each one, five in all, she found what she needed to secure the shed door. Using pliers from the tool board on the opposite wall, she yanked out each nail and stuck them in her coat pocket. Next, she lugged the frames inside the house and leaned them against a wall in the living area. While inside, she searched for a hammer and came across one in a bottom drawer in the kitchen.

Nailing the shed door shut, she stood back and admired her handiwork. Afterward, she put the hammer back and ensured all the lights were off inside the house. There were a few glowing embers left in the fireplace, but they would fizzle out soon enough. Even though the door was unlocked when they arrived, she turned the button on the handle and double-checked that it was secured. How strange that Andrea would lock her shed and not her house. What had she been thinking when she left?

After clipping her seatbelt on, she pulled out her burner cell to plug it into the charger. One missed call. Clearly, it was Ram. He was the only one who had the number. She'd call him when she got back into the city.

Cranking the radio, she headed out, whispering a solemn goodbye to the property. Leaving the cabin invoked an emptiness she couldn't explain.

When she reached civilization, she pulled into a fast-food joint for something to eat. As she coasted through the parking lot, she spotted a dumpster along the building's side. Remembering the sack of trash in the trunk, she stopped and parked nearby. With her hand on the bag, she eyed the footlocker. On impulse, she pulled out the items pertaining to *The Caretaker*, along with the electronics, and then threw the locker in the dumpster along with the household waste. If it held any meaning for Andrea, she'd apologize later. But instinct told her it served no good purpose to be kept around.

After grabbing a bite to eat and a coffee for the road, she continued to the city center, where she parked the car in a public lot near Andrea's apartment. Rather than heading inside, she walked over to the police station where Ram had left his car. She needed to get her stuff from the trunk, and the easiest way to do so, without speaking to him directly, was to ask for assistance.

A side door opened, and a handsome, sandy-haired man around her age emerged.

"Excuse me. Would you be able to help me get into this car? My overnight bag is inside, and I need to get to the airport. My friend is not answering his phone."

"Are you Allyson Marta?"

"Yeah, how did you know?"

"I'm Constable Sutter. I'm working on your sister's missing persons case. I recognized you from her pictures."

"Oh, right. Nice to meet you. Have you met with Ram Helm, the investigative reporter who's here with me? This is his car."

"I haven't, but I know he's out at the H0rr Studios movie lot right now, reporting on the nightmare we uncovered late yesterday."

"Nightmare?"

"Yeah. Why don't we go inside for a few minutes where it's warmer, and I'll fill you in."

"Okay, sure."

"We entered the premises at 10 p.m. last evening after receiving a call from the on-duty security guard," Sutter began his story as they sat down in his small cubicle. "He observed unnatural sounds coming from inside Building A while he was out making his rounds. He figured it was those Giver folks. They've been causing a ruckus since the studio shutdown. It got worse once the rumors of Roger Wotke vanishing started, with more than a few trespassing arrests made. The call triggered two patrolmen to be sent. They made entry, and we immediately lost contact with them. Our protocol had us sending in four additional units. Two went in but called for assistance shortly afterward. We lost contact with them too. Turns out the place was booby-trapped."

"What? Why? How?"

"All excellent questions. It's an active investigation, so I can't tell you everything, nor do I know all the answers. However, what I can reveal since you are indirectly involved is that those first two officers are still missing. The second set was killed when they fell through a secret hole in the floor."

Allyson's hand flew over her mouth, her eyes wide. "This is horrible. I'm sorry for their losses. What happened?"

"Broken necks. Died instantly. From what intel we've gathered, there's a tunnel running underneath the whole complex not included in the blueprints. *AND* we've uncovered rooms. A command center is being organized now. We're not sending anyone else in until we know what we're dealing with, but the intent is to search the entire area, starting with those rooms."

"What do the studio execs have to say? Have they released a statement or commented?"

"Only through their legal team, which is doing their best to derail us. They don't have a leg to stand on, though. The property isn't theirs, and we entered with probable cause. We're working on getting an FBI crew here soon to help speed up things, but it's a real shitshow over there right now, pardon my language."

Allyson waved off his apology. "Do you think my sister is inside the building?"

"We're reviewing the security footage of who came and went from the complex over the last two weeks. We haven't found any evidence pointing to her being there. I do know a third employee, Craig Guilford, has gone missing in Los Angeles. Do you know him?"

"Yes. I learned about his disappearance through Ram last night. There has to be a connection between Andrea and him, right? Not to mention Roger—even though the studio denies he's gone, too."

"Our working theory is these three knew something management didn't want them talking about."

"You mean information that could sink the company."

"Unfortunately, money is often the motive for murder."

"Murder?"

"I'm sorry. I don't mean to upset you, Ms. Marta. But the more time passes, the less likely we'll find your sister alive. I know that's harsh, but it's a statistical fact. The way this case is shaping up, with what we uncovered at the movie lot, clues are pointing to a much larger conspiracy."

Allyson patted the back of her head. "What can I do to help?"

"Honestly? Go home and let us work the case with our resources. Obviously, if you hear from Andrea or anyone else related to the studio or the missing individuals, let us know. Otherwise, we have to work our process and follow where the breadcrumbs lead us."

"Chief? They need you at the movie lot. There's been a development," a female officer stood at Jordie Sutter's office doorway.

"I'll be right there," he answered, stress lines creasing his forehead. "Can we get someone to help Ms. Marta? She needs an escort to the airport, and her belongings are locked inside her friend's vehicle outside."

"Yes, sir. Right away."

The constable stood and stretched out his hand. Allyson responded in kind. "Thank you for everything. I'll do exactly as you suggested—go home and wait for an update. Should I be worried for my safety?"

"Depends. Do you know something about H0rr Studios that no one else does?"

Allyson closed her eyes and pinched the bridge of her nose. "I guess I feel a connection to all of this because Andrea is my twin. If something affects her, it should affect me, too."

Sutter placed his warm hand on her shoulder. "My mother was a twin. I get what you mean. She often worried about such things, especially sickness. But my detective instincts tell me this whole situation is linked to the company and, more specifically, *The Caretaker* franchise. I believe you are safe, but exercise caution, and please keep in touch, either with me or with your local authorities in Seattle."

Outside, the same female officer who interrupted the constable's debriefing helped Allyson get her belongings from Ram's car. As soon as she retrieved her phone, Allyson immediately dialed her agent, Vince.

"Allyson! Where have you—"

"Vince! You need to get me the hell out of here. Now!"

25

UNEXPECTED

{ALLYSON}

"Psst, Hermana. Another suit is headed your way," Nina, the nosey neighborhood from down the hall, called through Allyson's door after a brief tap, tap, tap.

Allyson was back in her apartment, having arrived late from Vancouver the night before. Grace came a few minutes before Nina's knock, bringing along breakfast after Allyson had texted about her return. Grace wanted to know all the dirty details between her and Ram and their little getaway.

Allyson had just stuffed a bite of breakfast burrito in her mouth when Nina's warning came. "Who can it be now?" she mumbled, holding her hand over her lips as she finished chewing her food.

"Allyson Marta? It's Special Agent Irving Kingsley. May I have a word with you?"

Her shoulders sagged in relief. "He's Ram's friend," she whispered to Grace. "Do you know him?"

Grace's expression wasn't as relaxed. "Yes."

"What's with the face?"

"He's my brother—well, half-brother—different fathers. We don't speak, so this will be awk—*ward*," they sang.

"Allyson?" Irv banged on the door. "I can hear you talking. Open up. Err, please."

"Oooh. You got a *please*. You better go open the door," Grace smirked.

"Coming!" Allyson responded, chasing the food with a swig of sparkling water before standing and smoothing her tunic.

"Oh! It's you!" Irv stepped back as Allyson wrenched open the door.

"Surprise!" She giggled. "Not really Ram's new production assistant."

"Obviously."

"Surprise!" Grace drawled, coming to stand behind Allyson. "Not really Allyson's addict neighbor."

"Fuck me," Irv blurted out, slapping his hand over his mouth and shuffling back into the hallway before recovering his official stance.

"You look a little pale, Irv. You want to come in and have a seat?"

Irv and Grace made brief eye contact before he turned his attention to the floor.

"It's okay, big man. I will take myself back across the hall to my little slice of recovery paradise." Grace addressed Irv. "But listen, honey, don't think for a second you need to go anywhere or answer any questions that make you uncomfortable. You need me, you holler. You need your attorney; you walk right across the hall here and make the call. You have rights, even with the big bad FBI," they advised Allyson. Then they gave her an air kiss on each cheek before sauntering around Irv and slipping through their door.

"Come on in, Irv. What can I do for you? Is Ram okay? Although I'm pretty pissed at him, so I'm not sure I care. Well, I do care, but only to the extent that I wouldn't want anything bad to happen to him . . ." She was rambling. His countenance made her nervous. Grace's reaction made her even more nervous. "Can I get you anything? I have sparkling water, coffee . . ."

"I was actually hoping you'd come to the field office with me to answer some questions."

"Whoa. Am *I* in trouble? Is there really something wrong with Ram?"

"No, no. Ram is fine. He's still in Vancouver, covering the movie lot debacle. I guess this all makes sense now, however. You are the one he was traveling with, got too close to, and got into an argument with."

"Wow. And girls get all the shit for gossiping. Yep, you got me. We were there looking into my sister's disappearance, but you probably knew that, too."

"Well, I didn't know it was with you. I presumed it was a work thing. Strange, he kept that little detail to himself. Stranger still, I didn't put it together when you introduced yourself as Allyson the other day. I shrugged it off as a coincidence. It's a popular name. Anyway . . ." Irv trailed off. His eyes drifted around the room.

"Do you want the nickel tour?" Allyson asked as Irv wandered over to her framed photos and knickknack display.

He didn't answer her question but continued to move around the room as if he'd agreed. Unsure what he was searching for, Allyson went back to her breakfast. He was free to peruse as he wished. She had nothing to hide.

"What time did you get in last night?" Irv asked after a long silence.

"I'm sure you already know, being a Special Agent and all. But I believe it was around midnight by the time I stepped foot into my apartment. Caught the 9:45 out of Vancouver. Good thing they have flights practically every hour."

"What was the hurry to leave?"

"Vancouver? Umm, where do I begin? Ram being a fuckhead, the lack of any leads on my sister. And, oh! Haven't you heard? The movie lot is a big booby trap! But mainly, it was highly encouraged by Chief Constable Sutter. So, yeah, it didn't seem like the place to be anymore."

"Ram says his car was broken into."

"By the police. He had my stuff in his trunk. I needed it to come back. All proper laws were followed. Except for the shit he stole from Andrea."

"What do you mean . . . what did he have of Andrea's?"

"A sketch he took from her apartment."

"Can I see it?"

"If you go to her apartment. I brought it back on my way to the airport. Nobody has a right to her stuff until she's been found. Then, we'll talk about who gets what. Otherwise, what's hers is hers."

Irv smirked. "Well, I guess it will get bagged and tagged as evidence once the search warrant gets approved."

Allyson swallowed hard. "Why would you guys want to search her place now when you wouldn't do it when she was first reported missing?"

"It was a simple missing person's case. Now she's part of a criminal investigation."

"Why? What's changed?"

"The movie studio. Bodies have been found. With her and two other employees missing, there's a lot of dots begging to be connected."

"Bodies? What do you mean exactly?"

"Human remains were found in various rooms in the tunnels beneath the studio."

"Whoa," Allyson licked her lips and rubbed the back of her neck. "How many?"

"I'm told there are five thus far, in addition to the two missing patrolmen. They are still navigating, mapping, and searching the tunnel system."

Allyson whistled and shivered. "Five is a lot. Does the tunnel lead to somewhere outside the studio?"

"No word yet. Why do you ask?" Irv paused, holding Allyson's gaze.

"I don't know. I guess I was thinking about the homeless crisis in that city—really, along this whole area: Seattle, Portland. A tunnel makes for a nice place to make a home off the grid. Or maybe it was being used for something else? Human trafficking? Drugs? All of it? There's a train line right there, too. Easy access to transportation."

"Good points. I'll pass your thoughts along to the team. Which brings me to my next question . . . You said you met with the constable?"

"Yeah. To discuss my sister's case. That's how I got them to open Ram's car for me. Chief Sutter briefed me on the studio campus discovery. At the time, there were the missing police officers, and the tunnel system had been found, along with the booby traps. But I had no idea about the bodies. He told me to go home and stay out of the way, basically."

"So how did you guys wind up in the mountains if you were in Vancouver looking for your sister?"

"Following a lead. Turned out to be nothing, but it snowed, and we got stuck overnight."

"Why am I getting *The Shining* vibes?" Irv joked.

"Oh, it was nothing like that."

"You guys drove separately?"

"Obviously. Listen, where is this all going? I'm tired and would like to rest. Do you need me for something? Did you find my sister?"

"We have some leads, but we need your input."

"And you need me at a field office for that? Why is my bullshit meter reading in the red? Should I call my attorney?"

"Do you have one?"

"Silly question. You know who I am. My family has many attorneys at our disposal. Do I need one or not?"

"You're not under arrest. Therefore, Miranda does not apply, but if you feel more comfortable having counsel present, please make the call."

"I'd like to think I can trust you since you're Ram's friend. Not to mention Grace's half-brother! Hello? When was someone going to tell me?"

"I was unaware he . . . err . . . *they* lived here or had any connection to you."

"That does not instill confidence in me as far as the FBI is concerned if you have no idea where your own family is." Allyson crossed her hands over her chest and cocked her hip.

"With Andrea's case being lumped into the overarching investigation, it has allowed us more access to things than before. I need you to verify some records and give a statement. It has to be official. Ergo, it needs to be at our offices. If you'd like representation, you have the right to do so, but time is of the essence. As far as Andrea is concerned, too much of it has already gone by. The faster we can get answers, the closer we get to finding her."

Allyson puffed out her cheeks and rubbed the top of her head. Her short hair's velvety texture was soothing against her hand's palm. It had the same effect as a lovey might have with a baby. "All right, I'll come. But it'll be on my terms. I'm not riding in your car. I'm taking my control back. Too much has slipped in the last few days. Give me the address," Allyson demanded.

Irv pulled out a business card and pen, scribbled something on the back, and handed it to her. "Be there in an hour."

"No 'please, and thank you?' If you are trying to play your hand close to your chest, you give it all away with this tough demeanor. I've done nothing wrong, yet I feel like suddenly I'm a suspect for something."

"I'm just doing my job, Allyson. This whole fiasco is grating my nerves. The fact we all seem connected in one way or another is even more jarring. You have to appreciate the position I'm in."

"Back at ya, pal. I thought you were a friend—an ally. Now I get the sense I got it all wrong. But I'll come and answer your questions. I can't guarantee it will be in an hour. I have to see if someone on our legal team is available first."

"Why don't you call now while I'm still here? It will make me feel better about leaving without you and cover my ass should you decide to also . . . disappear."

Allyson rolled her eyes, grabbed her phone off the table by her break-fast plate, and scrolled through her contacts.

"Hello, this is Allyson Marta. I'm going to need an attorney here in Seattle—and within the next hour."

26

ATTICUS KING

{ALLYSON}

Allyson paced in her small apartment, wringing her hands and nibbling on a hangnail. When that didn't calm her nerves, she went to Grace's place and paced there.

"Wanna get high?" Grace offered.

"More than anything. But I think I need to keep a clear head for whatever the FBI might spring on me. I know they are going to have some surprises. The way Irv was acting, it's like he's got a smoking gun he's going to nail me with."

"In regards to what? Your sister? Does such a thing exist?"

"No way. I haven't done anything wrong—at least, not related to this crap with Andrea and H0rr Studios. I mean, I'm no saint, but I'm not a criminal either. They are wasting their time investigating the wrong person."

Allyson's phone vibrated in her back pocket. "Hello?"

"Ms. Marta, this is Marv, the building superintendent."

"Hi, Marv."

"There is a man here at the door. He says he's your attorney. Would you like me to let him up?"

"No. I'll come down, thanks." Allyson slid her phone back into her pocket and embraced Grace. "Wish me luck! The attorney is here. I'll have him bring me to Irv and get this shit over with."

"You let me know the minute you are on your way back, you hear? And if I can help in any way . . . like disappear my brother . . . or anything . . . you let me know."

Allyson held Grace's hands for a minute, her lip trembling slightly before she pulled herself together. "I've got this. Hell, I've stared death in the face. Four times! This is nothing."

"Damn right. Go get 'em, guuurrrllll!" Grace purred, swatting Allyson playfully on the ass as she turned to leave.

Allyson yelped and giggled, dashing out the door and down the stairs to an awaiting SUV with dark-tinted windows. A driver stood outside and opened the back door for her. As she climbed in, an authoritative, baritone voice spoke.

"Hello, Allyson. It's nice to meet you in person finally. I'm Atticus King."

As her eyes adjusted to the change in light, she let out an audible gasp. "Is this a fucking joke?" She fumbled for the door handle, ready to jump out.

"Unfortunately, no. But please remain calm, and I will explain why I'm here to assist you."

"Start talking, or I'm calling the police," she warned, pulling her phone from her pocket.

"I know you recognize my name from my work with H0rr Studios, but I actually work for your father. You are safe in my care, and to prove it to you, I will explain how I've been in the shadows working to protect you from the beginning."

The car started to move as if on cue. For a moment, only the heartbeat in her ears and the vehicle's engine were discernable.

"I've been working for H0rr Studios since shortly after your sister Andrea was hired ten years ago. Your father wanted protections in place should anything go wrong."

Allyson barked a dry laugh as she crossed her arms over her chest and raised her eyes to the car's ceiling. "You mean, he needed a fixer for when she got caught doing something, like, say, murder?"

Atticus mirrored Allyson's previous reaction with a dry laugh. "Well, now, I can't speak to your father's motivations. I only know what I was hired for—to protect his daughter's interests and his considerable investment in the company."

"Wait. What? Pa invested in H0rr Studios?"

"Oh, yes. He's the majority shareholder. I believe his total ownership is around 65 percent. So, you see, it benefits him to have a man on the inside representing him. That's me. I have also kept tabs on you since I'm based in the area. I'm sorry for your mental health struggles this last year. But you seem to have a great team behind you this time. I'm especially hopeful about your budding relationship with Ram Helm, everyone's favorite investigative reporter. And I'm incredibly excited to see your latest art installation at the Space Needle!"

Allyson sat with her mouth open and her mind spinning with Atticus' revelations.

"Are you okay, Dear? You appear unwell."

"I'm fine. I just need some air and a minute."

"Certainly," Atticus replied, reaching across from her to press the window control button, then behind their seats to grab a can of her favorite sparkling water. "How about some water?" he asked, grinning.

Allyson shivered as he handed it to her. "How did you know?"

"About what, Dear?"

"The water. How did you know my favorite brand and flavor?"

"Your father has little spies everywhere. He harbors tremendous guilt for not being more directly involved in your lives but feels his distance is for the best. It doesn't mean he doesn't love you both and wants to provide for you in any way he can. This water, me, we are a little piece of Anselmo's efforts to remind you of his love."

"A phone call or a Christmas card would work just as well," Allyson mumbled as she sipped her drink.

"What's that?"

"Nothing. So, you have worked for the studio for ten years while keeping tabs on our careers."

"Careers. Personal lives. All of it. If it appeared you needed help and I could provide it, I did so."

"How?"

"Well, we can start from today. At present, I'm here to guide you through this interview with FBI Special Agent Irving Kingsley. These last weeks, I've sent you Detective Davidson regarding your sister's disappearance and arranged for your apartment to be swept for bugs with 'Burns Pest Control.' I also sent those same men to help with the Roger situation at the hotel, although that was more for the studio. Most recently, they were directed to perform one final errand at a cabin in the woods, where, unfortunately, there was an incident with a gun."

Allyson inhaled sharply, choking on her water.

"Oh, my goodness. Are you all right?"

She swiped the back of her hand across her mouth. "What was the errand at the cabin?"

"I'm afraid I can't say right now. I suspect Agent Kingsley will have questions about your Vancouver stay."

"Am I a murderer too?"

"I don't know, Dear. Have you intentionally taken someone's life?"

"Absolutely not. But I did shoot a weapon recently, which is currently in the glove box of a car registered to my sister, parked in a public lot a block from her apartment."

"Good to know. Was the handgun registered to you?"

"No. I found it in the same place I left it. I'm assuming it was Andrea's. I only used it for protection. To scare an intruder off."

"Naturally, Dear. One owns such a weapon precisely for protecting their person and property."

Allyson swallowed hard, then rubbed her eyes. "Why would there be bugs in my apartment?"

"H0rr Studios has been secretly under investigation by various federal agencies for at least five years. Their recent decision to move production to Iceland didn't help matters. Think of the financial impact on our country's economy! Certain decision-makers are not pleased. With your father being the majority owner and your sister missing, their next natural move would be to look at you. 'What do you know? Do you have any knowledge they can use to help their cause?' It's what I would do in their shoes. Thus I came up with a little ruse so as not to raise suspicion and had my team search for surveillance devices. I do feel bad about all the drama it caused, however. Many of your fellow residents are in precarious positions with their recovery journeys, and any disruption to their routines could set them back."

"Seems like you know a lot about mental health treatment," Allyson commented while remaining silent on Atticus' revelations.

"I have some experience, yes."

"Do you know where my sister is? And Roger? Craig? What about the fiasco at the studio?"

"Let's discuss those things after our interview. While giving your statement, any current knowledge you have is impeachable. Afterward is a different story."

"I understand. Do you know what they are looking for with this interview? Irv was acting like I was a suspect."

"I don't know specifics, but I imagine there are circumstantial connections with you and the studio. Under certain contexts, they might look dubious."

"Do you think Ram threw me under the bus? The sketch he had in his car . . . he obviously thought it was important if he took it and hid it from me. All he had to do was ask if he could take it. I let him go through all her other crap. I don't get it."

"It's probably all a misunderstanding. If he found evidence he thought was damning against her, it could inadvertently hurt you. Therefore, he would hide it to protect you. This is only conjecture on my part, but he really is a decent fellow. I checked into him the minute I learned you might be working together regarding Andrea's disappearance. We all have a few skeletons in our closet, but his are more like cobwebs—a righteous fellow with a keen moral compass. How rare and refreshing! If you can see past the last few days . . ."

"Are you seriously shipping on us right now? Do you have a couple name already picked out? Ramyson, perhaps?"

Atticus chuckled. "Well, he's obviously a better choice than, let's say, Roger or the tattoo artist from the Reservation. Or your agent's sister. She was *unpleasant*."

"Oh. My. God! What don't you know about me?"

"Very little. And it appears we are here. Hold onto your anger. It will help you get through this process quicker. Whenever you feel uncomfortable with a question or are unsure how to answer, all you have to do is ask me. Not them. Me. I am here as your guide and counselor. Because even though they aren't charging you with anything, Miranda technically applies. Anything you say can and will be used against you."

27

EXCULPATORY EVIDENCE

{ALLYSON}

Security greeted Allyson and Atticus the minute they entered the non-descript two-story brick building along Lake Washington's shore in a quaint Seattle suburb.

"IDs out. Empty your pockets and place any possessions in these tubs—just like the airport. Laptops and electronics go in a separate container. You can keep your shoes on, but jackets off. They'll print a visitor badge for you once you are cleared here. Head through the metal detector and await further instructions. Next!" A tall, fit, middle-aged man directed visitors. He repeated the instructions to every other person in the short line.

"Do you think he gets a headache from repeating himself all day?" Atticus whispered to Allyson, who stood in front of him.

"I imagine he murmurs it in his sleep," she giggled. When the man in question frowned, she stood taller, squaring her shoulders and pursing her lips. Yet a slight tremble in her upper body couldn't hide her amusement.

"Sorry. It's a nervous reaction."

"Why would you be nervous, Dear?" Atticus grinned. "It's the FBI. Now, if it were the IRS, I'd be worried. Those people are the Devil's handmaids."

Allyson giggled more before covering her mouth. This place obviously took itself seriously with its rules and regulations.

Once their IDs were returned and temporary badges hung around their necks, they were greeted by Special Agent Irving Kingsley.

"Thank you for coming, Allyson. I see you brought representation. Wise choice. We'll be down the hall here." He waved his hand, indicating they should follow him. "Come in. Come in. Have a seat," Irv encouraged. He even gave a slight smile.

Atticus held out his arm to Allyson, like an encouraging gesture her father might make to get her to join in the fun.

"Before we get started, I must inform you that our session is being recorded with video and audio through the cameras there and there," Irv pointed to a ceiling-mounted camera in each corner of the room across from Allyson and Atticus. "Can I get you anything to drink?"

They declined refreshments and sat. Atticus placed his briefcase on the table, making a show of opening it and pulling out a legal pad and a shiny gold pen. It was an intimidation technique he employed often. The open case also served as a screen between them and Irv should they need a moment to confer in privacy.

"Can you state your names and titles for the record?" Irv asked.

"Allyson Maria Flores Marta. No title. Unless mixed media artist and identical twin count?"

"Good Enough. And you, sir?"

"Atticus King. Attorney at law and legal representation for Ms. Marta."

Irv's mouth curved into a sneer, and he snapped his fingers. "Now I recognize you. I thought you represented H0rr Studios?"

"I do! And many others."

"You've had your hands full lately," Irv probed.

Atticus tsked. "Such is life for someone in my position." Then he flashed Irv a wide smile. "Now, how can my client assist the FBI, Agent Kingsley?"

A banker's box sat on the table's corner with its lid off. All three glanced at it before Irv stammered, "Right. Well, let's get to it, shall we?" He slapped his hands together and rubbed them back and forth as if warming himself over a fire. "I asked Allyson here today to clarify a few points regarding this growing case involving H0rr Studios. How fortuitous we scored a bonus with your presence, Mr. King."

"Just so," Atticus inclined his head.

"For the record, due to the discovery of human remains and the deaths of multiple police officers at the movie lot rented by H0rr Studios, its three employees' missing person cases have been lumped in with the larger criminal investigation. As such, we secured a subpoena for their electronic records, including phone logs, banking transactions, travel, etc. It's standard procedure to examine whom a victim may have contacted prior to the inciting incident."

"To clarify, *for the record*, you're saying the FBI is pursuing these individuals' disappearances as crimes because you believe they are part of a bigger conspiracy?" Atticus asked.

"That's the question we hope to answer today."

"Through me?" Allyson asked, her voice raised in a pitch higher than her normal range. "What do I know that you all don't?!"

"While researching each missing person's phone records, we found a startling coincidence." Irv pulled out a file folder from the banker box, opened it, and set three pieces of paper on the table for her and Atticus to peruse.

"This first page shows Andrea's cell phone records from twenty-four hours before her missing persons report was filed . . . by you, Mr. King. Isn't that right?"

"I was acting on behalf of my client's interest and concern for an employee's well-being."

"Undoubtedly. Anyway, Allyson, I've highlighted a section on this first document. Can you confirm whether this is your phone number?"

"Yes, it's mine."

"Do you recall talking to your sister for five minutes twenty-four hours before she was reported missing?"

"I did talk to my sister the week I moved into the residence building . . . where you came by earlier today. I don't remember the exact date, and I couldn't pinpoint a specific timeline because I wasn't immediately alerted to her disappearance. But five minutes seems long for us."

"What did you guys talk about?" Irv asked, tapping his fingers on the table.

"I don't know. Probably how I was done with in-patient treatment and my shitty new place."

"She didn't mention her plans over the coming days?"

"If she had, this would all be moot, now, wouldn't it? She's spontaneous and unorganized. Except with work."

"All right. This next document is Roger's cellphone activity on the day he was arrested at the airport. Can you read the highlighted section aloud?"

"Encrypted message sent to my cellphone number via the *Doojigger* app."

"Can you tell me what the message said?"

"Obviously, that is protected information," Atticus interjected.

"I'm aware. But we are asking her to provide the information *voluntarily*," Irv replied. "Allyson? Can you share what Roger sent and maybe a little context as to why he would send *you* a message?"

Allyson scratched her cheek and cleared her throat. A peek at Atticus revealed him inclining his head imperceptibly. She had to trust the advisor her father sent her, so she pulled out her phone and scrolled to the appropriate app. "Roger said, 'An Albatross is found at sea. Love from your former devotee.' I wasn't sure what he meant, and because it was wildly obscure, I didn't reply. Later, I remembered there was this guy on social media who went by the handle Albatross69. He would constantly spam my posts. He was nothing but an Internet troll. He eventually stopped, and I forgot about it. When Roger used 'Albatross,' it threw me because it's such an unusual word. It was the only thing I could think of. But it made zero sense. I figured he was drunk, and it was all nonsense. Thus I ignored it and didn't receive anything else because he was arrested, and the rest is history."

"But why would Roger message you and use the word 'love?'"

Allyson puffed out her cheeks and referred to Atticus for approval. Again, he tipped his head in reassurance. "We were friends. Friends with benefits. For those listening who don't know what I mean . . . We had sex periodically. He wanted it to be serious. I did not."

Irv Adam's apple bobbed as he swallowed several times. He cleared his throat and sipped some water before speaking again. "Why didn't you want it to be serious?"

"Uh, duh. He was fucking my sister as well and worked with her 24/7. He wanted us both but for different reasons. He leaned towards me being the favorite, however, because I didn't need him. He loved the chase, where I like variety. I've never been keen on monogamy. I guess I share that with my sister. I've been told it's part of having borderline personality disorder. Who knows. But yeah, there it is. I'm a slut who slept with my sister's boyfriend. Satisfied?"

Irv pulled another folder from the box. "Can you identify this footwear?" He slid a photo toward Allyson.

She held out a shaky hand. "Ye . . . yes. They are Roger's. He fancies himself a fashion icon and has an impressive footwear collection. But these have been damaged. I bet he's pissed. What's inside them?" She lifted the photo to inspect it closer.

"Unfortunately, these trainers, men's size twelve, washed ashore two nights ago on Jedediah Island—the feet still inside. We're waiting on DNA confirmation, but we were able to authenticate ownership of this particular version through the designer."

"Oh my God!" Allyson shouted, throwing the photo back at Irv and covering her mouth with both hands. "How did this happen? I thought the studio sequestered him, right, Atticus?"

"Yeah, Atticus. Didn't Vanessa Rapaporte say in a statement that he was under the studio's supervision until his court date? What happened at the hotel? You left before I could question you and his security detail."

Atticus narrowed his eyes. "I'm afraid you are mistaken. We were questioned by an agent, Stephan Ackerman, and released. I have his card right here." He reached into the briefcase and, after a moment of shuffling folders and papers, produced a business card. "Afterward, I met with Vanessa, who reasoned that issuing a denial would keep the Givers from losing their heads and interfering with your investigation. It's a common tactic. Now, Agent Kingsley, I'd like a short recess with my client to allow her to put this new information into perspective properly."

"Allyson?" Irv asked. "Do you need a break?"

She rubbed her eye and sucked in a quick breath. "No. No. I'm fine. Well, I'm sad and confused and reeling. But I want to get whatever this is over with. I'll process everything in private later."

"Good. Moving on. Did you travel to Vancouver, British Columbia, recently?"

"Yes."

"And what was the purpose of your visit?"

"It was Ram's idea. He was helping me with Andrea's case. Didn't seem like the police were doing enough. He suggested the best place to find a clue might be there, where she lived and worked."

"So you visited her apartment?"

"Yes."

"And how did you gain access? Did you have keys?"

"I simply asked the concierge."

"Did you pretend to be your sister?"

"Are you going to pull my picture from that box? Because if you do, you better have Ram's too. *We* asked the doorman to let us in. He obliged, and Ram tipped him. We nosed about and left."

"Right. Okay. Did you find any indicator pointing to her whereabouts?"

"No."

"Nothing?"

"Correct."

"Why did you travel to the mountains after searching Andrea's apartment?"

Allyson slumped in her chair and crossed her arms.

"Asked and answered, Agent Kingsley. They were pursuing leads in her sister's disappearance," Atticus interjected.

"We're trying to establish a timeline of Ms. Marta's whereabouts while she was in Vancouver."

"Then you should be asking 'when,' not 'why.'"

"It's fine, Atticus. I found my sister's handbag, keys, wallet—everything—in her apartment. Ram suggested we check her car. It's one of those fancy electric ones. He thought going through her previous destinations might give us a lead. And it did, bringing us into the mountains, about two hours northeast of the city boundary."

"Where exactly?"

"A log home."

"This log home? The one owned by your sister?" Irv asked, pulling yet another file from the seemingly magic box and fanning out a new set of photos.

Allyson gasped. "When were these taken?" She raised one, showing a smoldering pile of rubble, and studied it. Then, she grabbed another, an aerial view date stamped three years before, and compared the two. Several more displayed property damage from various angles.

"This morning. A logger making his way through the mountain pass with a full load observed a significant amount of smoke through the trees and called it in. By the time support crews arrived, the place was a total loss. Fortunately, they were able to stave off its spread to the forest."

"I don't believe it! Before I left, I made sure the lights were off, and the door was secure."

"So, you were the last one to leave?"

"Yes, but . . ."

"You have no idea how a fire could've started? For example, did she have a wood-burning fireplace?"

"Yes, but I checked it. There were no live coals, and it was screened."

"You didn't leave a stove burner on accidentally or an iron plugged in?"

Allyson scoffed. "There was no food in the house, and look at me. Do I look like I iron?"

"How did you get back to Vancouver?"

"She had a second vehicle there. I drove it back and went straight to her apartment. Ram still had Andrea's electric car."

"You went straight to Andrea's apartment?"

"Actually, I was going to. But I left my weekend bag and passport in Ram's trunk. We hadn't planned to spend the night at the cabin. But due to the storm, we chose to play it safe. So before I went to her place, I went to Ram's car."

"And that's how you wound up at the police station and met with Chief Constable Jordie Sutter?"

"Yes."

"Did you only take what was yours from Ram's vehicle?"

Allyson clicked her tongue against her teeth. "I took my bag and a drawing Ram stole without my knowledge."

"A drawing? From where?"

"Yeah. A sketch of a tattoo. It must have been from Andrea's apartment."

"This tattoo?"

"Jesus. Is that another foot? What the fuck, Irv!"

"Yes. I'm sorry. This one belonged to Billy Walls. He was the Nisqually Tribe member whose remains were found two weeks ago and identified based on this custom tattoo. Is this the same art as the sketch you claim was your sister's?"

"It's hard to say if it's the *exact* design, but based on my recollection, it is similar."

"Where is the sketch now?"

"I brought it back to Andrea's place. Ram had no right taking anything without asking first."

"Do you recognize this photo?"

"Oh, for fuck's sake, Irv? Where are you going with this?" Allyson jumped up and paced the room.

"Well, that got a reaction. What about this photo is troubling?"

"It's not the photo!" Allyson spat. "It's this—*interrogation*! I don't see how these questions lead to finding my sister. Or Roger's killer—because I'm assuming if you have a picture of his feet, he's dead."

"We can't find your sister or Roger if we don't have all the data. Now tell me about this photo!"

Allyson thrust her arms in the air. "What does it look like?! It's a mask—one from my *Pretense* collection. I did a show in Vancouver with them about five years ago. Why? What does this have to do with anything?"

"Before falling to their death, a police officer at the studio mentioned a scary mask as they radioed for help. A broken totem mask, to be specific.

They said, 'Don't let the broken totem mask get me.' Sounds pretty similar to this one, don't you think?"

"Seriously, Irv? This is such bullshit." They locked eyes for a moment. "The whole collection consisted of twelve masks, representing various cultures from around the world. I was showcasing how we, as humans, no matter where we live, wear them to hide our true selves or to become someone else. I have no idea what the officer would be referring to."

"Where is the mask now?"

"Sold. The night of the show. They all did."

"By the same buyer?"

"No. I don't know. My agent Vince would be able to tell you."

"Do you know who bought this particular one?"

Allyson rolled her head from side to side to stretch her neck, then fidgeted with the photo. "Roger. It was Roger who bought it. We met for the first time that night in a rather awkward way. You can use your imagination—identical twin to his current lover. And . . . well . . . he purchased it as an apology for the misunderstanding. He always kept it on display in his Vancouver apartment as a reminder of our 'meet cute.' I don't see how any of this is relevant."

"I, too, am failing to see how these things are connected to the overall investigation into the crimes committed *against* the studio and its employees, Agent Kingsley. How do you think Allyson is involved exactly?" Atticus asked.

"She seems to be the one connection to everything. Including Billy Walls's feet."

"Because my sister sketched a design similar to his tattoo? You're really reaching, aren't you, *Special Agent*."

"No. Because he was Albatross69."

"What?" Allyson choked.

"These records confirm his social handle. Can you explain how your sister would have a sketch of an intimate part of a potential victim, one who Internet bullied and taunted you for years?"

"Are you saying he was murdered? I thought the Salish Sea feet phenomenon was deemed a naturally occurring event from people committing suicide and boating accidents."

"The only natural part is how the body decomposes in the water. How the victim got there remains open to interpretation."

"I had no idea they knew each other. But I can guess how they might have met. Bowe Bird. He's Nisqually and a very talented tattoo artist. We all met on the Seattle party circuit years ago when Andrea first moved back here from Atlanta. Through Andrea, Bowe eventually met Roger and inked several tattoos for him. He even did one for all three of them, Andrea, Roger, and Craig, to commemorate their time together on *Caretaker* earlier this year. He probably inked Billy Walls too, by the looks of it. By the way, Bowe helped me create the totem mask you think is connected. Maybe it's him you should be talking to! Stop wasting my time—time you should be spending on finding a kidnapper and a killer."

A knock sounded from outside the door.

"Excuse me a minute," Irv said, wiping sweat from his brow as he rushed out.

"I bet he's grateful for a reprieve. If the art world ever becomes a bore for you, you should consider becoming an attorney, Allyson! Bravo! If I were a betting man, which I'm not because games of chance are not games of chance at all, I would say you have them squirming, and I can't help but enjoy this a little."

Allyson groaned, stood, and stretched her arms over her head. "I can't believe Roger might be dead, and Irv knows my dirty little secret about him. Imagine Ram's reaction when he finds out! At one point, I told him I suspected Roger had killed Andrea before attempting to leave the country. I feel terrible."

"You have to admit, this all feels like a plot to a *Caretaker* season," Atticus mused.

"Seriously," Allyson agreed.

"Do you think we can go soon? I'm starving. I never finished breakfast and have a meeting with Vince to review the labyrinth installation this evening."

The door swung open abruptly, and Irv strolled back in. His face was ashen.

"What is it?" Allyson asked. "What's wrong?"

He held up his finger. "I have one final point to clarify," Irv said as he rifled through the pages on the table. "Ah. Here we go. You posted this photo the night Craig Guilford disappeared. Can you read me the highlighted comment, please?"

Allyson glanced at the photo and smiled. "It says, 'All obstacles vanish from my path.' I love Craig. He's such a spiritual guy. Many layers."

"What exactly does he mean?"

"It's an affirmation based on Zen philosophy. When trying to manifest a goal or an experience, it's hard to envision yourself as the person you need to become if you are overwhelmed with how-tos and what-ifs. My post was about my labyrinth project and how we can get lost along life's journey. He replied with this perfect affirmation."

"But how do you know Craig?"

"Aside from him working with my sister for the last ten years? We share the same agent, Vince Sasso. Craig is an amazing photographer on top of being a cinematographer. I introduced him to Vince at my show in Vancouver, and they hit it off. They've been working together ever since. So naturally, we follow each other's work and have even shown pieces in the same galleries before. We do *not* have the same relationship Roger and I had—in case you want to go there."

"You have no idea where he could be or what motive he'd have to disappear?"

"I mean . . . he had financial difficulties with an ex-wife and their kids always needing money for something . . . grad school, weddings, rehab, etc. But I don't think it was anything he couldn't handle."

"On a related note, I hope you can handle what I'm about to tell you."

"What? What is it?"

Atticus stood abruptly. "Dear, maybe you should take a seat."

"No. Uh-uh," Allyson murmured, shaking her head. "Just spit it out, Irv. My nerves can't take any more dramatic pauses."

"It's Andrea. Her body was found in Palm Springs an hour ago."

"No!" she interlocked her fingers on her head and gazed at the ceiling. "Are you sure it's her?"

"She was a guest at an exclusive wellness resort where privacy is all but guaranteed. It appears she overdosed. We won't know for certain until the toxicology report comes back. They'll perform an autopsy and interview the resort employees who had contact with her. However, the preliminary findings show there was no foul play. She was found alone and in possession of the drug."

"A wellness resort? What a load of horse shit. Andrea wouldn't be caught dead . . ." Allyson inhaled sharply. "This can't be . . . this can't be happening. I can't catch my . . ." Her eyes rolled back as her knees buckled, and her body went limp. Atticus dove forward and caught her before she hit the floor.

"Get Dr. Dean Santoli on the phone, now!" Atticus snapped.

Irv stood cemented in place.

"Agent Kingsley!"

"There's more."

"Well, obviously, now is the wrong time for surprises. The poor girl needs help!" Atticus yelled, gently laying Allyson on the floor, her head propped in his lap.

"Craig Guilford. He was found about an hour ago with what appears to be a self-inflicted gunshot wound to the head in the hills above his LA home."

28

WHAT DOESN'T KILL YOU

{ALLYSON}

D r. Dean stood at the foot of Allyson's hospital bed, his hands stuffed in his pants pockets, eyes fixed on her. Dressed in a gray suit with a white button-down underneath, he left the top two buttons undone, revealing tanned flesh. A troubled pout framed his face, hiding Allyson's favorite dimple.

"There she is!"

Allyson looked around dazedly. Dr. Dean's image seemed pixelated, like when the Internet signal goes out while streaming a favorite TV show. He came back into focus for a second, then blurred. Another second—he was jumbled again. When her vision sharpened for a third time, it was not Dr. Dean but Andrea standing there.

"I knew you'd come," Allyson murmured, her speech slurred from the sedative wearing off.

"It's time to make things right, Allyson," Andrea replied.

"Wait . . . What am I supposed to do?"

"Expose them. Lay it all bare. I should pay. We should all pay . . ."
Andrea faded, and Dr. Dean reappeared.

"You're the only patient I'd leave a date for," Dr. Dean's eyes sparkled.
"I understand you've had an absolute shock. How are you feeling?"

Allyson rubbed her face. "How do you think? Like part of me is dead."
She sat upright in the bed. "You had a date? How do you have time for a love
life? And why do I have a fucking IV in my arm? Is this necessary?"

"It is the fastest way to get medicine into you, should the need arise,"
he fidgeted.

"Whatever happened to the old needle in the ass? Always seemed to
do the trick."

"Not in my facilities," Dr. Dean replied, affronted.

Allyson rolled her eyes. "I want it out. Now tell me, what do
you know?"

"About what?"

"Don't play with me, Doc. I'm not in the mood. What did Irv tell you?"

"Ah. Right. Actually, Atticus King was the one who called me and
explained the circumstances. What a surprise it was to learn Mr. King rep-
resents you! And the FBI was questioning you? I was thrown for a second.
Anyway, I had them call an ambulance and transport you here. The EMTs
gave you a light sedative during transport, at my direction, which is wearing
off now," he said, pulling his sleeve back to reveal his watch.

"I gathered as much," Allyson groaned.

"While we waited for you to wake, Mr. King told me what happened.
He explained how Andrea was at a therapeutic retreat in Palm Springs run
by a well-known PhD, Dr. Bouchard. I'm familiar with his program. It's
highly regarded and *very* exclusive, with a year's waiting list. Apparently,
Roger and Vanessa Rapaporte both spent time there in the past. Andrea
was only halfway through treatment and was struggling mentally. We don't

know much more at this time because her therapy and their protocols are protected health information."

Allyson swallowed with difficulty. "Can I get a drink? I've got cottonmouth bad."

"Certainly. Here." Dr. Dean handed her a cup with a lid and straw.

As she sipped the cool liquid, the car ride with Atticus came to mind. "My father? Did Atticus call Pa?"

"I'm sure he did. He was here for a time, but he had to leave. He said he'd reach out soon. How are you really feeling?"

"Numb," she moaned.

"There's more if you want to hear it."

"Hit me while I'm down, Doc. It's the only way to take it," she smiled, but her lips quivered with the effort.

Dr. Dean told her about Craig.

"Jesus. What a mess. I can't wrap my head around how all three are gone—in a blink." She snapped her fingers. "Am I on a hold here, or can I go home?"

"Well, I'd like you to stay twenty-four hours to make sure you're stable. We can talk. Maybe even have a session with a grief support group?"

"I want to go home . . . well, I know the residence is not *home* . . . but it's my safe place. I want to be there right now. I need familiar surroundings, cuddling with Grace on the couch, binge-watching TV. I want pizza, ice cream, and a hot shower. I need time to process everything. Although deep down, I knew this is how it would end. You know, I felt great for a day or two after we talked about living life without Andrea's constant presence. Vince, my agent, said I was tethered. Flighty but grounded. I need to get there again so I can finish this project and deal with what's to come. I'm sure Pa is already making arrangements. I don't know how it will all play out or if Andrea even had an end-of-life plan."

"I get your need for safety and comfort during this time. However, I need assurance you will be safe from yourself and your thoughts. How can I do my job if you are not where I am?"

"I will go crazy here, Dr. Dean. Any meds you give me or talk therapy I participate in will only mask the pain. I need to feel it and sit with it. Let it sink in. And if I delay this installation project any further, they'll cut me out altogether."

"You can't worry about what you can't control, Allyson. Your health is way more important . . ."

"Than my career? Who am I without my art, especially with Andrea gone? My entire self-identity is tied to what I do and my twindom. Take them both away, and I'll have nothing—be nothing."

Dr. Dean stumbled backward as if Allyson had struck him. "Did I hear you right? Have you finally decided that being an identical twin is who you are despite how others see you?"

Allyson shrugged. "You're the head shrink. You tell me. What does this mean? Am I cured? Can I go?"

Dr. Dean opened his mouth to answer when Vince popped in. "Oh, my sweet Allyson. What are we going to do?" he cried. "With Craig gone too, I'm ruined!" He rushed to her side and gathered her hands into his as real tears leaked from his eyes.

"Why are you ruined, Vince?"

"Haven't you seen the news? They practically branded you the Zodiac Killer by connecting you to the three missing H0rr Studio employees and that other poor indigenous fellow, Billy Something. Holger is beside himself and wants to put as much distance between you and the Space Needle installation as possible."

"Wait. What? Who is reporting—oh, never mind. I know exactly who. That sonofabitch!" she sat up and swung her legs over the side of the bed. She attempted to stand, but Vince and the IV pole were in her way.

"Whoa, Allyson, relax." Dr. Dean moved to prevent her from toppling Vince. "How did you even know she was here?" he turned to Vince.

"Oh. Atticus called me. I told them at reception I was her older brother." Vince rubbed his bald head and smirked, his eyes still glistening with tears.

"Get out of the damn way, Vince." Allyson continued to struggle. "And don't you tell me how to feel, Dr. Dean!" Allyson snapped. "I just said art is my whole world. Now someone I trusted is throwing me under the bus in the most public way as an obvious grab for ratings and a career boost? I won't stand for it!"

"What will you do?"

"I don't know! Kick his ass? That feels like a good start! I'll get Grace to help," Allyson gestured to Vince, who smiled and clapped his hands.

"In a giant bowl of Jell-O, please," he added.

"Ram's report is already out there. The best you can do is not react. Let's call Atticus and see if he can *legally* finesse the situation," Dr. Dean suggested.

"I'm sure Ram covered his ass by saying I'm only a suspect. Leave it to the nightly news to taint the jury pool and try me in the open court of public opinion while hiding behind free speech! Some investigative reporter he is! How can Irv get away with constantly leaking info to him? The FBI knows I'm only guilty by association. Meaning I'm acquainted with people who work at H0rr Studios. That would make Vince guilty, and probably you too, Dr. Dean!"

"You should call Ram and demand he make this right. We could lose our biggest career opportunity yet due to his irresponsible reporting," Vince suggested.

"Great idea, Vince. Allyson, you could have Atticus demand retraction," Dr. Dean added.

"Didn't you just say the cat's already out of the bag?" Allyson retorted. "Opinions have already been formed, I'm sure. Admitting any error or fault will only make people think he was forced to say it, not because it's the truth. He has built his reputation on delivering factual information. No, the only way to fix this is to solve the mystery of who is behind these heinous crimes or create an even bigger story to suffocate the one with me in it. What that is, I have no idea. First, though, I need to leave. Dr. Dean? Can I? Please? And Vince, can you see if Holger Beitin will meet with us? I can assure him I am neither a suspect nor a criminal. Atticus could help. We can spin it that no publicity is bad, right? I mean, when Roger pulled shit, it made him a household name."

Vince looked to Dr. Dean, who frowned.

"Vince is my witness. If you let me go and I harm myself, no one will hold you liable. I am not in an emergent state right now. Definitely in shock but otherwise stable. You've done everything in your power, minus asserting an involuntary hold on me, which doesn't apply in this situation. I know, thanks to my past experience."

Dr. Dean exhaled loudly and pinched the bridge of his nose. "Okay, fine. You can go. But you call me or someone close to you *immediately* if you feel any telltale signs you want to hurt yourself. We will get you the help you need."

"For the first time in a long time, I have purpose. It's weird. I feel in control."

"I see you believe it, and I'm willing to grant you leeway. Many people need a catalyst in their lives to recognize how powerful they truly are. Maybe losing Andrea is that catalyst for you," Dr. Dean remarked. His brows drew together, and he bowed his head. "I'll go print the paperwork and have a nurse come to remove the IV."

"I'll call Holger and see when he's willing to meet," Vince added, following the doctor out.

"Hey, can you get me my phone first? I want to call Atticus," Allyson shouted after them.

"No need, Dear. I am here," Atticus announced, sweeping into her room past a startled Vince. "Now, let's get you home. Hospitals are up there with the IRS on my scale of disturbing places."

Several hours later, Atticus and Allyson were heading back to her apartment in a quiet, somber car.

"Are you sure you are well?" Atticus asked. "Mr. Beitin is a formidable adversary. This is a lot to process for anyone."

"I accept the things I cannot change," Allyson groaned. "We tried our best, but he had us dead to rights on the contractual stuff, and you know it. They've been bleeding money on this project, and the city is none too happy about the delays. Thank you for your efforts."

"I have an idea but need time to work through the details. All is not lost yet," Atticus assured her as his phone alerted him to an incoming message. "Hrm," he grunted.

"What is it?"

"Do you recognize this?" he asked, handing her his phone.

"Well, it looks like Andrea's handwriting, but I can't make out—wait! Ha! It's our twin language in handwriting. If you sound out the letters . . . Where did you get this?"

"I had an associate in Palm Springs verify the story the FBI gave us. They secured this journal from Andrea's room. The writing is unique. You can decipher it?"

"Yeah. It says, 'stupid fucking therapy.' Can't have therapy without a journal!" Allyson rolled her eyes and giggled. "I have a storage unit filled with them. Can we get it here?"

"It should arrive later this evening. Could you go through it and make sure it doesn't expose the studio or your father in any way?"

"Sure. But if I'm the only one who can decode it, what does that matter?"

"Risk. Exposure."

"Right. Will do. But why the rapid change in demeanor? You're making me nervous."

"I'm sorry. That's not my intent. However, there is a more serious matter to address. As you know, I am employed by your father and, therefore, by you, which establishes attorney-client privilege."

"Oh, no. Not you, too. I didn't do anything! I swear!"

"I know, Dear. I need to clarify what you found at Andrea's cabin."

Allyson stared at Atticus with a blank expression as she considered his question. "What do you mean, 'what did I find'? The place was sterile by her standards. You must know she wasn't the tidiest person, as was evident at her apartment."

"And the shed?"

"What about it?"

"It was broken into, was it not?"

"Yes. Wait. You sent those people. You alluded to that earlier."

Atticus bobbed his head.

"If you sent someone to break in, you must know what was inside. Besides, who cares? The whole place burned to the ground. You saw the photos!"

"Yes. Most unfortunate. Did *you* happen to look inside before you left?"

Allyson stiffened and shifted her gaze out the window. "Mmm-hmm."

"And?"

She reached across her chest and pressed her hand against her opposite shoulder in a one-armed hug. She then slid the hand to rest on her chest. "It was a shed."

"Stop with the games, Allyson! Did you find the trunk?" Atticus snapped, his gentle grandfatherly mask gone.

She jumped at his change in voice and hunched her shoulders. "Yes! I took it with me and threw it out when I reached the city's boundary. It seemed like the right thing to do!"

"Where?"

"A random fast-food joint. Big dumpster. Probably on its way to a landfill or incinerator by now."

"Did you look inside it?"

"Yes. It was nothing but junk—mementos and trinkets from who knows what. If a dumpster diver decided to have at it, even better, right?"

Atticus smiled. "I apologize for my firmness. But I must ensure all loose ends are tied off and tucked away."

"Which is why you torched the place."

"*I* did no such thing, Dear."

"Neither did I."

"It's a shame. It was such a lovely little oasis."

"Well, The property is still there. We can always rebuild."

"Indeed," Atticus assured her, reverting to his former genteel persona. "I need to ask you another question."

"Ooookkkaaayyy," Allyson dragged out.

"How much did you know about Andrea's—hobbies?

"Why do you think I am the way I am, Atticus? It's hard keeping others' dark secrets and being unable to act on them without hurting my entire family and myself. It was better for me to bear the weight of her secrets alone, even if it nearly killed me four times. What doesn't, makes you stronger, right?"

Atticus nodded and stared vacantly out his window for several moments. "And *The Caretaker*? Did you know about that too?"

"I suspected it as soon as the rumors started with the first film, but I kept brushing it off. It was a conspiracy theory. Too many people worked on those programs. It would be an impossible cover-up. When I got to know Roger, I believed it less and less . . . until . . ."

"Until what?"

"I don't want to go there, but it correlated with when I went into treatment this last time."

"About a year ago?" Atticus asked.

"Yeah."

"Something to do with your sister or Roger?"

"Neither."

29

EMOTIONAL WOUNDS

{ALLYSON}

"Oh, Grace, what a truly fucked and terrible day," Allyson cried, dropping heavily onto the sofa beside her friend. She leaned her head on Grace's shoulder as tears leaked from her eyes. "Andrea is dead, and my life is imploding thanks to Ram."

"I saw his report. I'm surprised you're here and not in jail for killing my best friend!" Grace chuckled, placing their arm around Allyson's shoulder.

"Ha! I wanted to, trust me, but I landed in the ER briefly with Dr. Dean after fainting during the FBI interview. They called an ambulance, then the good doctor. Can't wait for that bill."

"I can neither confirm nor deny that I may have heard something similar. How are you coping?"

"About as to be expected. Thankfully, I'm pretty numb from my everyday prescription cocktail, or I would most likely still be in the hospital—on the unit with all the padded rooms."

"I can only imagine. Talk to me. What is going on in that terrifyingly beautiful mind of yours?"

Allyson stared ahead, her chest rising and falling. "Have you ever been on a horrible date and stuffed yourself with food because if you didn't fill your mouth with something edible, you would have verbal diarrhea, pointing out exactly why your date was single, then rush home and collapse on the couch in despair because you are convinced you will die alone?"

Grace laughed heartily. "Not exactly, but I can imagine you doing something like that! Why?"

"Well, it's how I feel now. I had to leave the hospital, or I would lose my shit on Dr. Dean," Allyson grumbled. "I had to rush home from the meeting with Holger Beitin because I was going to rip him a new asshole, tell Vince to suck it for failing to protect me from such a dick, and fire Atticus for being unable to scare Holger into keeping me on the project," she let out a quiet sob. "I had to drop on this couch because I'm demoralized, knowing I will, in fact, be dying alone with Andrea no longer there to bug me to death." Hot tears streamed down her face, and she swiped at them angrily, offended at their audacity to show themselves in front of company.

Grace pulled Allyson close and kissed her cheek. "You won't die alone as long as you have me, Dear One."

Allyson was still for several beats. "You mean you won't take his side?"

It was Grace's turn to be still. "I refuse to choose a side because I know my friends. Ram never says anything he can't prove with facts. And you are no murderer or criminal mastermind. No offense. So somewhere in the middle, the truth must lie. Talk to me. You can trust me. We've seen each other through some pretty rough times."

"Indeed, we have. And no offense taken. I am far from a criminal mastermind, or I wouldn't be an artist!" Allyson exclaimed. She picked at her cuticles in a heavy silence for several minutes. "What I feel most guilty about is, for the majority of my life, I've wished to be a singleton and Andrea to be gone. Last week, I worked with Dr. Dean on embracing the world as plain old Allyson—no labels. I said I wanted her to go purgatory so she could revisit all the hell she's wrought on the world. AND I felt good about it for days after!" She shouted, the anguish evident in her voice.

"Shhh. It's okay. They say you don't truly love someone if you haven't wished them dead," Grace cooed.

"Who says that?"

"*Someone.* Anyway, it doesn't matter. I don't understand what you mean about purgatory and Andrea. Explain."

"What's there to say? We hated each other." Allyson hugged her knees to her chest. "I imagine she and I were like you and Irv, siblings by blood but not much else."

Grace frowned and stroked Allyson's back. "I can't imagine what it would be like to have an identical twin. Was it hard?"

Allyson scoffed. "I can't say what it is like for other identicals, but for us, it was a constant battle for supremacy. Pa always said we were two coins with the same side. I think he misunderstood the idiom, but the meaning is the same. Even though we were outwardly the same, people always noticed her first, then they'd say, 'Oh! You're twins!' like they were surprised by my sudden appearance even though I had been standing there the entire time. She always seemed to have an extra something that skipped me altogether. It often worked to my advantage, with people gravitating towards me because she was over-the-top or plain picky with whom she associated. I had more friends than her because I wasn't selective. Boys came to me first to test the waters with her. A few took me as a charity case, thinking I'd be grateful for their attention with a sister like Andrea stealing all the thunder. They weren't wrong. But they were always disappointed when they learned the quickest way to Andrea was *not* through me."

Grace clicked their teeth and bit out a short laugh. "Describes me to a 't' with all my siblings, but with me in Andrea's position. I mean, why would you spare any of those donkeys a glance when you can have this," they chided, preening as much as possible while holding a friend in one arm. "But I do think this is a case of dysmorphia. You don't see yourself the way others see you. You thought all those people gravitated towards you to get to Andrea. Yet having never met your sister, I see people all around you being pulled in by your genuine personality. Dr. Dean has championed you in ways I haven't seen him with other patients. There's your agent, Vince, sticking with you through your highs and lows. Look at our neighbor, Nina. She is always keeping an eye out for you. Ram was instantly loyal to a fault, and I believe even Irv had good intentions when he came here to talk first before getting you to go on record."

Allyson scoffed. "Yeah, and how well did that work out for me?!"

"I think there must be something else going on behind the scenes they don't want us to understand yet. It's the only explanation I can think of."

"I can't imagine what that would be and why they would risk shitting on my world without letting me in on the secret. But it all pales in comparison to the regret I feel. With Andrea gone, all our competition and hate seems pointless. You know she recently told me how she once consulted a priest about performing an exorcism to rid herself of me? She likened me to a possessed boomerang! I said she was more like a terminal cancer with an undetermined life expectancy, festering inside until she eventually killed me."

"Is that why you've attempted suicide multiple times?"

"I wouldn't admit that to her because she'd take it as a compliment, but she was almost always the root cause of my distress. All but this last time," Allyson trailed off. She chewed her bottom lip.

"What was the trigger?"

"Guilt."

"Over what?"

"So many things. Roger being one."

"Whoa, sista. Roger? Why?"

"Aside from Ram making me look like Roger's murderer with his scathing report and inciting the Givers' wrath?" Allyson's voice raised an octave. "Well, um, I know you are—were—a fan, and I don't want to diminish any of that for you. Or how you think of me . . . but well, we were sorta *involved* . . . while he was still with Andrea too."

"You nasty piece! You got sloppy seconds? Girl, I seriously underestimated you! S.E.R.I.O.U.S.L.Y."

Allyson's face burned hot, and she sat upright, shifting away from Grace's comfort. "I like to blame my borderline disorder on my promiscuity, but honestly, I just love sex!" she shrugged. "I enjoy how it makes me feel physically *and* emotionally. For those few minutes or hours, depending on the partner, I'm seen. I belong. I am loved. Roger was a fantastic lover, even if he was an asshole. By the way, he was the pursuer. Not me."

"See? That proves my point right there! You have as much mojo as your sister does—urm, did. Now, I need details. How did this come about, and why did you never spill this tea, especially with me?!"

Allyson pressed her palms to her cheeks. "What's there to tell? We screwed a few times a year when our schedules clicked."

"'What's there to tell'?!" Grace stammered. "How about everything? How did you meet? What was it like? What was *he* really like?! What was his kink? Because everyone's got one, at least."

"Are we doing this? How old are we?"

"Old enough to talk about sex with famous dreamboats. Now, dish it, gurl."

Allyson moaned but smiled. Waggling her eyebrows, she began, "We met at my *Pretense* show in Vancouver a few years ago. The one with the masks. He saw me disappear into a backroom and followed me, thinking I was Andrea. While I was wrestling him off me like a rabid dog, Vince came in and set him straight. He was incredibly embarrassed and quite drunk. As an apology, he insisted on buying a mask, but only if I delivered it to his flat the next day. He had lunch catered, and we spent the afternoon getting to know each other."

"I bet you did," Grace licked their lips.

"It wasn't like that. Surprisingly, one-on-one, he's not a terrible human, and we oddly had a lot in common, including how much we loved to hate Andrea. Few people knew he was from Argentina too, which was cool. His great-grandparents immigrated from Germany after the war, as did many wealthy and connected supporters of Hitler's regime. His mother died when he was young, and his father left him to be raised by his grandfather—similar emotional wounds make for strange bedfellows. However, we didn't actually become lovers for nearly a year. Unfortunately, for him, he was the serious one, and I *was not*."

"So how did Roger play into your last, you know, attempt?"

"Ugh. It's complicated, and all I'm comfortable talking about right now. Thank God Ram's report didn't mention our . . . affair. Should I call it that? The Givers are already clamoring for my head, thinking I did something to him! *As if*," she spat. "Can you imagine if everyone knew we were part-time lovers? With everything else unfolding, I couldn't handle being branded with a scarlet letter too!"

Her mood abruptly shifted. "You know what really chaps my ass?" she smacked her hands on her lap, her face red with anger. "Whatever happened to the journalistic moral code: minimize harm, be accountable, check your sources . . . I know there's more . . ." she trailed off, grinding her teeth.

"I know, baby girl. I am so sorry. I feel like this is partially my fault. I introduced you to Ram, thinking he'd be the one person to help unravel this mystery with Andrea. I even kinda hoped he'd be more, considering he'll never be mine. Instead, he's gone and lost his head."

"Let's change the subject. I'm hungry."

Allyson dozed off after pizza, ice cream, and binging a few episodes of an Anime series.

"Do you want me to stay over?" Grace asked as Allyson stirred awake.

"No, but thank you."

"Are you sure? I don't want to see a fresh carving on your precious skin tomorrow because you needed to self-regulate."

"I promise I won't cut. I need to be alone for the messy parts. No one needs to be subjected to that look," she emphasized the comment by swirling her hand around her face. "I do appreciate you being here tonight. Especially considering I could be a murderous fiend . . . like . . . like the Caretaker," she stuttered, taking Grace's hand in hers. "Listen, I don't want to come between you and Ram. If it ever comes down to it, always choose him over me. Promise?"

Grace cocked their head and glared at Allyson. "What is this nonsense?"

"I don't want to be a point of contention between you, is all."

"That'll never happen. Sleep well, Dear One. Tomorrow is a new day. Trust in the process of life." They bent and kissed Allyson on her forehead before sashaying back to their apartment.

"Hey!" Allyson called.

"What is it, Love?"

"Out of curiosity, what size shoe do you wear?"

"What a strange question," Grace laughed, glancing at their bejeweled thong sandals. "Size 12. Why? You got a thing for feet I didn't know about?"

Allyson giggled. "No, silly. I was thinking about Roger and the other Salish Sea feet. He was a size 12 too. Maybe Ram is right about a killer being behind it all. And they have a type." Allyson smiled weakly, waved to her friend, and shut the door. Her body ached from the emotional whirlwind. She reflected on the day's events while crawling into bed.

As her eyes slid shut from exhaustion, her cellphone rang. Groaning, she answered. It was Marv, the building super.

"I'm sorry to bother you so late, Allyson, but a package was just delivered for you, and they said you should have it right away. Can I bring it up?"

Bewildered by what it could be, she agreed to meet him by the elevator. He handed her a heavy-duty, canvas, tamper-evident tote bag, like the kind used to transport cash between businesses and banks. An address tag was attached to the secured zip tie-like lock with the words "For Allyson Marta's eyes only." She laughed softly at the absurdity of the exchange and questioned whether she might be dreaming.

"This is like something out of a spy movie," she remarked before thanking Marv and heading back to the apartment's safety. Fear crept up her spine as she shut the door like she was being watched. Hadn't Atticus mentioned bugs in her apartment?

Locking the door, she dragged a chair from her kitchen island and wedged it under the knob. She grabbed the kitchen shears, entered her bedroom, and locked its door behind her as an added security measure. Next, she snatched her phone off the nightstand and yanked the comforter from her bed before stepping into her small walk-in closet. She kept the overhead light off but switched on her cellphone's flashlight to have more control over the brightness. Then she wedged one side of the blanket against the door's bottom to block any light from leaking into her bedroom. She used the rest to make a nest to comfort herself against the tide of emotion the package might invoke once opened. Her scalp tingled as she clipped off the tote's security tag, and her hands chilled with a sticky sweat. She spent many childhood nights hiding in her closet, not afraid of the boogeymen that many her age feared, but of the one they had no idea existed—the one whose most personal thoughts might be lurking inside the bag.

30

STUPID FUCKING THERAPY

{ANDREA}

E ven though this was supposed to be a stupid fucking therapeutic exercise, I decided to take it seriously and write you this long-awaited
apology. Just kidding. If you've waited all these years for me to say sorry,
you are even sadder than I thought, and you obviously don't know me at all.

To ask for forgiveness is to admit wrongdoing, and I believe right and
wrong are subjective. I'm not responsible for anyone else's well-being. Have
I hurt people? No doubt about it. These days, looking at someone the wrong
way, or not looking at them at all, will send them into a state. However, their
response is their problem, not mine. You are the perfect example. You pined
over your trashy friend Callie, who would've thrown you under the prover-
bial bus in a heartbeat if it meant social advancement for her, spending the
better part of your life suffering from guilt and shame. It happened twenty
years ago! Let. That. Shit. Go! How's that for psychoanalysis?

I don't know why I'm even doing this. Why did I think coming to this
cloud cuckoo land would do any good? It worked for Roger and Vanessa.
Maybe it'd help me too. Scratch that. I might as well be honest while I'm

writing this. No one else can read it but you, anyway, and for all I know, if by some miracle it does make it to you, you might not even read it. But here it goes. The real reason why I came to Palm Springs? To make a case for my mental health because I know someone is onto me. And what better way to get out of a legal bind than to claim you're batshit crazy?!

Who is onto me, and for what? Well, I'm sure you can guess the what, as for who? That's the unsolved mystery. It all started after my last *guest* vacated the cabin in the woods. I started getting these messages. First, there were letters in my mailbox, so I stopped checking the mail. Then, flyers appeared on my car's windshield. I started parking in the secure garage. They stopped for a while but returned with a vengeance in my email and voicemail. They were cleverly disguised as sales calls and networking opportunities, but I read between the lines. I saw and heard the threats.

I thought it was those fucking Giver twats messing with me. But when I started hearing the voices and, eventually, seeing people who couldn't be there, I realized I was in serious trouble. It had to be the studio! Who else has that kind of technology? They must be trying to get me to confess and make me the scapegoat! Fat chance. And why now? Haven't I given them everything? I rescued them from financial ruin and turned them into the most successful trans-media franchise in the world next to those superhero-obsessed dingbats. Do you know who is the real superhero? Me!

Oh, shit. Someone is coming to check on my progress.

And I'm back. You wouldn't believe it here. Well, maybe you would. You've been through more treatment facilities than anyone I've ever known. I wonder if there is a Guinness record for that? You should look into it.

Anyway, let me start by saying nothing here is as it appears. Thus, the secrecy in writing this in *our* language. I'm almost 100 percent certain someone goes through my shit on a daily basis while I'm out for "therapy." And that word? What a joke!

The glossy brochures and interactive website showcase this exclusive resort with all the amenities a wealthy, privileged person has come to expect from such places. They tout the prodigious Dr. Bouchard's abilities as if he were a magician. And maybe he is since he did fix Roger after the first *Caretaker* movie. But something's not right here. Once you've signed the NDA, they've got you, and they can do whatever they want to you and call it therapy. That is definitely not a bullet point on the marketing materials.

Here's an example. The first night I was here, they forced me to eat this chocolate pudding. I told them I don't do added sugar, but they insisted. I won't go into details on how they convinced me, but needless to say, I gave in. As soon as I'd finished, I was stripped and placed in a small, windowless room with plush carpet and soft walls. Not padded, but supple to the touch. I threw a fit about being violated in such a manner. Their response was to wheel in a bed and strap me down by my ankles and wrists. That's when the real nightmare began.

I was a prisoner! I lost all sense of reality. One minute, I was lying there, and the next, I was trapped in the movie studio. I couldn't recall anything about my life except the distant past. I was desperate to find a way out. Before I knew it, I was back in the "treatment" room's utter darkness, vulnerable as a kitten on a four-lane highway. How is that legal? Where are my fundamental human rights?

It's been like this for God knows how long. I've lost track of the days, and time is an illusion. I'm in and out of different realities. Sometimes, I'm back in the studio, but not exactly as it is, trying to figure out its labyrinth design, only to "wake up" back at this place in awkward situations. For instance, I could swear I was weaving through set after set within the soundstage building. Then I blinked, and I was sitting across from Jorge, an Ecuadorian businessman who thinks he and I are chess partners! The crazy part is, before I got up and stomped off, I captured his king and shouted, "Checkmate!" When have you ever known me to play chess?

Another time, there was the dented head guy with no feet. He chased me through an on-set swamp before I found myself outside a replica of my shed at the cabin. Except it wasn't an exact copy. But it did lead me to the tunnels . . . the ones no one is supposed to know about . . . connecting my office to the sets in building two. I thought I was safe there until people, who were definitely dead in this reality, chased me through the complex! I had experienced stuff like this before I got here, but this has been more vivid.

Speaking of real, last week I would swear to you I was stuck out in a snowstorm, only to return to reality standing in the facility's kitchen, face-to-face with an old Chinese woman holding a giant wooden spoon like a baseball bat. She was screaming for help and later told the doctor I was threatening to kill her if I didn't get more pudding. What. The. Actual. Fuck?

At one point, I thought I could control these "trips" like a lucid dream. This one time, I stopped myself from trying to escape the movie lot. I thought I was still outside in that same terrible snowstorm. I was convinced I would freeze to death if I didn't find a way to safety. I discovered a lone truck in the parking lot and broke in to make a run for it. In my exhaustion, I regained my wits and realized I was actually here at the resort, only to find I had smashed the window out of the landscaper's pickup, slicing my arm pretty good. I threatened to claim rape if he told anyone but gave him my smartwatch as an afterthought for his trouble. Then, I walked away as if nothing had happened.

I spent two whole days afterward mingling with the other residents, swimming, and even trying my hand at golf. I made an excuse about my arm, and everyone bought it. Turns out, I didn't even need the excuse because my arm had healed completely. No scratch, scar, or anything. It was unreal. But which part? The cut itself or the fast healing? I don't know.

Eventually, the trips came back worse than before. They were full-on hallucinations. I saw more dead people, including Mummy Dear. I even thought I'd had a heart attack because my chest hurt like a horse had kicked me! I was convinced Dr. Bouchard planned to put a pacemaker in me while also surgically removing another man's feet just for fun! I was trapped in this purgatory straight out of Dante's imagination. I knew I needed to leave before I completely lost my mind. But isn't that what they'd want? Whoever put me on this path would like me to run because running makes you look guilty. And you know what? I *am* guilty. I'm culpable in many things, but so are they. We are all bound together by this mutual need. Theirs is based on greed, while mine is more feral. It is that base desire found deep inside, left over from some evolutionary impulse. I need to kill to feel alive. It's a power trip every time I get away with it. I'm like a soul eater. I crave it like food and water. Maybe more so.

Thus I've decided, to leave here with my mind intact, I need to beat them at their own game. But I'm going to need your help. I've never asked for anything from you, and you have every right to tell me to fuck off. But I'm optimistic you'll see by helping me, you'll also be helping yourself. Let's make things right, Allyson. We can start by taking down H0rr Studios from the inside out.

31

A NICE TALL TREE

{ALLYSON}

A loud bang and muffled voices stirred Allyson from her reading. She had been in a trance, so wholly absorbed in Andrea's narrative. She frowned at the time display on her phone. 3:00 a.m. Why were there voices in the hallway? Although she was still awake, she had good reason. What was their excuse? Then she smiled and shook her head. She honestly had forgotten where she was—in a building whose residents were all recovering, to some degree, from mental illness. The pharmaceuticals used to treat them helped with their symptoms, but the side effects, including messing with sleep cycles, were less than ideal.

"You think *you* were in cloud cuckoo land," she whispered to the open book in her lap as if it were her sister. "You have no idea," she chuckled. "Had," she choked, as an involuntary tear plopped on the page. "What the hell happened, Andrea? Was someone able to decipher this book and discover your plan? How does one go from devising a corporate takedown to OD'ing at a wellness retreat under a therapist's care? It doesn't make sense!"

Wiping away her tears, she refocused on the book, flipping through its pages. Many were blank, while others were filled with gibberish and random thoughts. Towards the back were several sketches. One in particular caught Allyson's attention: a stack of empty cartons and a spoon. Was that the infamous pudding they forced her to eat? And who were the faces staring out from the page? Other retreat guests or employees? Or were they from H0rr Studios? It would be nice to have more details of Andrea's stay.

Hours later, Allyson awoke with a start from a dreamless sleep. Her phone buzzed relentlessly. Disoriented, she fumbled with the screen buttons and accidentally declined the incoming call. It was late afternoon, and she had missed four calls from Ram, two from Dr. Dean, and one from Atticus. With 1 percent battery life left, Allyson needed to recharge the device before returning any of them.

"Ugh," she moaned as her bones creaked and the blood flow returned to her cramped muscles after being coiled in the closet overnight. "I'm too old for this shit. Note to self: No more sleeping in the closet," she complained, shuffling to the kitchen for a can of sparkling water.

As her hand stretched toward the refrigerator handle, her phone was buzzing again.

"Jesus Christ! Is the world coming to an end? Since when have I become the popular one?!"

She stomped back to her bedroom, where she had just plugged in her phone. "Hello?" she snapped.

"Allyson! Where have you been? I've been trying to reach you for the last five hours!" Ram spat.

"I didn't know I was on call."

"This is no time to be flippant. Have you seen Grace? I'm driving back from Vancouver right now. I should be in town within an hour."

"I saw them last night. Why? What's wrong?"

"They left a voicemail around 5:00 a.m. It sounded like a butt dial at first. The longer it went on, I could hear an obvious struggle, and they said the words, 'freaky mask" before screaming. Then the call ended."

"Well, did you call the police? Try Irv?" Allyson asked in a panic.

"Don't be so obtuse! Irv was the first person I called. He immediately requested a search warrant to ping Grace's cell and inspect their apartment. In the meantime, we thought you could help. Since I couldn't get in touch with you, he went ahead with obtaining the warrant and is probably parking outside your place as we speak."

"Why would the FBI come here?"

"Allyson! Pay attention! Grace is missing. They aren't answering their phone, and no one has seen or heard from them in at least twelve hours. The authorities are processing this as a crime and will come to get statements and search for clues."

Allyson sat with a thud. Her mind went blank, and her ears rang in a piercing octave.

"Allyson? Are you there?"

She swallowed hard to clear the lump in her throat. "Yeah, sorry." she replied hoarsely, "Grace offered to spend the night last night, but I told them to go home because I needed to be alone. Fuck! Maybe they needed *me*, and I couldn't see it because I was wrapped up in my own shit. This is all my fault!"

Ram was silent for a minute. "Where were you? I've been trying you since I heard the message."

"I needed a minute to grieve. I was sleeping in my . . . I was sleeping. You know, with my sister gone, and Roger, and the news . . . You motherfucker! You've ruined my life!"

"*I* ruined your life? Oh, sweetheart, you've done a fantastic job all on your own. And is it just me, or does it seem a little too coincidental that everyone around you keeps disappearing?"

"Too bad one of them wasn't you," she hissed.

"What did you say?" Ram retorted.

"I said, so naturally, this is all my doing, too, right?! Criminal mastermind here! This is such bullshit! I thought you were a good, trustworthy person. Turns out you're just another asshole! Maybe this is all *your* fault for spreading disinformation about me because a story this huge would land you a great big promotion," she yelled, rising to pace. She rubbed the top of her head as she continued. "You basically pinned the whole H0rr Studios nightmare on me from the movie lot debacle to Roger and Billy Walls. Perhaps whoever is truly responsible got a little jealous of my attention and decided to make a bigger statement. Have you considered that angle, mister big-shot investigative reporter?"

"I stand behind my reporting. You're connected to this somehow, Allyson, and you know it. You might be able to fool others, but not me. But, please, let's focus on Grace right now. They sounded in real trouble. Can you help?"

"How? What can I possibly do?"

"Run across the hall. Knock on the door. Check with your neighbors. Maybe Grace crashed with another resident!"

"Umm. Okay. But wait. My phone's going to die. I . . . forgot to plug it in last night before I fell asleep. Do you want to stay connected while I run over there?"

"Sure."

"Okay. Hold on."

Scurrying from her bedroom, Allyson yanked the chair she'd placed under the doorknob and tossed it aside. As she stepped into the hallway, she remembered the spare key Grace had given her when they moved in. They had made a pact to keep an eye on one another, including the ability to let themselves into their places should the need arise.

She retrieved hers from the hiding spot where she kept important items and rushed to Grace's door. As she inserted it into the keyhole, the door popped open without her needing to unlock it. Startled, she stood in the entryway, listening for any noises.

"Hello? Grace? Are you home?" It was unusual for them to leave their door unlocked.

With no answer, she pushed the door open fully and yelled louder. "Grace? Are you here?"

Still no response. Using caution, Allyson entered the apartment slowly. The floorplan was identical to hers, but a mirror opposite. It was dark inside due to the heavy drapes covering the windows. The waning daylight leaked around their edges, while a light above the stove was the only other source for her to navigate by.

"Grace? It's Allyson." She had an eerie déjà vu feeling, having already been through a similar scenario at the cabin. Her stomach twisted into knots.

"Psst. Hermana. Grace left early this morning. Told me to tell you not to worry if you came by looking for them. They seemed in a hurry and more than a little upset. Did you two fight?"

It was Nina, their other neighbor from down the hall. She was also the resident busybody.

"Did they say where they were going? When they'd be back?"

"No," the woman shook her head. "What's going on?"

"I'm trying to find out. Did you notice anything off about Grace before they left?"

Nina shook her head. "Wait! Sí! Oddly, they were dressed like a *man*. Normally, Grace is decked out to make an impression. You know their flare for the extraordinary. But they were wearing athletic pants and . . . and sneakers! I'd never seen them so . . . masculine!" Nina exclaimed.

Allyson blanched at the description. That was unlike the Grace she knew and loved. "Okay. You've been extremely helpful. Thank you, Nina." She walked towards the door as if to leave, hoping Nina would follow, then shut the door and locked it while still inside. Her intuition told her to be wary of her nosy neighbor. She shuffled back towards Grace's bedroom and searched their closet. Sure enough, there was a small selection of men's clothing and footwear. It wasn't uncommon because Grace was nonbinary, meaning they could feel feminine or masculine, depending on their mood. Yet Grace had never revealed that side to Allyson before.

She made a quick sweep through the bathroom and even under the bed to be sure she hadn't missed anything before heading back to update Ram. Allyson was no investigative reporter or FBI agent, but her impression was the authorities wouldn't find any critical clues at the apartment.

As she left, she made sure the door was firmly closed and locked. Turning toward her unit, a tingle swept up her spine when she spotted her door open. Had she left it that way? She glanced at Nina's door and frowned. She wasn't sure what she was expecting, but couldn't shake the feeling the woman was spying on her. For a second, she wished Atticus was right, and her place was bugged. It would be comforting to know whether her instincts were accurate. Shaking herself, she went inside and bolted the door before rushing to the phone. As she grabbed it from the nightstand, she glanced inside the closet and spotted the reflection of the setting sun glinting off the scissors atop her crumpled comforter. Had she left them there? What about Andrea's book?

"Hello? Allyson? Are you there?"

"Uh, yeah. I just got back. Hey, did you hear any noises while I was gone? Like someone moving around in my room?"

"I honestly wasn't paying much attention since I'm driving. Why? What's up? What did you find?"

"I ran into our neighbor, Nina. She had an interesting story," Allyson replied, repeating what she'd learned. "I think Irv needs to question that woman. If anyone on this floor is hiding what she knows, it's her."

"I'll mention it to him, but I need to let you go to do so. Stay where you are. Don't open the door for anyone but me, Irv, or Dr. Dean. I spoke with him earlier when I couldn't get in touch with you or Grace. He's doing his part to help figure this out."

"Okay. If you get any news before the calvary shows up, let me know ASAP! I can feel my nerves starting to fry with my adrenaline rush fading."

"Be safe, Allyson," Ram said in a tone Allyson couldn't quite identify. Was it worry? Sincerity? Or suspicion?

Setting her phone back on the nightstand, she stared into her closet again. The scissors' placement was bothering her. When she'd woken earlier, they were nowhere to be found. Squatting, she pulled the comforter out and resettled it on the bed. When she returned for Andrea's book, she panicked when it wasn't there on the floor. Neither was the canvas bag it came in. She moved items around until she spotted a storage tub's lid askew. In between folded concert T-shirts, she found the book nestled safely inside, but the safety pouch was missing. She must have moved it in her sleep.

She flipped through the journal again as she returned to the kitchen to get the drink she wanted earlier. In the daylight and after some sleep, she was hit with a new perspective as she revisited the sketches. It occurred to her Andrea was communicating a message through the images. Allyson was all but certain. It was ordered in a particular way, with seemingly random pictures to the untrained eye. One, an image of a man, reminded her of Grace. But she needed to go back to their apartment to be sure. Chugging the water, she scooped up her keys and the book, then crept back across the hall. A commotion came from the hallway just as she'd shut and secured the door.

"At the end is Nina Garcia Sanchez. To the right is Grace's place, and the left here is Allyson's." It was Irv's voice.

Before she could open the door and tell him she was at Grace's, Nina called out from her door and approached the men.

"Are you here about Grace and Allyson?" Nina asked.

"Yes," Irv replied. "Special Agent Irving Kingsley. This is my team. I take it you are Nina?"

"Sí. Yes."

"What can you tell me about Grace?"

Due to the lack of peepholes in the door, Allyson didn't have a visual on the exchange, but she had an overwhelming feeling to stay quiet and hidden for the time being.

"I saw Grace leave around 3:00 a.m. this morning."

"Did you speak to them?"

"Sí."

"What did they say?"

"Grace appeared upset and rushed. They were dressed in street clothes. Not their normal flamboyant getup. I thought it was odd, but again, it was 3:00 a.m. I asked if they were okay, and they assured me they were running an errand and would be back soon."

"An errand at three in the morning? That didn't strike you as unusual?"

Nina laughed. "In this place?"

"Right," Irv answered, clearing his throat. "What else can you tell us?"

"About ten minutes later, Allyson left. She was dressed in an oversized beige sweatshirt with the hood pulled up, so I couldn't see her face, but I knew it was her. She seemed to be in a hurry too. I didn't speak with her, though."

"She must be the person on the security footage leaving shortly after Grace," Irv commented.

Allyson fought to wrench open the door and call Nina out for her lies! She had been in her closet all night, going through Andrea's book! Marv, the building super, could at least verify the delivery!

"Is there anything else, Nina?"

"Well . . . I don't know if this helps, but I heard Allyson screaming at Grace earlier in the evening from her unit. It seemed rather heated at one point. A little while later, Grace left and went back to their place, but I didn't talk to them at the time. You know, the walls are so thin around here, you can hear almost everything."

Allyson fumed at Nina. Why would she lie to the FBI? It was making Allyson appear guilty! Goddamn Ram and his special report! He has tainted everyone against her.

"Thank you, Nina. If you would, please return to your apartment. Remain inside with the door locked until you are given the all-clear from me or one of my men. Do you understand?"

"Oh, Dios mio! I will. Sí. I will!" Nina wailed. Allyson could practically see Nina crossing herself as she rushed back to her place and slammed the door.

Next came a knock. Allyson jumped, but thankfully, they were at her door, not Grace's.

"Allyson? It's Irv. I'm here to discuss Grace."

She bit her bottom lip, trying hard to remain silent. She wanted to scream at Nina and berate Irv for being naïve enough to believe anyone in the building.

"Allyson! This is serious. I'm going to count to three. Then my team and I will be entering the premises. One. Two. Three."

Crack! Her door was kicked in, followed by shouts and commands. She was rattled. Holding her breath, Allyson pulled Grace's door open a sliver. No one was left in the hallway, leaving her with a chance to slip out. She ran for the stairwell and flew to the basement, where an unused and unguarded exit led to the alley between the buildings on their street.

When her bare feet hit the cold pavement, she swore. "Fuck! I'm still in my pajamas!" Over her shoulder, the door to her building clicked shut. "No going back now. Not without a scene."

Sticking to the shadows, she made her way between high-rises and businesses in her neighborhood, her mind a flurry of what-ifs and how-comes. Allyson eventually came to a park with a bad reputation due to those who congregated there. She sat on a bench to catch her breath, Andrea's journal still clutched in her hands.

She held it tight to her chest, closed her eyes, and tilted her head to the sky as if running her face under the shower spray. Gulping in the evening spring air, she ran through her options— none good.

"I've lost everything. And if I go back, I'll lose my freedom too. I've been set up. By who and why, though? The same people who were after Andrea? I wish I had those scissors. My skin is crawling!"

A broken piece of glass glinted in the street lamp's glow, which had just clicked on in the approaching dusk. She scuttled over to the spot, scooped it up, and glanced around to see if anyone was watching before sticking it in her pocket like a recovered treasure. Then she continued wandering.

The evening grew colder, and with it, her mood turned darker. Despair made her chest heavy and her legs weak. Her steps were weighty as they drew closer together. She was like a toy whose battery was dying.

Death. If there were a moment to greet San La Muerte, Lady of the Dead, it would be now. How would she do it? A week ago, she would have said the Aurora Bridge in Fremont. She was sitting in Dr. Dean's office, listening to the details surrounding poor old Billy Walls's feet for the first time. That seemed ages ago. As she considered the cause of his death, she was convinced it was best to go out in a cliché—a bridge jumper. Now, she wasn't sure. Maybe she needed to make a bigger splash. Suicide by cop, a.k.a. the firing squad? Nah. It would be unfair to traumatize people only doing their job.

She snapped her fingers. "I know!" she shouted aloud. "I'll prop myself against a nice tall tree here in the park and use this trusty piece of glass seemingly set out just for me. Report on THAT, Ram!"

32

CHANGE OF PLANS

{ALLYSON}

Allyson roamed the park in the dark, searching for the perfect tree. When she didn't find it there, she tried three more public outdoor spaces, but she still couldn't find the right one. Finally, she hopped on the light-rail and moved to a different part of the city. She half expected to find FBI agents stationed at each train stop, but no one seemed concerned by her pajamas or lack of footwear, and she detected no hint of recognition on any of the passengers' faces. Does no one watch the news anymore?

The more she walked, the stranger her body's sensations became. It was like her bones began to shrink. And it wasn't just her physical awareness. Everything around her seemed far away. As she walked along the sidewalk, it appeared to tilt on its axis. Leaning against a brick building to right herself, she ran her finger along the grout lines, mesmerized by their gritty texture. Slowly, she made her way through the streets. As people rushed to their destinations and made eye contact, their faces swelled into the shape of a helium balloon before retreating into tiny pinpricks as they passed. She struggled to remain upright, and it seemed her legs tangled themselves as they crossed in front of each other. The city's harsh noises made it hard for her to concentrate.

The wind whipped harder as she shuffled into another park entrance lined with large red oaks. The brown leaves, still clinging to the trees' limbs until spring, rustled in a way that caressed her weary mind. They sang a solemn lullaby, easing her lingering sense of urgency and confusion. They welcomed her with open arms.

She dropped with a thud at the base of the largest one in her vicinity and groaned. She pulled the broken glass from her pocket and flipped it between her fingers like her father used to do with his distinctive lucky gold coin with two heads.

She hadn't thought much about dear old Anselmo in the last twenty-four hours. Had Atticus told him the shocking news? Was he distraught or relieved? What would his other daughter's dramatic suicide do to him? Did she care one way or another?

Their parents must have loved them, but they rarely showed it, even when they were little. Patricia, their mother, enjoyed showing them off once they moved to Malibu. She dressed them in matching designer and bespoke frocks and paraded them around her social circles like prized cattle. They were always scrubbed clean within an inch of their life and smelled of lavender, bergamot, or some other crisp fragrance. It seemed as though Patricia was trying to scour the brown from their skin as a means to fit in. The joke was on her, though, because no matter how fair they were, they were still foreigners in a strange new world where people like them were typically the servants, not the masters.

Andrea became addicted to this attention and fed off it. In those early days, she learned to one-up Allyson, make her appear weak, and lose respect from everyone, including their parents.

One particular painful memory edged to the forefront, and all at once, she was thrust back to their last day of sixth grade. Before school began that year, their father insisted the girls be separated to help quell the constant bickering and competition. Allyson was assigned to the stringent Mr. Baker, who helped her discover she was a near-savant in math and science. She made it to a special national competition through the school's math club, a feat yet to be accomplished in its history. Her achievement was even captured in a tiny blurb in the *LA Times*. During the last day's awards presentation, she was called to accept a trophy for mathematical distinction. As she stood, a weird twinge hitched in her lower abdomen, and a trickle crept down her white, tight-covered legs. There were murmurs as she walked to the stage and delivered her acceptance speech. She sensed something was wrong and rushed through it in an effort to return to her seat. Rather than allowing her to leave the stage, her teacher held her back and called Andrea forward.

"We didn't feel it was right to single out just one of you extraordinary siblings, so we created a special award for you two to share." Mr. Baker beamed at Allyson as tears filled her eyes. How could these educators not grasp that twins already shared everything? The last thing the girls needed was a stupid award to share!

"For Outstanding Achievement of Identical Twins!" he delighted, handing Andrea a gleaming gold statue of two girls, conjoined by their hands, while their free ones held a pile of books against opposite hips.

Andrea accepted and turned to embrace her sister, inhaling sharply as she squeezed Allyson close. "Ohmygod, Allyson," she whispered, stepping back.

"What?"

"You have blood all over the back of you!" Her comment blasted throughout the room, thanks to Mr. Baker and his live microphone. "You got your period!" Andrea screamed. Her face contorted from jealousy to amusement until she covered her mouth to hide her laughing grimace.

Being singled out and in the spotlight was Allyson's dream. She had patiently waited for it and even worked hard to get it. She had imagined feeling triumphant and riding a heightened sense of self-worth. Instead, she learned two tough lessons: men will always betray you, and be cautious with your wishes, because they just might come true.

"I will forever gleefully live in my sister's shadow, the unstained one who didn't have menstrual blood all over her. The gracious one who accepted an unnecessary award while her sister's life disintegrated in front of the entire student body of Point Dume Elementary. The confident one who would always be the star of the family. The first at everything. I vow always to be second and no one important as long as Andrea lives." Allyson recalled the promise she made to herself that night in the safety of her closet, writing it in her journal like a contract. And for the most part, she'd stuck to it. However, in life's great irony, Andrea eventually became stained with blood too. Her victims' blood. She morphed into the ill-mannered and bad-tempered one. However, she was still the first in everything else, including the first to die. With her death, perhaps this self-imposed curse would be broken. Could Allyson use her newfound singledom to finally free herself as the secret keeper of Andrea's darkness? Isn't that what Andrea asked for in the end?

"But now you are here, and you've decided. This is the end. The only thing left to figure out is the how. You've failed before. If you're going to do it, do it right this time. No coming back. No more therapy," Allyson mumbled.

Holding the piece of glass firmly in one hand, she pushed her sleeve to her elbow and slid her forefinger over the veins and tendons of the smooth flesh. Then, she glimpsed the journal lying beside her.

She couldn't help but feel like a piece of Andrea was sitting there. Not the bad parts, but those precocious and purposeful ones. The ebullient and vulgar bits. Setting the glass in her lap, Allyson collected the book and flipped through its pages again, hoping for inspiration or an answer to her unspoken question. Instead, she gravitated to the drawings. What message was Andrea trying to convey? Could Allyson die not knowing the answers? More importantly, what if she failed again at taking her life? How many times could she disappoint the people around her before she lost their respect completely? And if she lived, would she be able to make things right? Wasn't it worth finding out?

For twenty years, cutting and suicidal ideation had been her crutches, her go-tos when life became too much. As Dr. Dean said, she was a repeat offender. There's a saying about doing something over and over and expecting a different result. Perhaps it was time to set those methods aside and try a new approach. Except with Grace missing and Nina lying to the Feds, Allyson had no one she could trust and to turn to for help. She'd have to figure this out on her own. Could she do it?

A helicopter roared overhead, startling her. It was time to find out if she could truly stand on her own. She could always return to this spot later if she failed. Her first task? To find a safe place to hide overnight. She needed to get off the streets and fast. But where was she?

Retracing her steps, she took a chance on the light-rail one last time and made her way further downtown, hoping to find a happy hour crowd to blend in with.

She planned to make her way to the condo she owned halfway between the Space Needle and the I-5 corridor. It was currently rented to a sweet young software developer. However, the bottom level of the parking garage was all storage units. Hers contained boxes of clothes and shoes she didn't bring to her current place, and it was also where she'd tucked the items she'd saved from the trunk she tossed out in Vancouver. It was larger than the closet she'd slept in the night before and would allow her to rest while also evading detection.

Once there, she'd change her clothes into something warm and spend more time poring over Andrea's journal. Could the documents and electronics she salvaged from Andrea's shed help decipher the drawings that had her so obsessed? Did she have the courage to make things right?

33

THE TRUTH ABOUT LIES

{ALLYSON}

"I don't believe it," Ram spat as Allyson pulled off her knit beanie and wide-framed sunglasses. "I didn't think I'd ever see you again. I figured you were halfway around the world. Perhaps Uzbekistan or Argentina, with your father."

"Why would you think that? Oh, I know because I'm obviously guilty. Strangely, it's an ego boost. I've always considered myself to be a failure. I like to blame my behavior and poor decisions on my BPD, but mostly my actions are driven by basic low self-worth and esteem. So being seen as a genius is rather flattering," Allyson tapped her chin as if in thought. "Yet a part of you doesn't believe it, or you'd be on the phone to the police by now. Let's set our mutual beliefs and disbeliefs about each other aside for a minute," she said, mimicking picking up a large item and setting it beside her. "And let's put your giant ego there with it. I came to tell you how you were right about me. I am hiding something, something big. I've been hiding it for a long time, and it's eaten away at me. It's why I'm such a fucking mess. But, it's time to make things right."

Ram crossed his arms and huffed. "How convenient. I suppose whatever it is, is all Andrea's fault or a combination of her and Roger's since neither can defend themselves anymore?"

Allyson stumbled backward as if Ram had punched her in the gut. She sucked air through her mouth and gritted her teeth. "Okay. This was a bad idea. I'll go. I'm sure Vanessa Rapaporte and Atticus King would prefer I hand over what I have anyway."

Ram sighed. "Don't try and bait me, Allyson."

"I am, and I'm not." She pulled Andrea's journal from a satchel hanging at her hip. "Do you recognize this person?" She showed him a marked page.

His face said it all before he schooled his features.

"That's what I thought. Maybe you can tell me why my sister would have sketched Grace while she was spinning out at the Wellness retreat. However, not the Grace I know and love, but a version perhaps you and Irv recognize."

Ram leaned out into the hallway. "You're alone?"

"Ya think?"

"Come in. My neighbors don't need to hear this." He opened his door wide open in welcome.

Allyson gave a curt nod and stomped inside, swiveling her head in every direction to ensure his hospitality wasn't a trap.

When Ram shut the door and walked to the kitchen, he laughed.

"What?"

"We went from besties to lovers to enemies who can't trust one another in the span of forty-eight hours. It's scary how alike we are."

"Maybe that's why Grace tried to match-make us," Allyson arched an eyebrow and walked to the window. "I have a better view," she bragged, running her finger along the sill. "And you need to dust," she rubbed her fingers together.

"From the residence building? You're joking. As for the dust, I'll let my cleaning person know. Oh, wait. I don't have one. Here, have a cuppa. You look like you haven't slept in a week."

"I'm pretty sure I haven't. Thanks," Allyson took the steaming cup and sniffed.

"Oat milk. Not poison. You're my meal ticket to stardom. Why would I poison you?"

"Why would you think I'm that paranoid? Because you thought about it?"

"Well, you did kill my best friend."

Allyson blanched. "Is there news?"

"Other than a bloody sweatshirt recovered from your closet? No."

"What?!" she shrieked.

"Thanks to a tip from your trusty neighbor, Nina, the FBI found it in their sweep of your place."

Allyson's hand shook with anger. "That *puta*! Why would I put a bloody *anything* in my closet? Especially if I'm a criminal mastermind running all over the Pacific Coast, killing people! Tell me our protection agencies are not that gullible!"

"Jaded, but not blind. You'd be surprised by the dumb mistakes criminals make to get caught. But it does look bad, don't you think?"

"Because it's supposed to look bad. Whoever is behind all this violence is looking for a scapegoat, and I seem to be the perfect sacrifice. It's clear they don't know me, or else they wouldn't have gone after Grace. What I don't get is how Nina is connected to this."

"Maybe she's the real mastermind," Ram offered, sipping his coffee.

"I doubt it. More than likely, she was offered money and/or affection. She lost her mind and her man during menopause, which is why she is there. She's a lonely old spinster who has her finger on the pulse of the building. They should be arresting her, not me!"

"Who said they want to arrest you? You got here without much trouble, didn't you?"

"Because I lived my whole life as a shadow. I'm invisible unless I want to be seen."

"Sounds like the perfect skill for a serial killer," Ram smiled over his mug. "Come, let's sit and hash this out. Tell me what you came to reveal. Is it worth protecting you or reporting you?"

"Oh no, first you are going to give me the juicy details on what you aren't reporting to the public, including what happened to Grace and their connection to my sister."

"You'll want to be sitting for that. Come on. Oh, are you hungry? I have a few day-old muffins I stole from the FBI's breakroom yesterday. They're from that little bakery down the street from their building. You know they're good if the cops eat them by the dozen."

Allyson's stomach growled. "Stop stalling, Ram. Spill."

He raised his hands in defense. "Okay. Okay," he said, sitting across from her in an old armchair.

"Where did you find that, by the way? The local dumpster? I thought an award-winning journalist would be raking in the big bucks," she commented.

Ram rubbed his hands on the chair's arms affectionately. "It came from Grace's mom's house. It was the first piece of furniture I owned when I left home."

Allyson hung her head. "Sorry."

"Don't be. It probably did come from a dumpster . . . thirty years ago. But it's got good bones. I've thought about reupholstering it, but I just can't bring myself to change it."

"Change is hard for people like you and me."

Ram stroked his chin and gulped his coffee before setting his mug on the table between them. He ran his hand through his thick hair, which was messier than ever, and locked eyes with Allyson. "Where do I start?"

"How about answering my question? How does Grace know Andrea?"

"I don't know if I'm at liberty to say. What I know was shared with me in confidence."

"Goddamn it, Ram! I'm being framed for multiple murders! My sister is dead, two acquaintances, and possibly a third. This is no time for secrets!"

"Says the pot," he snapped.

"Touché. However, I'm willing to share if you are. With guarantees, obviously."

Ram licked his lips and stared out the window. "Grace's real name is Osgood Kingsley, and *he* is an FBI agent. An undercover one, and a damned good one. They've been working on a RICO case against your father for the last three years."

Allyson gasped and stood.

Ram held up his hands. "Sit and let me finish before you go all batshit on me."

She growled but collapsed back into her seat, stuffing her hands under opposite armpits.

"You really are a petulant child."

"You tell me my father is a criminal, my best friend is an undercover FBI agent, *and* you insult me? Fuck you, Ram. I'd like to know how you'd react. You're lucky I haven't hurled this shitty IKEA table through your window."

He clenched his jaw and rubbed the back of his neck. "Anyway, Ozzy, that's his nickname from childhood, worked for H0rr Studios in Vancouver undercover for about a year. He tried to get close to your sister to collect evidence proving the connection between your father, the studio, and the RICO claims. He has had a few rough assignments over the years and struggles with addiction. Your sister partied hard, and he fell back into old, bad habits. The FBI removed him from his position and insisted he go to rehab. Then they got word you had attempted to take your life and would be spending your recovery in a program under Dr. Dean Santoli. It was a gift from the FBI Gods. He went back undercover, this time with the other sister, and as a bonus, he managed to get the treatment he needed while still helping the case."

"The best lies are the ones closest to the truth," Allyson replied, shaking her head. "I am an over-trusting fool."

"Listen, don't beat yourself up. Oz is amazing at his job. Even I couldn't believe his transformation into Grace. I only saw him once, the day he called about helping you. I honestly felt I was talking to a stranger. Irv agreed. When they ran into each other at your place, Irv almost blew the whole damn thing with his reaction. He wasn't surprised to see you, but Grace . . . We aren't typically in contact with each other when Oz's in deep, but since they were both assigned to this case, it was a possibility they tried to prepare for."

"You're telling me all those times we spent together, commiserating at our lowest moments, crying, and . . . it was all a lie?"

"Well, like you said, the best lies are the ones steeped in truth. Knowing Oz, his pain was authentic, along with his feelings. He adores you."

"But I was still their—his—target. His attraction to me was only part of his job! Wait . . . are they—dammit! Is *he* even in danger?"

"Oh, yes. We don't know where he is or what happened. And because he's a trained agent and a big person, for someone to get the drop on him? It has the Feds spooked. And it's why they stormed into your apartment when Nina subtly suggested you could be responsible. But then . . ."

"What? Then what?"

Ram cleared his throat and rubbed his arm. "Like I said before, I don't want to blow their case by giving it all away . . ."

"They gave it to you, didn't they? Why don't you grow a fucking pair and just tell me? You've already come this far. What more could you possibly say that will further destroy my faith in humanity and myself?"

Ram smiled, his lips parting slightly. "For the record, you are smart, strong, talented, and . . ."

"Ram!"

"Fine! The FBI was surveilling your apartment. They had tiny cameras and microphones installed in the common areas."

"Oh my God! Atticus was right! The other night! I sensed it. When Andrea's journal arrived, like a sixth sense, I had this feeling I was being watched. I spent the night in my closet!"

"They know, which is why there isn't a citywide manhunt for you right now. They could prove the hoodie was planted while you were checking on Grace's place *and* that Nina lied. Remember when you came back to the phone and asked me if I'd heard something while you were gone? When they found the sweatshirt, I told Irv to go and look at the footage during that window. Sure enough, a figure dressed in all black and wearing a balaclava swept in through your open door. They had a duffle bag in their hand and walked straight to your bedroom. They are running tests now to see if the blood matches Oz's or anyone else in the system."

"They didn't see where the person came from?" Allyson shivered.

"Unfortunately, there are no cameras in the hallways because it's a public space and, therefore, excluded from the surveillance warrant. The outside cameras are the building's property, and they showed no one coming or going during that time."

"Which means . . ."

"It's a fellow resident. Dr. Dean is cooperating with Irv's team to provide footage from the entrances and exits since the day you and Grace arrived to start your outpatient stay."

"Holy shit. This is scary. Maybe I need to disappear too."

"Not like the others, please. It didn't end well for them. Irv suggests you let the FBI keep you safe."

"He knew I'd come to you for help. I'm that much of a foregone conclusion? Ram, you and I both know how far the Givers' reach is. What if this person is part of their twisted club? What if they've infiltrated the FBI and are waiting to get me alone? No, I think I'm better off on my own."

"I would argue, but I'd either sound sexist or condescending. So I'll offer my help if I'm able. I told Irv you probably wouldn't agree to it anyway. Now, I've answered your question. It's your turn. Consider me your priest. Unburden me with your secrets."

"Hold up. I need guarantees I won't be implicated in any crime. I am simply the whistleblower."

"Well, I'm a journalist. My sources are protected, and there are whistleblower laws to help people like you."

"I need to understand more about why they are after my father and how RICO applies before I say anything."

"I don't blame you. Family is family, no matter what, right?"

Allyson stood and gazed out the window again. "Thank you for telling me about Grace, urm, Ozzy. And the investigation. If you hadn't, I would've thrown all my cards on the table and possibly done more harm than good."

"I had no idea about any of this until my report the other day. Irv provided me with all those details. He wanted me to be aware so he could use me in a situation like this."

"Figures. Sneaky, manipulating prick. Hey, speaking of . . . where were you when Grace/Oz called that day asking for help?"

"At work, and I think he was at the apartment in your building. Why?"

"Maybe the FBI isn't the only one surveilling the place."

34

A DEAL WITH THE DEVIL YOU KNOW

{ALLYSON}

"I have to admit, Allyson, it's a bit cliché having us meet at a park in broad daylight. Guessing you're a fan of spy thrillers?" Irv chuckled.

"It's the red oaks. They ground me." They sat on a bench near where Allyson had contemplated taking her life the night before. She glanced at the copse of trees and shivered.

"Are you cold?"

"I'm fine," she responded, shaking off the dark memory. "Anyway, thanks for believing I had nothing to do with Grace's disappearance."

"Well, the jury's still out where that's concerned. Nevertheless, Ram said you could help with the RICO case, so naturally, I'm open to hearing what you have."

"Did Ram also convey my need for impunity?"

"He did."

"Great. Tell me why you think my father is a criminal. Then I'll share what I have."

"That's not how this works. You show me yours, *then* I'll show you mine. Otherwise, you could run back to Atticus and Papa Marta and tell them everything while I'm left looking like a fool."

"Atticus is aware you guys are investigating them. However, he did fail to mention it was in regard to RICO. He even suspected my apartment was bugged. The pest removal people with the white van? Atticus sent them."

"Well, they did a horrible job, didn't they?" Irv smirked.

"Bugs are elusive. You think you've eliminated them for good, but they somehow manage to come back. Funny how that works, huh? I guess I made it convenient for you guys by trusting Grace with a spare key."

"It saved me from more paperwork, for sure," Irv leaned in with a half-smile and lifted his broad shoulders. They locked eyes for a moment before he moistened his lips and sat upright. "All right. Tell you what. I'll extend you a little unearned trust here due to our mutual connections with Ozzy and Ram. But don't take my willingness to answer your questions as a sign of friendship. And keep in mind, if this is a trick to get me removed from the case, even if I lose my badge, I am law enforcement for life. Yours will not be kind to you."

"No need for threats, Irv. Life has already been extremely unkind. I researched RICO and understand its concept. I learned it's an umbrella term used to go after high-value targets. Are you saying my father is a mobster? Because I see a successful, rich, non-Caucasian businessman being investigated due to his accent, skin color, and country of origin."

"Jesus," he tilted his head skyward. "The FBI doesn't have unlimited resources. That's the military," he smirked. "You can't imagine how many hours, personnel, and resources we dedicate to cases like these. They take years to investigate, and not to mention the paperwork—copious amounts. Forest-fulls. The attorneys' bills alone would wipe out the state of Texas if it were a forest. We took an interest in Anselmo Marta six years ago when a confidential informant named him a co-conspirator in another case—not because of his ethnicity. We looked into him, and initially his business dealings appeared legitimate. He was a copper miner who escaped political persecution with his family in the mid-'90s and entered the US under asylum protection. Considering his sizeable assets, the country welcomed him with open arms. He continued to work in metallurgy, lending his new government his vast knowledge of geology and chemistry. Your father is a genius."

"Must be where I got my math and science genes. Honestly, he never talked about what he did, and we didn't ask any questions as long as he kept us fed, clothed in designer duds, and living the Malibu life. We knew he worked with precious metals and had government connections, but beyond the basics, his day-to-day dealings were his."

"And that's what we thought, too. But we kept tabs on Anselmo anyway while the other case played out, and guess what? It turned out our informant was on to something."

"How so?" Allyson asked, jutting her chin and wrinkling her nose.

"Murder for hire, extortion, money laundering, bribing officials," Irv counted with his fingers. "The top four in RICO, if you recall."

Allyson shook her head. "I don't believe it!"

"Why would you? You said yourself you never paid attention."

"Listen, we came from a country where businessmen who do business the *RICO* way were a dime a dozen. You knew who they were and stayed away. My father—our family—we never associated with those types. They're one of the reasons we sought asylum."

"You want examples? Fine. I'll start with the money laundering. It's directly tied to his ownership stake in H0rr Studios. Bad money goes into the studio; good money comes out with an incredible ROI."

"I had no idea he even owned a portion of H0rr until Atticus told me the other day. Why do you think his money is bad?"

"Because he has other businesses that aren't legal. Human trafficking being a big one."

Allyson moaned. "No!"

"Yes. Across two international borders! Several of the smuggled individuals ended up at the movie lot as part of the construction crew and even the background actors and extras. We're waiting on a warrant to grant us access to the studio's HR files to confirm this."

"Let me get this straight. You *think* some of H0rr Studios' employees were illegals, so you jump to the conclusion my father was trafficking them? Why? Because he lives in Argentina? And you don't think my claim of race bias is valid? Come on, Irv! Have you only been watching Ram's reports? Here's a breaking news story for you: all of North America is struggling with an immigration problem. The presence of illegals does not prove human trafficking, only that people are migrating toward a hope for a better future."

"Don't get all liberal and condescending on me. There's more to it than I can speak to here, but the smuggling connects to the next serious charge, which is murder for hire. The majority of the recovered bodies from the studio were found in locked, hidden rooms with obvious signs of torture. Decomposition suggests they were there for months. Maybe even years. We're working as fast as we can to help identify the victims. What's clear is someone was hired to kill them."

"Another wild jump, Irv!" Allyson threw up her hands. "Hiring implies payment. How do you prove that? Their deaths could be the work of a serial killer using the underground space without anyone the wiser. Hell, it could be one of those Giver fucks!"

"Or it could be the work of your sister and her creative direction. And if that's the case, then we have your father on something called *respondeat superior*, which says corporations are responsible for their employees' crimes if they directly profited from them. Your father took his illegal money, invested it into the studio, and cashed in on large profits with each subsequent blockbuster, thanks to your sister's ability to create realistic torture porn. "

"I need a minute," Allyson whined. "My head is thumping." she put it between her knees to avoid hyperventilating. After a moment, she recovered. "If I have evidence proving what you say, at least the part about the execs profiting from crimes, can I be implicated somehow because I had prior knowledge and didn't tell anyone?"

"If it helps our case, the timeline doesn't matter. You could have simply tripped across paperwork while going through your deceased sister's possessions. Hell, I can say I found it in evidence boxes from Andrea's apartment or any number of places we have access to."

"Christ! This means going against my father, Atticus, and ruining our family name. It means wiping away any positive thing the studio, Roger, and Craig, ever did for the industry and through their philanthropy. It means mass hysteria for the Givers and the fandom. It will be on my head when H0rr Studios' house of cards disintegrates."

"You give me what you have, and no one will be the wiser as to where it originated."

"Isn't finding bodies hidden in a secret tunnel enough to bring charges against Vanessa Rapaporte and her executive team?"

"It's circumstantial. We need documentation demonstrating they knew about the crimes happening in the name of entertainment and profit. Because there's no repudiating solid evidence."

"I need more than your verbal assurance I'll be left unscathed from any legal drama. I'm not showing my hand until I can walk away clean."

"Considering you've been named a suspect in the three H0rr Studios employees' disappearances, I'd say that ship has sailed. Ram's report puts you in the center of anything related to the studio from now on. Some might even think you made a deal with the FBI in order to walk away safe and sound."

"You're a bastard! You used Ram and his platform to corner me."

Irv folded his lips, and the corners of his eyes crinkled. "Did I? Oops. Atticus isn't the only one who can move on this chessboard, Allyson. So what do you say? Give me what you have, and I'll protect you as best I can."

Allyson rubbed her hands on her face and scratched her head. "Can you get Ram here? If I had a witness who can swear to the promises you're making and keep you to your word, then we have a deal."

Irv slapped his hands on his thighs. "Yes! Yes," he dialed back his excitement and pulled out his phone. "Laramie. I need you to bring your sweet ass over here. Now. It's about Allyson. I'll send a car."

35

MIRANDA WRONGS

{ALLYSON}

"I have a question about WitSec, Irv," Allyson challenged. "Can you hold your excitement for a few more minutes and stay off the goddamn phone? Show some respect. I'm helping send several people to prison for a presumably long time."

"I am acting unprofessional, aren't I? I guess I needed the win, especially with Oz missing. It fucking sucks; excuse my language. I understand why you went with Ram and started looking on your own. The investigative process is arduous."

"In Andrea's case, her fate was left to the local authorities. At least with Grace, you have the FBI and its vast resources at your disposal. I'm sure that will make all the difference. Anyway, WitSec: Can you send someone to another country? A country where there is no extradition treaty with the US?"

"Your question is rather specific. Can you give me context?"

"You made Roger an offer too, didn't you? He changed his appearance and was headed to Uzbekistan after Andrea went missing. Even for him, that seemed out of character. How many people involved with H0rr Studios have you made a deal with? Was Craig on board too before he vanished?"

"Allyson . . ."

"Am I going to disappear too, Irv? How can I trust you or your people? Between the Givers and Atticus, it's clear people are willing to betray their professional loyalties." Then she gasped and put her hand to her mouth. "Oh. My. God. Does Dr. Dean have a deal with you guys, too?"

"Not here, okay?"

"Why? Don't you have people surrounding the park? Shouldn't this be the safest place in Seattle right now?"

"Technically, yes, although not everyone is at the same pay grade. Do you get my meaning?" he murmured.

A woman with two small dogs limped by and locked eyes with Allyson. The forced smile on her face had her considering Irv's veiled warning. "Okay. When Ram gets here, let's go somewhere a little more exclusive to hash out the details."

Twenty minutes later, Ram had joined Allyson and Irv. They were in Irv's car, with Allyson and Ram in the back, driving away from the city, where CCTV cameras and any other surveillance besides satellite were unavailable.

"How far out are we headed, Allyson?"

"Are you familiar with Browns Point Lighthouse? Probably won't be too crowded on a day like today." Rain was falling with varying intensity, and the wind lent a chill to the air, making outdoor activities less than ideal.

"Oooh. Isn't there a casino there? We could grab a nice meal on Uncle Sam's dime before we head back," Ram suggested.

Allyson shifted toward Ram. "What is it with you and food today?"

"I'm a growing boy!" he smirked.

While Allyson and Ram bantered further in the back seat, Irv navigated through the back streets leading to the lighthouse on the east entrance of Puget Sound.

"I did a tour here years ago. If you flash your badge, Irv, I'm sure we can get into the tower. Our very own Faraday-like cage," Allyson chided.

"It's a hollow concrete tower," Irv snorted. "Though, let's go see. It does have an old bell!"

Inside, there were three folding chairs leaning against the wall. The bell hung in the center of the room, a thick hemp rope tied to its clapper.

"If you like what I give you, Irv, I'll let you be the one who rings it. You were so excited earlier when I agreed to your terms. Then I denied you a proper celebration."

"Deal!" Irv beamed. "It's a childhood dream come true, huh, Laramie?" he said, clasping his hand around the back of Ram's neck and shaking him.

Like a switch, everyone's demeanor changed as they sat in a small circle, facing each other in their metal chairs.

"I'm unsure where to begin," Allyson launched into her speech, "I do need to make one thing clear: Andrea and I never got along. Extreme competitiveness and even violence worsened once we immigrated to the States. She was always the aggressor. It started as mean little torments and eventually grew into such hostility that she attempted to kill me at least twice before we hit puberty. My parents were busy with their individual pursuits and didn't notice much. Our housekeeper/nanny, Maria, did her best to keep us in line and alive," Allyson snickered.

"When we were twelve, Andrea committed her first murder. We were at summer camp, and the victim was my friend. My sister became jealous, and one night, while the entire camp was playing a murder mystery game, invented by me no less, Andrea made her move and killed Calliope Cameron. Yes, *that* Cameron family. It was deemed an accidental drowning. Everyone went home early and on with their lives—everyone but me. I couldn't cope. My nerves were frayed. The only way to self-regulate was by doing this," Allyson rolled her sleeves and showed Irv the scars on her arms.

"And this." She lifted her shirt, revealing more marks on her stomach. "Ram can attest to more. However, you get the picture. Andrea was actually the one who turned me on to cutting. She slashed my stomach with a kitchen knife during a fight. This one, right here. It changed my life. I could actually feel again! As expected, she ratted me out to my mother, who promptly deposited me in a psych hospital for treatment. That began my long, painful road through mental illness."

Irv had a small notepad out and was scribbling notes. Ram sat with his arms crossed and his head bent, staring at his shoes.

"When we were barely sixteen, my mother attempted suicide. At least, that was the story. Once again, my lovely twin was to blame. She knew my mother was developing a drinking problem and decided to swap out fairly harmless pills with a high-dose painkiller. When my mother chased it with her morning bottle of champagne, it had nearly catastrophic consequences. Patricia, my mother, was aware Andrea was to blame, as was I, yet we kept it quiet. She became a pariah within her social circle, losing several key friendships. Even though they relied on prescription pills and booze to get through their day, they had never considered something so 'desperate.' When her car went off the cliff in San Francisco a month later, everyone shook their head and said, 'If only she had asked for help.' Even the police saw it as an attempt that ended successfully. I can't be 100 percent certain Andrea was behind the accident. One way or another, though, she was responsible. Who would want to live in the same house as your attempted murderer? Or your evil spawn?"

Allyson rummaged through her satchel and pulled out a file folder overflowing with sheets of paper. She handed it to Irv.

"Andrea apparently discovered a new hobby when she moved to Atlanta after college about twenty years ago. This is what she left for me to find. Mostly, they are faces and scribbled notes, but they might still help solve a few cold cases around Lake Lanier. I'm uncertain if she committed any murders between sixteen and twenty-one, because I was in and out of hospitals. If you track her whereabouts, I bet you'll find a cold case or two with similar themes in those areas."

Ram appeared stunned, and Irv stoic as he accepted the bundle of documents. Neither spoke as Allyson continued.

"When the rumors surfaced about H0rr Studios, my gut said it was true. Yet I couldn't believe Roger, the crew, and the studio execs would go along with such heinous acts. Even after I met Roger, I had a hard time believing it. Roger was a fiend, for sure. We've all heard about his inappropriate behavior when he first found fame. However, actors are weird, and so am I," she shrugged. "So I put all those ugly whispers inside a box in my head where I kept all the other terrible things and let our relationship unfold as it did. It's unclear where they got these people . . . maybe they *were* trafficked by my father, as you suggested, Irv. For some reason, Andrea kept copies of their nondisclosure agreements and the final script for the first *Caretaker* movie, signed off by Vanessa Rapaporte." She reached into her bag and pulled out the items Andrea had hidden in the shed. "This should be enough to connect the execs and my father to crimes committed by the studio employees and put a shining gold star on your RICO case. Your team may need to spend time tracking down the cast members' names and whereabouts listed in each movie and subsequent serial shows. I'm positive you'll find the majority will be hard to locate alive. In addition to those documents, I found evidence of the bribery and extortion charges you mentioned. Here is a USB drive containing files and audio clips of a local doctor running a health clinic near the studio campus. She discusses body disposal, treating life-threatening wounds, and more. Her facility was culpable in concealing whatever went on during *The Caretaker* filming and other shows produced by H0rr Studios."

Ram stood and rubbed his face until it was dark red. "I can't fucking believe this! How could they all be involved in such a cover-up? How did they sleep at night knowing people were dying horrible deaths for *entertainment*?! Not only that, millions worldwide watched it, glorified the anti-hero, following him as if he were a God . . ." Turning to Allyson, he continued, "And you! You knew all along?! Slept with this man, befriended him, stayed in touch with your sister, and acted like nothing was amiss! I'm disgusted by you!" he spat.

"Hey, man, why don't you step outside and get some fresh air? This is a lot to take in." Irv stood and put his hand on Ram's shoulder.

"You can judge me all you want, Laramie Helm, yet you're one to talk. Your profession profits from reporting on this shit. You wouldn't have a job if people like my sister didn't exist. What drove you to be a journalist? Shit. Like. This. I guarantee. Don't deny the idea of covering this story has you excited. Killers are going to kill whether people like me know about it or not. And people like you get off reporting about it. We all make choices. Is yours any better than mine? Who's to say? Nevertheless, as much as I hated my sister, I couldn't be the one to turn her in. I had no proof. Coupled with my history of mental illness? If I came to Irv ten years ago when *The Caretaker* started, do you think he would've believed me? I doubt I would've believed me."

Ram stared into Allyson's eyes before dropping his head and rounding his shoulders. Then he walked out the door.

Allyson rubbed the top of her head and growled. "Fuck!" she shouted. It echoed in the lighthouse's hollow interior and rang in her ears.

"It's okay, Allyson. He just needs to wrap his head around this. I do too, but I'm not as personally invested. Thank you for everything you've provided, and I promise your name will never be mentioned. There's no reason. This stuff could've been found in Andrea's home, office, or random storage unit. It could even be Craig's or Roger's. I'll figure it out. You might reconsider making yourself scarce for a time, though. I've talked to my boss about arresting you and keeping you in protective custody. The only problem might be Atticus. He'll fight like hell to get you released, and he'd have access to you even if we can get a judge to deny bail."

"The way he had access to Roger after he got arrested at the airport?"

"Aww, hell, Allyson. That's not what happened."

"What did, Irv? You were pretty fucking spooked when Roger vanished from the hotel."

Irv huffed and puffed, kicking at a nonexistent rock on the lighthouse floor. "I'll admit, we did try talking to Roger. We attempted to work a deal with him but never got the terms right. I believe he intended to go to Uzbekistan and turn over evidence once he was safe from extradition and prosecution. I think he had such documentation with him when he was arrested. Yet when we went to the airport to collect his luggage, TSA said the Feds had already picked it up."

"Atticus!" Allyson said it like a curse word.

"That would be my guess."

"You're right. I need to get scarce and quick."

"Let me take you in."

"On what charge?"

"Oz to start."

Allyson groaned. "Break my heart, why don't you? The last thing I'd want to be blamed for is my friend's disappearance! And for the record, I don't like this idea, but my options are limited. So I guess I have the right to remain silent from here on out."

36

THE TOUCH

{ALLYSON}

"**W**here the hell is Ram?" Allyson asked as she and Irv exited the lighthouse.

"I'll text him," Irv replied, pulling out his cell phone. By the time they reached the car, he had a reply. "Damn."

"What?"

"It appears he took a rideshare back to the city. His text says he had to get to work on the evening news edition."

"He's not going to report about this," Allyson waved a hand between them, "is he?"

"No. He can't until I get these documents are validated."

"Validated? How?"

"Technology, obviously. There's a dedicated team. We always have to check our sources. Come on, let's head back. I want to get these in the proper hands and move this case in the right direction for a change."

"Don't you need to read me my rights?"

"Right now, you are only a person of interest in the disappearance of a federal officer. Once we get to the offices, I'll have you in a room like before, where we will talk about the last time you saw Osgood as Grace. Your answers are what will get you booked. Understood?"

Allyson rubbed her fingers together. The heat had been sucked from her extremities during the intense lighthouse meeting. A cold sweat trickled down her back as Irv talked about her connection to Grace as if he believed she was involved. Did she make the right decision to trust Irv? Why did Ram abandon her? She could use an ally right now. "Yes. I think so."

Irv's cell rang as four local police patrol cars, lights flashing and sirens wailing, flew past them as they merged onto the interstate.

"Wow. I wonder what's going on?" she asked, pointing at the scene.

Irv held up his finger and put a wireless earbud in his ear. "This is Agent Kingsley."

While Irv took his call, Allyson daydreamed about the last few weeks. Then, the only vexing details about her life were managing treatment and living in outpatient apartments. Now, she longed for them.

"Thank you for the update," Irv finished. His grip tightened on the steering wheel as his face turned into an icy glower, and his posture shifted inward. It was as if he wanted to curl into a ball.

"What's wrong?"

"It was an update on those police we saw. It seems another foot has washed ashore only a few miles from here."

"Oh, no! It's not Gra—Ozzy's, is it?" Allyson bit her bottom lip.

"No. The preliminary report claims it's a female's foot."

"Hmm. I think the other instances have been male."

"I don't follow those cases because the local agency within the discovery's boundaries manages them. Scientists!" Irv grumbled. "Ram could tell you for sure."

"It's too bad he left without us. Shouldn't you call him?"

"I'm sure he's already aware. There's a fucking app for everything now," Irv spat.

"I thought police dispatch and transmissions were encrypted?" Allyson asked.

"They are, but if you have a key, you can get access, as with most locked things. I let him in on the secret FBI stuff when I can. Otherwise, he does well with the local action on his own."

The car's intermittent wipers scraped across the windshield and echoed in the quiet.

"Hey, why did you get alerted to *this* Salish Sea foot incident if the local authorities have handled all the others?"

"Why do you ask so many goddamn questions?" Irv snarled.

"Whoa. I'm sorry. I didn't mean to upset you," Allyson frowned. Her eyebrows pinched as if she were in great pain or deep thought.

"It seems wherever you go, bad shit follows. I'm hoping to get back to the office in one piece. You're like Midas, except everyone you touch vanishes or winds up in pieces after you've made contact."

"Where is this coming from?"

"Gee, I don't know. Your twin sister—dead. Your former lover—dead. Your artist friend, Craig—dead. Some guy who may have Internet bullied you—dead. Oz . . ."

"Don't you dare say dead! Grace is strong and too vivacious to be anything but alive. They'll turn up. You'll see!"

"*His* name is Osgood Kingsley, goddammit! He's a man and a formidable FBI agent."

Allyson's eyes widened, and she pursed her lips as if she were going to whistle. Instead, she turned her attention to the roadside scenery. "Yes, of course. I keep forgetting. Osgood—Ozzy is amazing and will be back with an unbelievable story. I just know it." Irv was obviously agitated, and she didn't want to poke the special agent bear too much. She rubbed the top of her head and murmured a prayer.

"You better hope he turns up, or so help me . . ."

"Are you threatening me? I'm trying to help you, Irv."

"Are you, though? Or are you simply playing a role? You wouldn't be the first person I've met pretending to be something you're not," Irv snapped. "You have this whole tough-as-nails, yet vulnerable-as-a-kitten vibe you like people to buy into. Oz fell for it, as did Ram. Even I've been a victim a time or two. But there is something about you that is just not right. You are too good to be true, and I'm betting you're hiding more than a serial-killing sister."

"Don't forget my mob boss father. Or is he the cartel king? What's the difference between a mafia and a cartel anyway?"

"You can joke all you want. However, I've got good instincts about people, as does Ram. He sees through you now. It's why you went after Oz, isn't it? Because he'd begun to see the real you too."

"You have the footage from my apartment. I couldn't have harmed your brother because I didn't even leave until Ram asked me to check his place hours after he vanished. What has gotten into you? You were practically singing my praises when I handed you those documents. Then you get this mysterious phone call, and now, I'm Satan's spawn!"

His phone rang again. "For fuck's sake!" he shouted before tapping his earpiece. "Agent Kingsley," he growled. "Yes. Yes, sir. I'm almost there now. My apologizes. The traffic . . . Yes. I understand."

Irv steered the car off an exit too far outside the city limits to be theirs.

"Where are we going?" Allyson asked, gripping the door handle as Irv took a turn off the frontage road too fast.

"I need gas," he muttered.

Allyson peered at the gauges but couldn't get a clear read on them.

"I said I need goddamn gas!" he shouted, meeting her gaze.

She averted her attention back out the passenger window and nibbled at a loose cuticle on her thumb.

To his word, Irv slid into a crowded wholesale club gas station.

"Do you mind if I run inside to use the bathroom while you fuel up?" she asked.

"Don't take too long. We're on a tight schedule."

Allyson assessed the number of cars ahead of them and nearly commented on his station choice. "Sure. Can I grab you a hotdog? You seem hangry."

Irv narrowed his eyes and curled his lips in a sneer. Allyson threw up her hands in defense. "Okay. I'm going. Geesh."

Several black SUVs pulled in as she walked from the car through the parking lot towards the entrance. They were fanning out as if to cover a large area, and it struck her as odd. Getting a feeling like something was wrong, she turned back toward Irv, catching him pulling away from the line and swinging into a parking spot. He got out and walked to a sidewalk lined with knee-high shrubbery.

"What is he doing?" she mumbled.

Irv paced and rubbed his face before running his hands through his hair. He tilted his head towards the sky as if asking for divine guidance, then pulled out his phone and walked further along the sidewalk, away from the car.

Allyson turned back. The materials she gave Irv were sitting unguarded on the backseat. If they were crucial to his case, why did he leave them out in the open for anyone to take?

Once she got to the car, her eyes on Irv's position the entire time, she crouched as if to tie her shoe and tested the door handle. *Unlocked.* Opening it as little as she dared, she slipped her hand in and grabbed the items, stuffing them back into her satchel where she had stored them only hours before. When she stood back up, she searched for Irv. A cold chill ran through her body. He was nowhere to be found, and the black SUVs she'd seen entering the parking lot were now retreating and speeding away.

"What the fuck?" she whispered, spinning around slowly, twice, to survey her surroundings for any sign of Irv. He had vanished right before her eyes. Maybe he was right. She was Midas incarnate!

37

A WELL-PLACED BET

{ALLYSON}

"**E**xcuse me. Like a big dummy, I've locked my keys and phone in the car. Can I use yours to call my boyfriend?" Allyson asked the woman handling the service desk at the warehouse store from which Irv had vanished.

Allyson didn't want to raise any alarms by calling the police and claiming Irv might have been kidnapped in broad daylight. She wasn't confident about what had transpired. She also didn't want to stick around too long and get blamed for yet another missing person. The only one left in her shrinking inner circle who wasn't mad at her and could be trusted implicitly was Dr. Dean.

"If I ask you to come get me in Kent, without question, could you?" she asked him.

"Absolutely. Are you safe?"

"As safe as a wholesale club on a Tuesday can be, I guess."

"I'll park outside the exit. Look for me there in about thirty minutes," Dr. Dean assured her.

She thanked the woman and asked what time it was before heading to the bathroom for real this time. Afterward, she made her way to the seats by the small food court. With a giant pizza slice, she huddled at a corner table facing the exiting crowd of shoppers and waited for Dr. Dean.

Because she had time to kill, she pulled out a stack of documents she'd nearly handed over to the FBI and studied them. Everything pointed to Vanessa Rapaporte and her executive team as the guilty parties in the plot to generate revenue for the studio. The individual shareholders were missing from the financials Andrea printed out covering the last seven years. How would these documents help the FBI with their RICO case against her father?

"I think I dodged a bullet there," she murmured. "Without anything to link my father to the crimes mentioned by Irv, protection might be unnecessary. I need to learn more about my father's business dealings and figure out how to honor Andrea's wishes in the process."

With her thirty-minute wait nearly over, she stuffed the items back in her satchel and headed outside. It was twilight and time for Ram's first evening news report. Would he keep his word and avoid revealing her potential deal with the Feds? Was he back in Tacoma, already reporting on the latest Salish Sea foot? Why was he so freakin' mad at her? Didn't he get loyalty and her drive for self-protection?

As she walked to the curb, a black SUV came to a standstill and rolled the back window down.

"Allyson, Dear. What have you gotten yourself into this time?"

Atticus King.

"Shit!" Allyson swore behind a fake smile. "Atticus?! What are you doing here?"

"Playing your knight in shining armor, it appears. Come, get in!"

Allyson stepped back and glanced at the parking lot entrance. "Dr. Dean is supposed to be picking me up."

"Ah, yes. About that. Hop in, and I'll explain."

Allyson fidgeted awkwardly.

"He's not coming, Dear. I'm your only option."

"Where is he?"

"He's been fired effective immediately."

"You can't do that! I control my healthcare."

"I won't beg, Allyson. David, be a gent and go open the door for our lovely guest," Atticus instructed his driver.

Allyson groaned. "Never mind, David. I can get in all on my own, like a big girl."

Before she shut the door, the vehicle was moving. Allyson speculated on whether this car was from the entourage earlier. It crossed her mind that she'd again trusted the wrong person. Gathering her nerve, she locked eyes with Atticus. "Why were you talking to Dr. Dean?"

"I've told you before, among my roles as your family's counsel is risk management. When I heard about the recent events at your residential building, I spoke to him as the facility's owner. He agreed it would be in your best interest to step back as your caregiver in exchange for me leaving the medical board out of it."

"You threatened him," Allyson stated.

"No. I pointed out the errors he'd made in managing the building's safety and, therefore, its residents' welfare. He understood his profession's governing body might frown upon such misconduct. He admitted he could've handled many aspects differently and said you deserved better. It was a coincidence you called when you did. I offered to come in his place. He sends his regrets and best wishes."

"Is he still alive?"

Atticus shook with laughter. "Of course, Dear. Why would you ask such a thing?"

Allyson arched an eyebrow. "What happens now?"

"Dr. Dean suggested relocating you to a familiar place where you felt safe in an effort to keep progressing in your treatment. Naturally, I considered your primary residence. Asking your current tenant to leave without advanced notice seemed unfair. As luck would have it, a space in the same building was available. It's three floors higher, much larger, and an even better view. If you like it, there is a purchase option. I went ahead and arranged for your possessions to be moved tonight. However, the space won't be ready until tomorrow. I was hoping you'd stay with me instead."

Allyson shivered. "You're kind to offer, but I literally slept in my storage unit last night. I would happily crash on the floor at my new place."

"The movers are working through the night to expedite your transition. You'd just be in the way."

Allyson smiled. "My new neighbors will love me for that!"

"Neighbors? The entire floor is yours."

Her eyes grew big. "Larger indeed!" she chuckled. "I'd be honored to stay with you as long as you're sure it's not an inconvenience."

"No, Dear. I am humbled to be your host. It's the least I can do!" Atticus smiled, returning her jolly mood. "Have you eaten? We could go to dinner first before settling in for the night?"

"I grabbed a pizza slice at the store, but thank you." Allyson grinned, then turned serious. She glanced at the driver and back at Atticus. "When we get to your place, will we be completely alone?"

"If you'd be more comfortable, we don't have to be."

"No. No," she slanted her eyes back to the driver. "I want answers. Too much is unclear to me, and it would be best if our conversation were private. We'd have attorney/client privilege, right?"

"Certainly, Dear!"

"Okay. And you have liquor? I may need a little liquid courage."

Atticus patted her leg. "Courage? What for? Am I that scary? I am but a humble servant, and whatever I have is at your disposal. Mi casa."

Allyson resisted the urge to flinch at his touch. "Is your offer binding?"

"Are you sure you don't want to leave the art world and become a legal professional? You have such a natural attention to detail and a quick wit."

"If I'm unable to recover from the Holger Beitin–Space Needle debacle, I might have to contemplate a career change! Law school seems too harrowing, though."

"Not for someone like you. If you change your mind, I would be happy to help."

Thirty minutes later, they were in the driveway of a modest dwelling along Seattle's Arroyo Beach coastline. Allyson never imagined where Atticus might live, but a quaint multi-story mid-century modern home wasn't even close. Its street-facing façade showcased a simple front entry and a three-car garage, yet the water-facing view was spectacular.

"It's twenty minutes from the airport *and* no noise pollution! My only complaint is I don't spend nearly enough time here to appreciate it fully," Atticus commented, as Allyson stepped out onto the second-floor veranda, off the chef's kitchen.

"Do you have a family? I'm embarrassed to say I know little about you."

"Why? You've had no reason to. I am twice divorced and have four adult children."

"You don't look old enough," Allyson complimented.

"Flattery will get you everywhere with this old man," Atticus flashed Allyson a genuine smile, and it became clear how two women could fall in love with him. He was classically handsome.

"Can I pour you a glass of wine?" he asked.

"Sure. A full-body red, if you have it."

"A young woman who knows what she prefers. How refreshing. I have the perfect bottle. It's from a local family operation in Woodinville."

"Really? Which one? When I first moved here, I worked a few odd jobs to support myself, including a wine pourer at two smaller wineries there."

"Not this one. They don't have a tasting room."

"Us service industry folks were a tight community. We got together regularly and discussed the local vintages. I bet I can place it."

"What's the wager? I've told you I'm not a gambling man. For this, though, I'll partake."

Allyson tapped her finger to her chin. "How about complete transparency for the next hour? I ask a question about my father, his business, or what you do for him, and you answer."

Atticus whistled as he popped open the bottle. "No peeking! Wait for me on the balcony. I'll bring the first glass with some snacks, and if you guess correctly, I'll bring the bottle and do your bidding."

"Yay!" Allyson clapped. While she waited, she closed her eyes and breathed in the Sound's salt air. Even though it was cold by the water, a warm undercurrent in the breeze made it clear Spring was on its way.

"Did you just throw that together?" she asked when Atticus returned with a small charcuterie platter and filled wine glasses.

"Ha! My instinct is to say yes so you won't think less of me, but I'm starting the honesty now. I had a dinner party last night, and the caterers sympathized with the old bachelor who can't even boil water and left me a few provisions."

"A catered dinner party. Sounds fancy. I remember those days with my parents. Entertaining clients?"

"I'd use the word hosting. To entertain sounds more fun than it was."

"Oh!" she gave a short laugh. "I'm sorry."

"Whatever for?" he smirked.

"Making assumptions. Anyway, give me the glass. I can't wait to win this bet!" she changed the subject. Dramatically, she held the filled stemware to the light before sticking her nose past the rim and taking a long whiff. Then she swirled the nearly purple liquid and inhaled further before finally taking a sip and swishing it in her mouth.

"Are you trying to worry me with your showmanship, or is this a legitimate talent?" he inquired.

She swallowed audibly. "I guess you'll find out!" She smacked her lips. "This is tough because the grapes come from a common field several small operations purchase from. Three to five different varietals and a nice finish. I'm thinking the Thews Family vineyard, bottled last year or the year before."

"Incredible! You are absolutely correct. Did you see the bottle when I went to uncork it?"

"Why Atticus King! Are you accusing me of cheating?"

"You simply continue to amaze me with your hidden depths!"

"As an artist, it's second nature for me to hone in on detail. To be fair, though, I've had this before. Just recently, in fact—at my sister's cabin in the woods." Allyson gave Atticus a pointed look. His demeanor shifted from confident to concerned.

"Quick wit, indeed," he sighed, lifting his glass in a mock toast. "Let the questioning commence."

Without wasting time or mincing words, Allyson asked, "Is my father a mobster or involved in a cartel?"

"Wow! A big one right out of the gate. Are you sure you want to start there?"

"Quite," Allyson quipped, popping cheese in her mouth.

"All right. Maybe I should've opened the whisky instead," he murmured.

Allyson laughed. "The night is still young!"

Atticus set his glass on the table and cleared his throat. "Your father deals with various businessmen in the copper and mining industries in addition to his other ventures. Certain individuals are less honest than you and I are tonight. However, he does not head an organized syndicate, despite what the FBI thinks."

"Then you're aware of their RICO investigation."

"Yes. It appears you are too. I'm assuming Special Agent Kingsley tried to get you to agree to a deal if you turn your father in?"

"Hrmph. 'Coerce' might be a better description. I told him I had no idea about Pa's business dealings and found their claims absurd. I had no clue he was the majority owner of H0rr Studios until you mentioned it the other day. He didn't believe me. Now, it would seem they are using my friend Grace's disappearance as a ploy to pressure me. Have you heard about it?"

"A missing friend and a bloody sweatshirt. It's a good way to make a person feel vulnerable and without alternatives. People are prone to revealing more than they intend in those situations. Keep in mind, you can call on me. I am here to help. Please don't speak to Irv or any agent again without my representation."

Allyson considered Irv's vanishing act and smirked inwardly. She may not literally be able to speak to him again. "I should have called you right away. I panicked."

"Undoubtedly! Anyone would have in your position. Don't get me wrong. I'm not accusing the agency of any wrongdoing. I respect their position, not their tactics. Look at what they did with Roger!"

"What do you mean?"

"It was a little convenient his flight never left SeaTac."

"You think the FBI fabricated the security threat?"

"No. I believe they saw Roger's leaving as the threat and used their considerable reach to ensure he remained within their grasp. Once he touched down in Uzbekistan, he would've been inaccessible."

"Why was he a threat if he left the country? Did he have proof to validate their claims?"

Atticus scoffed. "Roger couldn't validate a parking token without assistance."

"You're not wrong," Allyson giggled. "I want your personal opinion, though. You seem to know him better than I do. Is my father involved in something illegal?"

Atticus's expression became pained. "My Dear, let's drop the pretenses, shall we? You knew about your sister's predilections. You're all involved!"

Allyson choked on a cracker.

"I'm sorry. My frankness startled you."

"A tiny bit. Could I go to jail?"

"It's unlikely the case will go anywhere. Their potential witness list is growing shorter, and all their evidence is circumstantial."

"That sounds ominous. Are you saying Andrea, Roger, and Craig were *silenced*?"

Atticus threw his head back in a hearty laugh. "Not at all! No one in H0rr Studios' entire organization would speak against your father. They exist and thrive due to Anselmo's ownership and leadership."

"I see. What about his other business ventures? Could someone from another entity speak against him?"

"They'd have no reason to."

"Unless they were put in a vulnerable position with no other options. I can't be the only one in that situation."

"You are not vulnerable as long as I exist. Rest assured, Dear."

"Andrea felt unsafe. I could tell from her writing. Did you get her into the wellness retreat?"

"She didn't need anyone's help to get in. All she had to do was pick up the phone."

"Why? Did she have a relationship with the doctor there with Roger and Vanessa's previous stays?"

"Because your father owns it."

"What?" she gasped.

"I think we need more wine!" Atticus stood abruptly.

"I'll come with you. Even though the view is extraordinary, it's getting a little too chilly out here for my taste." She collected the cheese platter and followed him inside.

After refilling their glasses, Atticus showed her to an intimate sitting area filled floor to ceiling with books. The air lingered with cigar smoke.

"Wow! You have an extraordinary collection. How do you have time to read?" Allyson quipped.

"Other than briefs and fillings? I don't. I'm acting as if, though. Someday, I won't have to pretend and daydream about sitting here with a whisky and a cigar. And when that day comes, they'll be here, waiting." Atticus gazed at his collection wistfully.

"Okay, back to the topic at hand. Why a wellness retreat?"

Atticus swirled his wine and took a long sip. "As with any smart investor, Anselmo's holdings are diverse. Among his acquisitions and investments are sprinkled in businesses based on you girls. The studio was with Andrea in mind, and the retreat was for you."

"I don't know whether to be touched or pissed. I mean, he could've bought me a gallery."

"I believe he meant it as a way to honor your lifelong struggles."

"No thanks to his other daughter's behavior. Again, a gallery would've meant more."

Atticus scratched his cheek, and his body shook with amusement. "I believe the Palm Springs property brings in more revenue, and it will be yours one day if you want it."

"Unless the FBI seizes it," she murmured into her glass. "Was Andrea aware he was H0rr's majority shareholder?"

"Yes. She's the one who brought him on board. She saw the potential for the company and worked hard to make it profitable. Neither dreamed how successful it would truly become."

"Does Pa understand the how and why behind it?"

"He doesn't need to."

"So Andrea devising and choreographing real-life murders for profit isn't a concern? I would think he'd like to know something like that!"

Atticus shifted in his seat. "That is a heavy accusation, Allyson, and only a rumor. Imagine the sheer number of people involved in such a cover-up. It would be nearly impossible to keep such a huge secret."

"Yes, I can imagine. It sounds like the foundation for a RICO case. I just can't wrap my head around my father willingly being involved."

"Now, Allyson. You sound like Special Agent Kingsley and his team."

"Ouch. It's my turn to be frank, Atticus. Andrea was a killer, and it wasn't only in her downtime. If my father knew about the studio's activities, the FBI would have a case."

"I say, prove it. It's a challenge I'd like to end my career on."

"End?"

"I'm an old man. I plan on retiring soon. As much as I love the law, I do have other passions."

"I'm sure. What about the movie lot discoveries? Doesn't that help their case?"

"My colleague who covers Canadian law is handling the finer details. So far, the only thing it has revealed is the FBI's ability to chase their tail. They have subpoenaed the studio for various records and are scrambling to help the Constable's office justify their entry into a private, secure building. Any losses they experienced were due to negligence on their part."

"What about the bodies inside the locked cells in the hidden tunnel?"

Atticus paled. "What? There were a couple of police officers the last I heard."

"Oops. I forgot I was supposed to keep that under wraps."

"Please go on," Atticus frowned into his glass.

Allyson cleared her throat and hesitated. "Irv mentioned that there were additional bodies discovered in a concealed tunnel beneath the buildings. They were in locked rooms and had been there for a while. The FBI has a forensics team investigating it to assist the local authorities."

"When did he share this information? I haven't been notified."

"Today."

"You were with the Special Agent today? Is that why you needed rescuing in Kent?"

"I was with Ram. There was another Salish Sea foot washed ashore to report on."

"Fascinating," Atticus said as if he were cursing.

"How so?"

It was Atticus's turn to appear abashed. "Is our hour over yet?" he smirked.

"Nowhere close," Allyson stated, not bothering to check the time. "I won fair and square, Atticus. What aren't you telling me?"

"Those feet. I was certain at least a few were from Andrea's . . . *experiments*. There was a similar phenomenon in Georgia while she lived there. Scientists used the same disarticulation theory—it was a natural occurrence as a body breaks down in the water. Except it was a lake and not the sea. Lake Lanier has a long history of tragic boating and drowning accidents. Thus authorities brushed each incident aside as another accident victim making its way shoreside as it slowly decomposed in the water. I assumed the occurrences would stop with Andrea gone." Atticus seemed troubled. "Did it fit the others' descriptions?"

Allyson shook her head, stunned by Atticus's revelation regarding the sea feet phenomenon. She repeatedly swallowed before her voice was steady. "Ram always said the feet were connected to a serial killer. Men's right athletic shoe, size twelve. Yet this one was a woman's. He might have more to report on the later newscast." Her voice was soft and dream-like. Ram was right about her. If she'd turned in Andrea earlier, Allyson could've saved those victims from their fate. Their blood was on her hands as much as her sister's.

"The scientists might have gotten this right, after all, and a few instances have been from accidents or suicides."

"No doubt," Allyson replied while trying to recall how many sea feet were alike, according to Ram. Was it ten? Twelve? Jesus! Her sister was a monster. "What . . . what will happen to Andrea and her possessions? Is there a plan for her remains or a will?"

"Your father wishes for her to be cremated. Once it's completed, her cremains will be flown to Argentina for burial among your people. It might be a few weeks before that happens, though, because I've been told there is a backlog at those facilities. Palm Springs is filled with retirement communities."

Allyson covered her mouth. "I never would have thought of that! How terrible." She helped herself to more cheese and crackers. "That leaves Patricia all alone in Westlake Village."

"Those were her wishes. Andrea's were less clear due to her age, hence Anselmo made the call. I'm assuming you'll want to attend any ceremony?"

"I'll have to think about it. I'm glad she's being cremated, though."

"Why?"

Allyson smiled ruefully. "While it may be silly, one of my favorite TV shows is a story about two brothers who hunt monsters. They say burning dead bodies prevents their spirits from staying around and creating more trouble. Especially the evil ones."

"Ahh, yes, I'm a fan too. Your concern is valid and practiced in many other cultures. Anyway, as far as a will, she didn't have one. Her estate will go through probate, and it will fall to your father to divide her assets after any debts are paid."

"I don't want anything of hers," Allyson stared at the floor, folding her arms in a self-hug.

"Well, you have time to decide. Anyway, did you find the journal I sent you insightful?" Atticus asked, grabbing a snack from the tray.

Allyson shook her head. "The majority of it was nonsense. It was a therapy journal the doctor made her start. Remember how I translated the first page to say, 'Stupid Fucking Therapy'? She mainly doodled and sketched staff members and other guests. I'm assuming that's who they were since none were familiar to me. It's nice to have a final remembrance, though, so thank you."

"I figured it would do better in your hands than with the authorities." After a moment of awkward silence, Atticus slapped his leg. "More wine?"

"Yes! Do you have a big selection? I'd be interested in seeing your tastes and tendencies."

"Absolutely! A little butler's pantry is on the other side of the kitchen. The mini-fridge has whites. The rack above contains the reds. They are all fair game. You'll find the really good stuff in the basement, though."

"Oh, I'm not falling for that! Even though I haven't seen my sister's movies or shows, everyone knows the heroine should never go alone to the basement. I'll stick with what you have available on this level," she laughed.

"Oh, you're the heroine, are you?" Atticus winked. "In that case, no running because you could trip and fall. Don't go *toward* the chainsaw noises or fall for the jump scare schemes. On second thought, I should come with you. Something always happens when the group gets separated!"

"Wow! You really know your horror genre."

"I *am* H0rr Studios' chief legal counsel," Atticus snickered.

After a few more glasses of wine and idle chit-chat about her father and Andrea, Atticus announced his departure. "I have an early morning," he said, standing and adjusting his gold wristwatch. "Let me show you to your room. I have an assistant who comes in the morning to get me and the house ready for the day. If you need anything, let me know, and I'll be sure to have it for you. You can stay as long as you like."

"I need my phone. I left it at my apartment. Do you think the FBI took it?"

"How about I get you a new one? I'll text my driver. He can grab one on his way to retrieve me in the morning. It will be waiting on the kitchen table whenever you wake up."

"Good point. If the FBI could bug my apartment, they could tamper with my phone. Thank you, Atticus. You've been incredibly kind, even if you feel it is your job. This," she waved around the room, "was above and beyond. It is noted and appreciated. Would it be weird to hug you?"

Atticus's smile was so unguarded a dimple appeared on his right cheek. "It's probably the wine talking for both of us, but yes, Dear, we can hug. And you are most welcome. While I can't say I am old enough to be your grandfather, I do feel an affinity to you and your sister."

"Will you join us for her services, whenever that will be, in Argentina?"

"If your father permits it, I would be honored."

"Then it will be so. Good night."

"Sweet dreams, Dear."

As Allyson relaxed in her plush bed with high-thread-count sheets, she reconsidered her feelings about Atticus. Despite crossing moral and legal boundaries as the family fixer, she believed that he was indeed a good person. She reappraised her father too, by running through all Irv and Atticus had told her about his business dealings. She was open to the possibility the FBI had a case against him. If Anselmo invested in H0rr Studios because Andrea asked him, what else would he have done for her? Bribe officials? Smuggle in humans for her various needs and desires? Extortion and murder for hire? Did that make him a loving father or a co-conspirator?

As her consciousness faded into dreams, a face emerged. It was a sketch from Andrea's recent journal. *Ozzy*. His true visage triggered a memory in her relaxed state.

Ten years ago, when Andrea first moved to Seattle, in a rare sisterly outing, Andrea asked Allyson to attend a party with her. She was meeting a group she had recently been introduced to. Bowe Bird was a rising star in the tattoo artistry world, and she insisted Allyson meet him. There were drugs. Lots of drugs. And booze. Loud music and low lighting. A small crowd gathered in the room's corner, laughing, drinking, and snorting cocaine off a man's abs. He looked like a cover model and was lying corpse-like on a long coffee table, shrieking in delight. Allyson and he locked eyes for a second. She returned his smile, holding her drink in a salute. As she revisited the memory, new details emerged from her subconscious.

The man lying on the table was Osgood Kingsley, a.k.a. Grace. More shocking than the fact she had run into Oz years before and hadn't put it together was another person there she didn't recognize until now. An indigenous male with beautiful, long dark hair worn in an intricate braid. He was showing everyone his foot. A new tattoo Bowe Bird had recently done for him. It was Billy Walls.

38

A CLEAR PICTURE

{ALLYSON}

For the first time in weeks, Allyson didn't wake startled, anxious, fearful, or grief-stricken. She stretched and lingered in the soft, warm bed in Atticus's spare room. The late morning sun streamed through the drapes, announcing it was time to rise and face whatever fresh hell awaited.

After redressing in the outfit she'd worn the day before, she padded to the kitchen to find a garment bag draped over the barstool with a note attached.

"New clothes! How thoughtful. And, naturally, they will all be in my size and style," she muttered, choosing not to check but to move to the new phone box sitting on the counter, along with another note.

As she opened the box to get the synchronization with her cloud data started, her stomach growled. A glance towards the double oven offered a third note. She laughed and smiled. It was nice to have her needs anticipated. Women's power was fantastic, and having independence was essential. Yet there were times when it was equally necessary to have things done for you, especially when you were overwhelmed and fragile. *Fragile like a school of piranhas.*

As she fiddled with the new device, eager to get back in touch with the world, she considered staying off the grid. She was less traceable without the electronic beacon. Yet her curiosity tugged at her. Where the hell was Irv? And was there any news on Grace? While grabbing a bacon slice from the plate in the oven and stuffing it into her mouth, she searched for a TV. If there were news about two missing FBI agents, it would most likely be a breaking story.

Roaming through the rooms, it struck her as peculiar that a man with his finger on the world's pulse didn't appear to have a single idiot box. Then she stopped outside Atticus's bedroom. She hesitated to enter. Looking through common rooms wasn't the same as entering an acquaintance's sanctuary uninvited. Yet she could see the TV mounted on the wall across from his bed. Surely, Atticus wouldn't mind her catching the news while her phone did its magic.

Tiptoeing inside, she hunched her shoulders and held her breath as if he would pop out and demand what she was doing in there. Sweeping the room, she searched for the remote and found it on his bedside table. She appreciated the masculine touches and his tidiness. She imagined him hiring a Feng Shui expert and an interior designer to get everything just right.

Switching on the TV, she noted what channel it was currently on—a twenty-four-hour news show, of course—and flipped through the options until she landed on Ram's channel, 12 Action News. It was almost noon. If anything were happening, he or someone from his team would be reporting on it soon. While waiting for the show to begin, she wandered toward the en suite bathroom, fighting between the instinct to remain respectable and her innate curiosity. Allyson hesitated against the doorframe as she took in its opulence. A massive walk-in closet branched to the left, while the free-standing soaking tub called to her. The rows of dark suit coats, neatly stacked sweaters, shirts, and even athletic wear drew her in like a squirrel to an acorn.

As she crept about, she resisted the urge to run her hands along each item but stopped to admire the footwear collection arranged by type and color in a floor-to-ceiling cabinet. Several designer and name-brand labels stood out, drawing comparisons to Roger's collection of highly covetable shoes. Moving on, she spotted, tucked in the corner between the cabinet and hanging space, a handsome luggage set, probably prepacked for emergent travel needs. It, too, was the best money could buy. Smoothing her hand across the buttery leather, her eyes went wide, and her heart stopped. The blood rushing to her ears nearly blocked the start of the mid-day show as she stared at another bag.

The carryall would've gone unnoticed by anyone unfamiliar with another person's possessions. It was the same brand as the others, with one subtle difference. The handles were wrapped in duct tape with little yellow Minion characters all over. The silly animated henchmen were a joke between her and, "—Roger!" she gasped in a shout. It was Roger's carry-on bag!

> "Good Afternoon, Seattle. I'm Tricia Cleveland, and this is 12 Action News at Noon. We start our broadcast this hour with a developing story. We go now to our air team coverage, positioned over I-5 at the intersections of King County International Airport and Swift Avenue. An early morning collision involving a semi and an SUV has left several dead and many more wounded. The freeway remains closed to investigators at this hour on the northbound side between exits 157 and 159. What more can you tell us from your vantage, Stu?"

Allyson couldn't hear what Stu had to say as her mind reeled and raged over why Atticus would have Roger's carry-on bag hidden in his closet. She recalled Irv complaining about the FBI's attempt at retrieving his belongings from Homeland Security only to discover another agent had already recovered them. Except it wasn't an agent at all, but an actor playing one.

"Atticus did it to protect the family," she reasoned aloud as her shaking hand pulled the bag into the room's center. She yanked her sleeve over her fingers at the last second to avoid leaving any fingerprints.

Unzipping it carefully, she used the same sleeved hand to rummage through its contents: Clothes, a toiletry bag, a strangely carved wooden box, and a leather-bound binder where Roger kept the latest *The Caretaker* scripts. Pulling each item out, she set them on the floor and sat cross-legged to go through them.

The binder indeed had a script. An identical copy to the one Andrea had hidden in the trunk Allyson had tossed out. It clearly showed Vanessa Rapaporte's signature, as well as a personal note to Roger saying, "Don't fuck this one up. We're all counting on you."

Hidden in plain view, between the 120-sheet document, were other pages, including casting lists with handwritten notes initialed by Vanessa, location shoots, filming schedules, and budgetary figures. Allyson was convinced the binder held no more proof her father was involved in the studio's day-to-day business when she discovered photos of Anselmo Marta at a shoot. He was smiling ear to ear, with either arm around Andrea and Roger. Cameras, boom mics, and workers milled about in the background. In another photo, her father held the clapperboard used to mark takes while filming. It clearly showed the production's name, the roll, the take, and some alpha-numeric characters associated with the scene enumerated within the script. Allyson bet she could match that information with what was already in the binder, proving her father was not only privy to the crimes being committed on set, but present for at least one.

"Jesus Christ!" she gasped. "How could either of you allow this to go on? AND look so goddamn happy doing it!"

This was the proof Irv was looking for and could put her father and many others in prison for a long time. "Why didn't Atticus destroy this and Roger's bag the minute it came into his possession?" she murmured. She considered every move the brilliant attorney could take with this damaging information. "Perhaps he was holding onto it as insurance in case Pa ever threatened him or tried to remove him in other ways."

The question now was, what would she do with the information? With Irv in the wind and all the mounting evidence pointing to her being wrapped up in all this nonsense, she didn't think handing over the materials to the FBI was the correct choice without some real assurances. Plus, it required stealing from Atticus and turning against the only family she had left. Conversely, countless families could get justice and closure, knowing how and when their loved ones died. It meant shining a spotlight on entertainment companies that put profits before the innocent, unassuming public. It equaled fulfilling Andrea's final wish.

Padding back to the kitchen, she grabbed her phone. It was nearly finished syncing. All her contacts were visible, and that's all she needed. As the news continued to ramble in the background, she called the one person who would use this information as intended. Ram.

39

RAM TO THE RESCUE

{ALLYSON}

"Thank you for meeting me," Allyson said, opening a side door for Ram. "I wasn't sure you'd want anything to do with me after yesterday."

"Don't thank me yet. You got my attention with claims about Roger and the H0rr Studios' crimes, yet I came because Irv says you ditched him at the gas station and took all the evidence."

"You've talked to Irv?" Allyson said with shock. "That fucker is the one who left me stranded! Atticus was kind enough to come get me, and I spent the night here because my life is a constant earthquake these days."

"Wait. This is Atticus's place?"

"Yeah. I figured you would've looked up the address before trusting me."

"Jesus Christ, Allyson!" Ram shouted, running his hands through his hair and spinning like a madman.

"What's wrong?"

"What's wrong?! Haven't you heard?"

Allyson shook her head, her insides turning wild with butterflies at the possibility of more bad news.

"He was killed this morning in an accident on the freeway: he, his driver, an assistant, and an unknown passenger. A semi truck switched lanes, clipping the front of Atticus's vehicle, causing it to flip and crash into the concrete barrier. A third vehicle couldn't stop in time and slammed into it, hitting the gas tank area. It burst into flames on impact. The semi driver is expected to be okay, but the third car's driver has significant burn injuries."

Allyson collapsed onto a nearby couch, her legs turning boneless.

"The FBI is probably getting a warrant to search this place with Atticus gone. We should leave."

Allyson shook herself. "We can't. Not yet. I have to show you what I found. In my opinion, Irv and the FBI can't be trusted. We should take and hide whatever we think is important to prevent it from getting into the wrong hands. Strangely, I think it's what Atticus would want. Besides, it is why I called *you*. You are the only one who will use this information for what it was intended for—to make things right. Come on!" She shot to her feet and ran to the bedroom.

Inside the closet, she explained to Ram how she had found Roger's bag and showed him what it contained.

"Go to the kitchen. See if there are any gloves for cleaning—the kind people use to wash dishes and such. You're right. We need to pack this stuff and take it with us."

"So you believe me and will help?"

"I don't want to spend precious time getting into it, but I do believe you're right about not trusting Irv. He may be compromised. And if he is, there is no telling who else within the FBI might be as well."

"I knew it! But wait. Can I trust *you*? Everyone I've put faith in so far has turned out to be a devil in disguise."

"You called me, remember? Besides, I'm the devil in plain sight. I'm not perfect, Allyson. Far from it. However, I have a good moral compass and believe in doing what's right versus what's lucrative or career-advancing."

Allyson scoffed. "Riiigghhhttt. Unfortunately, I have no one else to turn to unless I call a press conference and present the information myself. I'm afraid no one would believe me, though. I'm the crazy sister."

"A news conference might not be a bad idea. Let's put a pin in that for now. Get those gloves. I don't want to touch anything, and neither should you going forward. Although, your fingerprints would have more of a reason to be here than mine." He checked his watch. "Dammit. It's already late afternoon. My reporter instincts are saying before we go, we have an opportunity here."

"To look for more stuff?" Allyson asked.

Ram smiled. "Tell me you've already found something."

"While waiting for you, I had the same thought. If I easily found this bag, what else might there be? I started in the library and discovered a ledger and a stack of documents hidden among his books. In the cellar, along with an extensive wine collection, I found boxes disguised as more wine. When I opened them, they were filled with papers and hard drives! I put what I found in the garage. I'll pack this stuff. Go load your car with what I've set aside. I'm not worried about fingerprints. He was my attorney," she choked on the past tense. "I had the right to be here as his guest, and now he's dead. I was here the whole time and had nothing to do with the accident. It was just that—an accident. Unless . . ."

"Let's not go there. Focus. You finish inside here. I'll go grab the stuff you've gathered, and then let's get the hell out of here."

Working in tandem, Ram and Allyson collected what they hoped would be enough evidence to put H0rr Studios' execs away for a long time. Heading out, Allyson threw her garment bag and satchel in the backseat and hopped in Ram's car, all while balancing a plate of food. "What? Grief makes me hungry. Besides, if I left it there, it might rot in the oven. No need to make his beautiful place any less so," she shrugged, stuffing more bacon in her mouth. "Want some?" she mumbled.

Ram smiled. "Sure."

As they reached the end of the street, four dark-tinted, black SUVs sailed by, along with two vans and a sheriff's car.

"I guess they got the warrant," Allyson stiffened. "If they find out we took stuff, could we be charged with a crime? Like obstruction of justice?"

"In my opinion? They'd have to prove that what we have came from Atticus and that he didn't give it to me. I pulled the car into the garage so doorbell cameras or nosey neighbors wouldn't catch our movements other than a car coming and going. If they happened to see my license plate and I'm asked, the simple answer is I came to get you. Otherwise, it's none of their goddamn business. Besides, my hope is we can present all this information before they even finish logging the mountains of paperwork they must be buried in, with everything coming to a head all at once."

"Which is why I turned to you. We can control the narrative and make sure it's done right. The truth must be revealed in a way that makes it clear who is responsible. It's what Andrea wanted. Through you, through the media, is the only way. It's kind of poetic justice if you think about it. The media helped them rise, and it will be the media contributing to their fall."

"Since when do you care what Andrea wanted?" Ram asked.

"It's a long story. One that involves a journal she kept while at the wellness retreat in Palm Springs. I'll tell you later. Now, where are we going? We should secure this stuff so no one else can access it."

"I have the perfect place."

When they pulled into 12 Action News' gated parking lot, Allyson gasped in surprise. "This is the perfect place?"

"Thanks to the Supreme Court, information gathered for news stories is umbrellaed under the First Amendment. It helps that there is a secured war room in the basement only accessible by keycard, as well."

"Wow. Okay. But wait. Who hands out those keycards? IT? They'll have access too!"

"Thus one of us will always be there until we can pull this all together."

"Do I at least get an air mattress or a sleeping bag?"

"I can't make any promises. I can guarantee there will be all the coffee and donuts you'll ever want, though. Besides, I thought you were used to roughing it!" Ram stole a slice of toast from the plate Allyson was still holding and bit off half. "I may also have a little surprise in store for you," he smiled as he backed his car to a loading dock.

In the side mirror, Allyson glimpsed a tall man dressed in mud-colored denim coveralls like mechanics and maintenance people wear. He had a friendly, familiar air about him, but it wasn't until she approached him that it hit her. Her heart recognized him before her head did.

"Grace! I mean, Ozzy! You're alive! Oh, thank god!" she screamed, running towards him with open arms.

40

THE REVEAL

{ALLYSON}

"Good Evening. I'm Wendy St. Jahns, and you're watching The Mark, America's weekly true crime broadcast. What do the Salish Sea feet phenomenon, a dozen missing persons, and the most popular streaming service in the world have in common? Join us this week as Seattle's award-winning investigative news journalist, Ram Helm, exposes a serial killer in your living room and the team who helped them hide there. All this and more coming up on this week's episode: 'Lights. Camera. Murder.'"

"Are you nervous to see yourself on national TV?" Allyson asked Ozzy as they sat on the couch, munching on pizza and sipping their go-to beverages. It might have been any regular night at Dr. Dean's apartment building. Except it wasn't. After a few harrowing weeks dodging Givers and crooked cops, they were finally safe inside Allyson's luxury apartment, which Atticus acquired for her before his untimely demise.

"Naw. I'm oddly at peace. We did our best to ensure those who are guilty are getting what is coming for them. How about you?"

"I can't be concerned about what others think. If I didn't turn over what I knew, my guilty conscience would've killed me or driven me insane, like it did Andrea and Raskolnikov in *Crime and Punishment*."

"Oooh, gurl, I love the Dostoevsky reference. Beautiful, talented, and well-read. A triple threat!"

Allyson grabbed a pillow and smacked Ozzy in the chest. "Don't go all Grace on me now. That ship has sailed."

"Has it, though? I rather enjoyed them. Often, Grace was more me than me. Having no labels gave me a freedom I've never felt before."

"What's stopping you from embracing your alter-ego?" Allyson asked.

"It's trickier than just changing pronouns, especially in my new role in the cyber division."

"Like how it's risky to go on national television and tell the world your father, sister, former lover, *and* artist friend were all complicit in the largest murder-for-hire scandal in the history of forever?"

"Or how your brother was a crooked FBI agent? Yeah, something like that. Now, shhh. Ram's coming on, and we have to give him his due. He busted his ass to get this in the proper hands. This is his big moment."

"He who said he was more concerned with truth than career advancement," Allyson rolled her eyes.

"Those things aren't mutually exclusive!" Oz defended his friend.

Ram: "This story begins at the end. Twelve missing persons, a dozen more identified victims, and a list of killers who all met a similar fate. Were their deaths an attempt at a cover-up and a larger conspiracy headed by H0rr Studios' majority shareholder and copper mining mogul Anselmo Marta? Or were they all coincidences in timing? The evidence is damning. H0rr Studios' power and influence were extensive, even compelling an FBI agent to join their cause.

Allyson: "I couldn't understand how Special Agent Kingsley went from ally to adversary in a blink. It didn't make sense. Until I learned where his loyalties were. I was shocked to discover he had been working against the FBI the entire time."

Osgood: "I can't even wrap my head around it. Throwing away a prestigious fifteen-year career, all for a woman who was obviously manipulating him."

Ram: "Of course, former Field Agent turned Senior Cyber Analyst Osgood Kingsley was talking about Vanessa Rapaporte, H0rr Studios' CEO. Vanessa met S.A. Irving Kingsley early in his investigation into RICO charges against the studio's majority owner, Anselmo Marta. Relying on a jailhouse informant, their case hinged on proving Marta was directly involved in murder-for-hire plots, extortion, money laundering, dealing with obscene matter, and a host of other charges."

Osgood: "Everyone knows you can't rely on a convict's word. They'll say anything to get their sentence reduced! Yet this turned out to be the tip of a Titanic-sized iceberg. I can't imagine how trapped Irv must have felt when he learned the scope of what he was looking into was wider than the Pacific Ocean. I've got to sympathize with the man, whether he's my brother or not. I'm sure it was like those poor souls who signed on to be *The Caretaker's* victims. Once they were strapped on a table or face-to-face with a knife-wielding maniac, there was no going back."

Ram: "Naturally, Osgood is referencing the victims whom creative director Andrea Marta sourced from a complex human trafficking ring headed by no other than her father, Anselmo Marta. Records uncovered in our extensive investigation revealed they mainly targeted marginalized individuals—drug addicts, those struggling with mental health issues, LGBTQ+, and indigenous groups. One such victim, Billy Walls, whose feet had washed ashore earlier this year, has been recently placed as a murdered extra in the first *Caretaker* movie."

Osgood: "I remember him well. Before I was officially assigned to the studio case, I was working on another involving a cybercriminal group. The FBI had a lead they were based in Seattle and related to a specific party scene. I met Billy Walls there. He was a smart guy but troubled. He was a master with code, though, and a member of the ring. Andrea Marta ran with the same crowd. She had yet to start with H0rr Studios, and it seems Billy got sucked into her universe later on."

Allyson: "He was Albatross69 to me—a guy who started harassing me online about my artwork. I tried my best to ignore him, like they tell you to do with bullies. He kept claiming I was stealing his ideas. In hindsight, I wonder if Andrea selected him because she discovered his online identity.

It makes my stomach twist thinking about it, and I feel terrible for the family and friends he left behind."

Ram: "It's unclear how exactly Andrea Marta, the architect behind *The Caretaker*'s success, selected each person destined to be a 'one and done' actor for the show. Several have been tied to the Salish Sea feet phenomenon through cross-referencing studio records and DNA samples family members have provided. Up to half of the twenty-four cases reported since 2007 can be attributed to the disposal of *Caretaker* victims. Records also indicate it was Andrea's sole responsibility to vet, groom, and secure each victim for the series, even getting them to sign nondisclosure agreements containing language like, 'in the unlikely event of an accident, damage to one's self, or in the rare occurrence, death . . .'

Anonymous: "Secrecy is what makes the entertainment world work. If NDAs didn't exist, what you see on television and the big screen would be significantly different. These legally binding agreements clarify that any whistleblowing or breach will come at a great cost to the signatory. So why do people sign them? Because there is no shortage of people looking to become rich and famous. We all want to be seen and heard. We all want to be special."

Ram: In a recovered interview dated a month after the first *Caretaker* movie, Andrea Marta says this:

Andrea: "Our movie was financially successful because it had a low budget and high yield. Finding eager and cheap amateur labor is easy when you promise future roles, social media exposure, and product endorsements."

Ram: "Which is how Andrea Marta single-handedly saved the corporation from bankruptcy. A simple, evil plan to use cheap or even free labor to replace expensive, time-consuming props and special effects. The worst part? The audiences' bond with the content's emotional and visual 'realness' amplified their profits. Entertainment produced for and sustained by movie-goers and, later, streaming subscribers. Not to mention all the trans-media products, such as video games, merchandise, and sponsored appearances. People paid to watch fellow humans get tortured and murdered, then clamored to meet their anti-hero and shell out even more money to become him in virtual games."

Allyson: "I get shivers thinking about it. So many people watched H0rr Studios productions, thinking it was all movie magic when, in reality, people were losing their lives for their entertainment! Moreover, my family was funding it and inventing sadistic methods to depict it with each iteration."

Ram: "It was an ingenious plan employing thousands worldwide and grossing over $3 billion annually. So how did this all come crashing down? We'll dive into that after this."

"A commercial break already?" Oz cried. "I will say, Ram has done a great job tying together all the pieces from the information we gathered."

"I feel like the victims are still being victimized by how the program is sensationalizing the story. Doesn't this speak to the whole point Ram was trying to make there at the end? A media conglomerate and its employees profited by killing dozens of people horrifically. Why are they focusing on the bad guys and not talking more about the people who suffered at their hands?"

"Because the news is an entertainment business, too, Love. The bad guys *are* the story, unfortunately. They have a disclaimer stating they would donate advertising proceeds to the fund dedicated to supporting the identified victims' families," Oz pointed out.

"Beyond Vanessa, her team, and a few crew members facing jail time and fines, has any real change been made to prevent this from happening again?"

"There's a push by the ACLU to change how NDAs are used in the industry and legislation in the works to create more oversight on media productions. It's a start."

"It is. However, I think the real issue here is what we, the people, find entertaining. There's a huge community of bootleggers out there selling H0rr Studios' banned content, and people are clamoring to buy it despite legal consequences. Why do people find this stuff entertaining, especially knowing what went on to create it?"

"Because being fascinated with death and dying is in our DNA! It's one of life's great mysteries," Oz replied excitedly as the TV dimmed before Ram reappeared. "Perhaps all these true crime shows and torture porn are popular because we get to experience it secondhand. Maybe it helps us figure out how to avoid it altogether."

Ram: "Welcome back. Thus far, we've given you the run-down on H0rr Studios' rise to success and the players who helped them obtain it. Now, let's look at how the dominoes began to fall. We'll start with Andrea Marta's disappearance and subsequent death. It has been determined she died of an accidental overdose at an exclusive wellness center in Palm Springs. It was later revealed her father, Anselmo Marta, owned the resort, and one of its employees, Lars Berg, had connections to the Argentinian businessman and alleged crime boss."

Lars: "Andrea was a guest at the facility. I worked there as a concierge, which was a fancy name for a personal assistant. Wealthy clients came to the resort for stress management, burnout, addiction, and other minor mental health-related conditions. I kept them on their prescribed routines, ensured their needs and desires were met with expediency, and worked as a liaison between them and the supervising therapists and doctors. No one knew her father owned the facility, and she received no special treatment above and beyond what she had signed on for. Andrea appeared troubled from the get-go, and Dr. Bouchard was working to see her transferred to a facility better equipped to deal with her issues. Unfortunately, it didn't happen fast enough. I'll admit my family's relationship with Mr. Marta got me the job, but I kept it because I was good at it. I worked there for four years and never had a negative review. I'm not guilty by association. I only helped people become the best versions of themselves."

Allyson: "I find it hard to believe that a guest at such a private facility had access to drugs strong enough to overdose. Why wasn't she being watched more carefully if she was so fragile? Why didn't they order a 5150 and commit her to a psych hold? I can't tell you how often it's happened to me for simply crying in public."

**Anonymous
Crew Ass't:** "In the months leading up to her vanishing, Andrea acted more out there than usual. She was intense, but this was a whole other level. She became outwardly paranoid, accusing people of leaving threatening notes and messages. Then there were the people she claimed were watching her. Yet there was no one there! We were all a little concerned for her well-being. However, no one said anything for fear of reprisal. She was a difficult boss, and we all needed our jobs.

Ram: "Andrea's disappearance was reported by the studio's attorney and the Marta family's legal counsel in the States, Atticus King. He chose to keep the matter private until more could be determined about her whereabouts. Within days, another H0rr Studios employee and the star of *The Caretaker* franchise, Roger Wotke, became embroiled in legal troubles before mysteriously vanishing too."

Osgood: "We were alerted by Atticus King that after Roger had been transferred securely to an undisclosed hotel, he vanished. At the time, we—the FBI—thought it was a ruse by the studio. It turned out he had an accident in his room. Roger had slipped and fallen in his suite's bathroom and suffered a significant head injury. Due to a derelict guard, he lay unconscious for hours. When the guard found him and attempted to get Roger the help he needed, the actor simply snuck off. Doctors suspect he regained consciousness and, in his confusion, most likely from a severe concussion, wandered off and into the hands of a stranger, crazed fan, or another theory, my personal favorite, he simply fell into the sea."

Cheryl Guilford: "When my ex-husband learned through coworkers that Andrea and Roger were missing, he became nervous. He didn't say exactly why, but when the two people you worked closest with for ten years go missing within days of each other, anyone would become a little spooked and distrustful. He organized a dinner with me and the kids, who are grown and made a great effort to show us how much we all meant to him. Two days later, he was missing, and by the following day, he was found with a self-inflicted gunshot wound. I can't help thinking the stress of hiding what they'd been doing for *The Caretaker* production and his two partners' disappearances drove him to take this action. I blame his death on the studio."

Ram: "With the main creative team behind *The Caretaker*'s success dead, it seemed the execs at H0rr Studios had their hands full. It was about to get even messier."

C.C. Jordie Sutter: "Our department was asked to join an investigation involving an incident at the former H0rr Studios movie lot in Vancouver. A pair of officers entered Building Two when the campus security guard reported hearing noises coming from within the locked facility. We lost contact with them shortly after they entered, along with two others, before my team arrived. Turns out the building was booby-trapped like in one of *The Caretaker* movies, and there was a secret tunnel littered with bodies and torture chambers. The whole scene was haunting. We lost all four officers to their injuries along with what we found locked in these dungeon-esque rooms."

Ram: "Why would a defunct movie studio be booby-trapped? Turns out someone at H0rr had a conscience after all. Evidence gathered by C.C. Sutter's team pointed to Andrea Marta as the culprit. A note found in her studio office explained it as an elaborate scheme to ensure Vanessa Rapaporte and the executive team wouldn't be able to walk away with their hands clean."

Andrea: "They'll claim they had no idea what I did. I needed a fail-safe method to remove plausible deniability. This is it. Surprise!"

Ram: "They would've enjoyed impunity too, if it wasn't for encrypted communications intercepted between Rapaporte and S.A. Kingsley, the FBI agent mentioned earlier. How did he play into the cover-up? You'll find out . . . after this."

"Are you going to be okay during this next bit? I mean, I understand what it's like to have your sibling try to kill you. Having the whole world hear about it is a another level of trauma, though." Allyson took Ozzy's hand in hers.

"Remember the day I revealed Irv was my half-brother? I was honest when I said no love was lost between us. We are highly competitive attention seekers. It's built-in when you come from a large family and a single mother. We all fought to stand out. I don't begrudge him too much. He was hooked on this fantasy world of Vanessa and what it would be like to rub elbows with the rich and famous."

"Wow. You're more empathetic than I would be."

"Ever since that night, I've considered there was more than one active serial killer."

"What a chilling thought," Allyson shuddered. "What makes you believe so?"

"Irv had no real motive to kill me. My sole job was you, and you weren't handing over any juicy tidbits to your BFF, Grace, which gave me nothing on his girlfriend."

"He was trying to make me the scapegoat. When he brought me in for questioning, he thought he could make any random piece of circumstantial evidence stick. When that failed, he needed something more concrete. Killing you and framing me would have done the trick."

Ram: "Welcome back. To recap, we've discussed how H0rr Studios executives authorized and sanctioned its employees to find, employ, design, and execute kill scenarios for its movies and original streaming programs for profit. They made snuff films a household entertainment medium. When, by coincidence, three employees went missing, they panicked and tried to walk away from any wrongdoing by using a strategy of denial and influence.

"We've also touched on Vanessa Rapaporte's manipulation of an FBI agent in an attempt to avoid prosecution.

Her tactics were successful enough they turned brother against brother in an epic showdown. In his words . . ."

Osgood: "I first suspected S.A. Kingsley, my half-brother, was working for the wrong team when he started interfering with my assignment. I was embedded with a potential informant in order to gain their trust and convince them to help our cause. He went around me and put unnecessary pressure on this person, who was already vulnerable, to turn over evidence he planned to suppress or disqualify to help Vanessa and the studio. He intimidated this person and waged a public war against their reputation. It was outright defamation.

Afterward came the attempt on my life. We were to meet at a prearranged time and location. When I got there, I saw a figure resembling Irv. However, his back was to me. I didn't want to startle him, so I looped around the side to approach him from the front. When I moved into an area with poor lighting, I lost sight of him. The next thing I knew, I was being hit over the head. I turned to defend myself, only to find a masked figure wearing a gray hoodie holding a baseball bat or large stick by their side. My phone slipped from my pocket, which meant I couldn't call for backup. My best course of action was to fight with what I had available—my fists. I'm a big man, but this person was strong. Then they pulled a knife. It caught me in the ribs. Thankfully, it didn't go very deep because I had layered due to the cold. I screamed and used a defensive move, knocking my attacker down. When I turned to grab my phone, they took advantage of my distraction and fled. My phone was broken, and I was in a vulnerable spot. Not knowing who my attacker was or why I was their target, I decided to go to ground and hide until I could figure out what the hell was going on. Once I removed myself from the investigation, I had the freedom to explore the facts free from bias. It led me to the truth about my brother. He was working for the other side, and I could prove it. He was feeding Vanessa information through an encrypted app."

Ram: "The hardest part was still to come—finding someone he could trust with what he'd found."

A.S.A.C. Michael Joel: "Field Agent Osgood Kingsley and I have worked closely on several important cases. He could've had my job many times. However, he enjoyed and excelled at undercover work. It suited him. When he came to me about his brother, I was proud of his ethics and honored by his trust. His information immediately prompted a parallel investigation with select agents who gathered enough evidence to bring Irv in for questioning. We apprehended him while he was attempting to coerce Osgood's target into cooperating with him fully. We got there just in time too, because we found no evidence on him or in his vehicle. He was immediately suspended until formal charges were brought. This was a precarious position because the last thing we wanted was to have Kingsley warn Ms. Rapaporte he'd been found out."

Ram: "Up to this point, the FBI had pinpointed the crimes and discovered the mole within the ranks. How would they reel in the big fish they'd been working to catch for the last three years?"

Allyson: "According to Special Agent Kingsley—Irv—the FBI needed concrete proof tying my father to all these crimes to make the RICO case stick. I couldn't believe what they were saying about my father. My sister? Let me say, even though we were identical twins, we weren't exact in every way. I fully believed she was capable of what they were claiming about her work at H0rr Studios. I grappled with guilt and shame, as well as how I'd even go about finding hard evidence against my father. I was convinced their investigation was biased and unfounded. They were simply looking at the wrong man. Besides, could I be the type to turn against their own family? He was all I had left. I'd lost my identity as an identical twin and a big career opportunity thanks to Irv's public smear campaign. Now, I was being asked to turn against my father? I wasn't sure I could do it.

"Thankfully, I didn't have to make that choice. Through our family attorney, Atticus King, I learned documents were found in my sister's Vancouver place and Roger's apartment in the same building. It was damning and proved my father had first-hand knowledge of the movie murders and willingly supplied resources to Andrea and H0rr for over ten years. Atticus was preparing to meet with the FBI to represent my father the morning he was killed."

Ram: "A death too coincidental to be considered an accident."

Truck Driver: "He was in my blind spot. I'll never get that sight out of my mind. Four people died, and it was all my fault! I'm sorry. It was an accident! He was in my blind spot. I didn't see the car!"

Ram: "Looking into the driver's history, we found no relationship between Argentina, Anselmo Marta, or his other businesses. Nor any link between him and Vanessa Rapaporte, the other executives, or shareholders from H0rr Studios."

Osgood: "Nothing in his background was a red flag. He has been a trucker for about twenty years and has a spotless safety record. Not even a speeding ticket."

Allyson: "Seems suspicious to me. From a statistical standpoint, you would think driving on the nation's highways for a living would at least net him a minor incident—a taillight out, overweight cargo, following too closely for safe weather conditions. I guess, as with my sister's circumspect death, I have no choice other than to defer to law enforcement on this one. I've experienced such immense loss in such a short time I need to point the finger at someone and say: You! You did this!"

Ram: "In the end, there are not enough hands to point fingers. This cover-up is the largest in our legal history, and the number of people going to prison is staggering. It's estimated the court fees alone will cost the United

States billions—ironically around the same amount H0rr Studios banked annually during its time in the spotlight. And on that note, that's all the time we have. We hope you have enjoyed this episode of "Lights. Camera. Murder." Thank you for joining us. I'm Ram Helm, and for all of us here on *The Mark*, we wish you a good night and thoughtful viewing."

41

THE BIG PICTURE

{ALLYSON}

ONE YEAR LATER

The past year brought many changes for Allyson. She was nearly pharmaceutical-free, other than one maintenance drug to help with her anxiety. There was no itching to cut into her flesh to feel alive or self-regulate. And she only lived for the present moment, looking to future opportunities and endeavors. She'd lost weight, grown out her hair, and dyed it back to her natural shade with a few sun-kissed highlights. The biggest challenge was giving up pizza, which she hadn't fully mastered yet, but it was no longer the base of her daily food pyramid. Atticus had the foresight to move Andrea's assets into a trust for Allyson, and along with the one her father set up for her when she became an adult, Allyson had access to funds the government could not seize in their RICO case against Anselmo Marta.

Allyson had not abandoned life in the shadows completely. She switched locations every three to four months, carefully keeping a low profile, using her middle name as her first and her mother's maiden name as her last as an alternate identity. Yet each day brought about more positive self-discovery. Allyson had finally accepted she was all the labels assigned to her throughout her life and more.

A trustee Atticus appointed for her inheritance helped with plans, documentation, and distribution of funds as needed. Although she was not linked to the RICO nor H0rr Studios crimes and had escaped testifying against her father thus far, she didn't feel safe. It was anyone's guess who might be out there wanting to seek retribution for her part in Ram's exposé. It was a risk she was unwilling to take. She was a work in progress.

Sitting by the seaside, her legs propped on the pony wall that delineated her bungalow from the beach, she sketched an idea for a new exhibit. She would present her pieces within the next year, under a new agent's direction and using a proxy—someone she paid to pretend to be the true artist. A strong wind gust blew in off the surf, causing fine sand to stick to her eyelashes while her sketchpad's pages fluttered in her lap.

"Shit!" she swore, instinctively raising her hand to scrub her eyes. Then she dropped it, recalling a time as a child when she'd scratched her cornea doing the same thing in a much different location. Blinking rapidly to clear her vision, a shadow passed overhead, and a slight chill crawled up her spine. Odd, considering it was in the mid-80s.

Her cell phone's unexpected buzz caused her to jump and drop her pad. Loose sheets of paper escaped, getting swept up by the breeze. She grabbed her phone and ran after the stray pieces before they hit the water.

"Hello?"

"Why do you sound breathless?" It was Grazzy, as she'd taken to calling him after the confusion between his persona as Grace and Ozzy. Only he and Ram could contact her directly through an encrypted app. It was the most secure way to keep in touch with her without compromising her location, which was usually unknown, even to him.

"Stupid wind. Papers flying everywhere," she stammered.

Grazzy chuckled. "It's never a dull moment in your world, is it? How is my favorite artist?"

"Feeling pretty creative today. And warm. God, I love the warmth. The wind . . . not so much."

"Hmm. Warm weather, yet windy. Can I guess your location?"

"I'd rather you didn't. Besides, it's not like you couldn't find me in your fancy new role. I don't understand why the FBI has a cybersecurity division when there's the NSA and Homeland Security."

"It's complicated. And yes, I could find you if you needed finding, but I'm giving you the room to feel independent and invisible. I would only look for you for your protection."

"Thank you. I appreciate it. Anyway, what's the latest? How are Vanessa and the rest of the H0rr gang?"

"Since I'm in cyber now, I only get updates from Michael, the Assistant S.A. in charge. He tells me all the cases are progressing on schedule. As expected, your father's legal team is fighting like hell. And, you should rest assured, he's being held in the federal detention center's nicest section. It's relatively safe and has decent accommodations."

"I hate thinking about what he's going through. Admitting so makes me feel guilty. There are families out there going through much worse. I want my conscience to be clear. Yet he's my father, and I love him in this weird, twisted way."

"And how's therapy going?" Grazzy teased.

"What are you saying?" They shared another laugh before Allyson continued. "What about you? How's the job? Anything new with Irv's case? Has your family drama subsided?"

"Job is amazing. I love it as much as undercover work. However, there's the whole 'my life is in constant danger bit' that can't be replicated. That was always a real adrenaline boost!"

"Not funny, Graz."

"Too soon?"

"Ten years would be too soon."

"I hear you. Anyway, everything else is about as good as you can imagine. Half my siblings are glad Irv's in jail. The other half sees me as a traitor, even though he was the one in the wrong."

"Gotta love sibling drama!" Allyson sighed. "Although, I don't miss it one bit."

"I bet. Hey, speaking of your infamous sibling, there's been another Roger sighting! It's the eighth documented one in the last year."

"The Givers just won't let him stay dead, will they?"

"This time, there is a clear photo. I'll text it to you. You tell me if you think it's him."

"Where was 'Elvis' this time?"

"Good one," Grazzy chortled. "Mallorca."

Allyson's phone hand shook as she stood on the beach, gazing out at the water, her pages grasped tightly by her side. "That's . . . that is ludicrous," she choked, glancing back at the veranda. "Why would he be there of all places?"

"To be honest, I think it sounds like the most credible place for him thus far. It's a beautiful island, filled with people pretending to be private while flashing their money and prestige around."

Allyson hesitated before chuckling. "That's an unfair stereotype. You have the yogis, the hippies, and the soul-searchers, too. Oh, and don't forget the partiers. The club scene is intense."

"Sounds like you are pretty familiar with the place yourself."

"I've been there, did the things, bought the shirt," she joked. "Hey, listen. I've got to go, but stay in touch. Especially if Roger shows up, say, in Japan next. Talk about newsworthy. He'd tower over everyone there like Gulliver on Lilliput!"

"Will do. Stay safe, and call if you need anything. I sent the photo while we were talking. Check it out and get back to me."

"Sure. Back at you. Oh, and tell Ram . . . or I should say *Laramie* . . . I said hi. He's killing it on *The Mark*. Pun intended! Love you, Graz."

"Love you, too, Dear One."

Allyson turned back to her bungalow. The warm sand between her toes grounded her. She closed her eyes and listened to the sea waves lapping softly against the shore behind her. The water charged her. Native birds chittered to each other in the foliage that provided privacy along her rented property. Life was good.

"I should go for a swim," she muttered, opening her eyes and swaying as they readjusted to the brightness. As she moved to head inside to change, she was taken aback by a tall, dark figure standing by her chair, her sketchpad in their hands.

"Hello, Darling. Not happy to see me?" Roger placed his empty hand over his heart. "You wound me. Oh, wait. You wouldn't. You don't like to get your hands dirty with the details."

Allyson paled as the familiar voice that had haunted her dreams over the last year resonated deep inside. "How? What?" she choked on the words.

"Spare me the swooning bit. I know you better than anyone, including yourself. You had to have considered I'd come for you after the way we left things."

"You're dead. They said you were dead. Your feet . . ."

"Are still attached to my legs. How strange," Roger pulled his pants up from the knees to reveal his legs and bare feet still there.

"They had your sneakers!"

"Easily switched with the poor lad who offered to help me in any way he could."

Allyson shuddered. "The DNA. It was a match."

"Please," Roger huffed, crossing his arms over his chest. "Science is only as good as the people performing the tests. My Giver network has a much broader reach and more loyal people than Vanessa Rapaporte's. Now, stop with the demure act and come kiss me."

When Allyson stiffened, Roger did too. His eyes narrowed. "You can't stop, can you? You've been playing the damaged soul for so long that you don't know how. Come on, be a good girl, and offer me a seat away from the sun. This pale skin is a magnet for those cancer rays," he grinned, pointing at the sun blazing high overhead. "The ferry from Mallorca to here nearly killed me. Do you have any wodka? I'm parched."

Allyson coughed. Her throat was dry too from the heat and the tension. "Sure. Let's go inside." Throwing her shoulders back, her head held high, she marched towards the veranda. Roger turned and led the way inside. Allyson slid the glass door shut and locked it behind her. She pulled the drapes closed for more privacy.

"I caught your little charade in *The Mark with Laramie Helm* and was amused there was no mention of the other crimes your sister committed. Smart decision. You probably saved yourself millions in potential financial liability from the civil lawsuits their families might have leveled against you."

"Come on, Roger. You're the actor here. The show was about spinning a narrative. Andrea's extracurriculars didn't fit. It would've detracted from the real story—the biggest cover-up and RICO snag in the history of federal cases. The studio had to be stopped. They would've kept going without you, Andrea, and Craig. There is no shortage of people just as depraved as you lot. And it's not like the authorities don't know anything about Andrea. Those cases are being handled a bit more discreetly. Enough about all of that, though. Why don't you tell me how you faked your death? I can see you're itching to brag about it." She pulled out an unopened vodka bottle from the freezer and grabbed two short tumblers from the cupboard, waiting to settle in for his tale.

Roger waited until she poured, then took the glass filled with two fingers of clear liquid and tossed it back in one gulp. "Another, please. And thank you."

"Wow. Being dead has taught you manners. I'm impressed," Allyson remarked, fulfilling his request.

"I'm a different person around you. You always made me feel like I could be . . ."

"Not a sadistic asshole?"

"Yeah," he shot her a lop-sided grin.

Allyson's insides twisted. This was the Roger she had always been attracted to. He was devilishly handsome without his *Caretaker* persona.

"Sometimes, you liked my sadistic side. Especially when I was *in*side you."

"Generally, it was the *only time* I liked you. You weren't yammering on about yourself then. 'Poor misunderstood Roger.' People worshipped you despite what you did!"

"Don't pretend I'm the only one out there. So many rich and famous are the dark and dirtiest of us all, and the masses worship them. I mean, look at your family. Even without your sister, your father has blood on his hands. Yet he has no shortage of loyal supporters calling for his case to be dismissed."

"He'll have to answer for his choices, not me."

"Pfft! You didn't hold the knife, or the torch, or the clippers, or the . . ."

"Enough!" Allyson slammed her hand on the counter.

"That doesn't mean you are without sin," Roger finished.

Allyson glanced at the scar on her wrist. "Nothing is preventing me from starting now. I'm imagining how easy it would be to murder someone already dead and get away with it. So stop with your nastiness and get to how and why you're here."

"The *how* is a little blurry. I remember walking down the street in Seattle, my head hammering away like the drummer from Metallica was inside my skull when a car pulled up. You surprised me. You don't drive."

"Ironically, finding you roaming the streets naked, dazed, and confused somehow didn't surprise me. Also, 'don't' is a choice. It is not a synonym for 'can't.'"

"Your fake sincerity disarmed me. So much so, I didn't see the next bit coming."

"You mean the part where I left you in my friend's capable hands?"

Roger threw his head back and roared. "Capable, but not loyal. Once he realized who I was and what I could do for him, he was malleable enough. You have never been able to grasp the lengths to which someone's obsession will drive them. The Givers have always been my ace in the hole, my secret weapon. It's why I indulged them—went to those godforsaken conferences and fandom gatherings, posed for every photo, and signed every autograph. It wasn't for the appearance fees or the expensive one-on-ones. I was grooming the whole lot for a day just like today—well, maybe not exactly like today—but a time in the future when I would need to extricate myself from H0rr Studios and move about the world a little less encumbered by societal norms, local laws, or even a documented existence. You can't imagine the freedom I have roaming like a ghost, going where I please, doing whatever whim I can conjure in the moment." He ran his tongue over his bottom lip and let his eyes rove over her figure.

"You're saying you faked your death to become a ghost?"

"Ghosts are surprisingly adept at many things. Arranging a death here, an accident there, planting evidence, tying up loose ends with people who threaten your freedom."

"What exactly are you saying? Did you kill Andrea and Craig?"

Roger grabbed the bottle and poured another helping. "Drink," he ordered.

Allyson tossed back the liquid and banged her glass on the counter.

"I'm saying I'm responsible for all of it, my love. Andrea losing her mind and running off to get fixed by that quack Bouchard, burning down her house, Craig's presumed suicide, the movie studio discoveries, etc. . . . Everything the FBI is blaming on H0rr Studios, besides their role in creating their content, is on me. Even Atticus' accident. That trucker. God love him. He played his part well. Too bad there's no more *Caretaker*. He'd be a fantastic apprentice."

"You . . . You killed Andrea? Why? You loved her!"

"No, darling. I love *you*. It's always been you, even when I didn't realize it was you. Andrea's dark splendor turned me on. I won't deny it. She revealed in me a part I didn't imagine could exist. Yet it was you who bewitched me and made me as I am today. If it wasn't for you dreaming up *The Caretaker*, to begin with, none of the other stuff could have even happened. I wouldn't be standing here."

Allyson's eyes filled with tears, and a heat burned through her body. "She had no right to take my idea and make it into what it became. It was a teenage mental case's rantings. My drawings helped me cope with what was happening to me inside the psych ward, no thanks to her. The professionals tortured us, made us do unspeakable things, and left us with overseers who were barely human themselves. My version of *The Caretaker* was simply an outlet for my suppressed fears and frustrations!"

"And it was the perfect idea for a horror movie. A trans-media franchise! Who would've thought!" Roger roared with delight.

"You shut your goddamn mouth. I warned you before not to push me. Or ever speak about the origins of *Caretaker*. I've made things right for those people and their families. Everyone is getting their due punishment. Everyone. But. You. You're the last loose end, the only one who hasn't paid."

Allyson's face contorted into a mask of rage that made Roger stop mid-guffaw. He closed his mouth and drew back.

"Jesus. You look like Andrea. I could always tell the difference because you had this light about you, almost like a halo. But now . . . now . . ."

Roger was unable to finish his thought. In the seconds it took him to speak, Allyson grabbed the vodka bottle, smashed it on the counter's edge, and swiped its shattered neck across his throat, spraying arterial blood everywhere. The life drained from his eyes, and Allyson smiled as Roger's expression changed from confusion to acceptance. And was there a hint of pride?

"When will people learn to stop underestimating me? I'm the artist, *shitbird*. My hands are always dirty," she spat. Then she calmly washed them and cleaned up the mess.

"Scientists say the disarticulated body parts are a natural phenomenon when a body breaks down in seawater. They only float to the surface if they are attached to something buoyant, like an athletic shoe. Did you know that, Roger?" Allyson asked as she removed his flip-flops and wrapped his body in an area rug. "I'd like to test their theory. How about a little boat ride at sunset? Maybe we'll get lucky and spot the Great White people have been talking about!"

THE END.

ACKNOWLEDGMENTS

To my beloved, for giving me the space to explore my passion for storytelling. Your love and support is charished and appreciated beyond measure.

To my family and friends who are like family, you've listened to me moan and groan, complain and carry-on with this project for nearly seven years. Even though some of you doubted I'd get here, I appreciate your eagerness to press me about this project's status and even lovingly tease me about living the stereotypical writer's life.

To Wendy, my first reader, who patiently worked with me for eight months, reading as fast as I wrote, providing me invaluable feedback, friendship, and the freedom to explore my own writing methodologies. You are a gift!

To Charlie Donlea, author of numerous best-selling books with Kensington Press. You read my first ten pages seven years ago and gave me hope that the talent was there. I just needed more time with the craft. I appreciate you giving me that boost of confidence and direction.

To all the authors who've come before me, thank you for paving the way. And to those yet to become authors but dream of it someday, don't give up. In the (not exact) words of Marie Forleo: You have a gift, only you can give, that the world needs to see/hear/read.

If you enjoyed this story, please leave a review on your favorite reader sites, such as GoodReads, Amazon, Barnes&Noble, or wherever books are sold. Tell a friend, take to social media. The best way to see more from this author is to spread the word. You can also make requests at your local library!

For more information about K.T. George,
visit www.ktgeorge.com.